VICTIM OF THE GAME

They got out of their car and stood on the side of the road. They could just see a faint red glow a long way down below them.

"Christ, some poor bugger's driven over the edge."

He slid down the steep slope, his arms stretched out, trying to hang on to something, anything. He disappeared from her view. Then silence.

"Are you all right?" she shouted, feeling stupid and useless.

"Jesus!" his voice exploded below her. "There's somebody still down here."

"Shall I come down?"

"No, hold on," he shouted, and she waited as he clambered back up the hill.

"There's this guy down there sort of crucified? More like a butterfly with a pin through it. There's a branch stuck right through him." Then, as an afterthought, "He doesn't have any clothes on."

THE
SEVENTH
HEXAGRAM

A NOVEL BY
IAN McLACHLAN

BANTAM BOOKS · TORONTO · NEW YORK · LONDON

THE SEVENTH HEXAGRAM
*A Bantam Book / published by arrangement with
The Dial Press*

PRINTING HISTORY
First published in Canada by McMillan of
Canada, Ltd. in 1976
Dial Press edition published September 1976

Bantam edition / January 1978

*To my mother and father
in gratitude*

7. SHIH / THE ARMY

above K'UN THE RECEPTIVE, EARTH
below K'AN THE ABYSMAL, WATER

This hexagram is made up of the trigrams K'an, water, and K'un, earth.

THE IMAGE
In the middle of the earth is water:
The image of THE ARMY.
Thus the superior man increases his masses
By generosity toward the people.

Ground water is invisibly present within the earth. In the same way the military power of a people is invisibly present in the masses. When danger threatens, every peasant becomes a soldier; when the war ends, he goes back to his plow.

An army must set forth in proper order.
If the order is not good, misfortune threatens.
Let the eldest lead the army.
The younger transports corpses.

Part 1

1

It will end here, too.

Splinters of bone in an eye. The night soaked up the noise of gunshots. A body came running, white against the humid darkness, stumbling, falling, scrambling up and out of sight. Tires screamed on the concrete. The bushes were heavy with rain.

Now there was only the power, the sense of being in control.

He shifted down into third, the tachometer swaying up above the five-thousand-rpm mark as the car slowed to eighty on the downhill stretch of road. He had no separate identity; he was a part of the mechanism, functioning as automatically as the intermeshing gears. The exhilaration surged in him as the adrenalin pumped faster into the bloodstream. Nothing else mattered now. There was only the narrow road, the headlights cutting through the drizzle and glancing on wet leaves. A world that was all his own, in which he himself did not exist.

Then his mind slipped, for a moment only, spinning back into the scene that lay behind him. He pleaded with himself to forget it, cross it out. And in that moment he was cut off from the car.

The road was slippery after the dry winter. Oil had been dropped on it, had been rubbed away by tires and redeposited again, forming a film on the surface. He had driven over it many times before in all kinds of weather, and he knew, as he changed down into second before the tight, dipping, right-hand bend, that he was fifteen yards too late.

Normally it wouldn't have mattered; the car skidded round rather inelegantly, and he would have driven on more cautiously, shaking slightly. But tonight the rear tires broke sideways across the road, the front wheels started to follow them, and instinctively he accelerated, knowing this would be enough to drive the car out of its slide. Normally he would have been right. But earlier in the evening nearly four inches of rain had fallen in an hour. The water had poured, smoking, off the rocky hillsides, burrowing into the occasional patches of clay, spewing down towards the sea in a stinking yellow torrent. Somewhere far below him, far outside his own consciousness of all that was happening, part of the hillside had collapsed, burying alive more than thirty people whose rusty metal huts had, till tonight, clung to its slopes. Somewhere else, at the opposite end of the island, a home for crippled children had been built absurdly close to the sea, underneath an overhanging cliff. The water rushing down had met the incoming tide, coffee-colored mud seethed into the black salt water, rose to the second floor, stifling the panic inside.

Up on the road the rain had discovered a minute crack in the surface of the asphalt just before this downhill bend. The crack was explored, opened; the sides were broken away; the hole was driven deep into the rubble that lay beneath the surface—all in the space of half an hour, such was the force of the rain. And now, four hours later, there was this wide, irregular pot-hole on the left-hand side of the road nearly a yard across and a foot deep, full of mud and stones, a pond almost.

As the car drifted across the road, rubber squealing, the rear wheels starting to find the grip that would push it out of the corner, the rear near-side wheel slammed straight into the hole. The car was nearly five years old, and possibly even a new spring would not have withstood this sudden shock. As it was, the years of strain had pushed two of the metal leaves slightly out of alignment, so that the sharp, unusual pressure was focussed precisely on the point where the spring was weakest. There was a loud crack, louder by far than the unreal gunshots a few minutes earlier, and the back of the car seemed suddenly to collapse, to be made of damp newspaper. As the spring folded up in the hole, the car was pulled round at an angle of ninety degrees to the direction it had been travelling just a split second before, till it was heading straight towards the verge.

The situation had taken command, and all he could do was sit and watch. It wasn't, surely, happening to him, and there could be no danger in something that occurred with such ponderous inevitability. He felt no fear, certainly was much less afraid than he would have been had he just managed to control the skid and get round the corner. It was all as harmless and pointless as driving a Dodg'em in a fun fair. One couldn't be held responsible for such things. And wasn't that exactly what he was looking for?

The front wheels of the car rolled over the foot-high bank of stones and dirt. There was a drop of fifty feet on the other side, spiked with small, unfriendly trees that struggled for life amongst hostile rocks. As the car climbed onto the bank, the front part of its chassis projected over the drop, then the wheels followed, and with the noise of an oilcan rolled along a midnight street, its belly crunched down on the stones that had once formed a roadside wall. There it stuck, rocking gently: 2,934 pounds of metal and rubber, leather and glass, see-sawing slowly up and down.

It was a scene conceived in the mind of some despairing advertising man. For the car was still beautiful as it lay there, unsteadily, out of context. Its white, gleaming sldes still swept down from the enormous bonnet into the nestling cockpit and up again to the abruptly cut-off tail. Its headlights stared into the dark sky, swinging up and down. But then the weight of the engine began to tell. Each swing brought the beams of light farther and farther below the horizontal, until finally they caught the treetops like white, shiny flowers in their glare.

There was a tearing, scraping sound. The back of the car followed the front in a loop, the bonnet turning over and crumpling itself against the rocks, the top of the car bouncing behind it, the underside of the chassis rising in the air again, turning over and over, increasingly deformed, a stick of Plasticine, for fifty feet or more.

He was thrown clear as the car toppled, flying away from it, birdlike, until his forwards momentum was countered by gravity, and his body plummeted. His head caught the trunk of a tree—only a glancing blow—and it seemed for a moment that he might be cradled there. But a branch rose up, itself broken in a storm, its stump thrusting into his body just above and to the right of his genitals. It cracked into the femur neck, fracturing it, wood much stronger than the bone, the force continuing the fracture into the pelvis, splintering it and driving the splinter into the bladder.

And so he hung there, unconscious, speared,

6

blood seeping out of his body and being wiped away by the light rain.

"For Christ's sake, mind where you're going, Tom," said the tall blonde girl, bracing herself against the dashboard.

"Don't get so excited, doll," said Tom Price. "The car knows the way even if I don't. I bought it from a guy who lives up here."

In fact he was only vaguely aware of where it was they were going. Or, for that matter, of where they had come from. He had been to a party, that was certain. But he seemed to remember going to the party with a Chinese girl, and this one wasn't Chinese, was she?

Couldn't be.

Suddenly suspicious, he leaned across and peered at her.

"That's not a wig you're wearing, is it?"

No, it wasn't a wig. She had a long nose, too. Not too long, but longer than a Chinese one.

The car veered towards the side of the road, and the girl clutched at his arm.

"Watch it!" He looked out of the window and casually put it back on its course again. "Who's driving this fucking car, anyway?" Then, after a pause, "Better not answer that."

Concentrate. That was what you had to do. He squeezed his eyes shut for a moment, then reluctantly opened them. Now, where were they going? Was he taking her back to his place? Or was she just a nice girl he had offered to give a ride home? He would have to find out about that. The quickest way was simply to say, "Do you want to make out, baby?" That would clear it all up perfectly. So why was he so shy about saying it? Shit! You didn't even get to first base as a forty-seven-year-old free-lance photographer if you were afraid to ask a girl if she wanted to make out.

"Where are we going, anyway?" he asked.

"I thought the idea was I had to see these photos you took in Vietnam."

"That's right, doll, that's right. Almost forgot. Christ, wait till you see them, though. The trouble is no American magazine is ever going to print them. There are these shots of two young GIs just sitting behind a wall with tears streaming down their faces? Did I tell you about that? Not even trying to hide it. Maybe I'll try France. *Paris-Match*. The French like that kind of thing."

So that was cleared up. Etchings. Back to his place. Remember that. Now all he had to do was not pass out before they got there. In the morning he'd waken up with the most foul indigestion. Not a hangover, never got a hangover, just his whole gut filled with napalm. It would be hard enough to live with himself, let alone have all the problems of existing with another strange human being. Still, he had to now. Question of honor. Fuck honor!

He groaned.

Sally looked round, worried. "Why don't you let me drive, Tom?"

He shook his head, not just a brief, irritated jerk, but his orange beard swivelling about like a ship's radar.

She had heard about him from friends before tonight. Somebody—a girl—had said, "Tom Whatsisname, he's a sad little man." But then somebody else told her, "He's the funniest guy I've ever met." They were both people she usually believed.

Then tonight he had come into this party given by Morty Berkowitz, the American China-watcher. It wasn't very clear whether or not he had been invited, but he certainly didn't seem to feel any obligation either way. He spent most of the first hour he was there cursing the Americans. Every other empire had brought at least a simulacrum of civilization with it, but not you fucking Americans. The Romans brought roads and baths; the British brought law-courts and

dinner jackets, but all you've brought with you is anti-
personnel bombs that don't destroy buildings, only people, and a brand of gonorrhoea that eats antibiotics
for breakfast.

Nobody had taken offense. Tom Price was a
character; he put on a good show. She had watched
him standing in the middle of the room, a bouncy little
man, shouting at his host, the people clustered around
laughing at his insults, untouched by them. And, yes,
he was pathetic, and he was funny; the funniest sad
little man she had ever seen.

Then, in the space of five minutes—not so much
like a balloon that's pricked as one that slowly deflates
because of a weakness in itself—he had stopped rant-
ing and started to drink. The girl he had come with had
already been picked up by a distinguished-looking
young man with tinted glasses who worked at the
Swiss consulate. Tom had gone out onto the balcony
to sit by himself behind a rubber plant, and Sally followed him, sitting down on a cushion at his feet, listening to him talk about the wife he had left six years
before, seeing him soften with absurd pride in the
grown-up children who despised him, feeling for him
in his vulnerability.

Later, as they were leaving, Tom discovered he
had lost his shoes. Nobody could find them. They
looked in the toilet, in the rubber plant, over the balcony, in the oven. "Tom's shoes have walked out on
him at last." It was the sort of thing that people would
remember years later: "Do you remember that night
Tom Price—oh, God, you know, the Canadian photographer—the night he lost his shoes?"

Lights flashed on all over the house, in all the
rooms, momentarily startling those who had turned
them out. Finally, Tom made a ceremonial presentation
of his socks to the host, pointing out that they had
been made in China; only the holes were products of
the free world. With great dignity he stumbled out
into the rain.

In his bare feet he danced in the puddles. "You

fucking American house, eating up my shoes. What you need is defoliant poured down your chimneys!"

Then he turned to the tall girl with crew-cut blonde hair, gazing up at her in astonishment as if he had just noticed her for the first time.

"Jeez, you're so—so goddesslike," he said, kneeling down on the wet gravel at her feet. "You have the longest thighs and the smallest head in the world. That's my ideal." He squinted up at her, forming a view-finder with his fingers, making clicking noises with his tongue, contorting his body to get the best shot of her crotch. Leaning over to the side, he lost his balance and rolled into a puddle, giggling. He lay on his back, his belly whalelike in the air, flapping his hands on either side of him like a floating swimmer.

"I'm giving up," he called to her. "Ah'm jes goin' to lah heah in mah pool and watch yew-awl awl the day long. I'm not competing with you anymore. You're too tall. D'you hear?" he shouted. "You're too tall. You're six feet taller than I am. That's unfair competition. I shall only serve you if you buy me a ladder." He started to snore.

She stood above him, wondering whether to kick him in the ribs or fondle him like a teddy bear. Whatever was she going to do with him? She couldn't go to bed with him like this. Earlier, in the house, as they talked quietly on the balcony, she had decided that she might. He had been talking about his daughter, who sounded like a toffee-nosed little brat. "She's about your age, I suppose," he said regretfully, looking down at Sally as she lay with her hands under her head, her small breasts pushing upwards through the thin dress. He had seemed rather lost, and yet somehow not pathetic anymore; just isolated by some despairing honesty. She wanted to show him that not all girls of nineteen would despise him as a dirty, ridiculous old man.

But as he lay, pretending to sleep in the puddle, like a distended corpse dragged out of the sea, she wanted most of all to hurt him for having taken her in so; or, more exactly, for not having recognized the generosity with which she was willing to give herself to him, drunk and disgusting as he was.

She jabbed the toe of her shoe into the bulging fat around his waist. "Get up, you idiot. I'm fed up with your senile games. I want to go home."

He grabbed her ankle, pulling her down beside him, and she beat against his chest with her hands. "Why don't you just stay here and—and decompose?"

When he saw the tears mixing with the rain on her cheeks, he was suddenly the sentimental father figure again. "I'm sorry," he said, getting up and putting his arm around her shoulders as they lurched towards the car. "The older you get, the harder you've got to work to stay ahead of them."

"Them?"

"Yeah—the Furies."

"What do you mean 'Furies'?"

"Sanity, baby. Sanity."

And now he didn't even remember who she was. She felt cold and wizened.

She looked out the window, watching the glittering rocks on the hillside above her. As they came slithering round a turn, she glanced across at the road winding round to the other side of the small valley, hoping there wouldn't be any cars coming the other way. Tom had only just managed to avoid the two that had passed them. Suddenly she clutched at his arm.

"Stop, Tom."

The next moment she was nearly catapulted through the windscreen.

"Whassamarra?"

"Look over there. Don't you see? That light down from the road. What's it doing there?"

"Maybe it's somebody collecting water beetles," he suggested.

She glared at him.

"Okay, so maybe it's not. All we have to do is drive on round there and take a look."

The car jerked into reverse.

When at last they got out and stood on the side of the road, they could just see a faint red glow a long way down below them.

"Christ, some poor bugger's gone over the edge. He can't have had much of a chance."

"Hadn't we better look, though?" she asked.

"Nobody ever believes me when I tell them I used to be the most accident-prone mountaineer in B.C." He placed one foot carefully on a very solid rock. It tipped over, and there he was, sliding down the steep slope, his arms stretched out above him, trying to hang onto something, anything, nails breaking, a miniature avalanche of flailing limbs and dirt.

Helpless, laughing, she saw his bald head disappear. Then silence. She became worried.

"Tom, are you all right?" she shouted, feeling stupid and useless.

There was no reply. She started to take off her high heels.

"Jesus wept!" She heard a voice explode below her.

"Tom, what is it?" she shouted, irritated again.

"There's somebody still down here."

"Shall I come down?"

"No, hold on," he shouted back, and she waited amidst more curses, as he clambered up into the headlights, scratches on his face, blood dripping out of his arm.

"What is it, Tom?"

"There's this guy down there, sort of crucified? More like a butterfly with a pin through it. There's a branch stuck right into him." Now he was sober; gasping but sober. "I guess we shouldn't really move him, ought to get an ambulance. But, shit, he's still living. I felt his pulse. Unconscious, but he's alive. It'll be morning by the time they get an ambulance out here. We'll just have to bring him up ourselves."

He put his arm round her. "You'll have to come down, too," he said gently. "You're taller than I am." Then, as an afterthought, "By the way, he doesn't have any clothes on."

The Seventh Hexagram

It took them nearly an hour to get the body up to the road. How they even got it off the tree they could never really remember. Sally, on tiptoe, reached up holding the battered head in her hands, while Tom pushed like a caryatid from below. Then they had to pull it up the slope, rolling down with it again and again, holding with one hand onto blades of grass or spiky bushes and with the other onto the slack, leaking body.

Back at the roadside, Tom sat for a moment with his face in his hands, his heart bursting. He prodded the body with his foot.

"You prick! You've got me dying too now."

On the way to the hospital Sally sat in the back of the car with the head between her legs, feeling the wet blond hair against her thighs, looking at the long nose, the sunken cheeks, realizing that this was, after all, a man, not just an awkward bag of assorted bones. She held the right wrist between her fingers, feeling the pulse, not knowing enough to say if it was weak or strong, but clinging to it. Once she lost it, thought he was dead, started silently to weep, even prayed, until she realized that her fingers had slipped.

At the hospital they took one look at this old drunk and the tall, beautiful girl with mud all over her white dress and thanked them coldly for bringing it in. Of course, it would have been better if they had waited for an ambulance; they might have caused internal damage, ripping it down like that, like a wet sheet from a clothesline. But yes, it would live. No, there was no need for them to wait. Just leave your names and addresses, please.

Before going to bed they didn't even bother to look at the pictures of Vietnam.

2

My memories of what happened during that first week in hospital are impossibly tangled.

Some things I can remember precisely, trivial things such as fragments of a dream or the sound of metal scraping along a wall. Others seem a vast distance from me, vague and blurred. I had lost the power to discriminate between what mattered and what did not. The normal processes of perception were reversed: tiny issues penetrated deep into my consciousness, wounding, leaving scars that still hurt, even now, while what should have concerned me flowed smoothly over the surface of my skin.

The Seventh Hexagram

I can remember fragments of a conversation that was going on between two house surgeons while I was being examined in the casualty ward. According to the records I was completely unconscious. Yet when I talked to one of them later on, I was even able to repeat phrases that he himself had forgotten. It's as though certain words, some of them quite irrelevant to me, became lodged in my brain somewhere between consciousness and the subconscious, unable to escape into the freedom of one or the other.

Those two doctors must have been talking in the usual mixture of Cantonese and English, describing my case, talking perhaps of catheters and sutures, saline infusions, perforations of the bladder. On their own these words are clinical, unemotional; even when they apply to you yourself, there's nothing to fear in them because they're abstracted from the trauma of what has happened. For me they were not connected, either as cause or as effect, with the pain I felt.

But they are linked in my mind with other phrases that had nothing to do with me at all. Somebody says over and over again inside my head, "When he wanted to kiss her, she told him, 'If you want to do that, then you'd better find a European; Chinese girls don't do that sort of thing.'"

Fragments of gossip, they caused me almost unendurable pain. I had no idea what they meant, whom they were about, how they concerned me. And yet concern me they did, and do—splinters driven under a fingernail.

In dreams the phrases recur time after time.

I am standing in a field, astonished by the colors of trees and birds and flowers, myself the center of attraction. Then I see something—a leaf, a butterfly—that I want to touch, and I run towards it. Everything is open to me, mine.

But whichever way I turn, Mei is blocking my path, so tiny beneath my giant feet, the size of an ant, yet completely herself in every detail. On her face there is only trust and happiness. I cannot move without crushing her. To avoid her, I turn round to go in the opposite direction, but there she is again, still in front of me, like a child you see under the wheels of your car.

I turn faster and faster, but she is always in my way—cool, smiling, loving. And in my brain there are the echoes of the doctor's words, not in Mei's voice—she loves me, is ready to be crushed beneath my feet—but in the exact tones the doctor had used as he talked to his friend, the tones of the gossip, superior and cruel. The sound of his voice expands in the emptiness inside my skull, and all the time I am turning in panic, looking for a way to move without obliterating Mei, until finally I start to fall, tumbling over and over, for the whole landscape has tilted and the trees, which a moment before had been luxuriant and comforting, are now sharp as thorns, pointed like bayonets against me.

Or again, there is an enormous house without windows. I know that somewhere there is a secret door in the wall, and I probe everywhere for the button that must be pressed to open it. But the stones are made of flesh, and the search becomes increasingly erotic, caressing, orgasmic, until the aperture is found.

I push my way in, and there I see Jordan and Evelyne making love. It is not my orgasm but theirs that I have produced, and I see on Evelyne's face an expression of pain and delight as Jordan drives deep into her. I try to join them, enfolding them in my arms and legs, telling them that I love them both, but their bodies have become fused into a ball so slippery that it flies away from me.

They separate and turn towards me finally. On both of their faces I see a look of longing for me, and I run joyfully towards them. Their lips are moving in unison, and I embrace them trying to hear what it is they are whispering. But the voice is always the doctor's: "Go away. She doesn't need you; she needs me. That's why we're in bed together."

I press them tighter to me as if to stifle the words, but the door in the wall has closed, and I am holding, not flesh any longer, but rough granite. An overwhelming loneliness wells up inside me, and I circle the windowless wall, unable to find the door because now there is only stone that lacerates my hands.

Of course, I am distorting these recurrent dreams, rationalizing them. As they were happening, the sense of identity was much more fluid. When Evelyne was being fucked, for instance, part of the time it was I who was in her, part of the time Jordan, and it was only as I realized my own weakness in comparison with him that he became dominant, excluding me. But whatever was happening, there was this growing obsession with the doctor's words, as though they had been planted in my head like electrodes.

I worried over where they could have come from. I knew what they meant to me, but I needed to find some other meaning outside myself so that I could escape from their threat.

At last I managed to find the doctor who had admitted me after the accident. Although I told him all I had heard, he couldn't remember a thing. "You must be making a mistake. Accidents, drugs, you know, they play strange tricks on the memory." He really didn't have time to talk about it anymore.

But as soon as he had started to speak, I knew I was right: it was the voice in my dream. And when I insisted, begging almost, he finally did remember the nasty little anecdote he had been telling.

That, I was sure, would be the end of it. I went to sleep that night knowing I was safe. But the dream of Jordan and Evelyne recurred more intensely than ever. I wakened sweating, repeating to myself, "It's got nothing to do with you, nothing, nothing." And yet it had. The explanation didn't explain anything at all.

The next day, acute depression. But now, as time passes, the dreams have become less frequent, less searing. Others, of course, supplant them. Time is not a healer; it merely finds new roots of pain.

I talk of dreams and waking, conscious and subconscious, but during that first week the dividing line was erased by morphine.

The other patient in the room was, of all things, a police superintendent who had hurt his back playing lawn bowls. He was visited by a succession of other paunchy, hearty policemen who brought him bottles of whisky—even a crate of beer, which he ostentatiously hid underneath my bed.

Some of them seemed to recognize me. I knew none of them. They all seemed indistinguishable from each other, but they were still polite, even friendly in the sort of way I could never manage to be with somebody whose views I hated or despised.

One afternoon, I remember, I joined with a kind of hysteria in the usual conversation they were having about sports and bar-girls and promotion. But mostly I just lay in an amazed stupor, fending off their approaches with a bewildered grin.

It was as though I could tune in precisely to their conversations without being linked to them on any kind of social level at all. And at the same time I was able to be just as close to other people talking outside in the corridor, catching noises or words that normally I would never even have noticed. My sense of hearing seemed to be able to find the most astonishing beauty in quite ordinary sounds. The phrases I heard had a subtlety in no way connected with their content. I remember hearing a woman with a hoarse voice demanding to know where she could find a vase to put some flowers in, and the sentence seemed really fine and appropriate, like a line of poetry. And always I was able to move at my ease between one conversation and another, as if I were tuning the dial of a radio, not connected to any one of them, but aware of far more of their implications than any of the people who were actually talking.

All my senses were sharpened in the same beautifully accurate way. I could look at the badly made chair and be completely absorbed by the fantastic intricacy of the grain of the wood or the texture of the cheap material that covered the cushions. I could feel the rough linen of the hospital sheets under my fingertips and read it almost as a blind man reads braille. Everything was more real than it is in life, without difficulties or compromise.

But suddenly, it would change. Instead of ranging over the entire surface of experience, I was a diver crushed by pressure from all sides, crumpled into a tiny, defenseless knot of nerves. Voices, colors, shapes were no longer objects in a landscape that I moved through unobserved. They were directed against me; that was their only purpose. The minute rainbow in the corner of the mirror was set there specifically to attack my eye. Every trifling exchange in the corridor was a plot to bring about my extermination. I could never define how the change took place; everything was the same, and yet, without warning, the smile was scraped away to expose the bone beneath. I was on the verge of screaming, huddled in the corner of my bed, my knees pulled up into my stomach, naked as a snail without its shell.

It was, however, during one of the phases of euphoria that I had my first visit from the police. Presumably it was my second day in hospital. He wasn't one of the anonymous, good-natured chaps who came to visit their friend with the slipped disk, but an equally anonymous uniformed man with polished buttons and a polished face. He looked down at me sternly, and I smiled back at his wonderful buttons, which shone like stars into every corner of my brain.

He was on business. They had reason to believe that I could help them with their enquiries into the deaths of Dr. and Mrs. Jordan King. He had a mole on the right-hand side of his nose. It was speckled with tiny red dots, and one golden hair sprouted from the center, its edges glistening in the sunlight like a rapier.

19

They had been found dead on the verandah of their house on the same night that I had had my accident. My eyes flickered from the buttons to that one hair and back again.

"Did you visit Dr. and Mrs. King that evening, sir?" he asked.

"Did you visit Dr. and Mrs. King that evening, sir?" I replied.

"Look, I didn't come here to mess about. Just answer my question."

The words astounded me.

There was a fleck of white saliva at the corner of his lips. Then his tongue shot out like a shiny purple snake and gobbled it up.

I said very slowly, so that he wouldn't miss any of the beauty of it, "Look, I didn't come here to mess about. Just answer my question."

He moved forwards menacingly.

"You'd better leave him alone, Bob," said the policeman with the back. "You'll not get anything out of him for the moment."

"If he's taking the micky, I'll bloody screw him," said Bob.

"No, he's like this most of the time. What you call good company."

"Christ, I don't envy you him."

"It's better than having the commissioner yelling on the phone because his wife's got a parking ticket. Makes a change, anyway."

They laughed.

"Well," said Bob, "I'd better be getting along. But I'll be back. You know, they found all his clothes in the house, and he was bloody starkers when they picked him up after the accident. God knows what must have been going on. Not that I mind if the buggers go killing each other off. It makes life easier for us. But I suppose we'll still have to find out what happened."

I beamed at him compassionately as he left.

3

The red Mercedes taxi burped up the steep drive to the hospital, black diesel fumes spiralling behind it like a parachute in the still air.

Donald Winn was melting, wondering despondently how he managed to remain so enormous when so many pints of liquid oozed out of his pores each day. It wasn't as if he felt himself to be a fat man. On the contrary, the image in the mirror continually surprised him, not matching his small, hairless hands, his dainty feet, or his high-pitched voice in any way at all. It was not, he had to admit, a pleasant sight, not something that children should ever be exposed to; and since he liked children, other people's children, he resolved to diet, to take more exercise. Yes, he would play squash, become sylphlike. Yet when he mentioned it to friends, they would burst into wild laughter. "But we love you just as you are," they would say when he protested. Bloody liars, he thought. Don't know what love is.

The sweat ran down his face, collected in the folds under his chin, and dropped onto the pink shirt that adhered to his huge torso.

If I ever stay in one place, he thought, I might drown.

Really, the climate was unbearable. No wonder so many of the early settlers had died in those first summers like flies in winter. By accident, he had wandered into a cemetery one afternoon and had seen their names crudely carved on eroded headstones: "Mary Crawford, beloved consort of Thomas Crawford. In the prime of her life, in the midst of her labors, and in the meridian of her usefulness, she died suddenly at Hong Kong, July 12th, 1848, aged 23 years." Nicol McAllister, David Thompson, Agnes Miln: he remembered their names, since nobody else would.

The place had been uninhabitable then, a barren rock, fertile only in disease. And it was still as bad, he thought. Antibiotics and air conditioners had between them created an image of civilization, comfort, vitality, but underneath it all the same old festering monsoon island remained.

How little had actually changed in the hundred and twenty years since Britain had forced the Chinese to hand over this rocky island from which opium could be injected into China with impunity. Merchants had flocked here, unscrupulous crooks beneath a pose of Presbyterian self-righteousness. Most of them died of malaria, but those who survived grew rich on opium. Now, of course, the companies they had established were respectable, paternalistic empires; and yet when you looked at the kind of society that had mushroomed around them, there was the same aggressive self-interest and contempt behind the pretentions.

And whose side was he, Winn, on? Why, the exploiters', of course.

He tugged his trousers away from the plastic of the seat and squeezed himself through the door. And immediately everything was different again. The taxi had stopped next to some bushes covered in ringlets of tiny, whitish flowers. He stood beside them in the sun, sweat prickling, his eyes closed, feeling the perfume sweep over him. He ran his fingers lightly over his arms that somehow had become those of a slim young boy again. What one ought really to do was build a little wooden shack up here, like some straggly-bearded Chinese hermit, and then give the rest of one's life to contemplating these bushes and the view that lay behind them.

The mountainside fell steeply away from where he stood, dotted with white concrete buildings that shone, dazzling the eye, amongst fields of green. Far below there was a U-shaped bay between rocky promontories, with a small village set dangerously near to the shoreline. Undoubtedly, if you went down there, there would be the stink of poverty: pigs and dogs and chickens; naked children suffering from undernourishment, their skins covered with eczema; rotting refuse and urine in the gutters; oil and broken plastic sandals and glass on the dirty sand. From up here it was beautiful.

Beyond the bay he looked out across the estuary of the Pearl River, nearly fifty miles wide, dotted with hilly islands. The water around them was a light, almost silver blue, lighter than the deep blue of the sky. A few translucent clouds were hanging motionless above the horizon, their whiteness vibrating in the gently stirring surface of the sea. About it all was the peaceful but false sense that nothing would ever be any different. So he stood there trying to stare it into permanence.

From the bus stop on the road below, a thread of antlike people crawled up to the hospital. They filed between white buildings in the blinding sun: old women dressed in black, sheltering under umbrellas; young girls with tight, swinging buttocks in flimsy pink or light blue pyjama suits, laughing, pushing each other, giggling at boys; children strapped to backs; fishermen in dark brown oilcloth trousers and singlets stretched across knotted shoulders. They carried bags of fruit, flasks of herbal potions, and aluminum cans of cooked food, suspicious of the medicine and the diet in the alien hospital.

Donald Winn joined the endless stream and walked up the steps into the cool entrance hall, where two long queues had formed in front of the lift doors. An attendant came over and beckoned for him to go to the head of the line, but Winn glared him angrily away. The people around him looked merely puzzled. He must have plenty of time to waste. But Winn wasn't even conscious of their lack of faith. Warm with self-satisfaction, he fixed his eyes on an old man standing slightly ahead of him in the next queue. A body so fragile the lightest breeze would break him. His cheeks were hollow, probably from drugs, and a few grey hairs sprouted from his chin and upper lip. His deep brown eyes never moved from the back in front of him as he shuffled along, waiting, taking his turn, seeming to ask for nothing more.

Winn looked farther ahead along the line, and his sentimentality faded. Hadn't he recognized the back of a man who was just pushing his way in through the lift doors? He could be wrong; there were hundreds of men here dressed in cheap, light-weight trousers and white, open-necked shirts. But as the man turned, Winn caught a glimpse of the face and swore loudly. It was Kwan.

Kwan Wing-leung stood jammed into a corner of the lift, trying to draw his nostrils away from a towering European businessman who was shouting to his wife. What could have brought Donald Winn up to the hospital, Kwan wondered? It didn't worry him, it wasn't pressing enough for that, but it stretched his imagination slightly.

Winn wasn't following him. Quite apart from being too conspicuous, he was too important to do that sort of thing. Yet it was hard to believe he wasn't here on some kind of business. Hospitals were hardly his natural habitat. It was the peripheral things that interested him most: a gay bar, a second-rate fun fair with sleazy side-shows, a bourgeois gambling den with prostitution, male and female, on the side.

Yes, that's where Mr. Winn feels at home. Kwan caught a tightening in the muscles round his mouth and willed them back into relaxation. Disdain could be as dangerous, as distorting, as fear or hatred—or any emotion.

And, after all, how much did that kind of information really tell you about a person? There were times when everybody seemed to be following everybody else, tapping their telephones, bugging their lovers. But in the end, wasn't it all just gossip? Kwan knew he himself was followed most of the time, but he never even bothered to try and shake off the poor bastards who were doing it. Anyone who was given such a boring job would surely be too stupid to understand anything significant that he might accidentally stumble on.

Still, if it was all so pointless, why did you go on having it done yourself? Partly out of habit, he supposed, but mainly because you were so desperately afraid of missing something. If you had somebody watched, unless they were utter fools, you would discover practically nothing about their activities. But you went on hoping that you might, if you pieced all the scraps together intelligently, learn a good deal about their personalities: their desires, their vices, their tastes and habits. It was interesting and occasionally, very occasionally, useful. But finally it was still the sort of information that was almost always overestimated. Especially, of course, by Europeans.

The trouble was that you ended up with an enormous amount of knowledge you didn't really need anyway. After all, it was actions, not people, that mattered, and it was remarkable how frequently the two factors could be separated almost entirely. "I am not a blackmailer," Kwan had shouted recently at an informer who had come proudly in to tell him how this man Winn had been picking up young boys in a body-building gymnasium (a fact that Kwan had known, in any case, for a long time). "What I want to find out is where Winn's going to try to put the pressure on next. Knowing that he's queer doesn't tell me anything about that at all."

By now in fact (like it or not) he knew a great deal about this grotesque figure, Donald Winn. But that's just it, he thought. It was just this grotesque quality that was beginning to worry him: this mountain of flesh moving daintily as a ballerina, the dyed blond curls—dyed, so he had heard, because a spoilt little boy had said one evening in a moment of boredom or malice: "You know, I've just realized, I don't like brown hair; I wish you were blond, Donald." If he had said, "I don't like people with two hands," Winn would probably have chopped one of them off.

Kwan found himself smiling at the picture in his mind. And that was the whole trouble. Winn was so ridiculous you forgot to take him seriously. He was vulnerable and entertaining and so extremely kind in a quite unselfish way, feeling for people he hardly knew, going out of his way to mother them, help them, please them. In the process you forgot all too easily, though not excusably, the cold, destructive efficiency, the persistent ruthlessness he was capable of.

The lift jolted to a stop, and Kwan tried to edge his way round the carcass of the Englishman in front of him.

"Excuse me," he said.

The man paid no attention, just went on braying away at his wife. Kwan hesitated, then pushed him hard in the ribs with his elbow, knocking him off balance.

"Hey!" shouted the Englishman, and the hubbub in the lift suddenly faded. Trouble. The man swung round and saw the flat Szechwanese face staring up at him without apology.

Stewart had been lying surrounded by pillows, staring out the window onto the shaded balcony, trying desperately to keep his mind fixed on the outlines of buildings and hills that were visible through the bamboo blinds.

He was trying to ignore the banal conversation, full of pauses and false starts, that was going on between the policeman and his wife just a few feet away. But the more he concentrated on ignoring it, the more it intruded, underlining the sense of his own isolation.

At first, the feeling had been the result, quite selfishly, of the fact that nobody had come to see him; whereas these two ordinary, dull people had at least somebody, something beyond themselves. How easy, he thought with self-pity, to live like this, without ever facing up to any of the questions. So why did it seem to be so impossible for him?

But as he listened enviously to them, he began to realize there was in fact no contact there after all. They weren't really talking about anything that had any kind of meaning to either of them. He cringed into the pillows.

"I brought you some lychees, Joe," said Kwan softly.

The body under the sheets twitched round, startled, the eyes swinging to the other side of the room and back again, the brain not registering, and then a faint smile easing the drawn lips.

What a change there had been in the week since Kwan had seen Stewart last. Then Joe had been in control, his emotions strained, of course—whose wouldn't be in that kind of situation?—but held down by the will. Now, if there was any control at all in what he did, it was nothing more than a conditioned reflex that might break at any moment. The handsome, slightly flabby face had gone yellow and sunken beneath the bandaged forehead; wrinkles cobwebbed the eyes; the lips were grey and chapped.

Kwan's nostrils dilated at the smell that rose from

the plaster sheath, sweet as vomit. Just a flickering of
the nostrils that Stewart saw immediately.

"I'm sorry about the smell. There's not much I
can do about it."

Immediately Kwan was ashamed. What right had
he to this oversensitivity, like some old mandarin with
incense burners to shield him from the irritating stench
of misery?

"This place is making me very soft," he said aloud,
an arm on Joe's shoulder.

Joe Stewart winced as his body turned; then he
smiled and with both hands on Kwan's arm tugged
him down onto the wooden chair beside the bed.

"I've been feeling a bit rough. You know, the
shock, then the drugs. But really, you're the only
person I wanted to see, Wing-leung."

Kwan watched the tears that came too easily to the
corners of Stewart's eyes, the words stumbling. He
could feel the policeman and his wife openly staring
at them, puzzled. And then, with an effort, the woman
pulled herself back: "So I said to her, if you run away
from me on the beach ever again, it's the last time I'll
take you."

"I saw your friend Mr. Winn on the way up
here," said Kwan. "I think he's probably coming to
see you, too."

Stewart drew away. "What can he want? More
questions, I suppose." Then the eyes becoming restless
again. "Is that why you're here, too? Just to find out
what happened?"

Kwan smiled. "Of course not, Joe. It doesn't
matter to me. It's not my business. You can tell me if
you like, but I'm not going to try and make you. I'm
not an interrogator."

Winn was.

"But surely you want to know what happened to
Jordan." Stewart sounded almost offended now that he
wasn't being pressed, anxious that his secret should
not become unimportant.

"Look, Joe, I came to see how you were. That's

all. And to find out if there was anything we could do for you. I'll be honest with you: of course we're affected by King's death. It changes quite a few things. But that doesn't mean it upsets me; it doesn't even inconvenience me very much. Jordan was more in the way than anything else, and now he's out of the way, that's all. I'm not saying we're pleased he's dead—but, well, he wasn't as important as he thought he was. You knew that yourself."

Kwan hadn't been prepared for how shaken Stewart would be, and he was suddenly conscious of trying not to despise him for it. He had liked Joe ever since their first meeting at Jordon King's house. On the surface, to be sure, there had been the usual self-assurance that Kwan associated with most English socialists: the missionary arrogance that made them think they could dazzle the simple natives with their breath-taking platitudes. But underneath the racial mask there was something much more useful: an openness, a readiness to learn, a kind of enthusiastic doubt. That was what Kwan admired about him and found challenging. The doubt couldn't be allowed to become an end in itself, a refuge; that was the danger in it. Yet it had the advantage of honesty; it could be built on.

Even after a year of working together he still wasn't sure exactly how far Stewart could be relied upon; you had to remember that he wasn't much more than a boy, and his whole upbringing had accustomed him to a world where trust was nothing more than a matter of business convenience. But Kwan was still surprised to see him fold up like this, clutching any straw for consolation. And he hated this easy judgement that he found himself on the verge of making because it was in conflict with emotions he wished could be stronger.

He watched with a kind of relief as Stewart closed his eyes and seemed to relax.

"Listen, Joe," he said quietly, "there was something I wanted to say before Winn gets here. If he is coming, I mean. I remember you saying, before all this happened, that you didn't think you could stay here much longer, that you had to make a choice one way or the other."

Kwan paused.

The eyes opened unwillingly. "And you're trying to tell me that now I'm even less able to go on putting it off?" Stewart's voice was blurred, but he had seen, through the drugs and Kwan's own hesitancy, the line the words were taking. He had been drifting in the same direction.

"Yes, Joe, that's what I was getting at. Life here is going to be pretty impossible for you after all this. Whichever way you look at it—our work, or the police, or . . . Mei? You can't just start from where you left off. I haven't been able to find out yet how far the police will want to take things. Not very far, I expect. We've given them too many other things to think about. But anyway, we don't have to wait for them to make up their minds. We can make arrangements of our own. And if you did come to a decision—well, I think I could probably help." He patted Stewart's arm, trying to sound fatherly. "And you could help us, too, Joe. Much more than you could ever do here. This place is finished; you know that. I'm not trying to force you into anything, just telling you the road's still open."

The door of the room was flung inwards with a bang, and a shrill voice was saying, "Christ, that fucking lift! Stuck! I had to walk all the way up those fucking stairs."

Kwan had been leaning forwards, near to Stewart. Now he smiled and sat back. "It's still your choice, Joe."

As he spoke, he heard his voice become false and ingratiating. That was not how he felt; he cared what might happen to Stewart. But he was thankful all the same for the interruption.

"Hello, Mike, having a nice rest?" Winn waved at the policeman, who had opened his mouth to protest against the flood of curses and then closed it again when he saw who it was.

Who's that? said the wife's eyebrows.

"Name's Winn, ma'am," said Winn, bowing with insulting courtesy. "Donald Winn. Not had the—ah—pleasure."

She felt the watery grey eyes run over her and thought, as she was expected to think, What a horrible man!

Winn turned away. "How are you, Joe?" He tried to wipe the sweat away from his brow with his shirt sleeve, but to no effect. The sleeve was already soaked. He gasped for air and thumped himself on the chest. "You're looking all right. Better than me, anyway. And you, Mr. Kwan. Didn't expect to see you here. But it's a nice surprise. We don't often meet on neutral ground nowadays, do we?"

"There's very little neutral ground left," said Kwan. "Fortunately."

Winn smiled. "Oh, come. I would say 'unfortunately,' you know."

"If you want to be nostalgic. Or hypocritical. But then there isn't much room left for that either, is there? Not after all that's happened in the past year."

Stewart's eyes flickered back and forth between them, not keeping up.

Winn turned to him. He hadn't come to fight with Kwan. Not over this, anyway.

"I brought you these, Joe. I remembered you saying you could live on lychees, and I didn't think you'd get anything like that in this fucking mortuary. Stinks of formaldehyde or something. They're the small-stoned ones, the first this season."

"It stinks of me actually," said Joe, making an effort to meet Winn on his own terms. "But thanks, Donald. I didn't expect you to come."

"Well, I can't usually stand hospitals. They frighten the shit out of me."

As Stewart put the bag of lychees on the table,

Winn noticed an identical one, printed with the same big red characters, lying there already. He opened it slightly and laughed. Kwan was smiling, too. The bags both came from the same Communist store.

"Well, Mr. Kwan, at least I know where to buy the best lychees, don't I? Perhaps lychees are a kind of neutral ground, after all."

"No, I don't think I can let you get away with that." The voice was quite solemn, humorless. "They are a very . . . Chinese fruit."

"You mean they're nourished by the thoughts of the Great Leader and Great Helmsman, Chairman Mao? Like a kind of manure," said Winn sarcastically, pushing Kwan hard for a reaction of anger or embarrassment, anything that would show a break in the composure on the squashed moonscape of his face. It was such an irritating, incongruous face, with the thick black hair bristling out at the sides like a porcupine's, the smooth polished skin, and tiny nose, enormous in the complete flatness around it.

"Exactly," said Kwan, expressionless.

For a moment they watched each other across three yards of hate.

Finally Kwan said, "Come and sit over here, Mr. Winn," getting up from the chair by the bed and going to sit in an uncomfortable armchair in the middle of the room. "I expect there's a lot of things you want to tell Joe. Or ask him?"

Winn sat down protesting.

In his grandmother's house in Chengtu, Kwan had been brought up to suppress all show of emotion. Once he had broken a porcelain vase when he lost patience with a dull tutor who wouldn't answer his questions, and the old woman—she was his father's mother and ruled the family—had him locked up in a room for so long that he thought she was leaving him there to starve to death. So the anger that burned inside him now was no problem; he was used to it being there.

In any case, he had done what he had come for.

He could just walk off and leave the empty field for Winn to perform on, but curiosity held him back. He wanted to see how Winn would handle the situation, what he would make of it.

"You know Willie Muir, that little prick up at the university?" Winn was saying. "Well, he's been doing some research on drug addiction. Heroin. The bugger wanted to get some convicts to test it out on, but the government wouldn't let him. So he got a whole load of monkeys from Borneo. Gave them heroin instead of bananas. The trouble was, I reckon Willie was shooting himself up, too. Anyway, one night he forgot to look them up in their fucking cages, and they all got out. Can you imagine it?" The giggles rippled out of him. "Two dozen junkie monkeys? On the loose? They got right out of the lab and into the telephone exchange next door. Did five million dollars' worth of damage before they were shot."

Even Kwan had to laugh. Wasn't this just typical of Donald Winn? When you saw him like this, he seemed so innocent and spontaneous. He loved gossip for its own sake, a kind of mental embroidery he could decorate with his own designs. And yet, like everything else in his life, it became, almost by accident, a weapon, a means to a very specific end. This guileless, aimless chatter could so easily be used as a tool to wind a man round gradually, like a lock on a safe, until suddenly a gentle tap was enough to leave the door wide open.

Kwan could see only too clearly what was happening. But ironically, the growing sense of irritation that he felt was with himself. What he hated was this continual tendency towards suspicion. It seemed at times to be the driving force in his whole existence, and he despised it as if it were an alien infection. Basically he was sure that life was, ought to be, simple; there were a few simple choices that had to be made, and then everything should be clear. But here he was, puzzling over people, finding subtleties where you hoped they didn't even exist. You became involved, and soon there was nobody you could trust, not even yourself.

To shake off his irritation, he got up and went out onto the balcony, looking casually down on the nurses' home beside the hospital. Tiny and foreshortened from this height, a girl in an orange dress came down the steps, out into the bright sun, her dress luminous against the black Tarmac. She looked around, then started to run across to where a yellow sports car was waiting. At that moment a grey van with a rusty roof, wire grilles on all the windows, came round the corner heading straight for the girl. She jumped back just in time, stopped for a moment, then walked more slowly over to the car, got in, and was driven away.

Simple. From up here.

Kwan looked back into the room, where Winn was in the middle of acting out another story. Even from out there, Kwan could see the sweat trickling out of the blond hair, so fine and tightly curled that the pink scalp shone through. He sighed and went back in.

"Do your people have a grey van with a slightly rusty roof, Mr. Winn?" he interrupted.

Winn looked up at him, puzzled. "A grey van? I don't think so." He tried to think of something to say. "I don't expect it would be rusty, anyway."

The silence was quite empty.

"Well," murmured Kwan, "we don't have anything to worry about, do we?" He bent down towards Stewart, looking into the distant eyes that swivelled round towards him. "I'm sorry, Joe, I must go now. I'll have to leave you to Mr. Winn's . . . mercies. But I'll come back soon."

Joe whispered a reply, and then, as Kwan was closing the door, he tried to stretch his brittle voice: "I won't forget what you were saying."

Winn picked at a spot on his arm. "Well, what do you make of that? He's a weird old bugger, your mate Kwan, isn't he? What was all that about a grey van, I wonder. Half the time he talks like an abridged

34

version of Chairman Mao, and then, just when you know where you are with him, he goes and says something fucking surrealistic like that."

Winn reached for one of Joe's lychees. That was the whole trouble with Kwan. So many of his actions ran true to type, but the motives behind them were not typical at all, so you could never be sure of the final result.

Kwan was not in his heart a political leader. He was, by birth, by training, an intellectual, a product of the old scholar aristocracy, more at home with the subtleties of archaic jade, the ambiguities of late Tang poetry than with the slogans of the Red Guards. And yet last year, when he had been thrust into the role of an activist, chairman of the committee that had co-ordinated riots and terrorism, he had acted the part as if that were his true nature after all. There had been no weapon he was afraid to use: crude racism, bombs that killed indiscriminately, lies that not even the converted could have been taken in by. And he had come so near to winning, though to have won would surely have been a betrayal of all that he believed.

But that was the whole problem. What did Kwan believe? Now that an uneasy truce had been restored, he continued to argue with great persuasiveness and tolerance in defense of all that was still happening in China. And yet wasn't it an argument in favor of a society that had no need of argument or persuasion and least of all tolerance, since it was sustained quite simply by force? And it was here that Winn became most involved. How long could Kwan go on living out this compromise between his values and his actions? At some point a breach must come. And then what would happen to the rest of them?

He could feel himself becoming troubled and morose. What did it matter, anyway? All this intrigue and tension. And what was he doing in this stinking hospital? He supposed he would have to find out how King had been killed. But what was the point? He could guess most of the answers already. These fucking lychees tasted like flesh. But still, you had to be sure, even though you knew that certainty was impossible.

"How did you come to be playing cowboys and Indians up at Jordan King's?" he asked abruptly, knowing this kind of question would ruin everything, intending it, perhaps.

Stewart was jolted. "I knew that was why you came," he snapped, hysteria like a saw's edge in his voice. "Well, if you want to come and ask me that, you can bloody well wear your uniform."

"Oh, for Christ's sake, don't be so stupid, Joe. I didn't mean that at all."

Already Winn was sorry for the moment of irritation; ground that would have to be reclaimed. "Look, all I meant was you've got to talk about it sometime or other, and you might as well tell a friend as some moronic flatfoot." He looked over at the other bed. Mike Webb had gone to sleep. "I can help you, Joe, truly. I realize it was an accident, but we've got to know more about it than that. So why don't you tell me?"

"It wasn't an accident. That's all I've got to say." Stewart turned his head away.

"Jesus!" said Winn.

He paused.

"I suppose that was why old Kwan was up here, too."

No reaction.

"Or was there more to it than that, eh? You know, they were bloody glad to get rid of King. Blamed it on us in the newspapers, of course, but Jordan was just becoming a nuisance to everyone. So I should think Kwan must be pretty grateful. He wasn't offering you a free trip to Peking as a sort of reward, was he?"

Like a charm, he thought as Stewart fell for it, twisting around in surprise. Even a little afraid. Poor bastard. Something so obvious, but still enough to shake his nerves. Winn felt his irritation ebb as it was replaced by a feeling of power, then pity.

"Look, Joe, don't be taken in by Kwan. I know he's bloody convincing, but you know as well as I do there's no future in it for you. It's all right in the abstract maybe—lots of nice little peasants in blue uniforms covered with red badges—but after a month or two it would drive you out of your tiny mind. You know what freedom is; even in a dump like this, where there isn't so much of it after all. But over there you'd have none. You'd be a bloody idiot, I'm telling you. And I'm not saying that because it's my job. I'm saying it as a friend."

He watched Stewart draw farther and farther away and suddenly felt sick of himself. What right had he to break into people's lives like this? To take a man for whom he felt real tenderness and drive him so far into melancholy that all you could feel for him was disgust?

But then there was a reason, or at least an excuse for it. After all, it was true what he was saying, wasn't it? As true as any lie.

4

Mei left me ten days before Jordan King's death. I remember that first night without her. Now as I sit beside the lake—the water lapping, the buzz somewhere of a saw, the air sharp on my face but my body warm inside the blue kapok-filled jacket—I remember it, and it all seems impossibly diminished and unlikely.

I lay awake for hours thinking of the things I should have been able to say to her, turning over and over, listening to the drone of the air conditioner, hearing non-existent irregularities in it, the sheets getting tangled round my neck. As the night dragged on, the conversations in my mind became more and more repetitive. Sleep stalked all around me, but I was constantly fighting it off, forcing myself back over the old ground—old memories, new excuses—again, again, never getting to the end before I had to start once more.

I suppose at last I must have dozed off, a man walking backwards over a cliff, but I wakened almost immediately, feeling myself falling, trying to catch myself.

I could smell Mei still beside me, but when I stretched out my fingers, the bed was empty.

There was a place we used to go to, weekends usually, up in the country behind Kowloon, with a marvelous view along the craggy tops of the hills and down, over the town of Shatin, to the sea. It was just a shack really, set back from the road, with a rough garden and rickety chairs and tables. But in the tiny kitchen round the back, next to the smelly toilets, they made good, simple Malay food, and the garden was full of flowering shrubs and spreading flame and kapok trees. You could sit there with your eyes half closed, the sun trying to get at you between the branches, and almost forget the battle that was being fought just beyond the hills, in the streets of the city. One of the few places in Hong Kong where you could.

I remember one Sunday in particular. The temperature had fallen slightly, and the air was like a hot, dry towel against your skin instead of the wet flannel it usually wrapped you in. We drove out there with the roof down, the car rearing like an excited animal that's suddenly been let off its leash, Mei's hair blowing out behind her so that her face seemed somehow naked, alarmingly delicate and vulnerable in the middle of all this surging energy. When we stopped, I put my arm round her and pulled her against me, feeling so much more gentle, more protective than I knew I really could be.

We ordered beer and saté and fried noodles, the saté bubbling and spitting on the little charcoal grill between us, the lumps of crisp fat melting in the mouth, and the grease being washed away by the iced beer. The people round about us were mainly Chinese families from Singapore or Malaysia, most of them with young children, but they were far enough away not to come between us, the kids playing on swings at the side of the house or in the ditch that ran from there down towards the road.

I watched Mei as she ate fiercely, a different person from the fragile porcelain thing she had been in the car. Her hair fell down around her face, the ends curving in sharply towards her mouth, and it was a strong, firm face now, a handsome boy's. The cheekbones were broad and the lips wide and shiny with the grease on them. As she leaned in towards the table—her shoulders coming forwards, legs bent under her in the tight, faded jeans, feet bare, dust from the sandy ground around the nails—she looked young and careless of herself. But then, as she stretched back, her body seemed suddenly to swell, to grow self-conscious and satisfied, the Cardin leather jacket swinging open and her breasts pushing up through my old Fair Isle pullover, which she'd claimed. She rested one arm along the back of the next chair, crossing her legs, swivelling on the full thighs and buttocks, then opened her mouth and stretched her teeth forwards to pull the meat off the wooden skewer.

Her long tongue came out to lick away a drop of the peanut sauce. I watched her fiercely.

She caught my eyes and held them playfully. "What are you looking at?"

"We don't come up here often enough."

"We say that every time we come." She stretched lazily, sunlight and shadow flickering over her arched body.

"Well, that doesn't stop it being true; when I'm up here, I know what it is I want." Looking at each other, into each other, both of us wanting the same thing, wanting it more because we knew we'd have to wait.

She couldn't let herself take it too seriously, though; had been hurt too often when she had; by others, then by me. "Hey, that's how they ought to advertise the place, Joe. You know, the aphrodisiac mountain air; screw your worries away! They could build bedrooms out the back. Heavens, they're in the wrong business; they could make a fortune."

I laughed at the little-girl cynicism, but I wasn't going to be put off by it. "You know that's not what I meant, love. Well, not just what I meant." And as she smiled back, there was an ease in her, an acceptance of what I was offering. I tried to put it into words, knowing I didn't need to: "What I mean is, up here I can see the choice I have to make; if we stayed long enough, it'd make itself. Back there"—I pointed up the road as if to blame my own confusion on the city—"everything seems to be forcing me away from that—" I hesitated, "away from you."

She swung round and leaned towards me, a hand in mine. "We couldn't stay up here, though."

"No . . . but somewhere else."

"Do you want to go away?" Eagerly; no defenses now.

"Yes, sometimes I do." But then I had to modify it; it was getting too final. "But I don't want just to run away, Mei. I can't do that; that's the problem."

So she laughed again, but not bitterly, and looked up between the branches at the sun. "Look at those seedpods up there. Why can't I be like one of them?" Just words, the game of words, not really meaning anything by them, just using them lazily, as a reminder of contact.

I saw the moistness in her eyes as I looked down from the tough, crinkled pods, a foot or so long, with their rich brown skin stretched over the darker seeds.

"I can't think of anything you're less like."

"No, I mean it." Though she didn't.

"Why, then?"

She had to think for a reason. "Well, they're so much . . . themselves. Look, you look at them, and you can't think of any image for them, can you? They're just themselves, all worn and dry and wrinkled, and you feel they couldn't possibly be any different. They could stay like that forever. If something terrible happened to everything else, they'd still be the same." Her lips pouted. "Yes, I should like to be permanent like that."

I smiled. "Are you asking me to marry you?"

I had asked her once before, but she had laughed at the idea, wanted, she said, to be free.

So she laughed again. "That wouldn't be permanence. That'd be a slow decay."

And I laughed, too, released from my indecision, proud of her toughness among all the domesticated families round about us.

It wasn't enough, though; no strength was.

When I had paid the bill, we walked over to the side of the hill where the ground fell steeply away to the floor of the valley. We looked down at the confusion of tiny fields and houses, the long roads with the occasional lorry raising clouds of dust, the creeping disease of suburbia.

"Christ, what a mess."

"Why, what's wrong with it?" Surprise in her voice.

"Well, it's obvious, isn't it?" I was suddenly impatient. "Everybody comes up here, and they look at the view, and they say, 'God, it's so beautiful.' But it's not beautiful at all, not anymore. To say it's beautiful, you've got to ignore at least half of what you see. Maybe it was once, but now you've got to filter out everything that's been done to it."

She didn't say anything; silence that began to drag at my nerves.

"Just one fucking great mess," I insisted.

She ground a toe in the dirt. "Maybe it depends who you are. Where you're standing." The pattern she was drawing changed into a face. A thin girl's face. Pigtails. "But that's the trouble, Joe, I can't see what angle you're looking at it from. What I mean is, if you're a Communist—oh, or a socialist or whatever it is—something I'm not, anyway—how can you go and get all worked up about"—her nose wrinkled—"nature and beauty?"

Perhaps she had pushed me into a corner without either of us wanting it. Wasn't this, after all, just one more symptom of the double-talk I was always finding in myself, always denying? And perhaps that was why, recognizing it, I replied so vehemently, so pompously. "I don't think the two things need to be exclusive. I want men to be able to make the best of nature, not the worst."

"Well, then"—she jumped up on tiptoe, triumphing—"isn't that just what those people down there are doing? What you want them to do? They may not have any marvelous slogans, but they're struggling just as hard to make the best of what they've got."

She was still smiling, arguing half in fun, but the edge of it was sharp; and when we got into the car, we sat far away from each other, against the doors. We couldn't go back to talking about nothing anymore.

We had already decided to go on to an old walled village that lay a hundred yards or so off the road at the bottom of the hill. I had passed it often before, accelerating out of the ugly town, admiring the beautiful symmetry of its roofs from the corner of my eye, always promising that one day I would stop.

All the way down there, along the winding road with its marvelous views over to the right, neither of us spoke, blaming each other, behaving with a slightly exaggerated, stony normality to show that nothing was wrong. But then, as I pulled off onto a bumpy track, Mei leaned across and touched the lobe of my ear with her lips. Instinctively, I almost snapped at her, "Be careful," but just in time I drew back from the obvious childishness of it all and instead dropped my hand onto her thigh, squeezing it gently.

"I want you," I said.

"The natives'll be shocked."

"Let them be."

The wool was warm against the back of my hand,

her skin cool and dry on my palm, as I tried to work my fingers up to the hardness of her breasts.

She twisted away and opened the door. Over to the left dozens of people were riding bicycles round and round on a patch of open, dusty ground between shacks plastered with Coca-Cola signs, the narrow tires leaving tracks behind them like skaters on a lake.

"What the hell are they doing?"

"I don't know. I've never noticed them here before. Maybe they come out here and hire the bikes."

"They must be crazy. Why would anyone want to do that in a dump like this?"

"Oh, Joe, why don't we go over there, too, though? I haven't ridden a bike for years and years and years. The village can wait for another week."

"No, let's do what we came here for first."

And she came without arguing, holding my hand as we walked along the rutted track, then down some steps and along a concrete path that snaked between the marshy plots where watercress was growing, over to the arched gate of the village. Some kids were walking in front of us, transistors blaring, and Mei began to skip along in time to the music. Twenty yards away an old woman was working in one of the fields, up to her bony knees in the black water. Farther on, a couple of calves were tethered to a metal stake at the side of the path.

"It's like walking back into the past," said Mei as the walls of the village rose in front of us, larger, higher than we had expected them to be, with just a few small windows set into them.

"Aren't Chinese towns and villages supposed to be built on the same plan all over China or something?" I asked her. "You know, with the main buildings in exactly the same relative positions wherever you go?"

"Don't ask me, darling. I don't know a thing about China."

"You're just bloody ignorant." I kissed her.

44

"All I'm good for is sleeping with dirty old foreigners," she whispered.

But when we got to the gates, the first thing we saw was the rubbish. Old bits of newspapers or cigarette packets interwoven wtih weeds, worn tires, broken planks, tiles, plucked chicken feathers, ashes, and smashed pottery lay in heaps everywhere. And the buildings were just as bad. The eaves had once been decorated with painted dragons moulded in plaster, flowers and bamboos, gods and birds. Now only fragments remained, broken and scarred, a meaningless litter. I felt the happiness go cold in us.

For a few minutes we walked about, but the tiny houses had spread out into the open spaces and the narrow alleyways of the village, so that they were more like a series of private yards, chairs and birdcages and stoves and the ever-present rubbish lying about them, clotheslines stretched across from one building to another, hostile children peering out at us, until we both felt like the intruders we were.

From a narrow doorway came the sound of singing, a Sunday school with its Chinese versions of a jangling Christian hymn.

"Ancient China," I said grimly.

"I suppose we were expecting the wrong thing." Mei's voice was small and tired.

"Oh, don't let's start making excuses."

"It's not an excuse. It's our fault for being so sentimental about it to begin with, building the place up into something it couldn't be."

"But it doesn't have to be like this, all this filth and decay."

"Yes, but you're judging it by your standards, not by theirs."

"What are their standards, then? They haven't got any. All the traditional values have broken up, and the only new ones are those absurd bloody hymns."

"They survive."

"Like animals, yes. Not like human beings. What

they need is to be educated, to learn how to organize themselves."

"There you go again, trying to force them into a mould. Like all those old missionaries trying to impose their pretty little patterns on us from the outside."

"Okay, so what do you know about the inside? Just now you were saying you knew fuck all about China. You're no more Chinese than I am, love. Let's be honest about it."

About twenty children were gathered around us there, in front of the main gate, not understanding a word we were saying but fascinated by the hostility that was growing like a weed between us. Ashamedly we started to walk away, back along the path, past the calves trying to gnaw a few blades of grass from the bare mud bank, the old woman who still didn't look up as we went by, back to the car and the people riding round and round in circles on the sand, a cloud of dust hanging motionless in the air above their heads.

Silent again, I drove through the newly opened tunnel that pierced under the range of hills to the city of Kowloon and out into the grime and noise, the air tangibly thicker and dirtier than it had been just a mile behind us. It made you blink for fear you might be going blind.

My mouth was turning sour with the film of fat that had stayed there from the meal. We both knew that the row hadn't ended yet. Like a fire that had been damped down, it would burst out somewhere else, more vicious and pointless than before. There was still just a chance that a word of charity would extinguish it completely; it would have taken so little. But neither of us now could give even that, and the only alternative was for it to blaze up again, until finally it burned itself out. So we sat, pulses beating, waiting for it to happen, needing it almost as we had needed to make love just a couple of hours before.

I drove in through the rich suburbs, and already you could feel the tension of the city. People had been living with it for more than six months, the riots, the hatred, the violence, and they didn't know yet that it was nearly at an end. Their nerves were ragged: cars drove carefully around cardboard boxes that had fallen off the backs of lorries, afraid that they might be bombs; and only a few days before absent-mindedly I kicked a cigarette tin that was lying in the gutter and saw half a dozen people wince at the explosion that never came.

I turned left into the packed main streets, lined with their nondescript buildings, tall blocks covered with cheap ceramic tiles and old four-story tenements faced with pock-marked plaster, their once airy balconies walled in with wood and corrugated iron to make bed spaces for two or three more families. The crowds shoved anonymously past each other, spilling over onto the roadway, rushing through the diesel fumes and the din. Most of the buses still weren't working because of the antigovernment strikes. Instead, the streets were full of vans getting rich quick with passengers crammed in their backs. They darted in and out like dragonflies, spotting somebody waiting on the kerb and cutting across three lines of traffic to get there first. I wove between them, accelerating through gaps, watching for which lane would be the quickest at the lights, edging between a zigzagging learner-driver and the cliff of a lorry piled high with empty rattan poultry baskets that looked as though they would collapse at any moment, concentrating on the pointless game, enjoying it all the more because it allowed me to push the quarrel with Mei into a corner of my mind.

And then, in front of us, was a barrier right across the street. Hundreds of people were milling about, policemen trying hopelessly to push them back.

I pulled over to the side and got out. A police sergeant farther along the pavement was pretending not to see the crowds everywhere around him.

"What's going on here?"

He turned away as if he hadn't heard.

I began again. "I said—"

"It's a bomb in the middle of the road," came a

voice at my elbow. Thick glasses, a white shirt, black trousers, an ingratiating face: student, waiter, clerk? "They're trying to move it now. They say everybody should go home."

I went back to the car.

"It's a bomb. Let's wait and see what happens."

"Oh, God, Joe, don't be such a fool. If all these people get out of control, anything can happen. Let's go home."

"Okay, then, you wait here if you want to. I'll be back in five minutes."

Without looking round I heard the car door closing and then felt her hand on my arm. I pushed into the crowd, faces turning round ready to protest, then going tight-mouthed and hostile. At last we got to the front, and there, thirty yards away, in the middle of the empty road, was the bomb. More a carnival object than anything else: a biscuit tin painted bright red, with paper streamers tied to it, Chinese characters printed on them saying, "Patriots stay clear. Death to Imperialist Pigs." Hundreds of people stared at it, curious and sullen, willing something to happen, if only to break the silence.

Mei tried to pull me away. "All right, you've seen it now. Let's go. Please, darling." Her voice was strained, irritating.

"For Christ's sake, don't fuss. I want to see what happens."

"Look, I'm scared."

"Oh, don't be so bloody silly. It's probably not a real bomb, anyway. Just a fake."

Dozens of bombs were reported every day, but only a few were real. All the others were planted, according to which side you believed, by leftists who knew that even a fake would hold up the traffic for hours until a bomb-disposal squad arrived, or by anti-Communists who wanted to put the blame on their opponents, or quite simply by people who didn't like the police and wanted to see them sweat.

They were sweating now. One of them, in particular: an English inspector, a big man with red cheeks, an ungainly body, the trunk somehow not jointed properly to the legs, so that his bottom stuck out under the flap of his uniform jacket. From one of the buildings, he had borrowed a long-handled broom, and now very slowly he was trying to move the bomb with the end of it, prodding it towards a pedestrian island in the middle of the road so that the traffic could pass by on either side. The broom handle was thin bamboo; it shook as he held it, and maybe his hands —broad hands covered with ginger hair, blunt-fingered —were shaking, too.

"Oh, be careful," breathed Mei.

"He's a bloody fool," I said. "He ought to wait for the bomb-disposal people to get here."

"And I suppose you think the men who put it there are bloody heroes."

"No, you know I don't. Bombs are too indiscriminate. But all the same, you can see their point, can't you? I mean, just look at what's happening. Have you ever seen Kowloon like this before? They can disrupt the whole city whenever they want to, and nobody even needs to get hurt. They don't even need to be real bombs any longer; that's the whole beauty of it. It's becoming a kind of ritual, and everybody's laughing at the government because they can't do anything about it."

"What about those two little girls who got their heads blown off last week? Was everybody laughing at that?"

"No, that was a mistake."

"A mistake! God, Joe, you're a bastard. You're so bloody sure of yourself, aren't you?" She hated me, willing me to look at her, her lips white and compressed. And I hated her, too, blaming her for the way she was forcing me to defend something I knew ought to be indefensible.

Then it came. The explosion. I didn't see it. I didn't so much hear it as feel it, the sudden, shocking gust of hot air driving into my face, my hands going up over my eyes instinctively, the dust and grit blasting into my pores. The first thing I saw was a little girl about five yards away screaming as she took her hands down, her forehead covered in blood. Then the crowd surged forwards uncontrollably, curious, stretching on tiptoe to get a better view of what had happened.

Where the bomb had been, there was a dark, oily stain on the road. Yellowish smoke steamed into the air, and pieces of torn paper fluttered about like leaves. The policeman, or what was left of him, lay in a graceless, tangled heap ten yards away from where he had been standing when we last looked. His face was featureless, bloody; his carrot hair, burned; holes had been blasted into him, his chest, his abdomen, his thighs, and blood gushed and trickled and seeped out onto the torn blue uniform and the dirty road.

I pushed over to the left to see what had happened to the little girl. What I felt was not so much concern as guilt; and not guilt because of the bomb itself—nothing as simple as that—but guilt somehow for my own detachment, my inability to feel anything: shock, terror, compassion. I wanted to force myself to be moved. So I knelt beside her, taking my handkerchief to wipe the blood out of her eyes, her mother standing next to me, sobbing, hiccuping. But as I wiped the blood away, I saw that she wasn't hurt at all. It wasn't her blood.

I found Mei leaning against a barrier, her head hanging forwards as if she was going to vomit. But as I touched her tentatively, she fell into my arms crying.

We didn't need to fight each other anymore that day.

There's the smell of fall in the air, smoke from a fire, the end of a season.

At least there are seasons here; in Hong Kong all you could say was that it was hot or less hot, more or less humid. But there was life there. For a time. Shall I find any here?

They tell me the lake will be frozen in a couple of months. Some figures are moving far away on the other bank. The first people I've seen for—two days. They seem to be running. From or to what I have no idea. I can't even see what age or sex they are. I don't care enough to try and find out.

They mean much less to me than these memories I wrap myself in. This old jacket, with its padded sleeves.

I was always looking for the simple solutions. But when things simplified themselves, I didn't know what to do with them.

That night Mei left me, I lay stretched out right across the bed, feeling cold suddenly and unable to move, my muscles drained. The noise of the air conditioner, which a few days before had lulled both of us to sleep, drilled into my brain. I stared up at the ceiling watching the splinters of moonlight intersect. I began to shiver.

At last I got up and walked about the flat, out onto the balcony. The lights of the fishing boats down below me in the bay were closer to the shore than I had ever seen them before, right in near the rocks where the land fishermen cast their nets in the daytime. I could hear them shouting, their lights dancing in the fish-slurred water.

I wandered from room to room, touching things, until finally I ended up in the bathroom sitting on the lavatory, my head between my hands, looking at the mosaic floor and the white-tiled walls. So hygienic. The squares ran into each other, the lines between them vibrated, and for the first time since I was about fourteen, I was desperately, physically afraid of dying.

I tried to focus on the towels, the curtains, but everywhere I looked, their flowery patterns were full of leering faces, the crippled giants of my childhood. Then I saw the cockroaches.

When I had come into the bathroom, a dozen or so had scuttled away for shelter, but four were caught as I turned on the light.

The Seventh Hexagram

A year earlier, I would have taken off a sandal and smashed them under the heel. But I had done that once too often. One morning I had cornered an enormous cockroach in the kitchen. I must have hit it at least twenty times, each time standing back, seeing a leg twitch, and hitting it again, until I was really sure it was dead. I went to finish breakfast. But when I came back half an hour later, it was gone.

So I just sat and watched these four held in my mosaic net.

One was quite large, an inch long, pale brown. The other three were babies, darker, about the size of small beetles. I stamped on the floor to frighten them off, but they just stayed glued to the tiles, antennae waving.

I could have stayed there all night staring at them, waiting for them to move: objects to concentrate on; an escape from self-pity; religious almost. But the tap in the wash-basin started to drip, and my head lifted towards it. When I looked down again, they had gone.

One must have run straight between my feet to the knot of pipes against the wall; two others were frozen in the right angle between the bathtub and the floor where a blow would bounce away, missing them. But the largest was staring back at me from the opposite wall, exposed. Very slowly I took off my sandal and reached out towards it. Just as I was about to strike, it shot away and disappeared into a tiny crack beneath the water heater.

People talk about ants, their discipline, their organization. But ants destroy themselves deliberately in their adherence to order. With these small cockroaches motionless on the floor—so obvious that they became in time invisible—self-preservation was the only motive in what they did. You could watch them zigzagging about a room, and they would seem to be going nowhere, out of control; but as soon as they were threatened, they knew exactly what to do, when and where to move.

52

While I, of course, willingly self-destructive as an ant, haphazard as a butterfly, would never know.

That was the point I had already reached, ten days before I killed Jordan King.

Part 2

5

Maybe it was Jordan King's fate to live in an age when heroes, as soon as they are recognized, are seen to be fakes.

He was born at the beginning of it. In 1900, in Durban, South Africa.

His father was Cantonese, from a small village near the market town of Sheklung in the province of Kwangtung. In the 1870s, when the country was still suffering from the aftermath of the Taiping Rebellion, he had gone to Hong Kong to make his fortune. For three years he worked harder and ate less than he had ever done before, and still, at the end of it all, he had nothing to show for the effort or the suffering. He had learnt the deception of the city and the superiority of the foreigner, but there was no profit that he could draw from such wisdom. All he seemed able to do was carry a sedan-chair for those people who were born to ride in one: men with grey and purple skins, long noses, no culture. He wasn't bitter, just puzzled; and if it hadn't been for his pride, he would have gone home.

As it was, the only alternative seemed to be to go still farther away. When the chance came, he signed on as an indentured labourer for work in South Africa; a slave almost. His reasoning was simple: he did it, not with any idea of the possibilities he might explore there, only to escape from his own fear of failure. As he told his son years later, that was his one stroke of luck: he had been saved by his poverty. Had he been slightly better off, he might have ended up broke in a gold rush in Australia or California; Africa, however, made him a millionaire.

Those early years had been hard, and he never talked much about them. If anybody pressed, he would grunt and turn away. "I made money to be able to forget about all that." But long afterwards, when admirers tried to persuade Jordan that he ought to write the story of his own life—"It would be a crime not to leave a record of all you've seen and done; history will be the poorer if it dies with you," they would say—he would stretch back like a cat and smile.

"No, it's not my story I ought to tell. The only life worth writing about is my father's. I started with everything a man could have, and this is all I've ended up with"—a sweeping gesture—"but he started with nothing and never let so much as a grain of sand slip through his fingers."

He said it partly, of course, for the protests that inevitably came, the ripple of surprise that Jordan King, the egocentric old bastard, could be so modest and sentimental, but also because he was honest enough to recognize that in a very basic way it was the truth.

His father had started off by buying a few sweets to sell to other workers, then moved on to a stall in a Kaffir market. The profits were tiny. But he survived on the scraps that he found among the rubbish from the market while the other hawkers were getting drunk, and in time he had enough money saved for a real shop, then several shops, then a small factory.

Probably his greatest strength was rooted in the fact that unlike most overseas Chinese, he had not allowed himself to grow nostalgic about China. Dutifully he never forgot to send money back to his village, but he was a practical man, and to be homesick, to sit and dream of what his mounting fortune could buy among the flower-girls of Canton, was not in his conscious nature. What he wanted was power, not in any ostentatious sense (throughout his life he lived frugally, dressed badly), but power in the knowledge that you can, if ever you need to, prevent other people from interfering in your own life; power to take those people who would, if they could, meddle in your affairs and make them bow down before you. So he learned English, speaking it even to other Chinese, who thought him strange, till China became a small, overgrown garden in a corner of his brain.

And of course he became a Christian, too. The beliefs themselves always rather puzzled him with the emphasis they seemed to place on guilt, a feeling he could never admit to finding in himself; and the idea of a heaven struck him as faintly childish and quite unrelated to the central problems of this life. But all the same, Christianity had its uses for a Chinese businessman, business uses, and he was willing to pay for them in return. There was nothing cold or ruthless in such a move, no attempt to exploit or depreciate other men's beliefs. It just seemed to be the obvious kind of bargain to make. Some people made a bargain between prayers in this world and happiness in the next, didn't they? Well, then, all he was doing was recognizing that being a Christian could help him here and now, so what did it matter about God or heaven; whether they really existed was immaterial to their immediate usefulness. So he believed in them and would, after a while, have been quite taken aback had his professions of faith been challenged.

At the same time he changed his name from Wong, which was after all a meaningless sound, to King, its English equivalent.

Later still, when he had moved into other industries—textiles, cigarettes, biscuit-making—he began to look around for a wife, not so much to sweeten his old age as to testify to his material achievements. He had married once before, long ago in Hong Kong, and had children, but now he didn't even bother to find out if the Chinese ceremony that he had been through had any legal validity. It wasn't a matter for the law or for anybody else; not even for his own conscience. It could be settled in full by quarterly sums sent regularly without either meanness or extravagance.

It was his choice of a wife, though, that was surprising. Unlike most Chinese he felt no revulsion for the heavy-breasted, furry bodies of white women. On the contrary, these weird creatures seemed to him eminently desirable as a confirmation of what he knew he had become. So he married an Englishwoman, a girl from a middle-class family in Devon, who was not only young (less than half his age) but pretty, too, though in a rather wan way.

She had come out to Africa just a few months before, after hearing a much older and uglier woman describe the blood-curdling dangers that the faithful had to face in the process of bringing light to the Dark Continent. But when she got there she thought that maybe she had come to the wrong place: nobody seemed to want martyrs, sacrifices; and the people she met in Durban didn't seem so very different from the people in Exeter she was running away from.

She wrote back to her parents to ask them to send out her fare home, but then, two weeks before she was due to leave, she met this strange old Chinaman. He didn't have a pigtail or wear a long gown like the figures in her geography books at school; he wasn't so strange as to frighten her away. But he was different. There was a kind of stillness about him, a certainty that suddenly seemed to focus attention on the frivolity she had come out here to escape. He didn't try to rush her off her feet with romance; that would have been ridiculous. And he didn't try to blind her with his wealth, though he did tell her proudly, without boasting, how much money he had. In fact he didn't really say very much at all: extravagance with words seemed to him as pointless as throwing money away on cards or horses. But he took her out to his estate, showing it to her with care, making her feel that he wanted her to live there, too; so that when he asked her to marry him, the very idea, which sounded so crazy to the new friends she had made (they would drop her very quickly anyway), struck her as being entirely reasonable, even natural.

It was harder to explain in words, on paper, though, and here her husband's new name served one useful purpose, at least. It wasn't until five years later, after her father's death and shortly before her own, that she wrote to her mother to say that Mr. King was not quite English.

So that explains the second part of Jordan King's name. About the first part, however, there seems to be some doubt. According to Jordan, when his mother was pregnant, she was already sure that she would have a boy; the only thing she was doubtful about was what to call him. All the names she could think of were either too common or too obscure, ill-suited, every one of them, to the fierce uniqueness of the foetus in her womb. Until one day, she was sitting in her bedroom, absent-mindedly turning over the pages of her Bible, hoping to find the name she wanted there, glancing up from time to time to look out of the window on the black workers slaving in the endless fields. Looking down again, she came to a passage she had never read before:

And the LORD spake unto Moses in the plains of Moab, by Jordan near Jericho, saying,

Speak unto the children of Israel, and say unto them, When ye are passed over Jordan into the land of Canaan;

Then ye shall drive out all the inhabitants of the land from before you, and destroy all their pictures, and destroy all their molten images, and quite pluck down all their high places:

And ye shall dispossess the inhabitants of the land, and dwell therein: for I have given you the land to possess it.

That, anyway, was Jordan King's story. But when Stewart retold it to Donald Winn, he just laughed.

"I'd have thought anyone as inventive as old Jordan would have found himself a new story by now. The tread must have been worn right off this one, he's told it so often. No more grip. He's getting predictable in his old age."

"How do you mean? What's wrong with it?"

"Well, it seems to have been good enough to take you in, anyway. The only trouble with it is it's simply not true. Bullshit from beginning to end, like everything else about Comrade King. The old sod's a bloody good liar, though; I'll give him that."

"But how can you possibly know that?" said Stewart, getting angry. "You can't be sure."

"Of course I know. Don't be so bloody gullible. You just have to listen to the story to know it's not true. It's something Jordan made up for himself out of some kind of Deep South fantasy world: his mamma sitting there in her muslin dress looking out at all those Negro slaves picking cotton and just feeling in her womb the great revolutionary hero her son was going to become. It's like third-rate Tennessee Williams. Anyway, that's what it sounded like to me the first time I heard it. So I started asking a few questions. And do you know what your precious Jordan King's real name is? David Jordan King. And do you know why he was called Jordan? Because it was his mother's family name. That's all. The only name she got out of the Bible was David. So fucking original, isn't it? And even then she went and got the wrong one. It should have been Goliath. Or maybe Herod."

But much later, at the inquest, it appeared that there were in fact only two names on his birth certificate. And that those two were: Jordan King.

Perhaps, for once (unpredictable as ever) he had been telling the truth, after all.

After his mother's death Jordan was brought up for a few years by a governess; easy years that still, somehow, were marred by a puzzlement that he was never quite able to define.

It had to do with his father. Jordan had nothing to reproach him with or revolt against; there was nothing so obvious about it as that. The old man was kind and firm; he took an almost childlike enjoyment in watching his son grow up. And yet there seemed always to be a barrier between them, invisible and so all the more frustrating; a glass wall that cut off not so much sound as emotion. As an old man himself, Jordan King could still feel the mark of that glass like a scar across his forehead.

When he was old enough, he was sent to school in England. He learned little there apart from the ability to sail easily over the surface of racial prejudice, never revealing the slightest trace of pressure from those underwater currents. But when he came back home for a month each summer, this was an added bond that he tried to establish with his father, a bond of race. He wanted to talk about China, to ask questions that would help him to identify his own roots; yet here, too, he found himself not rejected but puzzled, unsatisfied. The old man liked to talk; he took a delight in asking Jordan about England, about his life at school, the other boys, the homes to which he was occasionally invited at weekends, how they were furnished, what they ate. But when Jordan, in his turn, tried to question him about Canton, Hong Kong, he became vague, almost dazed. "It was all so long ago, and I've thought about it so little—perhaps that has been a mistake; I don't know—anyway, I couldn't be sure any longer what is true and what is untrue. It would be wrong to talk about anything, anything at all, with so little knowledge. It would only give you a false picture that would mislead you or disappoint you. If, when you're old enough, you still want to know, you must find out for yourself."

So Jordan went back to school, then on to university to read medicine. He had thought somehow that his father would want him to go into the business, and he had been quite prepared to study engineering instead; but when he raised the subject, he met only a seemingly ungrateful reticence.

"You must do what you think best."

"But I want to please you, too."

"That is not what fathers are for."

"But surely, after you're gone, you don't want to see everything that you worked so hard for just disappear."

"When I'm dead, I shall see nothing."

"You know that's not what I meant." He was irritated but still persistent.

"And then, perhaps, as he saw how I was hurt," Jordan would say, "he began to soften slightly. It was almost impossible to tell with him, but just a little, I think. 'Yes, Jordan, I know what you meant,' he said, 'and it's kind of you, I suppose, to think like that. But it's not the way I think, and I'm too old to pretend. When I'm dead, I shan't give a damn what happens to all this.' We were standing on the verandah, and everything we could see, from there to the horizon and far beyond, belonged absolutely to him. 'All it means to me,' he said, 'is the power to go on living as I want to, and as soon as I lose that power, then all this becomes meaningless.' He was silent for so long afterwards that I thought he was finished, and then suddenly he turned on me. 'But don't you see? That's what you must look for, too; your own kind of freedom. Make up your own mind; don't let the past, or what you think the past was, make it up for you.'"

Jordan remembered the words when finally the old man died, but in his grief he couldn't really accept them. It couldn't be as simple as that. Still, everywhere he looked, he could feel his father's presence: in the fields, the offices, the house; in himself, too. He put off going back to England and stayed on, wanting to keep his memories alive, watching them fade. Every morning he went into his father's office, sitting there in the enormous armchair with its buttoned leather upholstery, his fingers trying to find a meaning in the intricately carved bevel of the mahogany desk. One by one the managers came in to him, standing in the middle of the slightly Oriental Axminster carpet, just as they had done with his father, never sitting (there was no other chair), waiting for his comments and decisions. He knew he could do the job; so much of it was obvious, unavoidable, governed by forces that you didn't so much create or control as exploit, the way a yachtsman uses wind. But there was no satisfaction in it for him. He had thought that by doing this he could come closer to his father; speaking, acting for him, almost like a medium, becoming him. But the words were empty, and the spirit he was looking for, if it still existed, had moved elsewhere.

And yet what was he to do instead? He could, of course, go back to London and carry on with his postgraduate work on TB. He had, so it was said, a brilliant future there. But though the brightness of the picture attracted him, its certainty, the definition of every detail, made it seem frighteningly predestined: academic, then professional success; a lavender-cool

English wife; evenings at Covent Garden, the theatre, the Savoy; a wisteria-covered country house and children, then grandchildren that he hardly knew; a knighthood, even. He could have it all so easily. So why bother?

One day he simply made up his mind. Afterwards he talked about it as the beginning of a quest for his lost identity, but at the time it was even more an escape from another identity that was all too certain and as a result—though dazzling—dull. Romantically he had come to believe that he could only really find himself in the unknown. So with as much speed as possible, he put everything on the market—house, furniture, land, factories—and bought himself a ticket on the next boat to Shanghai.

The only things he took with him were his mother's Bible and his father's chair.

Like the bubbles in a cesspool, commerce and politics seethed with equal intensity in the Shanghai of 1926. Jordan had, of course, already put commerce behind him, and as yet he knew nothing at all of politics. ("Nobody in England does," he said. "Nobody in England needs to," said Winn.) "I didn't learn politics out of a book," he would tell people. "I learnt it from the bitterness of my own experience."

At first, though, it was quite simply the strangeness of the place that struck him most. He had never come across a city so lacking in order or decorum. To walk about its streets was to be a spectator at a circus no imagination could ever have dreamed of. A city of crowds and noise and continual contrasts: noodle vendors with their portable, steaming kitchens on the backs of bicycles; beautiful Chinese ladies in long gowns slit tantalizingly up to pastures of creamy thigh; sweating coolies pulling carts of shit; wheelbarrows filled with gold bars; middle-aged Englishmen in motor cars off to the races or a cricket match; drunken sailors; pissing children; Sikh policemen, turbaned and hostile;

opium dens and banks; brothels and silk stores; pawnshops and expensive Russian restaurants—all crammed together and everybody shouting, yet communicating most intensely through the sidelong glance, the pressure of a hand, the word unspoken. It made Jordan feel like some peasant up from the country, as he walked about wide-eyed, bumping into people and being cursed by them, trying to understand and getting all the time farther and farther out of his depth.

His money, of course, would have clarified everything. He had only to let it be known how much he was worth and the whole chaotic city would have orientated itself around him; hordes of servants, White Russian mistresses, Korean bodyguards, and European flatterers would have swung into orbit like the spheres of a mediaeval theologian. The deafening noise would have resolved itself into an easy, refined harmony. But he had already made up his mind that he would have to find a better use for his father's money than that.

So he rented a small house, private and inward-looking, in the Chinese city and set about finding a job. With his qualifications there was no difficulty in that, and almost immediately he was appointed medical superintendent of a tuberculosis clinic. For three months he gave himself completely, passionately, sixteen hours a day, to his work, fighting to break down the preconceptions, the old-fashioned rigidity, the even more ancient superstition of his colleagues and subordinates. He plunged himself into it so totally that throughout that time he was hardly aware even of where he was; China had narrowed itself down to a hierarchical and inefficient hospital that shocked and exasperated him.

But then one day, by mistake, he happened to take out the personal file of his predecessor, an American with a dubious medical background who had stayed too long in China and only been prised out of the job by a third stroke. Flicking through it casually

Jordan suddenly saw what the old fool's salary had been: exactly three times the amount he was being paid himself.

He stormed out and round to the office of the Chairman of the Board of Governors, a polished Shanghainese businessman who dabbled in good works. He didn't have an appointment, so he had to wait for nearly two hours, secretaries and clerks brushing disdainfully past him: plenty of time to remember ironically how, just a few months ago, he had been running an organization that would have made this one look like a leaky freighter next to a battleship. His mind toyed with the most childish fantasies of revenge.

The Chairman, when at last he was shown in, was polite—a cigarette? a cigar?—but firm. "Really, Dr. King, I must ask you not to come here like this again. You can see how busy I am." He gestured at the gleaming desk. "Of course, the clinic is very close to my heart, but business must come first. Surely it could have waited till the next meeting of the board."

No, Jordan was afraid it couldn't. He explained. He hoped they would be able to put it down to an unfortunate mistake. Perhaps, too, the board might consider making an official apology? After all, if the British Medical Association were to hear about this.

The Chairman sat back in his chair and smiled a man-of-the-world smile. "But, Dr. King, I'm afraid it's clear that you have only been in China a very short while. I assure you that this is standard practice here. In every job in China there are two quite separate salary levels: a scale for expatriates and a scale for Chinese. Superficially it may seem to be a little unfair, I agree, but look at it another way: because of this differential, it's possible for many good jobs to go to Chinese that would otherwise be filled by Europeans or Americans. We gain in the long run, you know."

"But you're Chinese, aren't you? Or had you forgotten? How can you insult your own people like this?"

"*My* own people," the Chairman said pointedly,

"would not be insulted. You can't come here, you know, with your new ideas and expect everybody to fall into step beside you, just like that. You have to make an effort to adapt, too." He examined his lacquered fingernails. "And now that we're on the subject, the same thing has been rather worrying me at the clinic, as well. I don't doubt your enthusiasm, Dr. King, but you have managed to upset a very large number of people—people who have served us loyally for a great many years. I do wish you would show a little more tact in dealing with them."

So Jordan offered his resignation.

"I can't tell you how much I regret this," said the Chairman, relief in his voice. "I'm sure that once you had settled down, once you had fitted in with our way of doing things, we could all have got on very happily together. I've always thought of the clinic more as a family than anything else. But this is a matter of principle, I'm afraid, Dr. King . . . a matter of principle."

For the first time, in the following days, Jordan began to see Shanghai as it really was; not puzzled by it, as he had been to begin with, nor blinded to it by work, but clearly, bitterly. He saw the signs in the parks that read, "Dogs and Chinese not allowed"; the marble-stepped clubs where the only Chinese who were admitted were the servants; the residential areas of the International Settlement with their cool avenues, stately villas, and manicured lawns, all intended for the superior race alone; he saw a rickshaw coolie being beaten up by Sikh police with their lead-weighted batons just because he had accidentally splashed the white trousers of an elegant American drunk. He had come across racism in England and Africa as well, of course, but there he had been able to skim smoothly across its surface. Here the weight of it crushed him.

Till chance (or destiny, Jordan would have said) stepped in.

It so happened that just a few weeks before he left the clinic, Jordan had met a young clerk called Hsia Yu-hsiang, who worked in an import-export firm. Hsia

69

was a northerner from Shantung, a large, heavily built youth with hedgehog hair and a frayed shirt, a complete contrast to the smooth young men of Shanghai. He had come to see Jordan about his sister, who was a patient in the clinic. She was dying, and Hsia suspected that she had been receiving the wrong treatment. What was impressive about him was his determination to get at the truth, whatever it was, calmly, with a controlled anger; he had none of the ingratiating, apologetic manner that Jordan had come to look on and despise almost as a Chinese characteristic. He knew nothing of medicine, of course, but instinctively he didn't trust the doctor who was looking after his sister—rightly enough, as it turned out, when Jordan went into the case. The girl would die; nothing could save her now, though six months before, if she had been treated properly— "Well," as Jordan told him, "there might have been a chance of dragging it out a little longer, anyway."

Jordan had asked Hsia round to his house to tell him, expecting the inevitable outburst of grief and fury, the vows of vengeance.

"But he just sat there. At first he didn't say a word, just sat with those enormous hands of his folded in his lap, as though he hadn't heard a thing I'd been saying. And then, with his whole face quivering with emotion, he said, 'I ought to hate him, but I don't. I can't even blame him. Don't you see? It's not one man; it's a whole system. That's what we must hate.'

"Yes, it sounds incredible, I know," said Jordan as he read the disbelief on Stewart's face. "But I swear to you, Joseph, that's exactly what he said. His very words. I couldn't have forgotten; they made such an impression on me." He seemed to muse for a minute on some quality that had gone out of the world. "He was just nineteen when they killed him."

So now, once he had left the clinic, there was only one person in the whole of Shanghai he could talk to, only one man for whom he could feel any kind of respect at all. Respect: the one straw that he needed now to hold onto.

The Seventh Hexagram

When he got in touch with Hsia again, he poured out his own bitterness and anger and hurt pride. How, he asked, could the Chinese people endure this kind of treatment; why didn't they rise up and throw these damned foreigners out?

"That is what we've been doing for the past year," said Hsia.

Jordan described that evening to Stewart as they sat one night on the verandah of his house in Hong Kong, the darkness velvety around them, his eyes distant and seemingly sightless, his voice low and soft so that Stewart had to lean forward on the edge of the rattan chair to hear what he was saying. He was a fine actor, Jordan King.

"As Hsia talked," he said, "I realized that my own change of heart, my own awakening, really, wasn't just something personal. It wasn't something that isolated me from other people, as everything else in my life until then had seemed to. No, it was exactly the opposite of that. I suddenly saw that it was part of a whole national movement. I was just one among tens of millions of other people. For the first time I knew what it was to be Chinese."

Hsia told him about all the events of the past eighteen months when Jordan had been too involved in working out his own affairs to bother about China's. Back in May 1925 there had been a strike in a Japanese-owned mill in the International Settlement; some of the strikers were arrested, and a crowd of middle-class students demonstrated in protest. Just a tiny incident, but the foreign police panicked, and several of the students were killed. The ripples that spread outwards built up into waves that now were threatening to flood the whole country. All over China foreign goods were boycotted, missionaries were hunted down, a general strike paralyzed the port of Hong Kong; and together with the hatred of the foreigner there spread a growing contempt for the old warlord rulers in Peking, who didn't dare respond to this new mood of independence. From the republican South an army made

71

up of both Communists and Nationalists under the command of Chiang Kai-shek was advancing victoriously. China would be strong, unified, free again.

Hsia started to visit Jordan regularly after that, one evening a week, throughout those six crucial months from October 1926 to March 1927. And yet, beautiful though the memory of that awakening may have been, Jordan's response can only truthfully be described as passive, cautious to the point of cowardice. He read smuggled copies (in English, of course) of the works of Marx and Engels, and Hsia talked and talked and talked, sitting very straight in a corner of the deep sofa, refusing every offer of Scotch or port or beer, his eyes never straying around the quiet luxury of the room.

He insisted that this wave of hatred for the foreigner was only a starting-point, a catalyst, not an end in itself. "It's not the foreigners who are the real cause of China's oppression," he explained. "It's the Chinese. Every man in China lives at the expense of somebody else. One man wishes to get rich, so another must get poor. That's the basic problem that has to be solved. Once we learn to treat each other with respect, the foreigners will be forced to respect us, too. It's logical, isn't it? All this nationalism is just a starting-point; it's an easy way to bring the people together—workers, the army, the intellectuals, even the merchants. But once the movement is strong enough, then we can begin the real revolution; we can begin to build a new society in China."

Hsia used every argument he could think of to get Jordan to come in with them. Already the Nationalist army was advancing on Shanghai; an insurrection was being prepared in the Chinese city to overthrow the warlords so that when the army arrived it could take the city over peacefully and not give the foreign powers the excuse they wanted to intervene on the other side. Hsia was one of the two thousand cadres who were secretly being given the rudiments of military training in the French Concession. This time they had a plan;

it wouldn't be like the disorganized strikes of the past. And Jordan was almost convinced. Almost. He was almost ready to commit himself. But still he hung back, waiting to be sure, looking for some kind of proof; so that when, on March 21, 600,000 workers went out on strike and seized the police stations, the arsenal, the garrison, and then proclaimed a citizen's government, it seemed that he had waited too long.

He could never forget the look of triumph on Hsia's face, the flush under the fat brown cheeks, the hair bristling more than ever, the way he said almost contemptuously, "Now do you see you should have joined us?" Jordan would never forget his own bitterness, either. He could think of nothing to say, no way in which he could share this victory; and he found himself half wishing that the revolution had been a failure so that, absurdly, heroically, he might have proved himself after all.

He didn't have long to wait.

He never saw Hsia again. Chiang Kai-shek accepted power from the workers' army, but he was quick to see that this was a movement he would soon no longer be able to control; and so five days later he struck, arresting the leaders of the uprising, imprisoning, torturing, executing them, until five thousand had been massacred, Hsia anonymously among them.

So Jordan got the second chance that, instinctively, ashamedly, he had been waiting for. And it was here, in his instinct, that his greatness (if he was great) lay. He didn't react to Chiang's slaughters as the dilettante he had seemed to be. Instead, he threw himself euphorically into what must have appeared to be a losing struggle, setting up a hospital for the wounded in the International Settlement, smuggling those who had managed to escape arrest out of the city to the countryside, bribing, planning, risking his own life constantly, until he too faded away at the last moment, to turn up again in the next few months in Swatow and Canton. But unlike Chou En-lai, whom he never got on with (not even at the start), Jordan took little part in organizing the abortive seizure of these two cities; his talents seemed only to emerge afterwards, when the risings had failed and were being put down by Nationalist troops, when the remnants had to be held together and a new direction found for them.

"All I did was pick up the pieces," he said proudly.

And it was then, again, when everything was falling apart all around him, that this instinct of his proved to be triumphantly, almost uniquely, correct: this time in the speed, the certainty with which he came to recognize the importance of Mao Tse-tung. It must surely have been the most perceptive choice he ever made. Everything about him, after all—his background, his education, the way in which he had learned what politics he had in the context of an urban struggle —would have seemed to draw him to the conventional approach of the official Communist leadership who wanted, with Russian support, to go on emphasizing the need for a revolution centered on the towns and the industrial proletariat. But, in fact, what he saw in the uprisings of 1927 was enough for Jordan to realize that though they had the power to disrupt and even seize the cities for a short time, they were still not strong enough to control them permanently. He began to turn towards the country, a country that, ironically, he hardly knew at all. Partly it was an almost childlike hope; partly disillusion; partly, more simply, the fact that his own grounding in Marxism was so much less solid, so much more spontaneous than was the case with most other party members. But all the same, the decision he came to was remarkably prophetic.

It was just at this time, of course, that Mao Tse-tung had been expelled from the politburo for his insistence on an agrarian revolution. Mao himself came from a farming family; he knew vast areas of central China intimately, had studied its rural economy in detail. Jordan was an intellectual, and he had never been outside the large cities. It was a wild dream, but still he began to pin his hopes on this man who had been reported dead and was now supposed to be alive again, wandering with a depleted army somewhere in the southern part of Hunan province. And so in December 1927, with maps and money and a few rumours as his only guide, Jordan set out to look for him.

He travelled by steamer from the Portuguese colony of Macao, where he had taken refuge, up the Pearl River to Canton. The secret police were looking for him there, checking on all the trains. With the beard he had recently grown, he passed himself off as a Moslem trader, until he was able to get another, much more primitive riverboat from there to the town of Shao-kuan in the north of Kwangtung province.

"That was the first time, there on that dirty, smelly riverboat, that I really realized what China was. Until then I thought that Shanghai was China, but now I began to see that it was just as alien as I had been myself. At that time, remember, Kwangtung was probably the richest province in the whole country, and yet I had never believed that so much poverty was even possible. I was travelling in the cheapest class because I didn't want to draw attention to myself, but I had to change because of the food. My body simply couldn't adjust to it: just a bucket of very thin, watery rice for about fifteen adults. So I moved to the first class, where the only other passenger was a rich antique dealer who was travelling around trying to buy old jade and porcelain from farmers and landowners who were hard up. There was always far more food than the two of us could eat—chicken and pork all the time—and that pig used to throw what was left over the side. It made me sick, physically sick. And yet there was nothing I could do about it. It made me want to throw him into the river, too . . . anything, just to show him how much I detested him and what he stood for. But I couldn't risk bringing the police into it. So I had to sit there and watch him for three days, and he could see how I felt and went on doing it all the more to irritate me. But that was how I began to understand what the revolution could mean in China." A pause. "What I really couldn't forgive was the way the other people on the boat must have been identifying me with him."

Jordan stayed for more than a week in Shao-kuan in a small, filthy inn beside the river, where he had to share a room with five other travellers, one of whom stole his shoes. He tried to get some more positive information from the villagers, but they didn't trust him; he was a foreigner, and his Chinese made them laugh. They talked about bandits in the hills to the north, but he had no way of telling that in fact these were men from Mao's First Army.

So in the end, he rode on an ox-cart up over the mountains into Hunan and finally made his way to Changsha, which, he had heard, was where Mao came from originally. But the city was in chaos, full of beggars and unpaid soldiers and refugees from the surrounding countryside, whole families huddled together in alleyways, sheltering under cardboard boxes, selling everything—heirlooms, clothes, daughters—and still starving, freezing on the windswept sidewalks. Puzzled by it all, not knowing where to start, Jordan began making enquiries, but the hotelkeeper (the first man he asked) went straight to the police. He was arrested and imprisoned. Ho Chien, the governor of the province, who had never in the past shown any reluctance about ordering the deaths of many thousands of innocent people, hesitated now over Jordan's British passport and decided instead to send him to the capital, Nanking. So, barefoot, tied to a group of other convicts, he was taken to the railway station, where crowds of maimed and hungry peasants waited all day, every day, spilling over onto the tracks, hating and envying the rich officials and generals who stepped daintily down from the luxurious coaches. The criminals were herded into wagons along with groups of conscripts roped, like them, together. But Jordan managed to bribe one of the guards on the train and was allowed to jump out after only twenty miles.

Painfully, reluctantly now, he made his way back into the hills to the southeast. The weather was freezing, with drizzly rain and sleet; snow and frost lay in the corners of the terraced fields; mist hung in the valleys, and clouds swallowed up the higher ground. He had nothing to eat, his feet were soon bleeding, and though he stole a bicycle, he had to keep away from the villages where Kuomintang troops might be billeted, so that most of the time the cycle was more of a hindrance than a help as he carried it on his shoulders through fields and over rocks. Much of the land, he saw, was uncultivated; the spruce and walnut trees on the hill slopes had been cut down for fuel, and nobody had bothered to replant them: desolation everywhere, most of all in his own heart and belly. By this time, he had lost all thought, all hope of the revolution; all he wanted to do was to get out of here, out of China, alive, and then forget about it and its insoluble problems.

But then, without even knowing what he was doing, he stumbled through the Kuomintang front lines and was found by peasants from the first Chinese Soviet, which had been set up in the district of Chaling. They fed him on millet and vegetables and guided him to Mao Tse-tung's stronghold in the Chingkan mountains over in Kiangsi province. Jordan King, the hero, had arrived. By accident.

"It's hard to explain the change that took place in me there," he said. His large head tilted forward, and his hands were perfectly still on the rattan arms of the chair. "Probably only somebody else who was there could really understand. And yet you have to try, you know. Those next six years in Kiangsi were the most crucial of all. If you want to understand the Chinese revolution, that's where you've got to start.

"When I got there, I was too weak to do anything. But it only took a couple of days of that mountain air to get me on my feet again. And it wasn't just the air, either; it was the atmosphere—the peace. Now that sounds absurd, doesn't it? To talk about peace in a place surrounded by an enemy army. And yet that's how it was. The most peaceful place in China. Everywhere else I'd been, there was chaos and suffering. But here there was order, a sense of purpose. Even in Shanghai I hadn't felt that. I'd known what I was fighting against, but not what I was fighting for. But now, as I felt my body getting stronger again, I began to see what it was all about—the positive side, not the negative.

"Of course, it all started out from Mao's own personality in the first place. He was the only one who really knew where we were going. But there was no arrogance in his sureness. Quite the opposite: he seemed to have time for everything, everyone. And the fact that there was nothing condescending about it made it all the more impressive. He didn't give a damn about other people's reactions to him, what they thought about him as a person. Not on the physical level, anyway. He looked rather effeminate at first, actually—you know, rather fat and chubby, with very long hair flapping everywhere. But he would spend hours talking just to make you see a point. And you had to listen because it was so obvious that he knew what had to be done, and how.

"It was just about the worst place in the world to start an agricultural revolution, too. The soil down there in Kiangsi is red and acid. When it rains, it turns into a bright red glue; and when the sun shines, it gets as hard as concrete. But that was just the point, Mao said: it was the *best* place to start because the only way for the peasants to survive was co-operatively; individually they wouldn't be strong enough. That was how he was with everything; he could see how the most impossible situation could be turned into a solid revolutionary basis.

"And there wasn't anything one-sided about him either. He didn't just have this agricultural obsession and nothing else. Of course land redistribution was the most urgent reform that had to be made, but it was just a part of a whole new social attitude. Right there and then, with a war going on all around him, he was talking about education and the elimination of opium and prostitution—all at once; and not just talking about it, but putting it into practice from the very beginning.

"That was why Mao succeeded in the end. All ... e other revolutionaries I ever knew got their sup-p..t mainly on promises of what would happen in the future, *after* the revolution. Mao was the only one who saw that the revolution and the building of a new society had to go on simultaneously. They couldn't be separated."

And yet Jordan King, full of faith as he was, stayed in Ching-kangshan for only a few months in all those six years. Why?

"I would have given everything I had to be able to stay there," he said. "But they knew I was more use to them on the outside."

And that was true, of course. But the whole truth? Surely not. Perhaps, too, Stewart thought, there was an unconscious fear of becoming physically committed to a single place. Emotionally, intellectually, he was already totally committed, but it's the physical commitment, the roots in a place, that's the most primitive, the most essential, tie. Jordan seemed always to have shied away from that, finding plenty of perfectly valid excuses for a life of endless movement, adventure, mystery—all of which served as a more glamorous substitute.

So throughout that period, when the new Soviets were taking shape in the central provinces and the pressure on them from the Kuomintang army was constantly being stepped up, Jordan King travelled all over China, risking his life almost every day, making the art of deceit his finest accomplishment. He learned the various regional dialects, speaking them never as a native, always as an outsider, a man who came from somewhere else, and yet in a crisis invariably merging into the crowd like "a bayonet into reeds."

He started off by arranging food supplies for the beleaguered Red armies, then rifles and machine-guns, then machinery for a new arsenal, which he set up in the town of Juiching so that they would be able to avoid the absurd prices for grenades and shells that he was having to pay to the Jewish arms dealers in Shanghai. All of his father's gift for organization became apparent in him now, and something else besides —a kind of imaginative daring, the ability to aim so much higher than the Kuomintang agents could ever raise their eyes. Nobody, for instance, could have predicted that he would actually start building factories in the Soviet areas; but he did, breaking the machines down into unrecognizable fragments, smuggling them in in a hundred different ways and still ensuring that they all arrived at the same time at the same place. And who would ever have expected him to persuade two Kuomintang pilots to go over to the Communists with the most modern American planes in the whole air force?

"Even your friend Winn can't get away from that. D'you know what Evelyne overheard him saying the other day at my birthday party?" Jordan craned his neck to mimic Donald's squeaky voice. " 'Well, I suppose you have to admit one thing: he's the greatest *pirate* of the century.' " Jordan laughed deeply and looked across at Evelyne, who seemed to reflect his relaxation back at him like a glowing mirror.

For a moment Stewart felt excluded.

And then she smiled. " 'If nothing else,' was how he put it, Jordan."

He travelled everywhere by the most unlikely routes on foot, by mule, and most of all, on a bicycle. And still, at sixty-four, he had the thigh muscles to prove it.

He was caught three times—in Amoy, in Wuhan,

and in Chungking—and tortured, so he said. "But they could never hold me. I even talked three of my guards in Chungking into deserting with me."

He became a legendary figure, but more than that, too. All this time he was the main contact between Mao and the politburo of the Chinese Communist party at its underground headquarters in Shanghai and Hankow, and it was he who resisted most strongly the pressure that was being put on Mao by such theorists as Li Li-san, the party leader, who wanted a rapid military advance out of Kiangsi to attack the major cities.

" 'Our strength is in the people,' that's what I told them. 'It is not to be frittered away on melodramatic gestures!' "

And yet in the end, all the guts, all the intelligence, all the idealism were not enough.

In the early 1930s Chiang Kai-shek had been launching one campaign after another for, as he put it, "the final extermination of the Red bandits." One hundred thousand men, then two, then three hundred thousand were thrown against them; and every time the Communists allowed the enemy to advance deep into their territory before encircling them, wiping them out, putting them to flight. But then, in October 1933, there began the Fifth Extermination campaign, and this time the Kuomintang had mobilized an army nearly a million strong. Even that number could have been dealt with if they had offered themselves up for sacrifice in the same old way, but now, more seriously, Chiang was relying on his German military adviser, General Von Falkenhausen, for a change in strategy. Instead of trying to penetrate deep into the Soviet areas as he had done in the past, he surrounded them with his vast forces, building hundreds of miles of roads, thousands of fortified positions, establishing an economic blockade that even Jordan found difficult to break. Gradually, ponderously, the noose was tightened until, in the middle of 1934, the Communist leaders had to face a choice between starving where they were or breaking out to the southwest, giving up all that they had fought for in the past six years.

"I felt as if I had failed completely." Jordan rubbed the sides of his nose. "It was my job to break that blockade, but it was just impossible. Nobody could have done it. Nobody. I'm sure of that. For six years, the only thing I had lived for had been that damned Kiangsi Soviet. And now to have to just stand there and see it broken down . . . it was tragic.

"Of course we put the best front on it we could: talked about going to the northeast to fight the Japanese; Chinese shouldn't be fighting Chinese when there were foreign invaders on their soil—all that sort of thing. We dismantled the factories and loaded what we could onto donkeys, then buried the rest. And thousands of peasants and their families came along with us. But we had to leave most of it behind. Most of the people, too. That was the worst thing of all, really, knowing what would happen to them and not being able to do anything about it. Even Chiang Kai-shek admitted that a million peasants died before he got control of Kiangsi again. And I couldn't get it out of my mind that somehow I was to blame; somehow I ought to have been able to find some other solution.

"I even wanted to stay behind myself, but of course they wouldn't let me. It seemed like the end of everything."

So began the Long March, six thousand miles on foot through the mountain ranges of western China.

And now Jordan, shedding grief behind him as finally as a worn-out skin, found another role that he could play with a virtuoso's skill: that of the soldier.

He told Joe Stewart about that period of his life one night over dinner in his house. They sat there, the three of them, around the shining table with the chandelier reflected in its surface, Jordan hypnotizing Evelyne and Joe with the crystal and the silver that he moved at will about an imaginary China. There was something glorious, larger than life, godlike about him that night; something that set him quite apart from the tetchy, vicious has-been that he could seem at other times to be. Usually he was a man who fed on flattery, who intermittently had enough self-knowledge to see that that was all it was—flattery—but who went on all the same, using it like a drug. But that night, Joe was sure, praise or blame could have made no difference to him because he was absolutely certain of himself, what he had done. When he had been talking about the earlier years, there was a tension in him, a kind of bullying over-emphasis, a jealous self-protectiveness, that would creep now and again into what he was saying; but here, you felt, he had found a place where he could relax into the past and be wholly at ease with it.

True, when Stewart went to the history books, he could discover very little mention of Jordan's part, but that could be explained, surely, by the backwater his life had turned into later on. And even when Kwan became evasive and said, "Well, perhaps he wasn't quite as central as he likes to make out," the memory of that evening was still stronger in Stewart's mind; the calmness of Jordan's voice, the ring of truth, though how one could be more precise about it than that he would never know.

Unlike most of the Red Army commanders, Jordan had had no military training. "I was just an amateur," he said, smiling. But a brilliant one, by any standards. He had a talent for detail, for painstaking organization; and he started out, unglamorously enough, in charge of the transport. But at the same time there was another side to him, too: daring and deceit combined, amounting to a kind of wit.

"Of course, I didn't know anything at all about it. Like most other people, I'd been taken in by all the mystique about higher strategy. They made it sound like some sort of metaphysics. But I soon found out how simple it really is; a matter of common sense.

What it comes down to in the end is getting what you want without letting the enemy know you want it. That and keeping your men together."

It wasn't, though, until they came to the Yangtze that he finally got the chance to prove himself.

Chiang Kai-shek had seen or been told that his main objective must be to prevent the Communist forces from getting across the great river that cut the country in half. If he could keep them bottled up in the south, he could drive them gradually farther and farther into the wastelands of Tibet. But if they managed to make the crossing, he might not be able to prevent them from fanning out into the less stable regions to the northwest. So he organized his troops in defensive positions to block any rapid advance on the river and, at the same time, ordered all the ferries to be drawn over to the north bank and burnt.

"The first thing we did was to give the bastard the biggest fright of his life. He was controlling everything—or at least, that's what he thought he was doing—from right down in Kunming in Yunnan. He thought he was perfectly safe down there because it was in exactly the opposite direction to the way he expected us to be heading. So we made a diversionary attack straight down towards him: two hundred miles in four days to just outside the city. It must have put the fear of God into him; it was so unexpected. Anyway, he drew all his troops right back and scuttled off with his wife like a couple of cockroaches along the railway line to Indo-China.

"But while all that was going on down there, our main force had turned northwards towards the river, making for the nearest crossing-point at Lengkai. It must have made Chiang think that he'd be able to get even with us again because he knew that all the boats had been destroyed and he'd be able to catch us with our backs to the river where we couldn't outmaneuver him. And mind you, there were a good many of our own people who wanted to make a stand there, too. One decisive battle." He shook his head slowly. "Perhaps we could have won it; I don't know. But I was sure it was the wrong thing to do, playing Chiang at his own game, doing what he expetced, what he wanted. Anyway, they listened to me. That was the great thing in those days, Joseph. People listened. I got the engineers to start building a bridge—all very obvious and out in the open so that even *their* spotter planes wouldn't miss it—just to make Chiang quite sure that we were going to dig in and try to fight our way across. And then, at the same time, I took another battalion, and we marched eighty-five miles all through the night and the following day, back eastwards to another crossing-point down here at Chou Ping." His finger found the spot on the table.

"Eighty-five miles. You should try that sometime, Joseph; be good for you. Take Donald Winn with you." He laughed happily.

"By the time we got there, it was already late in the afternoon, so we waited a couple of hours more and dressed up in some captured Kuomintang uniforms. Then we marched straight down into the town and disarmed the garrison before they even knew what was happening to them. And then, Joseph, when I looked over at the other bank, I saw what I'd been gambling on all along. They had taken all the ferry boats over there, just like Chiang Kai-shek had told them to . . . but they hadn't burnt them. I knew they wouldn't. I was sure of it." More than thirty years looking at it from their point of view, you see. They thought we were a hundred miles away, and they knew that if they burned the boats, they wouldn't get any compensation for months afterwards. And the whole livelihood of a town like that—the inns, the shops, and so on—depends on the ferries operating. They must have thought they would make a fortune if they didn't burn them and all the other crossing-points did. Their greed, that's what I knew I could rely on.

"Anyway, from then on there was nothing to it. All we had to do was wait till it was completely dark and then go down to the river with the headman. We made him shout across to the guards on the other bank to send a boat over for some government troops that had just arrived. They fell for it, too, of course, and over we went. Just one boat was enough. We got out at the landing stage and marched up to the garrison and walked right in the front door. They were all sitting around, drinking and playing mah-jong, and we just took the whole place over without wasting a single bullet. They wouldn't even believe us at first when we told them who we were because they thought we were three days' march away. It took us nearly half an hour to convince them!"

So the Long March continued: next, the heroic crossing of the Tatu River; then up over the sixteen-thousand-foot passes of northern Szechwan, where thousands died of cold; down again into thick jungles and rain-soaked swamps, where many more drowned; until finally, a year after they had set out, they came to the province of Shensi, from which, a decade later, Communist power would spread outwards again across the whole of China.

In October 1935 it would have been normal to predict the most brilliant of futures for Jordan King. Only Chu Teh and Lin Piao were closer to Mao; his loyalty was beyond doubt; his skill and versatility, unquestioned. And yet from that point on his position became increasingly peripheral, so that when Stewart finally met him at the end of 1966, he was the sort of figure about whom people are always saying: "Good Lord, is he still alive? I thought he died thirty years ago."

How does one explain his failure to cross the threshold of history? It was no use asking Jordan, in any case, because he would never even admit that that was what had happened.

Probably in the end, though, it comes down quite

simply to the fact that he was not Chinese. Only a handful of men have done more for China in the twentieth century. And he had come all this way, through starvation and prison, war and torture, to claim, prove, his identity. But still that wasn't enough.

In Shensi, more even than in Kiangsi seven years before, what was needed was the man who would be totally committed to the place. And in this Jordan failed, just as he had before. Intellectually, theoretically, sentimentally, he could see the importance of the social reforms that had to be put into effect. But he couldn't bring himself to settle down in a village, lost in this irrelevant corner of the world for years, maybe a lifetime even, and work and watch as peasants were eventually convinced of the truth of what he already knew to be true.

"The life of significant soil," thought Stewart. Perhaps that was what he lacked.

And possibly, too, another factor that was involved was his honesty. It seems strange to say that about somebody as prone to deception and self-deception as Jordan King. He wasn't the sort of person one can usually accuse of being honest. But when, in 1937, the Japanese invasion of China forced the Communists and the Kuomintang back into each other's arms, it was something that he just couldn't bring himself to accept. He couldn't agree to this alliance with men who had destroyed all that he had worked so hard to build. Perhaps, again, you would have had to be Chinese to accept it.

So in 1938 he turned up in Moscow. On the face of it his position there was of enormous diplomatic importance: to ensure that the Russians would understand and therefore support the policies of Mao Tsetung. But in practice there was very little room for subtle manoeuvring with a man like Stalin, and in the end he probably would have been of more use back in a cave village in the loessial plateau of Shensi.

For the first time in his life since he was a student, he had time to himself, time, in a way, for the kind of life that he had tried to avoid so long ago by not going back to London after his father's death; time for culture, time for love. He tried his hand at writing, in English; and the novel that he produced, *A Bridge of Chains,* about the crossing of the Tatu River, became, with its heroic and elegant simplicity, a best seller in the Russian version. He went frequently to the ballet—a tall, graceful, distinguished man in his neatly tailored Chinese uniform—and there he fell in love with a young dancer in the Kirov, Nastasya Sharonova. They married, she bore him two sons, and then he watched the three of them die slowly of malnutrition in the siege of Leningrad. Jordan survived: he had learned to live on less.

From then on his life was fragmentary, episodic, full of events but lacking any central function.

He travelled widely on official duties, but the more trivial the business became, the more vehemently he protested its secret importance.

In 1950 he was married again, to the eighteen-year-old daughter of a French steel magnate, and soon afterwards they came to live in Hong Kong in a big Spanish-style villa with a view that stretched almost as far as the coast of China.

"I wish they didn't still need me here," he would tell those who came to sneer or flatter. "What I really want to do is to go back to Peking and retire in one of those small walled houses near the center of the city, with a few flowers and flowering trees."

An old man, windy with history.

6

There's a phrase of Jordan's—of his father's, rather, that Jordan told me—that sticks to my mind. It was when Jordan was worried, uncertain about his future, trying to get his father to make the choice for him. They were at lunch, the servants padding in and out, and there was one of those long silences as the old man seemed to drift away into a space that Jordan couldn't locate at all. He only spoke when Jordan's thoughts had already moved on to some other problem. There was no advice, no consolation, nothing you could hang onto. He just said, "We live with what is going to happen to us long before we allow ourselves to face up to it."

As Jordan remembered those words one night in Hong Kong, he said, "I put them aside. They were no use to me, Joseph. I didn't even know what he meant. Now I think I do." For a moment his voice was morose.

And now I remember them, sitting here alone beside this grey lake, and I wonder what they can mean for me.

Everything is grey now. It's only four o'clock, and the evening is closing in fast. There's a deep gunmetal grey in the sky, and the lake is choppy and threatening. It's turning cold, and tonight there will be snow. I wear a glove on my right hand, and when I stop writing because my fingers are going numb, I put one on my left hand, too. In half an hour I shall go in.

This morning, though, as I finished writing about Jordan, the sky was a bright blue, white cloud swirling across it. I was full of exhilaration; something was complete, I thought, and I walked out along the edge of the lake, round the point, past the other cottages boarded up for the winter. The leaves crunched under my feet, then thin layers of ice on the puddles; and as I came near to a clump of ferns, two pheasants rose out of it with a tremendous flapping and disappeared into the forest.

I carried Jordan with me. When I passed the headland where the lake widens out so that you can hardly see the other side, I came on him, sitting on his own on a rock, the wind trying to tug the white hairs out of his skull. I sat down beside him, and he started to talk again: of the past, the Long March, new stories, stories I had never heard from him before, drawing maps with the end of his stick in a patch of sand. The words flew up and away from him like gulls.

I came back full of his death.

I write to deny that death, to make him live one last time. Not out of love, but from the need to know.

Yet how much can I ever know? I can people this whole landscape with Jordan and Evelyne, too,

Donald and Mei and Kwan Wing-leung. I see them so vividly all around me that I can talk to them, repeating, controlling our old conversations. But when I reach out and try to touch them, they fade away. I'm left with the grain of the table, the pores of my skin.

I look at my hand, purple and blue with the cold, and I can't believe there's anything beneath the surface. I look again, and I see no surface at all, just a mess of nerves, muscles, veins.

Is this all that can survive, this twitching instinct? I have tried to be so objective. Keep everything at a distance, I told myself. Set it all down as if the "I" didn't exist. But even as I began to write about Jordan, I was using him, using his stories, to turn away from a horror I still couldn't face up to: blood in a little girl's eye. "It's cowards who make heroes," Jordan used to say when the flattery got too cloying for him.

I know there is only one way to stop this swinging about, dangling, between extremes. To write about the past and make it whole for the first time. I know what Jordan's father's words meant to him. I must discover what they mean for me.

It is dark. I can't feel the pen any longer. I shall go inside. Back to a beginning.

Winn was the first of them I met. Inevitably. He seemed to know everybody, everybody's business, in Hong Kong.

"That's my job," he said.

"You mean your vice, darling," said Kramer.

"You haven't met, have you?" asked Donald, ignoring him. "This is Klaus Kramer, the queen of the German telly."

We nodded.

I had found them sitting in a bar in Wanchai, full of American sailors and bar-girls in tiny cotton dresses. I had gone there for the company, really. I still didn't know many people in Hong Kong, and I didn't want to know most of the people that I had met. I found the Europeans too isolated in their artificial worlds, living the kinds of lives they wouldn't have been able to afford back in Europe; and the Chinese, the middle-class ones I had come in contact with, seemed merely conformist and tasteless, concerned with money and nothing else. So I spent a good deal of time hanging around the bars, liking the arrogant image of myself as the detached observer. Sometimes I would buy a couple of drinks for a girl, take her out for a meal, then back home to bed; but it was all very mechanical, and though in a sentimental moment I may even have promised to go back for her again the next night, I never did.

I had heard Winn's high-pitched voice from farther along the bar as he talked to the supercilious, powdered little man next to him.

As he turned round and saw me looking at him, his face suddenly contorted into a wink. "Hi, Joe," he shouted.

I turned away. Everybody was called Joe in the bars.

But I could feel him getting up, coming over, then the smell of him; the thick, buttery sweat.

"You're Joe Stewart, aren't you? Look, why don't you come over and join us?"

"What did you mean, about it being your job?" I asked, sliding onto the bar-stool beside him.

"You've been in Hong Kong long enough to see that it's more like a village than anything else, haven't you? Well, I'm the village gossip. Par excellence. The only difference is I get paid for it."

"Who pays you?"

"Oh, that's a long story. Anyway, what does it matter as long as the money keeps on coming in. Let me line you up another beer."

As he talked, he breathed deeply, panting, every little movement seeming to bring him to the verge of exhaustion.

He sighed. "How do you like Hong Kong, anyway?"

"All right, I suppose. I don't think I've really

come to terms with it yet, though." I tried to think of something new to say but couldn't. "It seems so ingrown as a place. Nobody's interested in anything that goes on anywhere else. I still haven't got over that. I thought—you know?—that here I'd really be able to find out more about China, but now it seems even farther away than it did in London."

"Yes, and you won't find much to interest you on the paper, either, I don't expect." He looked at me coyly, waiting for a response.

"How did you know I was working there?"

"I told you, I know all about you, Joe." He punched my shoulder.

"Well, it's not the job that interests me, of course." I felt that I had to justify myself, to give an excuse for the dull mediocrities that I found myself working with; the only news that ever got reported first hand was when there was an accident in the street outside the office. "But I've got a job as a stringer to write a series of articles for a couple of quite big English provincial papers as well; that ought to be more worthwhile."

"Yes, I know," he said, though this time I don't think he really did.

I hesitated, sensing somehow that I shouldn't tell him any more. But I had to impress him (he could always count on that). "And then I thought it might be a good place to get some of my own writing done, too."

"What do you write?"

"Oh, poetry mainly. I was publishing quite a bit back in England. But it all started to seem too personal, too irrelevant." I was trying to sound intense; I wasn't sure if he was really interested—probably not —but I wanted to break out of the net of slightly mocking omniscience that I felt him wrapping me in. "Writing in the West is too narcissistic; what it needs is more objectivity." I sucked my beer. "Politics perhaps. Something more than just the individual, anyway."

"Hey, Klaus, did you hear that?"

"No, what?"

"Joe here's a poet."

"Is he now?" said Kramer with studied boredom, looking away towards the gaudily decorated ceiling.

"Don't mind Klaus; he's just a tasteless kraut."

A girl brushed past us, and Donald swung round and grabbed her by the shoulders. "Ooh, you honey-pot." Tiny, boneless against his bulk, she giggled up at him, and then he patted her on the bottom as she slipped away.

"Look at that arse, Klaus, sweeter than yours."

"If you like that sort of thing."

"You know what your trouble is, Klaus, you bugger? You're too conventional. No taste for experiment." Then, as Kramer sniffed, he went on, "Oh, for Christ's sake! I'll get you what I promised you. Don't worry so much; it'll give you wrinkles." He pinched Kramer's cheek. "I'll be back in a minute, Joe."

He pushed over through the couples who were rubbing themselves against each other on the small dance floor in front of the jukebox and disappeared into the shadows on the other side of the bar.

Two minutes later he was back with his arm around a small, rather fat black sailor who walked like a white man's image of a Negro, flexing every muscle in his body with each step.

Donald called Kramer over to the end of the bar, out of earshot, and a whispered negotiation went on until Kramer and the black turned and vanished out of the door.

"Well, that's got rid of Klaus, thank Christ," said Donald. "Even he ought to be satisfied with that. The biggest cock in the Seventh Fleet. Bloody German gluttons!"

He glanced at his watch, a big cheap one with large numerals on a purple dial. Another sigh. "Jesus, I'm late again. Look, Joe, I've got somebody waiting for me. But why don't you come back to my place and have a drink?"

I didn't know him well enough to be sure if he meant me to go or not, but I went, anyway. I was puzzled by him, unable to be sure whether I liked him or not. In one sense, I was repelled by him: by the showing off and the childish desire to mystify, by the feeling I had that one would be picked up and squeezed emotionally, then dropped again at the slightest whim. But there was something else there, too, something contradictory and perhaps more genuine, that I still wasn't able to define. And, of course, more immediately, he wasn't dull; that was all it took to make me follow him.

He lived in an old, pre-war building next to a garage, and we had to climb up a narrow, dark staircase to his flat. The wooden steps were worn and dirty, with rubbish lying in the corners; and in the light that cut through the concrete slits from the street lamp outside, I could see a tracery of looped electric cables along the walls. It was a strange place to live for someone who didn't seem to be short of money.

"You're late, Donald," said the Chinese boy in his early twenties who was sitting elegantly cross-legged on the sofa. He was wearing a sharply cut suit, a flowery shirt, his hair slicked back impeccably: a complete contrast to the breathless, dishevelled Winn.

"Yes, I know. I had to fix Klaus up; otherwise I'd never have got away from him. And then I met Joe." (Had he brought me home as an excuse for being late?)

As soon as he had entered the flat, he seemed to soften, bustling about maternally: "Have you had anything to eat, Gary? D'you want me to get you something? A salad? Or there's some pâté in the fridge. I could make you a sandwich." He turned to me proudly. "He never eats. He would starve if he didn't have somebody to look after him." I expected him to put on an apron even, it was so much like an absurd parody of a mother. And yet touching, too, almost vulnerable, especially in relation to the object of these attentions, who sat there just shaking his head, a thin smile etched across the carved, slightly pock-marked, self-consciously beautiful face.

I felt cut off from it and yet involved enough to be embarrassed. It wasn't simply that they were queer, though that might have been why I felt left out. No, there was something else here that I couldn't understand, something to do with this half-mocking, half-serious domesticity and with the way in which Winn should seem to choose deliberately to leave himself so exposed; to use that, even, as some kind of basis for desire.

I looked around the room, trying to think of something to say. "How did you ever manage to find a place like this, Donald?" I'd never seen anything like it in any of the new, matchbox blocks that I'd been taken round when I first arrived. The rooms were large, with high ceilings, and he had obviously rented the flat above as well because a hole had been knocked in the ceiling, with an old, wrought-iron circular staircase painted bright orange going up through it. It seemed completely lived in, and yet there was nothing settled about it; the walls were dirty and peeling, cobwebs in all the corners, and there were a couple of large packing cases lying behind the door, with straw spilling out of them. The furniture was a complete jumble: two or three plastic inflatable chairs, a Madame Récamier-style sofa that Gary was reclining on now, tables made from doors, African masks, a large portrait of Mae West, a Chinese scroll of a tiger, enormous paper flowers, a dying rubber plant.

"It was just an accident," he said. "When I got here, I looked around all the vacant flats that were advertised, but I couldn't stand any of them. Rabbit hutches with standardized furniture in exactly the same position whichever one you went into. Everybody eating at the same time at the same tables, shitting in the same lavatories, screwing each other's wives in the same beds. Not me, baby. I like to be able to make my own environment. Then one day I was with this friend who stopped at the garage downstairs for petrol. As I was sitting there, I looked up and saw that these places were empty. So I found out who owned them and got two whole floors for less than the price of one new flat. The government didn't like it very much, said they wouldn't do any repairs or decorations, but I don't want those buggers snooping about, anyway. Gary says he's going to do it up. He's an interior decorator."

"So you work for the government," I said, disappointed, slightly deceived.

"Half and half. I'm on secondment, really—"

"What was Klaus doing?" Gary interrupted suddenly.

Donald turned to him, his voice condescending, slowing down as if he was speaking to a child. "We had a few drinks in the Neptune. Then I fixed him up with Lulu."

"Lulu has a beautiful sense of rhythm, hasn't he?" Gary turned to me like a lady at a coffee morning.

All I could do was nod.

But what, I wondered, could be the contact here? Sex, of course; yet how could that be enough to bridge the oceans of difference that must lie between them all the rest of the time? The question bothered me: for somebody like Winn to put up with this incredibly stilted relationship, the physical satisfaction that he drew out of it must somehow be so much more powerful than anything I had ever known myself.

"Joe has a new sports car," Donald was saying. "Actually, it's more like a plane. You feel as though you're taking off in it."

"Is it an Alfa Rómeo?" asked Gary.

"No," I said, "it's an old Jaguar that I bought second hand."

"I like Alfa Rómeos best."

"It's not Rómeo," Donald explained abruptly. "That's a character in a play. It's a Roméo. Alfa Roméo."

Silence.

"Where were you before you came here?" I asked.

"Oh, I've travelled around quite a lot. Kenya. Cyprus. I was in Aden before I came here."

"What *do* you do, then?"

He smiled. "Intelligence."

"Christ! How did you . . . I mean, how did you ever manage to get into something like that?"

"You mean, being gay?"

"Well . . . yes. But not only that. You just don't seem to be the type of person—"

"Oh, God!" Another deep sigh. "Look, there's no such thing as types; only people doing jobs. If you're a fucking writer, you ought to know that, at least. And that's all this is: just another job. Not cloaks and daggers and that sort of stuff at all. It's more a matter of filing systems and forms in triplicate."

"But how did you get started in it in the first place?"

"By accident again. Everything in life happens by accident really, doesn't it? It seemed like a cushy job when I went into the army for my national service, and then I got sent to Cyprus because I read classics at university. I told them there wasn't much of a connection between ancient and demotic Greek, but nobody seemed to care. So I ended up as an interrogator, of all things. Actually, I turned out to be quite good at it because I'd always been interested in piecing together scraps of information; in the end I just stayed on because I couldn't think of anything better to do."

"I think I shall go and have a bath," said Gary solemnly.

Winn turned to him. "You know where the towels are, don't you?" he said. And again I found myself looking in his voice for some hint of how much of this was real. But I just couldn't tell where he stood. What made it difficult were these abrupt changes in mood; the way he seemed at one moment to be utterly bored, irritated by everything around him, so that the only thing to do was to make fun of it all. And then, a minute or two later, he was full of enthusiasm, conviction, love, leaving himself wide open to other people's mockery.

"What did you mean about politics when you were talking about poetry back there in the bar?" he asked when Gary had gone.

"Am I being interrogated?"

"I shouldn't have told you that. It always stops people from talking freely. No, I was just interested, that's all." The light grey eyes stayed fixed on mine.

"Well, what I meant was that in England if you want to get away from writing about yourself all the time, there's nothing much else to write about. There aren't any social issues that really matter, and if you try to blow them up, it all starts to seem deliberately artificial. There was a poem I wrote about the break-up of a love affair. I didn't want it to be just something private, so I tried to open it out by bringing in a lot of imagery of Hiroshima. Most of my friends thought it was great at the time, but after a while it made me sick. I was just exploiting Hiroshima; it wasn't something I really cared about. Not enough, anyway."

"So that's what you're looking for," he said coldly. "Something worth fighting for."

"What's so wrong about that?" I asked defensively.

"The only things worth fighting for are people; that's what's wrong about it. Everything else is lies." He pouted, and for a moment I saw his face as it must have been when he was a child: chubby and clever and spoilt.

"How can you say that, doing what you do, of all things?"

"I don't try to justify it in terms of a cause. It's still just a matter of people, personalities. When you're interrogating somebody, it's not a matter of ideologies anymore; in a strange way, it's still the relationships that count."

"A rather twisted way, I should have thought."

He took no notice of me. "Once, in Cyprus, some French officers from Algeria came over to see if they could learn anything from us. 'What success rate do you get?' one of them asked me. 'About sixty per cent,' I said. 'We get ninety,' he said. So I asked him, 'How do you manage that?,' although I already knew the answer. There's only one way you can get a ninety per cent success rate. 'Oh, it's simple,' he said. 'You just get a blowtorch and hold it to the prisoner's balls.' Bastards! Those are the sort of people who believe they're fighting for something: God, the motherland, Karl bloody Marx. And all they have to offer is a fucking blowtorch!"

I was surprised by his vehemence, not convinced. "Surely you don't expect anyone to believe that nobody ever got tortured in Cyprus."

As quickly as it had built up, the façade of anger disappeared. "No," he laughed, not ruefully, but happily, "we left that to the fucking Turks."

Gary came back wearing a maroon silk dressing-gown artfully left open down to the waist to reveal the lean, taut body underneath. He sprawled down on the sofa, resting on one elbow, kneading his thigh with the other hand, and I could feel myself getting an erection, not because I wanted him, but because I knew Winn did; another man's lust stirring in me.

I was just about to leave them to it when there was a clatter in the corridor and a big black Alsatian galloped into the room, its claws skidding on the polished floor. It jumped up at Winn, licking his face, and out of the corner of my eye I saw Gary draw back, disgusted.

"How did you get out, you sexy beast?" asked Winn, rolling the dog over on its back, scratching its belly.

"Why don't you take him for a walk, Donald?" tittered Gary, a malicious smile spreading across his face.

"That's an idea. D'you want to go for a walk, boy?" Winn was laughing, too.

The dog's ears pricked up.

"Joe, watch this," said Winn. "In spite of his name, Rover is the craziest animal in Hong Kong, aren't you, boy?"

"Rover?"

"Yes, I got him from a schoolteacher's family that left about a year ago. They wouldn't recognize him now." He stood up "Walkies, Rover, walkies."

The dog turned and ran back into the corridor, away from the outside door.

"Where's he going?"

"Come and see."

In the darkest part of the corridor the dog was scratching and whining in front of a door.

"Walkies, Rover?"

The yelps became frenzied.

And then Winn opened the door. Inside there was just a small broom cupboard, but the dog jumped in and curled itself up in the back, cringing. Winn shut the door.

I heard Gary exploding with hysterical laughter behind me.

"He'll stay there for hours like that," Winn grinned.

"But how——?"

"He's schizophrenic. When I got him, he was perfectly O.K. of course—dreadfully normal, in fact. Used to go wild about being taken for a walk. So I thought it would be an interesting experiment to try and channel all that energy in a completely contradictory direction. It was just a simple process of conditioning really. But what I rather like about it is the irony of keeping the same trigger.

"Walkies, Rover, walkies," he whispered, and the dog whined inside the cupboard.

I turned away, tight-lipped. "I must say, I can't see the point of it." The pleasure on their faces annoyed me, made me feel self-righteous; and as I looked at him, I could feel my face trembling with anger.

"Oh, for fuck's sake, don't get all sentimental about it. It's just a bloody dog. But that's what you intellectuals with all your talk about ideologies do to *people*. You twist them until they can't think straight and words start to mean the opposite of what they used to mean. Animals are dispensable, but that fucking dog in there's a warning of what can be done to human beings, too. I know because I've seen it happen. Don't you see, Joe? That's why people have got to be protected."

But I didn't trust him; I was sure of that now.

"Well, I've got to be going, anyway."

"Oh, come on. It's just a joke. Jesus, I wouldn't have shown you if I'd known you'd take it like that. Look, have another drink."

The same old weakness that made him human again: he couldn't bear people not to like him. Or rather, he was only prepared for people to dislike him so long as he could control the terms of their dislike.

He pressed me back into the chair, got me another drink, and we sat there silently drinking.

"Hey, I know just the man for you," he said suddenly. "Have you ever heard of Jordan King?"

"Jordan King? Wait, I've heard the name—" My memory dredged up a book that had impressed me a few years ago. A paperback. Published in East Germany. "You mean the writer? But he's dead, isn't he?"

"Not so as you'd notice, no. He was quite important in the thirties, but then he faded out and ended up in Hong Kong with all the other flotsam from the Chinese Revolution. He's a kind of mascot for the local lefties now. Shows off like mad, and he's an awful old phoney, but he's certainly not dead. And wait till you see his wife; she's a real sweetie. Though how Jordan keeps her satisfied, I don't know.

"Jordan can't stand me, of course, because I see right through him. But he loves to play the man of the world who can charm his enemies, so it satisfies his ego to have me around. Suits me, too.

"Next Wednesday's his birthday. He says he's sixty-six or something, but I doubt if that's the truth. He's as vain as an old queen. But look, why don't you come along to the party and see for yourself. They'll love all this crap of yours about a cause."

Abruptly he stood up. He had made up for the dog business, and now he was tired of me. It was as simple, as clear as that, and I rather liked him for not disguising it.

"Good-bye, Joe. Do come again," simpered Gary.

Donald picked up a big flashlight that was lying beside the door and, with his arm around my shoulders, guided me out onto the dark landing.

"Can't have you breaking your neck on these fucking stairs."

He switched on the torch, and as I stumbled from one step to another, he trained the light just a little too far in front of me. I looked up and waved, but as I did so the beam jumped back into my eyes, blinding me.

"You bastard!" I shouted, laughing at the obviousness of it all; and as the light poured over me, I heard him laughing, too.

7

"Fucking pyramids," he muttered into the wind.

"What did you say?" I bent towards him, trying to catch his words above the noise of the car as it pulled up through the steep curves.

Donald Winn didn't look towards me, just settled deeper into the fur coat he was wearing. "Actually, what I really wanted was one made of hair—human hair," he had said when I picked him up outside his flat. "You'd think you'd be able to find something as simple as that in a place like Hong Kong, wouldn't you?

"I said it's like a fucking pyramid," he shouted,

104

waving at the lights of the city that climbed up the steep slopes.

I nodded, watching the road.

"Well, isn't it? It's like a concrete fucking mountain. The bigger you are, the closer to the top you live. But God help you if you're really poor, baby; you'll drown in all the shit they pour down on you from up here."

"You're becoming quite a politician, Donald."

He didn't bother to answer for a couple of minutes. We had risen above the mid-level of apartment blocks, and the road wound between the houses of the wealthy that sheltered behind terrace walls and shrubberies. The air was fresh up here.

"No, the rich buy their own punishments," he said at last. "It was summer by the time you got here, wasn't it? Well, just wait till you see what it's like in the spring." His voice filled with a gleeful malice. "I'm telling you, Joe, these buggers buy their houses up here so they can look down on everybody else. But then in the spring the cloud level comes right down around them. It doesn't lift for three months. For three months, Joe, you can't see a fucking thing. Like a London fog. All their filthy little kids get bronchitis."

He paused for me to laugh. "Okay, you think I'm exaggerating, but I'm not. I promise you, it's so damp the water just runs down the walls." He stroked the fur on his arms. "They have to employ extra servants to mop it up."

The fairy lights on Jordan's house glittered in the cool November air. A servant came running out to show us where to park, and as he opened the car door, Donald bowed and said, "Thank you, comrade!"

Jordan was standing in the entrance hall talking to a group of men I recognized vaguely as left-wing journalists. Donald nudged me with his elbow and strode towards him, arms flung wide. "Many, many happy returns, Jordan!" he squealed, smothering him in fur and banging him on the back with his fat little ring-covered hands. Everybody else melted away, leaving Jordan on his own to try and free himself, but it was as hopeless as struggling against a bear's embrace.

When at last Donald let him loose, Jordan turned to me, out of breath. He was tall, as tall as Winn, taller than me, but thin and slightly stooped. His head was bony, disproportionately large and solid on top of the body that dangled down from it like a puppet's. And the nose, hooked and birdlike, seemed somehow out of place between the small, yellowish eyes and Oriental eyelids; out of place, that is, in a human face, though not, I thought, on a hawk. His hair was long, pure white, and curling.

He stretched out both hands and clasped mine in a grip that was hardly noticeable; in contrast with his voice. "And this must be the Mr. Stewart you phoned me about?" It came out astonishingly deep from such a thin frame, controlled, resonant, patronizing.

I nodded, but he didn't let go of my hands. "I'm very pleased you could come, Joseph—I have got your name right, haven't I? Yes, the more young people we get up here, the better we like it." He looked around the room, seeming to hesitate. "Now, I don't suppose you know many of our friends here, but we can't very well rely on Mr. Winn"—a fragile smile—"to tell you who's who, can we?"

All the time he was drawing me into the room, not looking at me and yet not seeming to want to let go, waving absent-mindedly to anonymous groups as we drifted between them.

"I wonder where my wife is. She'll see that you meet everybody you ought to. Mind you"—he bent confidentially towards me, whispering into my ear while I felt his eyes roaming like spiders over the rest of the room—"you may not find all of them particularly interesting, to be quite honest. They're good chaps, of course, but not always particularly interesting." He hummed a little. "Ah, there she is over there." He turned me towards the corner where she was fending off Winn's advances.

Evelyne.

Even Mei, the first time she met her, said to me afterwards with a mixture of envy and awe in her voice: "I wish I didn't have to admit that women like that could be so beautiful."

It wasn't a particularly fashionable beauty, though. She was—looked at coldly (which wasn't really possible)—almost too fat, big-boned, brawny even, overripe; those fine legs opening out suddenly into wide thighs and hips, a waist spreading ever so slightly, breasts just beginning to be pendulous. It was a body that could so easily have relaxed into vulgarity: a rich woman in her mid-thirties losing a grip on herself, not caring quite so much any longer. But immediately there was her face, full of strength and pride, just the sort of feeling that the great potters of the Tang dynasty managed to put into the long, passionate heads of their horses.

I'm struggling to describe her as she was then, that first glimpse I had of her; and yet somehow I keep feeling that it ought to be easier than this, if only because the thing that struck me most at the time was the way she seemed to show no change, no response at all. All kinds of different things were happening around her in that moment: Donald hugging her, trying to press her backwards into a corner; Jordan coming towards her across the room; and behind Jordan, me. But there was no trace of amusement or irritation on her face, no relief or recognition or interest, just this sense of somebody so fully herself that other people couldn't help or hurt her. How could anyone be so still?

As Jordan introduced us, it was her skin I was conscious of first. Even after I had seen and touched her hundreds of times, it still drew my eyes hypnotically. Stretched tight, close textured, so perfectly smooth: underneath it there could be nothing so mutable as muscles, blood, nerves. There was something incredibly fluid and soft about the way it seemed to fit so truly over the mould beneath. I suppose she must have spent hours in the sun to have turned the deep, rich color that she was, hours that would have left most women looking burnt, dried-up. But with Evelyne the pigment had welled up to the surface from somewhere beneath, spreading outwards and fading into the creamy hollows of her eyelids and under her chin. It threw the whole structure of her face into a strange, negative relief: where you expected grey shadows, there was soft whiteness instead, surprising in such a strong, almost masculine face.

Abruptly Jordan left us together, and she took me and passed me on hastily, like something held at arm's length, to an old banker who was standing alone on the balcony.

"Is that one of the Communist banks?" I asked him.

"One of the patriotic ones," he corrected me and went into a long monologue about how, forty years before, he had traveled on a liner to America and nobody had even bothered to tell him that the spoon he was using for his soup was really meant for the coffee. "I have always felt nervous about European food ever since," he said and fingered his tweed tie.

I seemed to spend the rest of the evening trying to make contact again with what was happening around me. Without my knowing how, it had slipped out of my grasp; and yet the feeling kept on recurring that I ought to be able still to find a pattern in it, one that I could fit myself into as well, and that all that was needed was some kind of simple effort on my part for everything to resolve itself as clearly as iron filings in a magnetic field.

Jordan fascinated me. Just that whisper about his friends had been enough to draw me in closer to him, making me imagine there would be something more important to follow it up; and yet whenever I bumped into him for a moment, he would wave as if he couldn't quite remember who I was, and then say, "Make yourself at home, Joseph, make yourself at home," as he slipped off in a different direction.

It was the same with everybody else as well. Most of them knew each other already, and though they seemed perfectly friendly, as soon as I moved away, I got the feeling that they were going straight back to some conversation I had interrupted. "You must try the Yunnan ham," they would tell me as I joined them, but when I looked back from the other side of the room, what they were saying seemed to be so much more intense and serious than that.

I felt frustrated by it all. And then I noticed Evelyne standing momentarily on her own and began to push over towards her. I had been watching her already, catching the little glances that passed between her and Jordan—what struck me as questions in his eyes, reassurance in hers—and now as I came up on her from behind, I was determined not to talk about ham and coffee spoons any longer.

"Are you interested in politics, Mrs. King?"

"Of course. I have to be, don't I?" The answer came out immediately, unnecessarily cold, as though she was holding tightly onto invisible reins.

"But you must have interests of your own, too."

"Music, yes. But I'm really rather a dull person, Mr. Stewart. You shouldn't bother about me."

I shook my head; my gigolo smile.

"Will you excuse me? I have to see to something in the kitchen."

She walked away. Fuck this, I thought. But in the same instant she turned and came back to me, closer, her hand warm through my jacket sleeve.

"I don't want you to be bored here," she said.

"I'm not."

"It can be very interesting, you know, but it takes a little time. I can remember how lost I used to feel myself." Her face broke into a nervous little smile. "But there are other things to do here besides talking." A pause. "Jordan has a very good library, you know.

You ought to go and look at it if you get tired of the party."

Then she was gone—somehow, in my imagination, younger, less self-possessed than she had been just a second before.

And I did go to look for the library an hour or so later, not so much because I was bored any longer, but more as a way of expanding that moment of contact.

I must have opened the wrong door, though, because I found myself looking into a small, brightly lit room with just a single bed and a cheap dressing-table in it. Jordan was perched on a stool, and opposite him, sitting on the edge of the bed, there were three men whom I hadn't seen at all at the party. They were wearing working clothes, but all I had time to notice was the large oil stain on the trousers one of them was wearing. They were speaking in Chinese; I didn't know enough then to understand what they were saying, and in any case they stopped when they saw me, Jordan jumping up, a hand on my arm, turning me away.

"Are you looking for the loo, Joseph?" We were out in the corridor already.

"I'm sorry. No, the library."

"It's the next door on the other side of the corridor. Over there."

As I walked away, I could hear the key turning in the lock behind me.

But ten minutes later Jordan came into the library after me.

"Ah, it's nice to get away from it all for a few minutes." He flopped down into an armchair. "I wish I could spend more time in here, but the older I get, the more work there seems to be for me to do."

"I was looking at this first edition of your novel," I said, not turning to him directly, the scene I had just intruded on making me awkward.

He came over and took it from me, weighing it in his hands. "I don't suppose you've read it?"

"Yes, I have. I think it was a Seven Seas paperback edition that I picked up in Collet's a few years ago." I turned to him now. "I liked it a lot."

"Really?" The pleasure flickered like neon across his face. "Let me tell you a secret, Joseph." The ghost of a hand on my shoulder. "I still read it myself from time to time. Does that sound terribly narcissistic? Maybe it does, maybe it does. But every time I read it, it comes as a surprise. It . . . excites me; it's a part of me that I keep on forgetting."

He sounded as nervous and enthusiastic as a child, and I warmed to him; though once I knew him better, looking back, I wondered if it wasn't just a little contrived, laid on specially for my benefit.

"It must make you want to write another one," I said.

"I don't have time, Joseph, that's the trouble. I've got reams of notes, but I never have time to settle down to them properly. Look at that filing cabinet over there: it's full of . . . embryos, and so's my head. But other things keep getting in the way."

He got up and started to pace about, picking up an old pair of scissors from the desk and hacking nervously at his nails with them.

"At some point, my boy, you have to make a choice between yourself and something bigger than yourself. You live either by one or by the other; never by both."

"I should have thought the two could be combined," I said. "Or rather, that one could give strength to the other."

"No, they destroy each other. Believe me, they do. I know."

My eyes stayed fixed on him as he roamed up and down obsessively. I could feel the strength in him, felt I could touch it even: the strength of his will and a physical strength, too, that the frail, gentle body couldn't contain. Its intensity attracted me, but it was somehow frightening at the same time, especially as I glimpsed the pressures that were working in his face, distorted by the light from the one reading lamp in the large, dark room.

When he spoke again, the voice, too, seemed different, twisted. "But what about Evelyne, eh?"

I looked at him questioningly, but he didn't see me.

"That makes up for it all, doesn't it? Have you ever seen her before, Joseph?"

"Why no!" I said, surprise in my voice. "No, of course not."

"Yes, you have, you know. Yes, you have!" It was almost a shout. "Just wait till you see this." He dragged a chair across the room, catching one of its legs in the fringe of a Bokhara carpet, tugging it away impatiently. Then he clambered up on top of it to pull a big art book from a shelf, muttering, "Just wait till you see this." When he brought it back to the desk, it fell open at a large reproduction of Botticelli's *Birth of Venus*.

"There," he said triumphantly. "There she is. That's Evelyne."

It was as if he had been picked up by some monstrous wave in his mind and swept away from me, so that I felt suddenly at a loss, alone, as I leaned forwards, looking at the picture. Venus? There was nothing of Evelyne King in that slender, delicate face.

"No, I can't see the likeness, I'm afraid," I said irritably.

"No, no, not Venus. Here." He stabbed excitedly at the farther of the two cherubs in the top left-hand corner, the points of the scissors tearing into the paper.

I looked again.

"Yes, I think I can see it now." I must have sounded hesitant, as though I was humoring him. But what I was thinking about, the thing that was so striking, was how close the likeness really was. Not just in the superficial sense, though even there you couldn't miss the same broad face, the same small, full, determined mouth; but beneath that, what surprised me was the way in which the picture somehow expressed the feeling I hadn't been able to define in Evelyne earlier: a strong sensuality that she seemed to be trying to suppress. But it came out much more clearly in the painting because of the contrast with the spiritual, fragile Venus.

"That really is something, isn't it, Joseph?" Jordan was saying, sitting back, proud of himself as a cat with kittens. "D'you know how old I am? Sixty-six. But thank God I can still fuck my wife!"

"Did you get a look at Evelyne, Joe?" asked Winn in the car afterwards. "Isn't she wonderful? Like the Sleeping Beauty. Jordan's never wakened her, has he? But, God, I'd like to have her for myself. I'd waken you, baby, I'd waken you. I'd hang you up on the wall, naked, in a great big plastic bag. Just think of her, full of juice and honey. I'd lick it out of her every day."

He shivered and pulled the fur coat tight around his neck as we came over the brow of the hill and saw the millions of lights of the city, the harbour, Kowloon on the other side, spread out far below us like galaxies.

From that night on I saw Jordan and Evelyne two or three times a week. At first Jordan would phone me at the office, asking me to come round for a drink or for supper; then later it was just assumed that I would go.

Initially it was Evelyne I went to see. During the party I hadn't been thinking of her in a particularly sexual way, but afterwards, as I thought back, the warmth of her hand through my sleeve, what Jordan had said in the library, and Winn's fantasies in the car built up in my mind. I say "in my mind" deliberately; it was a mental kind of lust, other men's images of her, that stirred me first. And then, seeing her alone or with just a few other people, I had time to look at her in the moments when she wasn't conscious of being watched. Like a voyeur, I would browse on the swell of her breasts. And she would suddenly feel it and try to switch herself off, but not too hard because she wanted it as well.

And all the time Jordan talked.

"It's good to be able to talk to young people," he would say. "I don't feel anything in common with old men. Look at the Cultural Revolution. The people I feel closest to are the Red Guards. They won't let the revolution die."

At first, though, with the memory of that scene in the study fresh in my mind, I was suspicious of him; young myself, I looked for all the weaknesses, all the hypocrisy that I could find in him. And I found plenty, as I would have done in any man. But as I listened to his stories, I became caught up in the sheer size and freedom of his life; he had done so much more than I could ever hope to do. And so I envied him, though admiration outweighed the envy. I had come from a country where distances are measured in miles, crowds in dozens; and Jordan's talk of thousands, millions, carried me away. He would bring out maps and photographs and spread them all over the vast dining table, and then Evelyne would come in and say, "This is my favorite one," pointing at a faded sepia picture of Jordan, young and slim, on a tiny mountain pony with his feet almost touching the ground on either side. And my eyes would move from the maps to the photo and from there to Evelyne's long, strong fingers.

I suppose that my lust for his wife drew me closer to Jordan, too. In any case, I grew to like him as well, liking even the sides of his character that at first I had been critical of. After all, didn't a man who had done so much have the right to act out his life, to boast about it in his old age? It was all right to be honest when you had nothing to be honest about, I told myself, but maybe you had the right to lie when the truth itself was so fantastic.

Yet none of that explains why Jordan should

have forced Evelyne and myself together. It couldn't have been merely accidental; no man accidentally pushes his wife into the arms of someone more than forty years younger than himself. And yet it couldn't have been deliberate, either; not, anyway, in the sense of Jordan wanting Evelyne to have an affair with me. He was too jealous for that, just on the simple level of personal property. He had surrounded, cushioned, his life with objects, some valuable, some worthless; but he could never give anything away, never throw anything out. He would complain about them constantly—"The only things that really matter are the things that you can carry on your back over a mountain pass"—but he still clung desperately to his possessions, Evelyne most of all.

In the end, the only reason that I can think of for the way in which he pushed us together is that he did it out of a longing for danger, to return to a world where risks were taken. He didn't want us to make love, I'm sure, but he wanted to play in his mind with the possibility that we might. Maybe it made him feel young again.

"Old men become dangerous," he said to me once, talking of what was happening in China. "They become dangerous because they start to feel responsible only to their own egos."

Donald Winn said just the same thing about Jordan. Though finally, of course, it was true of us all in our own ways and had nothing to do with age.

Anyway, it began with Jordan saying Evelyne ought to go out more; he didn't have time to take her, but would I mind? So I used to call for her, and we would leave like a couple of teen-agers and go to a cinema or a concert and then come back home to find Jordan waiting, not seeming to have done anything all night. I would listen to him reminisce, and Evelyne would say she was tired and go to bed, and about three in the morning Jordan would walk out with me into the drive with his arm around my shoulders and stand there waving as I drove away.

It couldn't, of course, continue. Both Evelyne and I knew that we were going to make love; putting it off only added to the pleasure. She used to question me about the various girls I had slept with, and so we went on blowing up such a balloon of lust around ourselves that it had, sooner or later, to burst.

Finally, one night we were supposed to be going to see a film when she said, "Take me to one of your bars." It came out like an order, arrogant and determined.

So I took her to one that was called the Universal Bunny Bar and Nite Club. It was a quiet night because there were hardly any American ships in the harbour, and you could see the place for what it really was without any of the false glamor, the noise, the phoney romance that drew the tourists and the sailors. Some of the girls sat around reading magazines; others were playing poker or just talking or eating or wandering about. They kept on glancing at us curiously, but a few minutes was long enough to make us a part of this world, as uninteresting as everything else. And it was this, I told Evelyne, that I liked about the place: its essential, infectious boredom; the sense of isolated lives, freed from having to mean anything at all.

"Like one of Lautrec's brothels," she agreed.

A girl came in from outside with a bag of melon seeds in her hand and lounged against a table where two of her friends were playing cards. They talked raucously, splitting the seeds between their teeth and spitting the shells out on the floor. An old servant came over with a brush and started shouting at them for making a mess.

"That's the only kind of crisis in a place like this," I said. "It's all very harmless. Cushioned."

"That one over there is very beautiful, isn't she?" said Evelyne.

I nodded.

"Have you ever slept with any of them?"

"I don't think so," I said. "They're pretty good at camouflage."

"But you would like to, wouldn't you."

"I'd rather be with you." I tried the gigolo smile again.

"You don't have to do that," she said impatiently.

"Do what?"

"I mean you don't have to . . . leer at me. You can have me if that's all you want."

I hadn't expected it to come like that. Bringing her here was another step forwards, but I had expected that we would drink, dance, hold hands, kiss, savor the lengthy prelude, rather than this cold directness.

I ran my fingers through my hair. "Right now?"

She stood up, smoothing down her skirt. "Why not?"

In the car, as I drove back to my place, I put my hand on her thigh, but she pulled away; and when I tried to kiss her in the bedroom, she pushed me back. "Let's get undressed first."

For a moment I was angry. What did she think she was trying to prove? I could feel myself getting small, and I kept my underpants on. Sitting irritably on the edge of the bed, I watched her step out of the orange linen skirt, fold it up neatly on the chair, then unbutton her shirt and shrug it off.

But liking or disliking her became irrelevant. She seemed to be quite deliberately showing off as she reached back, her breasts thrusting against the bra, to undo her hair. Dark brown, it fell down to her shoulders, the first time I had seen it out of its tight knot, and she shook it, grinning suddenly, human again, as it tickled her skin. Then the bra, and her creamy breasts swinging loose, heavy, pendulous, but tilting up strongly to the large brown spread of the nipple. Then pants, stockings, garters, standing there at last naked, challenging me to criticize any part of her.

As she leaned down on the bed, I rolled over towards her, but she shoved me onto my back and straddled me, pushing down my underpants, parting the thick pubic hair with her fingers.

She smiled. "Now I've got you."

I laughed nervously, not really believing it yet. "Are you always so bossy?"

"I'm old enough to be your mother," she said very solemnly.

"No, you're not."

"I'm thirty-four."

"Child-mother."

I stretched up and pulled those breasts into my face, but she pushed me back again.

"No, I want to look at you properly."

The insides of her thighs curved elastically away from my fingers.

"Did I shock you?" she said.

"No. You surprised me, though."

She began to move up and down, long, firm strokes, her hair falling down into her eyes.

"I wanted it to be different. That's why I wanted to go there, to that bar first, so that you'd see the difference. It's not just a game for me, Joe."

And there it was again: that awful arrogance of hers, this wanting to be different, setting herself apart from the poor little tarts she had imagined me with before. And for a moment I almost drew away from her, repelled, but I didn't have the strength. She had made me so easily hers, sucked me out of myself and into her, so that I wasn't a man, nor even a penis, any longer, just a new part of her body that she was intent on manipulating, pleasing, exciting. But I couldn't think of that at the time; I wasn't able to think of anything just then. It was only afterwards, when she had taken a taxi home, that I saw how it had been and felt slightly, self-indulgently, disgusted with her.

That's how unfair I was. There, at the beginning, the only side of her I wanted to see was the strength. I wanted her to dominate me; that's what *I* was looking for, so I couldn't allow myself to see the uncertainty, the need to be sure, that lay beneath the surface of her words.

I could feel myself getting near, and I reached my fingers down to her, but she pulled them away.

"No, I don't want to come now. I want to watch your face."

And that's what she did, controlling me, seeing my face crumple like a crushed-up ball of paper, then rolling over beside me and holding me tight against her body. But later, when I came on top of her, into her again, the orgasm had to be wrenched out like a root.

8

Days passed. Bones, tissue, skin began clumsily to knit together. Joe was able to get up and swing himself along the hospital corridor on crutches, a giggling, plain little nurse beside him saying, "We'll have to keep out of your way once they take the plaster off." Grunting, sweating, the pain spreading upwards along both sides of his body, he was sickened by the very idea of sex.

They had cut the drugs down gradually, so that he began to feel the pain, not just when he got out of bed, but lying absolutely still, the different parts of his body stretching out tentatively towards each other, linking up like tendrils. Just breathing in was enough to wrench them apart again. It was almost unbearable, and yet he repeated it deliberately, holding his breath, drawing in his abdomen, feeling the nerves scream, then relaxing out of cowardice because he couldn't stand it any longer.

Without torturing himself like that, he couldn't really be sure that he even existed. He would lie there for hours quite normally, and then suddenly begin to feel that his body and his head were horrifyingly empty, like the inside of a shell.

One night he dreamed he was standing alone in a planetarium with the stars circling up above. He was shouting his own name, but there was no reply; until, looking up, he knew the planetarium was the inside of his own skull. Up there somewhere was the roof, the bone, but he couldn't see it; it seemed transparent, opening outwards onto the whole universe. Stars, planets, galaxies. Then gravity tilted. Terrified, he was spinning into the emptiness, praying for an end to it, a wall to hurl himself against.

Bone breaking. Pain connected.

Part 3

9

Outside there is nothing but snow.

I sit with my feet on the rail around the cast-iron stove. From time to time I open the doors to throw on more wood, and as I bend down, I feel myself drawn into the fire roaring inside. I stare into it until my eyes water and I can't focus any longer. Then I bang the doors closed, feeling the heat radiate from the dull black box.

Mrs. McLaren has just left. I stood by the window and watched her go, stumbling up through the drifts. As she reached the top of the hill, she turned to wave, not seeing me, but waving to where she knew I would be; a vigorous, scrubbing motion of her whole arm. Behind the frosted window I raised my hand.

Mrs. McLaren is the only contact I have with an outside world. She and her husband, Gord, rent me this cottage, and she comes down once a week or so, "just to see how you're coming along." She always brings a casserole and a cake. "Can't have you living out of cans all winter," she says. "It's not good for you, all these additives. They cause a lot of the cancer that's around."

My silences puzzle, but don't bother, her. They've become part of our routine.

She bustles in, covered in smiles; and I make a gesture at politeness, offering her cocoa, a coffee.

"I'll just put these away first," she says. "Get things ship-shape, eh?"

So I sit here by the stove or over there at the table next to the window, watching her as she washes the dishes, plumps up the cushions, puts my books straight. All the time she talks.

"Don't mind me, Joe. Just you go on with what you're doing."

I grunt.

"What's that you're writing? A book or something?"

"I'm not really sure," I say.

She looks round at me, worried by this English accent she can never quite trust, searching my face for sarcasm. A man ought to know what he's doing. But now she has found the right approach. She treats me like a young child—or a very old invalid.

"Are you sleeping good with those new pills you got?"

"Better," I reply. "But the ice kept me awake last night."

The lake is freezing over, light blue expanses reaching out to each other, linking up. At night, as it stretches, the ice groans and grumbles or cracks like a gunshot.

"Mind you don't go walking out on it yet, eh?"

she says, coming over. "It's real treacherous this time of year."

We look out of the window together. There are still some black pools of open water a hundred yards out from the shore. In the bitterly cold air, steam rises from them as if they were boiling.

"It was just this time last year Nancy Sullivan went through. That's their marina you can see across there, behind the island? Used to be; Pat sold up this summer. You can see where she was, right in a straight line with that clump of cedars. The water's still open there. Lord knows what she was doing so far out. There were some people said she did it deliberate, like, but I'd never want to say that about anyone myself, even though she was a bit . . . strange at times. I'll admit that. Nobody noticed her till she went through. Wayne Crowe saw her with that big telescope of his. Said her clothes were holding her up in the water like a parachute and she was trying to get out, scratching at the sides of the hole, but the ice kept on breaking away. Wayne ran down and got some of the boys to go out with an aluminum rowboat. Pushing it with their feet? Young Mick Cavan went through right up to his waist, the ice was so bad. And when they did get out there, she was gone, no sign of her at all, just the grooves her fingernails had made around the edge. She must have dug in so hard there was blood in them, they said."

She turns and goes back to the sink. "Maybe I'll make some cocoa now."

"What about her body?" I ask. "Did they find it?"

"No. Not right then, anyhow. The police tried diving for her, but the current's strong in there. And by the next day the hole was sealed right over. It wasn't till the ice went out she washed up down the narrows. Gord was one of the ones went down to get her. It made him sick to his stomach just to see her—all black and blown up twice her proper size."

I warm my hands on the mug.

She laughs to break the spell. "You be careful, Joe, eh? Wait till it's real hard?"

I smile back. "I'll stay close to the shore."

But just a year and a half ago I was able to bang on the table and say with so much certainty, "What this place needs is a revolution!" Though even then the violence in my voice was only half real.

I was sitting with Kwan at the upstairs window of a small, dirty restaurant in Shaukiwan. "The fishing village of Shaukiwan," the tourist guides still called it; and perhaps that was what it really had been a few years before: a pretty, isolated fishing village on the edge of a curving, rocky bay. But now the city had stretched out its tentacles and turned the village into a mess of tenement blocks and factories and slums.

We sucked in the greasy noodles and looked down on the scurrying crowds below, watching as though from another planet as they crushed blindly between trams and lorries, stumbling, bumping into each other, threatening each other's eyes with umbrellas, holding sodden newspapers over their hair, fighting to get onto buses.

"Look at them down there. They're not running because they're late or in a hurry or anything. It's sheer habit, that's all. Movement for the sake of movement."

I waited for Kwan to say something, but he just sat there smiling, letting me run on, too.

"There's so much energy here, and it's all wasted. It just pours into the gutters, and nobody gives a damn." I wanted to draw some show of agreement or concern out of him, but the eyes went on watching me, gently amused. "Christ! I should have thought *you* at least would want to do something about it."

I felt I had to be angry with him, but he seemed somehow protected from other people's moods. And it was just this protectedness, this acceptance of everything, that was getting on my nerves. I wanted him to share my anger, but the more I tried to whip up my own emotions, the more placid he became.

Finally he said, "We don't *need* to do anything about it. It's you who're in the hurry, Joe. You Europeans live on a different time-scale; that's what you're forgetting. You speak as if the next year or two are always going to be the most important, but that's not how we look at things. We know how to wait."

"It sounds to me like a pretty obvious excuse for doing nothing."

Yes, I felt so sure then, didn't I? It was as though I was driven to prove myself to him. Yet not to prove myself as I was, but as some simpler, more extreme version of myself.

As I look back at Kwan, I'm full of regret: regret at the loss of someone more genuinely tolerant and gentle than anybody else I've ever met, regret for the falseness with which in the end we treated each other. And yet from the very beginning there was something between us that forced me into these artificial gestures: something in me that took pleasure in them, certainly, but something in him, too—another kind of weakness—that encouraged and invited them.

It began at Jordan's. Not the birthday party or any of the other parties they gave—Kwan never seemed to turn up at them—but one night a couple of months or so after I first made love to Evelyne, I went up there, and she said that Jordan was in the study with somebody important.

"It's you I came for, anyway," I whispered.

We went out onto the dark verandah and sat down in the deep rattan sofa. I put my arm round her and pulled her towards me, meaning just to kiss her lightly, patronizingly. But I met her mouth wide open as if to swallow me, the smell of sex on her breath as noticeable as nicotine, her whole body opening wide. I could feel her hand inside my trousers, and I jerked myself away.

"We can't. Not here."

"Why not? Jordan's busy." She tugged me on top of her, pulling up her dress.

"The servants."

"Damn the servants!"

So I let myself be drawn into her—immersed, she was so moist and deep—lying there with her legs folded up around my back, her arms stretched out on the seat not even holding me. She seemed almost unconscious, frighteningly so, as she lay with her eyes closed, moaning slightly as I thrust down vertically into her.

But then suddenly I felt myself thrown off and away into a corner of the sofa, and simultaneously, or so it seemed, I heard Jordan's voice inside the room calling her name. And there, now, was Evelyne, sitting up coolly, as if nothing had happened, while I, in a panic, struggled with my tangled trousers and shoes.

"I'm out here, darling," she called, smiling at me as though we had just been eating cucumber sandwiches on an English lawn.

When Jordan came out, I was sitting a couple of feet away from her, hoping the night would hide me.

"Joe was just asking me about how we met, Jordan," she said, reaching out for his hand.

"Ah, Joseph, no one told me you were here." He gestured absent-mindedly. "No, don't get up, my boy, don't get up."

I hadn't even thought of trying to, wasn't sure that I could. Then I saw somebody standing behind him, and Jordan followed my eyes.

"Oh, you don't know each other, do you? This is Mr. Kwan; Mr. Stewart. You should have a lot in common, being in the same . . . game." He looked around uncertainly. "Let's get some more light on the subject, shall we? It's so dark out here, Evelyne." He touched her gently on the cheek, and she looked up at him warmly. "My wife likes to sit in the dark. I think she finds it romantic."

If I had to put my finger on a single point where I could say the nightmare started, that would have to be it. It's a melodramatic way of putting it, of course, but even now, I can focus on what we did and said that night and can say, yes, that's where we started to destroy ourselves. At the same time, though, I find it increasingly difficult to explain how and why it came about. On the surface everything stayed the same: a casual domestic scene, friends talking on a verandah in the cool of the evening, Evelyne getting up to go for a cardigan, the servants bringing coffee. Yet underneath we were sinking into a world where we couldn't be ourselves any longer, where we were forced to become dismembered fragments of what we truly were or had once been. All we could see of each other from that evening on were the glimpses we caught of strange underwater shapes, changing constantly according to no laws we could hope to discover, while all the time we went on pretending that everything was just the same—normal, under control.

It was Jordan who suffered most—or so I thought, not seeing myself at the time. It was as if he had been driven out of himself, leaving only this empty, posturing husk behind. I'm not sure why it should have happened just then. Perhaps the only explanation is that somehow the presence of Kwan and myself together, forced him to impress each of us with his power over the other. But as it was going on, as I sat there, full of my own treachery, it seemed more mysterious, something in the night itself—a lingering vision of Evelyne and myself screwing wildly on the sofa—that he couldn't quite see and yet couldn't scrape away from the surface of his eyes.

He was always an arrogant man, of course; and I had seen him mad, I'm sure, once before. But then I was just watching. Now I was committed to him, drawn in by my own sense of guilt towards him.

He paced along the clay tiles of the verandah. He wouldn't, couldn't, sit down.

"Why don't you sit down?" I said casually at one point, and as he whirled round, I thought for a moment he was going to hit me.

"I don't need to sit down," he snarled.

He went on just standing there in front of us, boasting all night long, not about the things he had a right to be proud of, but about the petty triumphs of an old and envious man.

"You know, Kwan, people come up to this house, and the first thing they think is that Jordan King has sold out, become a capitalist. That's what they say—I know; I'm not such an old fool as they think I am. But they don't use their eyes properly. Look at the bar, for instance. People come in there, and they think: why should a Communist have a bar like that? Well, I had the colonial secretary in there once, and I said to him, 'D'you know what you've done by coming in here?'

" 'No,' he said.

" 'Look up at the ceiling,' I said.

" 'Yes, it's very pretty,' he said.

"And I said, 'But don't you see anything special about it?'

"So he looked again. 'No,' he said, 'no, I can't see anything special about it.'

"Then I said, 'Count the number of stars. How many are there?'

" 'Five,' he said.

" 'That's right,' I said. 'That's the number of stars in the Chinese flag. Five stars: the symbol of China. And you're standing underneath it, Mr. Colonial Secretary. That's just the way it should be.'

"That's what I told him, Kwan. And that's the way you've got to treat these people. You're too reticent, you know. That's your trouble; you let them get on top of you. But you've got to keep them in their place."

He turned by the verandah wall, the lamp, with moths fluttering around it, between us.

"It's the same thing with the swimming-pool down there. The same symbol in the tiles. I won't be happy till I see it all over Hong Kong. And d'you know, Joseph, I built that swimming-pool with my own hands.

I blasted the rock away, and I poured the concrete, and people still say that Jordan King has sold out. But they'll learn; they'll learn soon enough."

My whole face was electric with shame and sorrow for him, and oddly I felt this protective instinct all the more intensely when I remembered how I had been betraying him just an hour before. But when I looked across at Evelyne, expecting to find the same tangle of emotions in her, all that I saw was a mask responding, smiling, nodding in all the appropriate places.

It was then, by contrast with the rest of us, that Kwan established himself in my mind. It's hard to describe the first impression he made—he was so carefully unimpressive—but he seemed, as the night went on, to be the only honest person there. He sat there smiling, too, but it was quite clear that his silence didn't imply agreement. Just his presence was enough to make the rest of us appear selfish and hypocritical, Evelyne most of all, so that I began to hate her—not Jordan, nor even myself—Evelyne; or rather, this clusive, ambivalent figure she was disappearing into.

I found myself turning more and more to Kwan, watching him, fixing on the striking ordinariness of the man as if it were the one thing I could grasp. He wasn't tall or short, handsome or ugly; he didn't seem especially brilliant, but he wasn't shy, either. His clothes were nondescript, and his body looked rather clumsy and out of condition (though later I learned he played squash twice a week to keep in shape). You would have lost him (he would have lost himself) instantaneously in a crowd.

That was the Kwan I saw then, though looking back, I wonder whether that ordinariness wasn't false, too. Wasn't Kwan's simplicity just as much of a deliberate act as Jordan's self-inflation? Perhaps.

I suppose the main difference was that he never wallowed in himself as Jordan did. As I do. It didn't seem to be important who he was, where he came from. "All that matters," he said, "is what you do."

Later, it's true, he told me (because I pressed him) a little about his early life; but even then it was something he made didactic, impersonal. There was the lonely childhood; the mother, a second wife, who died before he knew her; the distant, aged, mandarin father; an uncle who was viceroy of Szechwan. He had been educated strictly in the traditional pattern—"I can still write rather good, utterly meaningless poems"—and then, with the Japanese war, had come a sudden breath of freedom. He left home to attend a Westernized university, studied French literature for a year, translated Rimbaud. Getting involved in politics, he dismissed literature as an irrelevance, moved, started to study medicine, changed again, and ended up in Chungking at the end of the war as a mechanical engineer and a member of the party. The British government gave him a scholarship—somebody from his social background must obviously be trustworthy—and he went to England to do research on metal fatigue, but he tired of that again and wandered about the wreckage of Europe for a couple of years. "By that time I was more interested in the cracks in capitalism than those in metals."

When he finally returned to China, he decided to become a journalist. He had already started to write again, but saw his own abilities clearly enough to know he would never be a great creative writer. In any case, he told himself, that wasn't what he would have wanted even if it had been possible. It seemed inevitably too self-centered a way of life, too antisocial. Communicating other men's originality, interpreting, explaining was what he was good at; and very soon he caught the attention of Tao Chu, the brilliant, ambitious intellectual who was to become the virtual ruler of South China. Tao planted Kwan in Hong Kong—literally, "Take root there," he said.

"But it's the end of the world," protested Kwan.

"The best place to start," said Tao. And by the time I met him, though Tao had been overthrown, Kwan had survived to become the managing editor of the largest left-wing newspaper group in Hong Kong, a faceless, powerful man.

By the time we finally left Jordan's house that night, neither of us seemed able to think of anything to say. I was exhausted, my legs trembling, but even then I didn't want to be the first person to start pulling Jordan to pieces behind his back. In a sense it was just superstition. I was deceiving him enough already as far as the big things were concerned without the little betrayals as well.

So it was Kwan, tactfully, probingly, who brought the conversation round to the direction we both knew it had to go in.

"You have to remember that Dr. King has done a great deal for China." His voice was neutral, but it provided me with the excuse I needed, *that he knew I needed*.

"Christ! That was a disgusting bloody performance, wasn't it?" I jerked the gear-lever forward angrily.

Kwan was quiet for a minute. When he spoke again, his words were still reticent, tolerant. "He's getting old, and he still works like a slave, you know. Too hard. There's been a big change in him in the past couple of years."

"But the frightening thing is you could never rely on somebody like that. After seeing him tonight you could never really trust him, surely?" And as soon as I had said it, as well as feeling guilty because I knew it was unfair, I sensed that somehow this was what Kwan had been wanting me to say; not my words or even his, but those of a figure that just his presence could shape me into.

From that point on I was at ease with him, free, the words flowing and mingling as though some common secret were drawing us together. Perhaps, I said, I ought to see less of Jordan. And yes, Kwan said, he could understand that; not that he had anything against Jordan, of course, but that kind of world could be very narrow, hermetic. What I really needed, I told him, was to get involved with what lay beneath all that, something more ordinary perhaps, but more real, too. So he thought for a bit, and, yes, he said, yes, there was a place he would like me to see, the worst in Hong Kong; that was where I ought to start—next weekend?—at the bottom.

As I came into a steep downhill corner, he caught my eye just for a moment. "I don't usually like taking foreigners there; it seems rather—voyeuristic? But you're not a tourist, are you, Joe?"

We both laughed, and as I guided the car smoothly around the tight bends, the dishonesty of the evening seemed to be rising away from us like mist.

We walked down away from the tram tracks towards where the sea should have been, past the back of a cinema and curbside stalls selling needles and fruit, cloth, plastic toys. It was one of those heavy days when you know it's going to rain, the air full of humidity already and low clouds just above the rooftops of the multi-story factory buildings. No day of rest here, just three days' holiday at Chinese New Year, and the rest of the time the continual clanging of machines and the thump of pile-drivers thudding into the smelly clay as more factories were built. An expanding fungus world with no laws other than the simple ones of maximum profitability: put your money in, and get it back doubled next year. Cotton, plastics, transistors, toys, watch-cases, wigs, cameras, pullovers, furniture, sequins, food. It didn't matter what you called it all; one word was enough: dollars.

Where the factories stopped, the slums began. Land was too good, too expensive for the poor. They had to live on the sea. We came to a breakwater where once there must have been a beach. With the tide out all I could see was ten yards of foul-smelling black slime: oil and mud and vegetable skins and excrement, rotting in the ooze. On top of that were the houses, hovels, rising on spindly matchstick legs: branches, driftwood, slats of boxes nailed illogically together, not a straight line in sight. The walls and roofs of the shacks were made of the first thing that came to hand, rusty metal, oiled paper, canvas, cardboard, wooden slats, a fifty-year-old ad for Singer sewing machines. You might have found it framed on the wall of a chic Parisian flat. Not one of these buildings would have stood up on its own, but together, hundreds of them huddled against each other, they survived, until the next typhoon.

We crossed over from the roadway on some narrow wooden planks, not looking down.

"This is the main street," said Kwan, pointing at the three-foot-wide alley that twisted away in front of us. Almost immediately, we had to press ourselves in against the wall as an old woman staggered past, bandy-legged, with two large aluminum cans of water hooked on a bamboo pole across her shoulder.

"There isn't any water here, of course," Kwan went on. "It has to be carried from the stand-pipes back there opposite the cinema. That woman probably lives off the few cents she makes by carrying other people's water for them."

"The poor exploiting the poor," I said self-righteously.

"They don't know much about politics," he said gently, "but they know they have to survive."

"There are better ways of surviving."

"Yes, Joe, you may know that, and I know it, too. But, then, it's not our problem." There was a slight edge to his voice, not sharp enough for a rebuke, but a reminder.

Some of the houses were three stories high: three stories, anyway, in the sense that they had three floors stacked on top of each other, but the ceilings were so low that by looking up just a foot or two, I could see into the top floor. All around us the smoke from cooking fires hung in the heavy air, mixing with the thin mist that drifted in from the sea. We strolled along, looking down even narrower side alleys, until we came to a sliding door that was open at the level of our knees. Inside, the box was about five feet by three, the floor covered with worn green linoleum, the walls three feet high and hung with photographs of babies and grinning children, a wedding group turning sepia. An old woman, fat, in flimsy pink pyjamas, crouched there like a battery chicken, not even looking up as we passed; and you felt that she could never move from that position, her muscles atrophied.

Farther on, Kwan had paused at a slightly larger box painted white, with Chinese characters in black. "This is a doctor's surgery. Not a Western-style doctor, an herbalist. The notice is an advert for the things he claims he can cure: kidney disease, appendicitis, backache, a weak heart, insomnia, just about everything, in fact. It's closed at the moment. He's probably got half a dozen other places like this that he goes to in rotation. On a good day he might make anything up to two thousand dollars."

We went on and came to the sea—brown water lapping against black slime; paper, empty cardboard boxes, a rubber tire, waterlogged cabbages, the skeleton of a fish bobbing rhythmically up and down. The houses were even more rickety, and the planks twisted haphazardly between them. One shack had been made out of the wreck of a small rowing boat (it still had a rudder) on which a patched canvas tent had been erected. A child's face peered out through one of the holes, snot streaming down its chin. It didn't wave or smile or stick out its tongue; there was no sign of curiosity, just a blank, unblinking stare. And then it was joined by the equally expressionless face of an old woman. She looked about ninety but could, I suppose, have been half that.

All the same, the air was slightly fresher, the smoke thinner. Down from the boardwalk, on a platform just above the water, a young woman with a baby strapped to her back was kneeling over a small metal bowl cleaning a tiny fish, nearly all bone. She looked up as we approached and smiled; Kwan nodded, and she stood up, her hands on her back, a plain, stocky woman with a plump, lively face. Kwan asked her if she was cooking the lunch, and she laughed raucously, speaking so fast I couldn't catch any of what she was saying.

"She was asking me if I had only been in Hong Kong a few weeks because I speak Cantonese like a 'foreign devil' with the tones all wrong," said Kwan. "So I told her I had been here for fifteen years, and she said I must be very bad at listening to other people."

He grinned, and they went on talking, Kwan not condescending at all, the woman not deferential. Instinctively he seemed able to make her feel that he was interested in what she could tell him, listening to her properly, not looking past her at the small boats that rocked hypnotically on the water, but nodding, asking questions, following her gestures.

Then he turned to me. "She says her husband works in the textile factory over there at the bottom of the hill. They've lived here for six years now, and they rent this house from one of her husband's uncles. She used to work in a plastic factory, but she gave it up because of the baby."

"Do you like living here?" I asked stiltedly, trying to make contact, too, but the flood of her reply went sweeping past me.

"She says that's a funny question. Nobody lives here because they want to. But it's better than sharing a bed space in a tenement, and then the air's better out here."

I looked down at the evil-smelling water and up at her face again, but there was no trace of irony on it, just a broad smile as she listened, uncomprehending, to what Kwan was saying.

Then she started again. "She says that since you're a European, would you ask the government to put electricity in the village. Then they wouldn't always be afraid of the children falling in the water in the darkness, and they might even be able to have a television set."

We walked back towards the shore, the children

waving and giggling till we were out of sight, past a small bakery with thick grease hanging in tarry drops from the wire netting that covered the windows and a forge where a man tossed red-hot metal rings onto a growing, cooling heap. It started to drizzle, then rain in great drifts of water, and we began to run back in the direction of the main street. But as we turned a corner Kwan pointed towards a figure crushed into a doorway: an old man, terribly emaciated, his knees up under his chin, his cheeks so hollow there hardly seemed any room for a mouth. He was leaning against the wall, groaning. We crossed over, and Kwan bent down beside him, asking him what was the matter; but the man didn't show any sign of understanding, just went privately on with his pain. Kwan called to an assistant from the cooked-meat shop next door. The boy shrugged and turned away; Kwan repeated what he had said and finally got a short, abrupt answer.

"They say he's been like this for years. Nobody knows what's wrong with him."

That was the image that stayed in my mind as we ran in and out along the crowded pavements, under the dripping awnings, Kwan just in front but looking round to make sure I was keeping up with him. And as we stood in the restaurant laughing, gasping for breath, brushing the rain off our clothes, then sitting down and Kwan ordering, I was still trying to sort out how I felt about it all. One thing I thought I was sure of: the more I saw of Kwan, the more I was drawn to him, to his openness with other people, this unemphatic kindness that seemed to leave a small circle of warmth in a vast, cynical city. Sentimentally I wanted to throw myself into this world of human contact. But then again there was something passive about it, too, wasn't there? I wanted to remember the woman we had spoken to, her friendliness, the natural dignity about her; but my mind kept on coming back to the old man in the doorway, the grandmother in her chicken coop, the blank stare, the futility of being poor.

Along with my attraction to Kwan there was a

vague, sour anger: with him, with that woman, with everyone who went on accepting this awful life as a matter of course, without protest. True, they didn't give up; they made the best of it. But wasn't that even worse? Kindness, love, warmth—they didn't do anything to change the basic situation; they just made it more tolerable.

The anger I felt was most of all with myself and my own inability to help, though when Kwan said that what I needed was to understand the Asian time-scale, their capacity to wait, it was much easier to turn it against him.

"It sounds to me like a pretty obvious excuse for doing nothing." I leaned forwards heavily on the table, and it tilted wildly, so that we both had to hang on to stop the plates from sliding onto the floor.

"No, it's not an excuse, Joe. You're quite right in one sense: the only thing that can change this situation *is* a revolution. But you can't make a revolution out of nothing, just by talking about it. You've got to have a solid political basis for it, and we just don't have that here."

"All right, then"—I struggled to fit a slippery mushroom between my chopsticks—"but what's being *done* about it?"

"Well, we've got a lot of people in the factories. But even there what they really want is better wages and shorter hours."

"But that's exactly the point I'm getting at. You get them better wages, you get that woman back there her electricity and her television set, and all you've done is to make their conditions more bearable; you've made them less dissatisfied, which is the opposite of what you want, surely?"

Kwan took a long time to reply, and when he did so, his eyes were turned away from me, looking down out of the window at the never-ending crowds in the street. The rain had stopped, but the water was deep in the gutters, the drains blocked with rubbish. An old man went by, bent over a pushcart with wooden wheels, his trousers rolled up above his knees, a bright leather money belt around his waist.

"No, I don't think any cause is helped by insisting that people must be kept unhappy."

The words were precise and sure, and their obviousness made me ashamed of how I'd been trying to impress him by being so orthodox, so doctrinaire.

"I'm sorry," I said, "I was being stupid."

"The thing you've got to remember, Joe"—his chopsticks hung in the air—"is that this isn't China. The people may seem the same, but politically they're primitive."

"That's what I mean," I said. "A few miles away you've got the whole Cultural Revolution going on—society being taken to pieces and re-examined like a clock or something. But here people just seem to go on putting up with this completely feudal kind of situation. Nobody seems to ask any questions about it at all."

"Well, I'm not saying the Cultural Revolution won't have some effect even here—in the long term—but the conditions are totally different." He probed his teeth with a toothpick. "And in the end it all depends on what's in China's interests. We can take Hong Kong whenever we want it, of course, just by putting the pressure on. But for the moment Hong Kong is useful, economically useful. A revolution wouldn't be to our advantage, not right at the moment."

And so the image that I had made of him crumbled almost as soon as I had built it up. All this kindness, this charity; but in the end what counted was power, power politics. A party man after all?

"So the interests of four million people don't matter?"

"It depends. Not if they conflict with the interests of seven hundred million."

Safety in numbers. But for whom?

Just a few weeks later, at the beginning of May, all that was to change completely. Or perhaps nothing did change finally; perhaps we just began to see how things really were.

A strike was taking place at an artificial flower factory in the most dismal and overcrowded part of Kowloon. The great celebrations of May Day had come and gone, with their rousing, patriotic speeches, their variety shows, their enormous, elaborate dinners; but none of the glamor had rubbed off on the day-to-day reality. This wasn't a strike about important principles or political ideals; the workers were quite simply protesting in the only way open to them—not a very effective way, at that—about the new shift system that had been introduced and the fact that their pay was stopped whenever any of the rickety machines broke down.

So all one steamy Saturday, while the beaches were crowded, the workers sat on the pavement outside the factory in the foul air that was blown across to them from the nearby power station. They had come to talk to the bosses, but the bosses didn't turn up. After all, it wasn't a serious strike, not worth spoiling your Saturday for. The police were there, though, waiting around corners in trucks, wire grilles over the windows. Just in case there was trouble; just in case they could make trouble.

As the day went on, the good humor of the morning turned to sullen frustration. The strikers stuck handwritten posters all over the concrete façade of the factory. They shook and banged the metal gates and shouted at the few scared workers inside, then turned to the "running dog" police and hurled insults at them. Why the hell was it never the interests of the people that the police protected?

At twenty past four a lorry pulled up outside the factory, and one of the foremen, a man they all hated, pushed the few unwilling but faithful workers forwards with crates of plastic rosebuds that had to be loaded onto a ship that night.

Suddenly, all was confusion: fists, knees, heads,

the police moving in from behind with their riot guns and batons and rattan shields, a wall closing in around the crowd.

That was the spark. The fire didn't burn itself out till December.

10

Sally didn't like hospitals; they made her feel scared. She wrinkled her nose at the smell, the coldness of it all, even on this steaming summer's day. It was the sort of place you wanted to run out of as soon as you got in the door. God knows why Tom had wanted to come. Her eyes flickered around the room, not concentrating on the two men: Tom bent forwards, talking, talking, and Joe, this man she had helped to save, his face so ashen, pain in his eyes as he tried to push himself into a fresh position.

"D'you want me to fluff up the pillows?" she asked eagerly, getting up.

A look of surprise. "No. No thanks. I'm okay now."

So she sat down again, useless, trying to sit still. What was that on the bar under the bed? Something brown. She shivered, lit another cigarette. And still Tom went on talking.

She had moved in with him the day after the accident. She was always making love to people she felt sorry for. That first morning when she woke up so relaxed from the sound of waves breaking all night and found Tom sitting at the table in the kitchen, his head between his hands, groaning, it had seemed natural to stay and look after him. "What's the matter, love?" she asked, her arm round his shoulder.

His eyes slid back beneath his elbow, catching sight of her thin body and the blonde pubic hair; he belched loudly and groaned again. "There isn't even any fucking coffee."

So she went down to the shops on the street below and brought back a jar of coffee and some bread and a good ripe papaya. Then she moved in, settling as best she could among the tape recorders and the movie cameras, the enlargers and the bottles of developer.

Tom wasn't working, and she couldn't think of any good reason why she should either, so they had been spending every day on Tom's boat. His flat was a cheap one in a dirty old five-story tenement; the rooms were cramped and cluttered up with the gadgets he was someday going to make a fortune out of, but it was right down on the edge of the harbour with a typhoon shelter for yachts and junks and sampans just five yards away from the door. He had bought a boat, a twenty-eight foot, clinker-built life-boat converted into a cabin cruiser, inelegant, slow, and rotting, but one way of getting away from a phone that never seemed to ring. To confirm its function, he changed its name from *Adonis* to *Marie Juana,* and the Marine Department had written it down without even a smile of recognition.

That first day had been the best, though; the best

of all days. Monday lunchtime, with everybody else in the city stuck in their claustrophobic little offices for another five hours. Sally had put on a tiny white bikini that made her cream skin look rich and tantalizing (it looked anaemic in a black one), and Tom had seemed to her like some old Mediterranean fertility god in his long blue shorts, his thin legs, his barrel of a body.

It started badly, of course, as good days do.

"Just hold it like that," Tom had said, putting her hands on the steering wheel.

And she had watched him happily as he opened up the engine and poured what seemed to be oil all over it from a plastic detergent bottle. Then he straightened up smiling, looking at her looking at him.

Suddenly he sprang towards her. "Christ! You fucking idiot!"

She thought he was going to hit her and raised her arms to cover her small face. He got his fingers on the wheel just as they ran into an anchored boat. They were both thrown onto the floor, and when she looked up, she saw the side of a smooth red speedboat going past with a great gash in it.

"We'd better piss off out of here as fast as we can," Tom said, helping her up.

They chugged out of the harbor, past freighters surrounded by cargo junks and barges, little men clambering all over them, past ferries and fishing boats and hydrofoils, until at last they came to a small, crescent-shaped beach with long grass growing up the hill behind it and trees casting shadows across one corner.

As Tom steered in between the rocks, he told her to go up to the bow and throw in the anchor when he shouted. She swung herself out onto the side, holding one of the metal struts that supported the cabin roof. But suddenly the rusty strut wasn't there anymore, and she found herself falling with it, clownlike, into the water.

She couldn't swim; she remembered that as she went down. But she didn't panic, didn't feel that she was going to die; and so she was able to watch the water getting darker and wonder, quite objectively, if she would ever come up again. There wasn't any of this business about the whole of her past life flashing up in front of her eyes, only an awareness of the beautiful translucency of the water; and then the green got lighter, lighter, her head broke the surface, and for a moment she saw the sun. She splashed a bit and shouted, and then she went down again, remembering that the third time you weren't supposed to come up anymore. But still she felt she had all the time in the world to think about this, to wonder if it was true, even as the thinking told her there was very little time left. Then up to the surface again, and still it didn't feel as though this was her last chance to look at the sky; a very ordinary sky with a few wisps of cloud. In the distance she saw Tom plopping into the water like a frog, and she laughed, just as her head went under. Her mouth seemed full of water that she couldn't get out of it.

After that it wasn't so clear what happened, but Tom was tugging her up to the surface, and there was his face so close, his beard dripping with pearls. She clung on. How she loved him, the only man she had ever loved. Just to remember it again, sitting in this antiseptic hospital, made her want him now.

"Let go of my fucking arms," he said, so she let go, trusting him, suddenly floating as he pulled her towards the beach.

They lay there gasping in the shallow water, Tom even more exhausted than she was. But she was brought back to herself by a loud grating noise, and looking along the beach they saw the boat had driven itself up on the sand, its propeller shuddering in mid air. Tom got to his feet and staggered towards it and tried to climb in and turn the engine off, but it was too high up for him, and all he did was cut his leg. He limped back.

"Fucking boat!" he said, standing over her, blood trickling down his shin, the water spreading it out among the hairs. She pulled him down beside her.

"Where's the rest of your swimsuit?" he asked, and she realized she had lost the top of her bikini. She hadn't thought of bringing any other clothes with her, but it didn't matter, anyway, not with the sand so dry and burning, the sea receding. As they kissed, the salt water trickled from their nostrils, and then Tom licked her small breasts and her thighs and her feet, the salt water in her cunt.

Later, he helped her into the boat and told her how to turn off the engine. Then they walked up a pathway behind the beach, curving up under cool trees, until they came to a little fisherman's house on the headland. There was nobody there, and the poles that projected out over the rocks and the sea obviously hadn't had nets hung from them for at least a year. The door was blocked with an elaborate contraption of bars and stones, and the well at the back was covered over with heavy cobwebs. In front of the door stood a thick tree with knotted branches, fresh green leaves. In between its roots dozens of joss-sticks had been planted, their ashes still black on the ground.

"That's the kind of god I like," said Tom. They found a piece of joss-stick that was only partly burnt and lit it, and stood there for half an hour until the last of the smoke had climbed up into the still air, the peacefulness of the place surrounding them.

They slept on the beach that night with the cushions from the boat, and in the morning a junk towed them back to the harbor.

It had never been so good again. Not bad, either, but somehow there didn't seem to be any further discoveries to make. Every day they went out on the boat, but she didn't fall in again, and in any case, Tom was teaching her to swim. They made love, of course, but that, too, seemed to have gone back to normal, which for her meant the old unsatisfactory struggle to keep up. She didn't like to come on her own, leaving a man lost up there; but trying to match her rhythm to his, she began to worry, to hold herself back, and in the process most of the pleasure went out of it. And afterwards, back in the flat, there were long, dismal evenings when Tom would draw into himself, fiddling with the tape recorder, cleaning his camera, or just staring morosely down at the harbor, his heavy head slumped forwards on his chest. When she tried to make contact, he didn't seem to want her, shrugging her away.

It had happened to her often enough before; yet still, desperately, she didn't want to recognize that kind of inevitability. She was ready to give herself so completely; why couldn't things be simple, free, a game you didn't get tired of?

Understanding people was so much more difficult than it needed to be. This morning they had planned to take the boat out for a couple of days and sail to a remote island Tom knew, with basalt cliffs and caves and eagles. But when she got up as he was coming in from the shops, she had sensed immediately that it wasn't going to work out. He was taking things from a bag and putting them, item by item, on the table. Without looking round at her he said, "Look, Sal, I was just thinking, maybe instead we ought to go and see that guy in hospital."

"What? Today, Tom?"

He nodded.

"But why today?" They had talked a bit about Stewart at the beginning, because Tom knew some people who knew him, but that was days, weeks ago.

"Well, it gets pretty lonely in hospital. I heard somebody talking about him the other evening. Seems he got fired just a couple of weeks before it happened. They thought he might have been trying to commit suicide."

And that, Tom had known, was enough to bring Sally round. Lame dogs were her specialty. And she, for her part, knew that that was what he was counting on, and even then she didn't mind. She just wondered vaguely why Tom really wanted to visit Joe Stewart in the first place.

There were no questions in Stewart's mind, though. For the first time since the accident he was beginning to feel there was an ordinary reality that he could touch, make contact with. Despair, apathy; these were the phases he had passed through, but now for the first time it began to seem almost possible that he might be able to pull himself, or be pulled, out of them again.

It wasn't a matter of faith, politics, religion; nothing like that. On the contrary, it was this recognition of ordinariness that he had needed most.

Both Winn and Kwan had carried on visiting him, and he had grown almost to hate them for it. Admittedly he was being unfair to them because they cared for him genuinely and wanted to help. He knew that, too. But he couldn't avoid the feeling that in the end he was just an object they were fighting over, not because he was important enough to be *worth* fighting over, but as a way of breaking a deadlock, a way for one to prove that he was stronger than the other, even by so minute a margin.

There could be nothing of that kind as far as this visit from Tom and Sally was concerned, though, could there? What had drawn them together—all three of them—was something simple, pure almost, in the sense that accidents are uncontaminated by human motives. When Joe had tried to thank them for saving his life, Sally had broken in and said, "Well, *we* ought to be just as grateful to you; after all, it was you who brought us together, really."

True, they weren't probably as interesting, not nearly as intelligent, as Winn and Kwan. But Christ! Winn and Kwan, Kwan and Winn—they had become so predictable that he knew what they were going to say even before they said it. Even when he was drugged half out of his mind. Of course, Tom and Sally were predictable, too, but it was in a different, more open way; not because they were all the time trying to conceal the truth or manipulate it. They weren't afraid of seeming to be what they in fact were.

He was simply feeling closer to life than he had for weeks.

He remembered playing as a child with the other village children around a disused colliery not far from his grandmother's cottage. And one day some of the older boys had taunted him into letting himself be winched down the shaft.

"Yer jest a wee furriner," they would say.

And he, white in the face, would shout at them in his English accent, "I'm not. I'm not. I'm as Scottish as any of you."

"Prove it tae us then."

So he let them put him—gently; now they could be kind—into a large metal bucket and wind him slowly, creaking down, large flakes of rust falling into his eyes as he looked up at them.

It hadn't been too bad at first, but as the circle of light above his head got smaller and he could no longer see the features on the faces hanging out from the sides, the panic came over him in waves. It was the smell most of all, the coal dust that seemed to be building up in his nostrils until he was sure he wouldn't be able to go on breathing; his ears, his mouth, his lungs were filling up with it, and they were going to bury him alive in coal dust.

It was the same sort of panic that had been closing in on him for weeks now. He had reached a point where he had to be pulled back up, out of himself, and it didn't matter any longer how dull or banal the reality up there was.

Take Sally. She was pretty, even beautiful in a depersonalized, mass-media way, with the long legs and the thin body magazines would call "willowy," the small, oval face perched on her neck with the cute awkwardness of a Modigliani. As he looked at her, he could see her lucidly enough to know that normally he would have felt hostile towards her. She was the kind of girl that, as a student, he had grown used to seeing in rich students' sports cars, cool and remote on the surface and—as he told himself enviously—empty underneath. He could see all the symptoms: the way she sat there trying to look so self-possessed, smoking too much, not knowing quite what to say or do, looking to Tom for a lead, the sentimental phrases she came out with. An essentially trivial person.

Yet all that was irrelevant to the emotions she stirred in him. The two-dimensional world would be enough for Joe Stewart for a long time to come; if only he could just hold onto something and not slide down again, he would ask for nothing more.

That was what Sally seemed to do for him, and he was grateful to her, almost loved her for it, for her silliness and her sentimentality. Tom, too. Ever since he had come in, he had been talking, trying to keep things moving, papering over the silences. Talking about himself mainly, so that even Sally was finding out things she hadn't known about him. The bad time he had had in the late forties when he was sacked from his job as a cameraman with a government film unit because he was a Communist. The nervous breakdown that followed.

"Christ! I know what it's like, Joe. I've been through it all, too. They said I was a fuckin' paranoiac, and I said, 'I'm not a fuckin' paranoiac; it's just those bastards who're trying to destroy me.' "

Stewart saw him clearly enough for what he was: an entertaining little man, basically selfish, but finally pathetic because he was so obviously a born failure. Yet there was a resilience in him, too, surely, because it *was* true, what he said; he, in his way, had been through it all and somehow or other had come out on the other side. His wife had left him, and he had spent years driving about Canada, living in a trailer, going around schools taking pictures of kids. But he had survived; as his third-rate self he had survived, and here he was with sweet, superficial Sally to prove it was possible.

Joe smiled, and as she saw the smile breaking into his colorless, pinched face, Sally smiled back at him.

Tom, though, was talking about China: "God,

153

there's money to be made there. I'm not a Communist anymore, but I'd give anything to go there. What I'd really like to do is stay for about a year. I wouldn't mind working for them even, provided I could move around and take some pictures. You could name your own price for a movie like that, eh? Not that it's just the money. I really believe in what they're doing over there, but what they need is somebody who can show it to the rest of the world for them."

He looked at Stewart and saw him smiling. Then, as if he had only that moment thought of it, he said, "Hey, Joe, maybe you're the guy who could do it for me. You've got lots of contacts with them, haven't you? Well, if you could introduce me to someone who could help me to get in there—"

So that was why he wanted to come, thought Sally. And Joe saw it too: that's what brought them up here. But he didn't mind; it didn't change anything because it was all so obvious. Tom hadn't tried to hide his self-interest; he wasn't pretending, as Winn and Kwan would have done, that it was all completely un-selfish, all for somebody else's benefit.

With someone like this what was the point in keeping things secret yourself? "Yes," said Stewart, "I was thinking maybe of going there. For good."

"Oh, I'd be a bit careful, though," Tom said quickly. "What you really need when you're getting over something like this is familiarity. It's the best cure. Haven't you noticed how when you're ill, it's what you ate as a kid that your stomach seems to need? Well, it's the same with the mind. That's what I found, anyway. What you need is the language, the faces you grew up with. Look at me for instance; you know what I'd do in your place? I'd go straight back to Canada. It's just what you need at a time like this. Somewhere you don't have to be involved, but where things are familiar enough to fall back on them when you need to. Really, Joe, it's worth thinking about." Thought creased his brow. "Yeah, maybe it's not such a bad idea, even though I say it myself. I've got some friends who live up in the lake region about a hundred miles north of Toronto. I could write to them, if you liked. In the fall it's the most beautiful place in the world up there."

Floating.

Before they left, Tom had found out that Stewart didn't have anywhere to live when he left the hospital in five days' time.

"But, Tom, it's obvious," whispered Sally. "Why doesn't Joe come and stay with us?"

"The more the merrier," said Tom.

And Stewart lay there in the chipped metal bed with the coarse sheets and the stained blanket, knowing he would be saved.

For two weeks Joe did absolutely nothing, allowing himself to be convinced that a vegetable was all he needed to be. Sally and Tom had thought of everything that anybody could do to cushion him, giving him the bedroom, where he would have peace—apart from the inevitable noise of the mah-jong from the flat next door—moving into the living-room themselves. Still, for the first couple of days he struggled around on his crutches, sweating, getting tired quickly, feeling out of place; but Sally had to have somebody to help her with the cooking, and Tom needed to explain what he was doing with the tape recorders: a sound picture of Hong Kong, splicing, re-recording, superimposing. "There's got to be a lot of money in it somewhere," he said. "You know, trade fairs, exhibitions, all that sort of crap."

Three totally different human beings living on top of each other, bumping into one another all day long, but there was no strain in it; it was more like a game, Sally thought; and whenever one of them started to feel depressed, the other two were always there to turn it into a joke.

Later on, when she and Tom decided to take Joe on the boat, it was even better. They had to carry him down the slippery stone steps in the quay wall, and even then, even with them so close to him, just for a moment as he found himself in the boat, he felt that terrible panic sweep over him again. Somehow he didn't seem to be able to get enough air into his lungs. His muscles tensed up, and he looked around for something to hold onto: what was he doing here, all this space? But then Tom began kicking the engine because he couldn't get it to start, and the moment was past.

From then on, he spent all day every day lying on the front of the boat, Sally bringing him cans of cold beer and rubbing suntan oil into his skin, running her fingers deliberately along the ugly purple scars that at first she had hardly been able to bring herself to touch. She felt towards Joe as she would towards a brother, even when one day he twisted his head round and kissed her between the breasts as she was leaning over his back. It didn't matter because they seemed somehow to have drifted, all three of them, beyond sex.

They had stumbled, she felt sure, onto something important in all this, because now she could see clearly that the basic social unit wasn't two people; it was three. It made you more tolerant, less possessive, and her only worry was that it might not last.

Donald Winn didn't fit in at all, though. Sally couldn't stand him, with his little fish eyes that never seemed to focus on anything. He came round to the flat on a couple of evenings to talk about the inquest, but he seemed completely out of place, too big, patronizing and yet unperceptive. Joe hardly listened to what he had to say, shrugging off his advice and not bothering to follow all the arrangements he had made, the people he had talked to, to make sure that everything would go smoothly and not too deep. Noticing Joe's reactions made her feel a little more secure.

But one morning it was time for the inquest after all, and Sally and Tom were suddenly irrelevant, lightweight. It was the first day it had rained since Joe had come out of the hospital, and Sally tried to stop herself

from feeling it was ominous as she looked out and saw
the low, thick clouds and the rain sweeping across the
harbor. Winn was waiting downstairs with a car. They
went down to the entrance with Joe and watched
anxiously as he edged himself into the back seat, his
clothes already drenched by the time he got inside. As
he was driven away, they waved to him, and he looked
back with what she said to Tom was a desperate expression on his face. Then there was just the rain
splashing down like bullets in the sea, rattling on the
plastic covers of the boats, forming opaque puddles
smeared with oil.

"Don't worry, Joe," said Winn. "It'll soon be
over." Then you can go back to mother, he thought.
"You don't have to worry about a thing. It's all fixed
up perfectly. The only witnesses will be the servants
who found the bodies, the police, the pathologist, then
you. All you've got to do is stick exactly to the statement you gave the police when I was there with you.
Nothing else."

Stewart was staring out the window at the crowds.

"Look, did you read through that copy of the
statement last night like I told you?"

Stewart nodded.

"That's okay then. Just so it's fresh in your mind.
And for Christ's sake, you bugger, none of this business about it not being an accident." He tried to look
into Stewart's face, but there was nothing there. "Promise?"

Another nod.

The magistracy was a huge new building, deliberately designed to frighten ordinary people. Colonial
courts had always been built on neoclassical models,
with great pillared galleries and domes. But the more
recent examples seemed closer to German blockhouses
than anything else, with flat walls, small haphazard
windows, large square doorways at the top of flights
of concrete steps.

Crowds of poorly dressed people stood about in

knots in the corridors, interspersed with strutting policemen in neatly pressed khaki uniforms, belts and holsters shining. Donald pushed a way through to the coroner's court, which was already full of young men chattering to each other, all of them seeming to Joe to have a far clearer idea of what was going on than he had. But very quickly they were resolved into a loose kind of order, the reporters settling down on the brightly polished wooden benches at the back, the clerks drifting to their desks in front of the rail. Donald sat him down at a table and immediately started moving about from one person to another, gossiping, giggling, leafing through papers, taking control of the proceedings. He was obviously enjoying himself enormously.

Joe could feel other people's eyes on him. As he looked around, he tried not to meet their gaze. The room itself was depressing enough: erratically tiled with soundproofing blocks, soot congealed around the air-conditioner outlets. The bright green Venetian blinds tilted at odd angles. On the wall above the coroner's seat was a wooden crown and the letters *EiiR,* the lower arm of the *E* half broken and hanging down. A neon tube directly over Joe's head flickered constantly, like a nerve in the corner of his eye.

The three-man jury came in: two Chinese merchants in the inevitable charcoal-grey suits and a European civil servant nattily dressed with a magenta shirt and a purple floral handkerchief.

Winn came over and slumped across to whisper in Stewart's ear. "Don't let the buggers frighten you. I've got files on all three of them." He sat back in his chair and waved at one of the Chinese jurymen.

They were followed by the coroner, a fat little man with a few wisps of hair brushed across the top of his head, who glanced about nervously, unused to so much interest in one of his cases. When he spoke, his Welsh voice was thin, little more than a squeak; and he addressed himself directly to the jury, ignoring the reporters who craned forward trying to hear what was being said.

"You are required to fill in the *pro forma*s that you have on the table in front of you. Later, at the appropriate time, I shall explain the categories of death to you."

The categories of death! This was how they made death meaningless here, transformed it into something that society could tolerate without pain or loss. Joe looked around anxiously, not worried for himself, but feeling shut in, stifled. This had nothing to do with him, or with Jordan and Evelyne, either. Everybody was writing everything down—the jury, the clerks, lawyers, the coroner, reporters—miles of straggling words that kept the system going, a paper wall to keep reality out.

The only person Joe could see with whom he felt any contact at all was a very old, scraggy-necked Englishman, who sat bent forward in the public benches with a metal goblet held against his ear and an angry expression on his face as he strained to hear.

The witnesses came and went; no surprises to interfere with the routine, no sense of the immediacy of two people's deaths. It was all dragged out interminably by the coroner, who insisted on writing everything down word for word. The gold pen shook in his hand, and from time to time he would look up tetchily and say, "I'm a slow writer, Inspector Goddard. Wait for me."

At last it was Stewart's turn to take the stand, everybody listening more attentively, a girl reporter starting to sketch the sunburnt, chunky face and the remote, almost evasive eyes, then shading in the sunbleached hair. (Sally had trimmed it the night before, wanting him to look his best.)

He answered the questions slowly, as though he was unused to speaking, but he seemed completely at ease. Too relaxed, Winn thought, for a man who's talking about the violent deaths of his mistress and her husband.

They brought him the photographs that had been taken in the mortuary: could he identify them, please? And now it all came back in a flood. In these glossy pictures he saw them as he had never seen them before; this was the reality of what had happened, that he had been trying to escape from, aided by pain and drugs. Two bodies naked, unnaturally white in the mortuary spotlights, the limbs distorted by the camera angles and the hard shadows. Evelyne's breasts like pastry, with three tiny, seemingly harmless wounds, stretching down a line from the left nipple to the middle of the abdomen. Jordan with the whole side of his face blown out by the bullet that—as the pathologist explained—had entered underneath his chin. Part of the cheekbone splintered up through the eye.

Joe swayed, dizzy. One of the photographs slipped out of his hand onto the floor. He stared at the other one, his sunburnt face yellow, and the words came out more quickly, in sudden, stabbing bursts; yet still, by some final instinct for self-protection, keeping to the story Donald had approved.

The appearance of reality. So who cares what the substance is, Winn thought. It couldn't have gone better if he'd been doing it himself.

After it was all over, he took Joe out to celebrate. They went to one of Donald's favorite places, a teahouse that in the evening was converted into a blaring, second-rate nightclub for tourists and American servicemen. But in the middle of the afternoon it was a limbo, elaborate, deeply carved dragons on the walls and lots of little waitresses walking round the tables with trays of tiny dumplings.

"Well, that all went off very nicely," he said in the tones of a self-satisfied headmaster and wiped his sweating face and scalp with a steaming-hot towel. "Mind you, I was a bit worried about old Dai Jones. Dai the Death, I suppose he ought to be called," he giggled, taking a big gulp of thick, brown *bo lei* tea. "Ah, that's better, keeps the bloodstream moving. He's a shifty little bugger. Kept on talking about it being a matter of principle. Fuck principle! I said. If you mess this up, Jones boy, I'll bloody screw you. Anyway, he didn't."

He stopped talking as a girl came past with some more *ha gau*. She must have been about fourteen, with a younger body and an older face, wearing a white blouse and a stained black miniskirt. Her shoulders and tiny breasts were thrown back by the weight of the tray she was carrying, her pelvis thrust forwards, as she stopped in front of him with her legs stretched apart. He looked at her for a moment with a smile, then asked her softly for two plates.

"If I was ever fixing up an orgy, d'you know where I'd have it? In a place like this, with lots of these little birds strolling about naked with trays of *dim sum*. Stimulates the appetite."

He looked down at the round wooden plates with the steaming, crescent-shaped *ha gau* lying on a piece of lotus leaf in the bottom, pink shrimps bulging against the thin, white, translucent paste. He picked one up in his chopsticks and dipped it into some hot pepper sauce, then swallowed it.

"Yes, and you were just beautiful, too, Joe. Couldn't have done it better myself."

He felt benevolent. Hadn't he done all this for Joe, just to help him? And being so pleased with himself made him feel still more benevolent.

"Anyway, what are you going to do now? You can't go on staying with Tom Price forever."

"Well, I still haven't really made my mind up about China."

"Oh, Christ! Look, I told you you'd be fucking crazy to do that." He speared another slug of *ha gau* and felt its contents burst against his palate. Bloody Stewart! Drifting along, one day in a nightmare, the next in a dream. Why couldn't he waken up enough to see sense for just one moment? "Why don't you go to Canada, for fuck's sake?"

11

"Darling," Wai-ling had said to Mei, not looking at her, of course, "I'd never have come if I'd known it was going to be like this. It's so dead. The same old faces. I've been through them all." Her eyes ran eagerly round the room once more. "Oh, a million times."

Though Mei couldn't stand Wai-ling and liked Donald Winn, she had to agree. It was a typical Winn party. The cobwebs hadn't been brushed down, the hole in the ceiling was still unfinished, the packing cases and all kinds of other rubbish were still lying around; but more than a hundred people had been sucked in, seemingly at random: a couple of South American consuls, an Australian drag queen called

"Miss R and R," a fashionable hairdresser, a professor of anthropology with a snake around his wrist, a highly placed civil servant with his Thai boyfriend, fashion models galore, aging beauties in old-fashioned, tightly fitting cheongsams, Filipino pop musicians, Chinese movie stars, American marines, dollies from everywhere in see-through dresses, male prostitutes, a stockbroker from Merrill Lynch—all of them saying, "Darling, it's so dead," and watching each other every second like hawks ready to swoop,

A vacuum? she thought. No, more like a kaleidoscope; shake it a little, and you find yourself with something that seems to be totally different, beautifully impermanent. So, why, she wondered a little sadly after her fourth gin, why did it all have to be so bloody boring and predictable?

And then she had come into what seemed to be Donald's bedroom—just by accident, because someone had locked themselves in the loo—and here was this man she had never met before; nobody the least bit like him. An old man, very tall, very thin, long white hair, deep burning eyes that never seemed to blink, wearing—of all things—a light grey Chinese tunic with a Mao badge on his chest. At first she had thought he was just another kook, but then she saw that he was serious, not even afraid of being serious. And who else here could you say that about?

There were half a dozen people around him: a couple of very intense, rather square-looking American students; J.C. Chan, the television producer, with his ever-silent girl friend; a stocky, quite handsome young man she had seen once or twice before with Donald —somebody had said he was a reporter, but now he was standing in a detached way at the edge of the group, as if he couldn't make up his mind whether he wanted to stay or not. When she got there, they were talking about the Cultural Revolution and this latest wave of strikes in Hong Kong, the clashes just this afternoon with the police. J.C. was saying something about agitators, infiltrators; and the old man looked at him very precisely and said, "These are meaningless words; a fish isn't an agitator in the sea; a bird doesn't infiltrate the branches of a tree." A rich, resonant voice; it even rhymed! Of course she stayed, and after a while the American girl started asking him about the Long March (she was writing a thesis on Chu Teh) and some quarrel in Szechwan that Mei had never heard of; but soon it turned into a monologue, with all of them squatting or lying around on Donald's immense circular bed and the old man—Dr. King seemed to be his name—propped up like a doll against a pile of multicoloured cushions.

"Oh, my Gawd, it's an awgy," scoffed an English girl, poking her head round the door, but none of them took any notice.

"There's an area in China near the border of Tibet," Jordan had begun. "It's called the Grasslands. That's the literal translation, anyway, but the name's all wrong in English because it gives you an image of something like the steppes or the prairies. And in fact it's nothing like that. Just the opposite. It's a great swamp that stretches for hundreds of miles, and it's the most frightening, lifeless place in the world, worse than any desert.

"All you can see for days on end is this ocean of wild grass growing out of a sea of black mud. The grass grows in thick, matted clumps that have their roots in decomposing clumps beneath them. It's like some horrible parody of the birth-life-death cycle because there seems to be no purpose in it at all. There's no life there: no bushes or trees or flowers, no birds or animals; you don't hear the sounds of crickets or cicadas; there aren't even any stones. Just this grass growing high over your head and the stink of it rotting under your feet. You never see the sun through the clouds—they're almost as thick and black as the mud—and it rains all the time in torrents, with a terrible, cold wind that drives it right the way through your body."

Mei wiggled her toes into a fold in the sheepskin that covered the bed.

"Well, we had to come down through there towards the end of thirty-five to get from Szechwan to where we were finally heading for in Shensi. We were all very weak after coming over the mountains, and all we had left to eat was some dried grain and tea. And even the grain wasn't any use to most of the men because their stomachs couldn't take it; they came from the rice-eating part of China in the south, of course, and the grain just went straight through them like a handful of pebbles. And on top of all that our clothes were in rags. The tribespeople round the edges of the Grasslands told us we'd be frozen to death if we tried to get across like that. But we had to. There wasn't any alternative.

"I'll never forget that first day. It dragged on and on endlessly, and you fell into a kind of daze, so that you couldn't be sure any longer if it was really happening. We marched for ten hours, completely soaked and frozen, in single file along this narrow path. The rain was so heavy, and the noise it made beating down on that thick grass all around us was so loud, that you couldn't hear the voice of the man in front or the man behind. Not that anybody had anything to talk about. Even the people who usually sang all the time were dead quiet. At night we tried to light fires with the wood we had brought, but it was soaked through; so we just lay down where we were on the frozen path, tying the grass on either side into a kind of shelter above our heads. But it couldn't keep out the rain . . . or the wind. I don't think anything could. A lot of people didn't get up the next morning. And that's how it went on for eight days."

Jordan paused to sip some of his whisky, holding his audience with his eyes; and Joe Stewart found himself remembering an old man in his grandmother's village who had had this same kind of gesture, the same power beneath it. Auld Davie his name was. He'd been trapped down the pit in 1911 in a fall that had killed eighty-seven men immediately and left five more, Davie and four others, cut off in a pocket of air. Twelve days later, when the rescuers reached them, the other four were dead; but Davie was still half alive, lying on a ledge high up near the roof, where a whiff of sour air reached his nostrils. He lived, until his death, on the strength of what had happened to him then; the management gave him a soft job at the pithead, and every evening he went around the pubs cadging beer from the young miners. But Sunday was his true day of glory: every Sunday afternoon he would sit in the square in the middle of the village, on a brown-painted wooden bench between the verges of forget-me-nots and marigolds, wearing his best black boots, a dark grey suit, a tweed cap from Abercrombie's in Falkirk; and he would tell the young boys how he survived, ten, twenty, thirty years before. It irritated some of the older people who sat looking out across the square from behind their lace curtains—"Auld Davie? Och, he's jest an auld blether. Ye cannie believe a word he sez."—but the children who listened to him never doubted this story that they knew almost by heart.

Until we grew out of it, Joe thought sadly.

Jordan had started again. "Then, on the third day, I had to watch a man, who had saved my life, die.

"Back there in the mountains I must have become dizzy with the exhaustion and the thinness of the air— we were over fifteen thousand feet up at the time—because suddenly I found myself slipping away down the ice. I shouted, and this fellow in my platoon threw me a rope and pulled me up. But then, when I got onto my feet, I found I'd twisted my ankle and just couldn't walk at all. I told them not to wait for me, just to let me rest there for an hour and I'd probably be able to carry on and catch them up, though we all knew I wouldn't have lasted ten minutes. But this man—Yang was his name—insisted on helping me, more or less carrying me for the next two days right up over the pass. I hardly knew him at all, but that was the sort of thing that happened a lot then; there wasn't time to think about yourself, to be selfish; and anyway, selfishness wouldn't have helped you to survive. You needed each other constantly, just to keep going.

"Well, on that third morning in the Grasslands Yang was about two hundred yards behind me, looking after one of the pack horses. I didn't see what happened, but apparently the horse reared up without any reason at all—just the madness of the swamps—and knocked him off the path into the mud. He went right under, and when they dragged him out, he was unconscious. One of the men came up for me, and I went running back with him, and there was Yang lying in the middle of the path, black all over with this foul slime. I tried to pump as much of it out of his lungs as I could—it really made you hold your nose—and he came back to consciousness for a few minutes. I gave him some of my own grain—he'd lost his in the swamp—but he couldn't chew it, so I put the grain back in my pocket and waited for him to die. It wasn't long, and we just buried him there beside the path. But, you know, when we stopped that evening, even though I was starving, I still couldn't bring myself to eat that grain I'd taken back from him. It seemed as though it still belonged to him."

Jordan paused again and looked around into the eyes that were fastened on him. From the other room came the noise of two queens who were trying to see which of them could scream the loudest.

"Well," he said, "that's probably made you all want to get back to the party."

"Oh, no, please," said Mei, who had been sitting with her chin between her hands, looking up at him. "It's a fabulous story. Please don't stop now."

"All right, my dear, if you bribe me with a good strong whisky." He held out his empty glass and glanced at her appreciatively as she turned away with it, his eyes running over her naked back.

All through the story Joe had been watching him

suspiciously from a chair in the corner of the room. He told himself that he didn't want to fall under Jordan's spell again, having freed himself from it once already. Ever since that night when he had first met Kwan, he had been trying to stay away from Jordan's, going up to the villa perhaps only once a week and, even then, usually when he knew Jordan would be out. And Jordan had noticed it, of course, and been hurt. Just tonight he had said, "We don't see you very often these days, Joseph."

"It's just that I've been working very hard the past few weeks."

"Ah, yes, I thought that must be the reason." And the sad pride in his voice had made Joe feel sorry for him for a moment. But, Christ, it was Jordan's fault, after all, he had told himself, for being such a self-centered old fool.

It wasn't, though, really as simple as that, he could see now, because what he hadn't wanted to admit was the fact that it was Evelyne he was trying to avoid. In a sense he had become almost afraid of her, and it was her spell rather than Jordan's that he really wanted to break. He was obsessed with her physically, and the erotic dreams that he had in the morning, just before he wakened, were always full of her, so that her body stayed with him for the rest of the day. But there was no satisfaction in it. When he phoned to tell her he wanted her, she would say she couldn't speak; and when he asked her to come out with him in the evening, there was always some reason why she had to stay at home. However, the next day the phone would ring, and it would be Evelyne, saying, "You must come up now, Joe. I can feel you so hard in me already." And he would run after her like a little dog chasing a big bitch in heat. The only need she thought of was her own, and she couldn't be bothered to understand that anybody could need her when she didn't want them, or not need her when she did. He hated her for it, her selfishness, but at the same time his own pride wouldn't allow him to admit that she had this kind of power over him. And if she didn't have any power over him, what reason could there be for avoiding her? She was just a good fuck and nothing more; something to be grateful for whenever you got the chance.

So it was Jordan's egotism that he blamed, not hers. And all he had to do then, of course, was to think back to that night with Kwan for clear-enough evidence of that. All that boasting—it was just romance embalmed in the amber of an old man's pride.

But here, tonight, he could see that that wasn't really the truth, not the whole truth, after all. When Jordan had been talking to Kwan, for instance, it wasn't so much his pride that had driven him to make such a fool of himself; rather it had been something like a temporary loss of pride. Pacing up and down on his verandah, he had been an old man, unsure, trying to assert himself, to prove his superiority over the two younger men. It was the unsureness that had made him ugly and pathetic. But there was none of that tonight. He was proud and confident. The stories were not just romance; they were real. Joe could see the old tricks—the pauses that always came at the most dramatic moment, the fullness of the voice fading to a whisper—but that didn't detract from the reality of what he was saying; it only made it more immediate. It was more real than this party, and you could feel the awareness of that fact in the atmosphere as everybody, ten of them now, sprawled around waiting for Jordan to resume, chatting about other things but knowing that they didn't really matter very much.

Joe felt himself drawn again into the circle around Jordan, getting up and going over to sit on the end of the bed, catching Jordan's eye and seeing a flicker of recognition there. He found himself pressed up against the girl who had come back with the whisky—a very pretty Chinese girl in a purple silk trouser suit—and for a moment they smiled at each other, feeling virtuous, perhaps, because they were being so serious and not giggling at the impromptu striptease that was starting next door.

Jordan glanced at his audience, then began again. "The Grasslands. Yes." He rolled the harsh whisky round in his mouth. "I don't think I've ever seen so many men die as I did during those eight days. The whole of that path seemed to be lined with corpses. One morning, I remember, I wakened up, and one of the men in our group seemed to have disappeared. So we looked around, and we found him quickly enough. He hadn't gone far. All of us had diarrhoea, and he must have got up in the middle of the night with it, because when we found him in the morning, he was frozen stiff just squatting there, with a little pile of frozen, undigested grain covered with white frost underneath him. It was a terrible way to see men die.

"We thought we'd never get out of there. But then on the sixth day, in the evening, the clouds lifted just a little, and away in the distance we saw the outline of a low line of hills. And suddenly everybody started shouting and singing, even though we knew quite a few more of us would still die before we reached them.

"And then, the next day, I found a stone. Just a small stone at the edge of the path. Nothing special about it—the colour was dull grey—just a nondescript garden stone, but it struck me as being the most beautiful thing I had ever seen in my whole life because for the first time I felt sure that I wasn't going to die in that godforsaken swamp. I picked it up, and I kissed it; and I've still got it in my garden, in the rockery.

"I'm the only person who knows which stone it is.

"At last, on the eighth day, we came to the dry land again. It's impossible to describe how wonderful it was; we just went mad. In a way I think we were probably the most disciplined army that ever existed in the history of China—certainly we had a clearer sense of purpose than any other I've ever heard of—but for an hour or two we went completely crazy. I can remember us all rushing up to eat the short, juicy grass on the hillside, and then we found some bushes covered with thick clusters of berries. I don't know what their name is, but they were the color of goldfish. And we just stuffed great handfuls into our mouths, the juice running down all over our faces and our hands. Actually they tasted rather sour, and they weren't really edible at all, but that didn't make any difference; we thought they were the most delicious fruit we'd ever tasted, better than . . . lychees."

"Yes, but you couldn't go on living forever on grass and berries," said the solemn American girl.

Jordan nodded. "No, of course we couldn't. And that was our biggest problem by that time. Food. I was in charge of the supplies, and I had to spend the next few days scouring the countryside to buy up anything I could find. But it wasn't very successful because the local tribesmen were afraid of anybody Chinese and ran away when they saw us coming. We had taken over a deserted tribal village—all the houses were made of yak dung—and we discovered that some of the larger houses had secret storerooms built into the thick walls. So we broke them open and distributed what food there was, and some of the soldiers even boiled the cowhides for twenty-four hours and ate them as well.

"But the best find of all was in the religious halls that were built onto the houses of the rich families. They kept all the old family documents and Buddhist manuscripts there, and at one end there were these altars with lots of carved figures of gods and animals painted green and red. Well, one evening I came back from trying to scrape up some grain, and there was a strange kind of feeling among the dozen or so men who were billeted with me. They were all very subdued, not asking questions about what I'd managed to find, like they usually did; and yet underneath it you could sense a sort of suppressed excitement. I couldn't make out what it was. Then, as I looked around, I noticed one of the figurines on the altar seemed to be missing. So I asked them what had happened—just for something to say, I think, really—and it all came out. They brought me a large metal bowl full of steaming wheat porridge with a great chunk of butter melting on the top. Butter! I'd forgotten what a marvellous thing it was. That was the best food I've ever had in my life." He rolled his eyes and drained the last of the whisky. "What had happened was that they had knocked over one of the figurines by accident, and when they picked it up, the paint was chipped, so that they could see that underneath it was made of a solidified mixture of wheat and butter. Marvelous!"

He swung his legs over onto the floor and stood looking down at them. "That's the only time in my life I've ever had any use for religion."

Mei was thinking about coffee bars. Not very intensely—you couldn't think very intensely about coffee bars, after all, for heaven's sake—but enough to have made up her mind that they were too—well, insecure. A friend of hers named Bruno, a French hairdresser, had been trying to get her to put some money into opening a new one. So she had come in here to this absurd, pseudo-Mexican place called the Acapulco to see what the competition was like. Competition! Dingy, dirty; weak grey coffee; weak grey men staring at her. She shivered. You couldn't invest in people like that, could you?

Just as she had made up her mind, Joe Stewart came in. She had asked Donald his name before she left the party, so she must have been interested in him, though it couldn't have been for anything in himself, particularly—she didn't know a thing about him, after all, just his name. No, it was more the feeling that had flowed between them as they sat next to each other listening to that old man, Dr. King; something exciting and yet—it was the combination she couldn't remember feeling before—at the same time serious, too. Instinctively she waved.

It was Evelyne, though, that Joe's mind was full of. The bitch, the bloody bitch that she was! He had been trying to phone her, just had to see her; but the servant kept on saying she wasn't in, though he knew she was.

So he had come out, anyway. Anything to get away from that bloody office.

The newspaper he was working for was more geared to advertising supplements than news, and now everybody was running around in circles trying to discover what line they were supposed to take on the dispute at the flower factory. Joe had found out through Kwan that some trade union leaders who had gone to the police station to ask for the release of the arrested workers had themselves been arrested and beaten up, but Middleton, the editor, had said, "Look, Stewart, we all know what's happening. I've lived here a damn sight longer than you, you know. But we can't print this. It's too inflammatory. It would just stir things up."

"Maybe that's the only thing left to do."

Middleton bent one of Joe's paper clips in half. Then he said, "You're forgetting. We've got a tradition of responsible journalism to live up to here."

Fuck responsible journalism! Joe was still fuming when he came into this dingy coffee bar, but even then, the first thing he noticed was the girl sitting on her own over by the window, all the men in the place coveting her out of the corners of their eyes. He didn't recognize her to begin with behind the enormous sunglasses, and he was just going to sit down by the door when he realized she was waving at him—me?—all those eyes swivelling round and reproaching him. So he went and sat beside her and, without even bothering to introduce himself or ask her what she was doing, started to pour it all out, the whole filthy business: "God, how I wish I hadn't signed that bloody contract last month! At least I could go and try to do something worthwhile somewhere else. You never know, there might even be a place where you could tell the truth once in a while."

As he ran on, he realized his anger was evaporating with every movement of her body.

"Nobody tells the truth, though, Joe," she said very seriously when he slowed down. "You couldn't afford to."

Looking at the frown on her face, he saw her really for the first time. Listening to Jordan, he had noticed her, how attractive she was, but it was something he didn't bother to define because what really interested him was his own response to Jordan. And coming in here all worked up, though he had noticed her again and been pleased when she waved, it was himself that he was still involved with. But now, suddenly, he saw her for herself: the mischievous, teasing face that could so quickly turn sincere or troubled; the body that never stayed still, shuffling around on the seat, fingers tapping on the table, the slender legs in the long white leather boots crossing and uncrossing, and yet not seeming nervous or bored; no, the opposite, a kind of pulsing concentration flowing out of her.

"What d'you do to make you feel like that?" he asked gently, trying to touch her.

But she slipped away again, laughing. "Why, don't you know? I'm a career girl. That's what *your* paper called me anyway."

He remembered. "Oh, yes, of course. It was on the women's page, wasn't it? A sort of profile? Teen-age tycoon stuff. But how did you get involved in all that?"

She shrugged. "I s'pose I started off at school really. It was the only way to get away from those dreadful nuns. D'you know, when I was a very little girl, I used to think God was a loudspeaker because that was what the prayers came out of four times a day. Well, at first I was sure I was going to be a poet; I wrote tons of it, all very truthful and silly. But the nuns got hold of it somehow and said I was terribly sinful, so I never wrote anything down anymore. But then I thought I'd be able to get away from them in the more concrete things like sewing and dress-making and domestic science, though even there they were always telling us how we must prepare ourselves to be obedient wives. Put me right off marriage. When I was thirteen, I swore I'd never get married if that was what it was going to mean—" She bit the end of her thumb. "What on earth was I talking about?"

"How to succeed in business?" he suggested.

"Oh, yes. Well, when I left school, lots of people said, 'She's very fresh and pretty,' and took millions of photographs of me, in between trying to lay me. Then I thought to myself, You're not going to last very long like this, my girl; there'll be somebody fresher and prettier and easier next year. So I decided I ought to begin doing some of the exploiting myself. I started a model agency first of all; then a boutique. And then I thought, Why should I be making a fortune for other people selling their rubbish for them when I could be selling my own, for heaven's sake? So I opened a factory. But you can't grow very big on the local market, so we started exporting. Now we've got lines going in America and Britain and France and Germany, and it just never seems to stop."

She paused, bit into a salami roll, and chewed it hungrily. "It really scares me at times because I think, It's not me doing this; it's somebody else."

"Well," he said, enjoying her now but laughing at her, too, "that all sounds pretty truthful to me."

"No, I really meant that, Joe. I don't mind talking about myself; people aren't important. It's what you do that matters, isn't it? I bet you could never get me to tell you what my profit margin is."

She looked at him challengingly, but underneath she was feeling that, yes, maybe she really did rather like him. She wasn't sure what it was about him; he wasn't her type at all—whatever that meant. Perhaps it was quite simply the way in which he seemed to take himself so seriously. She really did believe what she had been saying just now about people not being important; it was only your actions that had any effect on the world around you, after all. And most of her friends—Donald talking about conditioning, Wai-ling

175

with her "new morality," Bruno sounding like a paperback summary of existentialism—all of them, in fact, seemed to look at life in pretty much the same sort of way as she did. They could make it sound terribly honest, of course, and stoical, too, but in the end what you came down to was something fairly boring and self-indulgent; maybe just an excuse for doing anything you wanted to do without having to think much about it. Whereas Joe seemed to start out from himself: that was what really mattered to him, she could see. With him everything would have to be involved, she suspected, ingrown; and perhaps there were as many dangers in that as in anything else, but God, at least it was a change, wasn't it?

They found themselves in the middle of a silence.

He was afraid that she would go. "Have you ever met Jordan before?" he asked quickly.

"Who? Oh, yes, you mean the old man at Donald's party, Dr. King? No, never. But he *was* fabulous, wasn't he? Terribly sexy and virile. He made all the other men there seem so dull and feeble." She didn't bother to apologize. After all, it was true—well, almost true—she thought with a smile. "And all those stories about the Long March—I don't know anything about it, of course, but they make you feel rather ashamed of what we all do with our lives now, don't they? I mean, you bitching about your paper and me boasting about my 'career' or something. It's all so petty, isn't it?" Her forehead wrinkled. "And yet it's hard to see what else you can do—"

"Would you like to meet him again?"

Good heavens, yes, that would be fabulous, she said. When? Well, why not now? he asked. No time like the present; using Jordan as an excuse for not letting go of her.

Being with her was like holding a tiny wild animal in your hand—a mouse or a live fish—knowing that if it got away, you would never catch it again. His instinct was protective: to shut her up in some affectionate cage.

When they got there, the sun was stooping down towards the mountainous islands, the few thin clouds already tinged with red. Jordan was dozing on a lilo in his swimming-pool while Evelyne wrote letters under a multi-colored umbrella; a picture of domesticity.

She touched her lips with an elegant, painted finger, her voice distant and almost hostile. "He's supposed to be resting."

"Why? Is something the matter?"

"Nothing serious. But he's been getting very worked up about these strikes, and he had some kind of a row on the phone with Kwan on Saturday. Then he went to that party in the evening, and after he came back, he couldn't sleep, just kept lying down and getting up again and walking about, starting letters and tearing them up all night long. Yesterday morning he said he felt awful, so I called the doctor, and he came and gave him a sedative. His blood pressure's too high. He's supposed to rest for the next few days."

"We'd better go then," said Joe, and it looked as if Evelyne was going to agree when they heard Jordan shouting from the pool.

He was leaning on his elbow, the other arm drifting in the water.

"We just dropped in for a second as we were passing, Jordan," said Joe.

"No, you didn't." Jordan paddled towards them. "Nobody comes here by accident. So now you can just sit down and have a drink. Can't have one myself, though. Don't let Evelyne frighten you away."

Dripping, he climbed out of the pool, his eyes on Mei. "I know you, my dear. I remember you. The girl at the party. That's right, isn't it? Evelyne, this is the young lady who kept me so late at the party. She's the one you should have given the row to."

Mei looked at Evelyne anxiously, slightly overawed. "It wasn't me really. Everybody wanted him to stay."

"But you were the one I stayed for," said Jordan, rubbing himself with a towel.

"Oh, Jordan, stop embarrassing the poor girl," chided Evelyne.

Later the sun became a gigantic orange ball that looked at though it were impaled on the jagged peaks of the mountains. As Mei stared at it, the mountains themselves seemed to melt away, the ball expanding, consuming everything. The sea far below them was flat, shining, not a boat crossing it; patterns of orange reflected down from the clouds and were drawn about by the meandering currents. The islands rose vaguely out of the sea, a few lights twinkling on in the villages, the mist in the valleys a dark purple.

A plane slid in across the sunset, black as ink, like a tadpole, a red light blinking under its belly.

Jordan had drawn his deck-chair close to Mei's, turning the back at an angle to Evelyne and Joe, stretching forwards and tapping her now and again on the thigh to emphasize a point as he lectured her on the Cultural Revolution.

"Don't you see the importance of it, though? A whole generation's being taken on the Long March this time. All the young people in the country. It's something that'll have to be done in every generation, too, because it's not something you can tell people about. They've got to be made to do it for themselves."

Mei was hesitant, out of her depth. "But it seems such a pity. You know, all these old things being destroyed—"

"That's the typical bourgeois line." He jabbed his finger at her knee, then smiled. "I'm not saying that to get at you, m'dear. You've got an excuse—the way you've been brought up and so on. But there are lots of people who don't. People who claim to be on our side and who still think like that basically. Lots of them in Hong Kong especially. They don't grasp the simple fact that you can't have revolutions without things getting broken. They're full of statistics to prove that we're not ready for a revolution yet. They'd never be ready. Joseph's met a few people in Hong Kong

178

like that, haven't you, Joseph?" he called over his shoulder.

Joe and Evelyne had been sitting quietly, half listening to Jordan, half just watching the disappearing sun. Only a few words had crossed between them.

"I tried to phone you this afternoon," he had whispered.

"I didn't know."

"Why did you tell the servants to say you were out?"

"I had other things to do." She turned away from him.

He watched her, watched Mei, his feelings confused. If Evelyne was beautiful, then Mei couldn't be, surely? She seemed broken, fragmentary, full of pieces from different puzzles that couldn't possibly fit each other—eager, silly little girl; shy, tongue-tied boy; self-possessed business woman—bits and pieces that she had picked up from other people without even bothering to weld them together. She talked about having been a model, but that didn't seem to imply the usual kind of poised remoteness. Moods, ideas swept through her as openly as images on a movie screen, and as she sat, she seemed to jump about excitedly, constantly surprised by the newness of everything. One moment she was scowling and ugly; the next, wide-eyed, innocently pretty; so that he found himself watching her, trying to catch a repetition of some fleeting expression that he couldn't any longer be sure he had really seen at all.

It made Evelyne seem monumental. Everything about her was so controlled, classical, and yet there was that strength of sensuality beneath the surface that he doubted Mei could ever match. But even then he found himself beginning to feel increasingly hostile towards her. She knew so much more than Mei physically, emotionally, intellectually, but why did she need to keep such a tight grip on everything? It was Mei's vulnerability that attracted him by comparison.

Evelyne, he knew would never be caught out; Mei frequently would, but would never care.

They came back to themselves with the sound of Jordan's voice rising.

"But the thing I like about it here," Mei had said, "is that I'm free to be myself. Even if I am a mess," she giggled.

"There's only one kind of freedom in Hong Kong," Jordan told her, "and that's the freedom to exploit. Well, my girl, we've come to the end of that road. There's going to be no more exploitation here. It's gone on too long, but now things are going to change. There'll be blood in the gutters before there's any more exploitation." His voice was rising towards hysteria, and Mei drew back, her chair squealing on the tiles.

"I think he's getting tired," Evelyne said softly, touching Joe's hand, the closest they had been all afternoon.

As they left, the thin clouds above their heads had thickened and turned an ugly, dark violet, bruised color against the deep blue of the sky.

"He's sweet really," said Mei, "but I still don't think he's right."

"That's because you've got too much to lose if he is," said Joe.

A strange love scene. At the beginning, anyway. They were walking slowly along the beach behind which the block of flats he lived in projected out of the hillside. The beach was empty now, after the packed bodies, the blaring transistors, the rancid suntan lotion of the daytime. All that had been blown away by the cool evening breeze. There was the smell of salt water and the perfume of flowering shrubs from the gardens on the other side of the beach road. The only noises were the distant barking of dogs, the clattering of mahjong tiles from a boarded-up café where the waiters were gambling for the day's tips, and of course, loudest of all, the sea, so constant you ceased to notice it.

Barefoot, they zigzagged down across the powdery sand to the water's edge, then followed the curving line of foam until they came to a breakwater. Behind them the bamboos and pine trees that grew along the back of the beach hissed in the wind. Out along the horizon was a line of dotted lights where the fishing-junks had found a shoal.

Mei skipped a little in the water. "Look at the moon. Isn't it marvelous?"

He looked up and saw it, the newest of new moons, etched in finely under a black cloud.

"Let's swim out to the raft," he said.

"What about bathing costumes?"

"Come on, we don't need them."

She dipped one foot into a breaking wave, looking away from him.

"Shy?"

As an answer, she turned putting her arms around his neck, kissing him, her tongue firm and strong as it ran over his gums and teeth, then darted like a lizard far back into his throat. Startled, struggling to respond, he slipped his hand under her jacket, finding she wasn't wearing a bra, didn't need to.

"The raft?" he whispered urgently.

"No, I want to go home with you," she said drawing him up the beach, arm outstretched.

Making love to her was like making love to a child. In comparison with Evelyne's, her body was like a young girl's, with those small breasts; slim, pliant thighs; naked, almost hairless cunt. Yet her buttocks and hips were wide and rhythmical, her nipples hard and larger, more erotic to the touch, than Evelyne's. Fascinated by her ambiguity, he wanted to look at her, examine her with all the lights on.

She lay there smiling up at him, surprised by his tenderness. She had expected him to take her quickly, selfishly; and that, she had known, was what would have happened if they had swum out to the raft. She had done that once before, the water soothing and impersonal around her body, so that it had spoilt everything for her when the man she was with had come into her from behind before they even got there, his nails pinching her, scratching her breasts, salt water in her nostrils as they bucked and heaved. She hadn't wanted that again.

They sat side by side for a while, playing with each other like a couple of teen-agers, afraid somehow to start something that had to have an end. Then they turned into each other, her knees around his waist, so relaxed it seemed that it would last all night. She stretched round behind her, her fingers running through the ringlets of blond hair on his thighs, pulling his legs up so that he had to lean further and further back until his head was resting on one of her feet.

"Hey, this is new," she said softly. "I've never been here before."

He looked up at her, up between her thighs, her face far away, black hair flung out around it on the pillow. With his right thumb he kneaded the moist red lips, his other hand stretching up towards her breasts, reaching only her navel.

"Next time, we must get some champagne," she giggled, turning round on her elbow so that her right nipple brushed against the cool sheet. "It's the only position for drinking champagne."

But when she came, her body twisted back with the agony, so that he jumped out of her like a spring.

"Oh, damn!" she cried, "I wanted you in me. I'm always such a flop," one tear running down and mixing with the laughter.

12

When I got back to the flat after the inquest, I couldn't bring myself to say a word to Tom and Sally. I knew now why they had taken me in; I was sure of it. Somehow or other—it didn't matter how—Winn had manipulated them, as he manipulated everybody, into pretending to care for me, using them to keep me away from Kwan.

I recalled Tom's words in the hospital: "In the fall, it's the most beautiful place in the world up there." Those words I had held onto; they made me sick.

I shut myself in my room feeling betrayed. But the aloneness that filled me went far deeper than that.

My mind kept on coming back to those photographs in the coroner's court: two naked bodies on a mortuary table. Ever since the accident I had been running away from them. Now the image had caught up with me. It made everything so final, finished: those two bodies pinned down, flattened by the glare of the spotlights. I had never seen either of them motionless before, even for a moment. Hands had always moved, hearts and eyelids flickered.

Without my presence they would still have been alive. Legally maybe, with some help from Donald Winn, I wasn't responsible, yet I knew I was to blame. The image clutched at my throat.

I swallowed some sleeping pills and tried to escape again. But Jordan and Evelyne were there, too.

We are sitting in an enormous cinema, though nobody seems interested in what's happening on the screen. People keep on getting up and strolling around: Jordan's friends and Donald's, all mixed up together. The old Communist banker comes walking towards me, the light from the screen reflected on his face, and at first I'm only vaguely aware that there's something strange about him. But as he comes closer, I realize he's wearing a tight silk cheongsam and high-heeled shoes covered in sequins.

I am sitting in the back row fondling the girl I'm with, and it's all very warm and adolescent. As I kiss her, I realize it's Sally, and I feel very close to her, dependent and protective at the same time. But her body is too full for Sally's; the breasts, the thighs I touch in the darkness are Evelyne's. Yet there's nothing disturbing in the awareness; it only adds to my happiness because I can go on having Evelyne, even in Sally. I lie there with my head on her shoulder, my feet draped over the back of the seat in front of me; but as I focus on the screen, I know that this sense of security is all a sham. The film is quite simply a series of shots of Jordan's and Evelyne's dead bodies, the camera exploring every imperfection, every cranny: Jordan's shrivelled penis, Evelyne's navel, the beautiful red wounds that stretch up from there like whorls of paint in an abstract picture.

Fascinated, I try to freeze every frame in my mind so that I will never forget, knowing desperately that I will. Then I see Donald Winn walking across in front of the screen, the images gruesomely flickering on the fur coat he's wearing. I dash towards him, angrily trying to push him out of the way; but he just opens his arms and draws me in to him, his body hot against mine, a wide smile across his face, knowing, as I know too, that I want him. I start to kiss him, his face rough on mine; but as I do so, the film on the screen behind him begins to crinkle at the edges, as a film does when it becomes jammed in the projector and is burnt by the heat of the bulb.

The bodies melt away, and I am outside the cinema again, propped against Sally, crying bitterly. I know I can't pretend any longer that she's Evelyne, but all the same, I still feel I can trust her. She takes a small pad from her pocket and gives it to me, saying, "Rub this on your eyes, it will stop you crying." But it makes my eyes sting terribly. I throw the pad on the ground and suddenly see that it's actually a large beetle-shaped insect, light turquoise in color. It scurries away towards the gutter, and I run after it and kick it, hating. But as it turns over, its legs jerking in the air, I realize there are a dozen tiny ants underneath it, tearing at its body; and I know, too late, that it is something beautiful, full of grace, which I have helped to destroy.

I slept fitfully for the rest of the night, the dream repeating itself, the people in it changing constantly. From time to time I half wakened, my muscles twitching separately, one after another, then dropping off to sleep again until, with light coming in through the blinds, I heard Tom and Sally making love next door. I lay there listening to them giggling and grunting, Sally whispering, "Don't make so much noise, for goodness' sake."

"Why not?"

"It might waken Joe."

"Do him good," he said breathlessly.

Then a little series of bird noises from Sally, a great sigh from Tom, and silence. They had left me with an enormous erection, cold, lifeless, like a piece of wood.

A few minutes later the door was banged open, and there was Tom with a cup of coffee, a self-satisfied grin all over his face. "Come on, Joe. Time to get up. We're going out on the boat."

I turned away towards the wall.

"Oh, for God's sake, Joe, snap out of it. We've got a lot to celebrate. It's in all the papers." He sat down on the edge of the bed and put his arm around my shoulders, his voice coaxing a difficult child. "You don't know how lucky you are. Now you're completely free. Just think of it: you can do whatever you like, go wherever you want to. You can make a completely new start, Joe."

So I went with them on the boat and lay all day in the sun, but there was no happiness in it or relaxation. My body seemed to have no weight, no thickness; it was like a jellyfish caught by the tide on a rock, slowly disappearing in the sun.

Part 4

13

May 22. Monday. That was when the violence began for me.

Before that it was just theory. I had never even been close to violence before. The war was only a void filled slightly by other people's stories of what they felt I should be taught to remember. Other than that, the images are trivial and disjointed, a shy child's.

Glasgow bus station on, I suppose, a Saturday night. A fight between a group of miners and some American airmen; a man, a bystander, with blood suddenly spurting out of his chest and down a white wall. My Auntie Agnes hurrying me away.

A football game and in the middle of it, without

my knowing how, me on my back with another boy on top, the older boys standing round us, shouting him on, my own blood in my mouth: "D'ye giv in"; choking, "I can't breathe"; laughter, "He cannie breathe"; "No, he caun't breathe"; He cunt breathe"; "Heh, heh, heh."

Kwan had said, "We must do everything we can to avoid violence that we are not able to control."

Words. But how, Kwan, how?

Monday the twenty-second. Already there was no doubt that the confusion all around us was bringing Donald into his own. Though the government might go on pretending that the situation was under control, in actual fact they were running scared, at one moment assuming a cool liberal tolerance, at the next, unpredictable and ruthless. In the daytime officials would make careful, placatory assessments for reporters; but at night their wives kept "getaway cases" under the bed, packed tight with passports, bank drafts, birth certificates, open airline tickets, and jewelry.

It was the kind of situation Donald Winn thrived on.

Ever since he had come to Hong Kong, he had been written off as a weird, peripheral figure in a community where everyone naturally wanted the same thing: to make as much money as they could as quickly as possible. He had been treated with condescension and suspicion. But now they needed him. Suddenly his network of unlikely contacts penetrated into every area of society; the information he had hoarded so indiscriminately gave him a key to the most carefully locked doors. More basically, too, he was only really at ease when everyone around him was in a state of panic or contradiction. He might talk a lot about order, yes, but his own life was itself so contradictory, seeming always to verge on hysteria, that it was when those qualities were everywhere uppermost that he finally revealed himself as a figure of power and insight. An absurd figure still, of course, a clown, but that was where his danger lay.

I didn't take him seriously at first, though; least of all that morning when I ran into him at nine thirty in the main street.

I was standing on the curb as a crowd of demonstrators marched past, six abreast, about two hundred of them all together, men and women, boys and girls, practically indistinguishable with their short hair and white cotton shirts outside dark grey or blue trousers. They were chanting quotations from Mao Tse-tung, and all of them carried the little red, plastic-covered book in their hands and wore a red-and-gold portrait of him pinned above their hearts. People applauded as they went past, but they just marched straight on by, grim faced. Only a few of the stragglers, children, catching sight of this Englishman, turned for a moment to point at me and shout that I was nothing but a paper tiger.

"What we need," Kwan had said at the meeting the night before, "is a way of showing our strength, our force, without being drawn into the kind of brawl that the government wants. In Kowloon everything was allowed to degenerate into violence and aimless destruction. Hooligans were hired by the police to throw stones and light fires so that we would be blamed. Now we must show them that, in Chairman Mao's words, they have lifted a rock only to drop it on their own feet. Our response must be to step up the protest marches on the island. We must take the fight to them. We must have ten thousand workers, even a hundred thousand, marching through the center of the city and up to Government House, until nobody can ignore the power of our movement any longer. We will carry on for as many weeks as it takes them to listen to us. But everything must be kept under control; that's essential. Even if they can't keep order, we must."

I walked along beside the group of demonstrators,

passing behind the people who stood at the edge of the pavement watching. Some were silently hostile, but most applauded or called out encouragement. As I stopped for a moment, a couple of young clerks next to me were joking about the girls in the procession: "Look at the way that fat one swings her arms; she's going to knock herself out if she's not careful."

"Yeah, but take a look at the tits on this one coming along on this side. Hey, darling, why don't you stop a moment and give me a feel."

The girl blushed furiously, but an old laborer standing in front of me—hair cropped close to a scarred skull, his vest rolled halfway up his chest—glanced round threateningly, fingering the heavy bamboo carrying pole on his shoulder, and they shut up immediately.

Yes, Kwan had been right. It wasn't any sense of spontaneity or passion that made these demonstrations so exciting and frightening at the same time. It was just the opposite of that: a feeling of controlled strength; two hundred ordinary, small people becoming strong together in a city where everybody until now had been weak and isolated. I began to clap to the rhythm of the chanting.

"What d'you think this is?" came Donald Winn's voice from behind me. "A fucking theatre?"

I turned to him happily, pleased at the irritation on his face. "Why, Donald, is it getting to you? Upset that nobody cheers when the cops go by?"

"Personally, Joe, I don't give a bugger. But there's going to be trouble with this little lot; I can tell you."

"Why? *They*'re not causing trouble. If there is any, it'll be your fault, not theirs."

"Jesus wept, Joe, use your bloody head. You can't have thousands of these morons wandering up and down the streets all day long. It's a breach of the fucking peace." He gestured to the back of the pavement, the doorways of buildings, where hawkers had emerged like cockroaches from the side alleys to set up their stalls as soon as they realized the police were being tied down by the demonstrations. "Can't you see what you're doing? The fucking chaos? Look at that." He pointed to an old woman kneeling in the doorway of a bank beside the row of razor-sharp cooking choppers she was trying to sell. "Look at those bloody things. Lethal. Nobody's going to be safe in their own beds around here pretty soon."

I smiled condescendingly. "You're getting paranoid in your old age."

He pulled a vast colored handkerchief, more like a sheet in size, from his pocket and tried to mop himself off. As he did so, my eyes went down to his feet and the two big straw shopping baskets he had dropped there. They were full of cans of food.

"What have you got there, then, Donald?" I asked, laughing already.

"None of your fucking business."

"Come on, what are you hiding?" I leaned down to look into them.

"Trough," he said challengingly, pushing me back with one hand.

"Trough, Donald, trough? Christ, that's great, that's just beautiful. There's the governor coming on the radio every night to say, 'Don't panic, kids. Don't hoard food supplies. Remember the spirit of Dunkirk. Don't listen to panic scare spread by treacherous wogs. We'll look after every—' "

"Listen, baby," he interrupted me viciously. For a moment I thought he was going to hit me. "Even if all the rest of you in this goddam town starve, I'll be buggered if it's going to happen to me. You and your fucking friends, you're gloating right now, aren't you?" He stooped to pick up the baskets, but the handle of one of them gave way under the weight, and dozens of cans of spaghetti and luncheon meat, baked beans and stew and tomato soup went spilling all over the pavement.

As I bent to gather some of them up, with him chasing the others right along the gutter, cursing and kicking out at them, aggravating the mess, I noticed that they all had labels from the main Communist department store.

"Hey, what's this, Donald?" I held one of them up to him. "*Communist* cans? Trading with the enemy? I thought you were paid to be on the other side. Aren't you scared they'll try to poison you?"

He snatched the can from me and hurled it down on the pavement again; a dull thud and a dent. "Listen, Joe, you fucker," he shouted, gripping me by the shoulders so that passers-by paused to watch, hoping for a fight. "All this stinking crap that's sold in the Chinese stores in Hong Kong is subsidized by the state, right? That's why it's so cheap?"

I nodded, puzzled. "Well, yes, I guess so."

"Right, then, you bugger!" he shouted triumphantly. "If I eat enough of it, they'll go fucking bankrupt, won't they?"

Instantaneously his good temper flooded back into him; he laughed, winked at me coyly, and then casually, half turning away, said, "By the way, what's all this I hear about you and old Kwan starting up a newspaper together?"

He had caught me completely by surprise. Just yesterday Kwan had talked about the buildup of government propaganda that was being repeated without question by all the English-language papers. "You may argue that it doesn't matter what the English say or what the English think, but that's a dangerous fallacy. This is not a racial struggle; this is a political struggle, a class struggle, and it has global implications. So far the only English writer who's come up with an objective assessment of the situation has been our friend here, Mr. Stewart. But he's been taken off the news staff of his paper and transferred to the business section. He's also managed to file a couple of stories with an English provincial daily, but their effect can't be more than marginal, and in any case we don't know how much longer papers of that kind will find his viewpoint acceptable."

So Kwan had been voted the funds to publish an

English-language weekly himself, and I had agreed to do all that I could to help him. "All we need to do is to give the people the facts," he said at the end. "We don't need lies or threats or promises; that is our great advantage over the government. If we go on giving them the facts, the people—even the most confused of people—will begin to listen. History is on our side; the truth, too."

Everyone at the meeting had been completely trustworthy, but twelve hours later Donald Winn knew all about it. I couldn't hide my astonishment. "How the hell did you find out about the paper?"

And now it was his turn to laugh. "Oh, we have our little ways," he said, very pleased with himself. "But, seriously, you want to be careful what you get mixed up in. This isn't a game, you know."

"What d'you mean by that?"

"Well, it stands to reason, people are going to get hurt, aren't they? It's just that I wouldn't want it to be you, Joe." He pinched me on the cheek, then bent down and got his arm around the basket with the broken handle. "Can't even get a fucking taxi nowadays," he grumbled and staggered off along the crowded pavement, bumping into other people and muttering at them under his breath.

Even with the threat so clear in my mind, I still couldn't take him seriously.

By midday, though, I was trembling with the knowledge of what he stood for.

Let me try to get the events straight as I remember them; they seem so clear in my memory, and yet as I see them, project them into the present, I can hardly control my responses.

At ten I was in the office, still slightly puzzled by Donald but mostly amused and complacent. Then, just after eleven, as I tried to work on an advertising supplement on tourism, Jimmy Cheung, one of the reporters, came running in. I was closer to him than to any of the others on the staff; he was young, with an elaborately cynical defense against the world; Bogart with a Chinese accent.

"Quick, Joe, can you get out of here? There's going to be trouble along outside the Hilton."

We ran there together, excited and invulnerable.

It was at the crossroads outside the Hilton Hotel that all the groups of demonstrators came together to advance up the hill to the governor's house in an irresistible tide. That was how it had happened in the past week, but this morning they must have got there to find an army of police barring their way. In front, facing them, there would be several files in normal uniform; then the riot squads, looking like hard-shelled beetles in their helmets and gas masks. They carried rattan shields and riot guns and tear gas shells. Behind them were several rows with rifles at the ready, and right at the back a line in running shoes, ready to sprint after a crowd as it broke and fled, to separate out the ringleaders and arrest them.

Farther up the road there would be armored cars, truckloads of reinforcements. The demonstrators would have no defenses, no weapons at all. Just their badges and their books.

The image of it was in my mind long before we got there.

As we ran along the main street, which an hour before had been full of marching, determined people and now was almost empty, we could hear the roar of the crowd rising and falling and the synthetic tones of police loud-hailers warning them to disperse or tear gas would be fired. Before we reached the corner, Jimmy tugged me by the arm towards the lobby of the hotel. "If you stay out there in the street, you'll be half a mile away from all the action. You won't see a thing. If we cut through here, I reckon we can come out directly above them."

So we elbowed our way in through the lobby packed with milling American tourists. One of them grabbed Jimmy by the arm as we pushed past. "Hey, boy, not so fast. What's going on out there?"

Jimmy turned, shook his arm free, looked up at the big man, his eyes rolling; a mock Negro accent: "The slaves is risin', suh!"

The noise inside was almost as great as the noise outside. Men were shouting at each other, at their wives, at the girls at airline counters as they tried to move their reservations forward, at cringing clerks as they bargained for overpriced clothes and jewelry and fake antiques. We pushed on through, and sure enough, Jimmy found a door that led out onto a balcony. As we opened it, the hot, sticky air burst into the air-conditioned hive, the roar of the crowd wiping out the noise behind us.

"Man, this is fantastic," said Jimmy, his voice dropping to a whisper.

Just twelve feet below us the front line of the demonstrators was pushing up against the police, a sea of white shirts against a khaki wall, caught in a delicate equilibrium.

Disruption was what we'd been forcing our lives towards. All of us, not just Winn with his love of confusion, but Kwan, Jordan, myself, that whole city; for all of us that balance had to be destroyed.

From somewhere—an incident I can't place in time—Kwan's voice comes to me again: "Only somebody from a country that had grown rich and irresponsible from its exploitation of others could believe that politics was a matter of choice rather than necessity." But that was how I had been brought up: to believe that the free exercise of choice was the summit of political action. The ballot box, a piece of paper with two or three names printed on it. There, I pass my power on to you, my chosen, my elected, and as quickly as possible wash my hands of all responsibility. But these crowds had come out into the streets determined to assert their freedom: not just to choose, but to act.

What was it Jordan had said to Mei? "A whole generation's being taken on the Long March." That was the myth that carried us all along. "It's something that'll have to be done in every generation," he had told her, "because it's not something you can just tell people about; they've got to be made to do it for themselves." And each of us had to make that march in his own way, stumbling, getting lost, yet knowing, too, that all that could bring us to an end was the kind of commitment Jordan's stories preserved.

So why are the stories that I have to tell so different from his? How I envy him their simplicity and force, their achievement. They moved with such sureness in one direction only, and only one conclusion was ever conceivable. But mine divide and divide again, and every end is knotted in with all the others. True, Jordan's stories might have been full of his own ego, but they weren't just his; they stood on their own, full of history. Mine seem only to be mine now, falling so far short of the myth we tried to imitate.

In the coffee bar after his phone call, Jordan's hand shook so that the cup rattled against the saucer. "Damn doctors! Want to put me on sedatives. I told them I'll cure myself." The voice was rasping, jagged. Then, jerkily, he pushed his face, long-necked, like a turtle, into mine. Red cobwebs in the eyes. "I've got to know whose side you're on, Joseph."

I drew away from him. "What d'you mean, Jordan? Whose side in what?"

"Don't try to tell me you haven't heard." He looked at me suspiciously, as if all the world must know. Then, seeing the puzzled look on my face, he went on like a man who knows the lines by heart: "There was a meeting last night to set up a joint struggle committee. Didn't even have the courtesy to invite me. No sense of what I've done for them. And do you know who they agreed on as chairman? Kwan! Of all people. Kwan Wing-leung. They're fools, Joseph, fools. They just don't know what they're doing. I could have the British out of here in ten days. Shoot the top men; that's all it needs. But Kwan! Oh, he may be all right in his place; I haven't got anything against him. But he's an intellectual, Joseph, a—a dawdler. He'll never be able to take the initiative. I know; I've seen his kind before." His eyes glazed over. "They always break at the crucial moment."

He sat back and watched me desperately, openly pleading now. "That's the choice you've got to make, Joseph. Simple enough. Him or me?"

I tried to laugh it off. "I thought we were all on the same side, Jordan."

"No, no, no!" He hammered the table so noisily that the two English businessmen in the next booth momentarily forgot the plunging stock market. "No, we have to get this cleared up once and for all. The consensus is over, Joseph. Those who're not for me are against me. You'll have to make up your mind." He sat there stubbornly, not willing even to talk about it.

And that filled me with irritation. If he'd got as far as me, how many people must have turned him down already? It was all so artificial, this having to choose, when what lay beneath was just personal pride and pique.

"For Christ's sake, Jordan, why do you come to me? What do I matter, anyway? Look, you can see for yourself. I didn't even know what you were talking about. Nobody even bothered to tell me there was a meeting. So how can what I decide possibly alter anything?"

His reply came out with a false sureness as he tried to keep a grip on the situation; on himself. "If there's one thing I've learned, Joseph, it's that everybody matters. Nobody's so unimportant that you can afford to ignore their position." But he wasn't telling the truth now; I knew it, and so did he. He was just trying to cover up the fact that he hadn't been able to get anybody else's support; that was all. And instead of causing me to sympathize with him, it simply made it easier for me to turn him down, too.

"No, Jordan," I said, getting up. "I'm not going to let you force me into this. Can't you see? This is the worst possible time to start fighting each other. If we don't work together, we won't stand a chance."

A self-righteous platitude. But I knew I was right. I had chosen not to choose, or rather, to let the events themselves make the choice for me instead of trying to pretend it was a personal, private decision. I felt the power of the moment running through me. I was responsible to the act, not to the individual—Jordan or Kwan or even myself.

And so I was able to get out of there leaving Jordan behind me, his eyes looking down, not focusing, the litter on the table, the saucer half full of coffee, rejected even by this young foreigner whose support would have meant nothing anyway.

I ran straight to Kwan.

"Yes," he said, "I'd already heard he'd been going around like this. To be honest, I wasn't sure what to expect from him, Joe, but not this. I mean, why? What's wrong with him? I tried to talk to him, but he wouldn't even listen. I did speak to his wife, though. Have you heard what the doctors' diagnosis is?"

"He just said they wanted to put him on sedatives, but that he wasn't going to take them."

"Oh, that's typical." The exasperation showed through Kwan's voice. "I suppose that's what it must be, some kind of nervous break-down. But this is the worst time it could have happened, Joe. We can't afford to have something like this getting out. Even a hint that we're not completely together. . . . Anyway, he's all on his own, as far as I know. Still"—he shook his head—"I'll have to keep an eye on him. . . ." A silence as he drummed his fingers on the side of the chair.

But then, building up out of that frustration, there was an anger, a passion that I hadn't sensed in Kwan before. It stood out most clearly in that dingy office, with its cheap steel desk and the overflowing bookcases. Over the next few months he would work and wait and sleep here, and perhaps what kept him going through all that pressure was the total unpretentiousness of these surroundings—no stars in the ceiling, no rhetoric, just books and papers piled up everywhere and a scroll of Mao's calligraphy tied, as if by an afterthought, to one of the bars across the grimy window.

"Joe, listen, this is only the beginning. We've reached a point where the struggle becomes self-generating. Nothing can stop it now. Not even the government wants it to stop here. They're stepping up the pressure on us all the time. It's that old nineteenth-century colonial attitude: everything has to be done on their terms. There wasn't any rioting before the riot squads moved in, was there?" He paused at the window, his back to me. "Well, if they want trouble, we'll see they get it, more than they bargained for. They think they're still dealing with people who'll kneel down and beg for another chance. But all we need is one chance, Joe; we've got it now, and we'll take it. On our own terms."

He turned round, and I felt the strength in him then: not the easy friendliness, the slightly mocking watchfulness that I'd always been aware of and liked, but a strength I hadn't really caught in him before. I could see it in the round face that I'd thought of as somehow soft and blurry round the edges; something just a little spoilt and self-indulgent about it. But under the harsh light from the neon tubes in the ceiling, the features were firm, a hard stubbornness beneath them.

He went on. "Oh, they say they want peace, of course. They've got to say that. But they're going about it the wrong way if they do. They arrested two of our cameramen who were covering the riots over in Kowloon. And one of my reporters was beaten up as he was on his way home the night before last. They left him in the gutter with a fractured jaw and a couple of broken ribs. They must want us to respond to that, surely." And then suddenly he smiled as if he was embarrassed at letting himself get carried away. "They're such children, Joe. I should hate to disappoint them."

He came and sat down, and there was a silence between us, but there was no nervousness in it now. A boy came in with a metal teapot to fill up the tumblers of tea on the table, and after he had gone out, there was still the silence.

Kwan picked up his tumbler and rolled it between his palms. "So, where do you stand in all this, Joe?"

"Come on, Wing-leung, you know the answer to that already," I said, wanting to remind him how I had come to these conclusions before him. "Remember that day you took me down to Shaukiwan? Our talk in the restaurant? Why should I have changed my mind since then?"

Suddenly he was the concerned friend again, a note of worry coming into his voice as he said, "Yes, you were right then; I give you that. We were a lot closer to the breaking point than I thought we were. But I don't see how it can be an easy decision for you to make all the same. Theoretically, perhaps . . . not in practice. It means turning against your own people."

I could see the doubt in his eyes and wanted to find a way of dispelling it. "They're not my own people. They feel like a different species most of the time. Even if they're the same race, they're not my people. If all this was happening in Britain, I know which side I'd be on. It should be the same here. Race just doesn't come into it."

Now, as I write it down, I can feel the euphoria that certainty injected into me. Long after the situation that made it necessary has disappeared, I know my answer was the only one possible. And I find myself looking out this window into the emptiness of the evening, wishing such questions might still be asked, feeling out of place with the knowledge of the answers so vibrant inside me.

Inevitably, though, for Mei and myself this certainty of mine, which she couldn't share, opened up all the uncertainties between us.

"Joe, you're not really serious about it, are you?"

"Oh, yes, I am. I've never been more serious about anything in my life."

It was two days after my talk with Kwan, Saturday, and we were driving past Government House, this strange, unbalanced heap of stone and stucco that the Japanese had put together during the occupation, not quite anything in style, marked only by its whimsical ugliness. It had always struck me as fitting that this nondescript monstrosity should have been chosen as the palace of the queen's representative, a cage for the stuffed white linen suit, the plumage of ostrich feathers, the empty authority of the governor. Now there was more life around it than there had ever been before. Hundreds of demonstrators had gathered in the road outside the large, iron-spiked gates to chant their quotations and howl for him to come out and hear what they were demanding. "We are going to force him to acknowledge us," Kwan had said, and he had come up himself on Friday afternoon in the middle of a crowd of singing marchers. Who could tell? Maybe somewhere inside, in one of the marble-floored rooms, somebody was listening. But there was no sign of His Excellency's presence, let alone his concern. Governors do not show their concern. All together tens of thousands of protesters had marched up here and handed in their petitions to the guards without any apparent effect at all. So now they were sticking posters across the gates and the walls and the railings, climbing on each other's shoulders to reach the tops of the pillars, cheering every time a new set of demands was stuck up.

The police didn't dare to interfere. Their order had broken down completely, and the demonstrators had organized their own crowd control, leaving the police, in true colonial fashion, to look after a temporary car-park. As we drove past, we were stopped dozens of times by workers leaning in to shout slogans and hand out leaflets, but the tone behind it all was good-natured, like a carnival, because they were sure they were going to win.

We were held up opposite the gates, and as I looked at the cartoons and tried to read the posters, I began to laugh with the sense of release that everybody was feeling. "It's so beautiful. This ugly old place; it's always been so dead and oppressive. Look at it now. It's like a Buddhist shrine covered with paper prayers. It's fantastic, Mei; they've made it human and holy at the same time."

I put my arm around her shoulders and felt her shivering; her whole body.

"Why, what's the matter, love? You're not afraid, are you? Everybody's so friendly."

She pulled away. "No, I just don't like crowds."

"But this is the most marvelous thing that's ever happened in Hong Kong. Nobody's ever paid attention to these people before. Now they've got to."

She didn't respond; just looked out the window on her side.

"Well, isn't it?" I asked accusingly, not leaving her alone.

"It's . . . exciting," she said half-heartedly, still not looking at me.

"You know, love"—I pulled her round towards me, my fingers in her far shoulder working against the inertia of her body—"this is the first time ever that the workers have been on top here. In the past it was always the British, and then it was the local middle class, but they were only half Chinese, even at their best. All their values, all the objects they looked up to were foreign; only their prejudices were Chinese. But now it's them"—I gestured with one hand as I steered between groups of marchers swarming up the hill from the city. "They're making people like you and me irrelevant."

"So what happens if I don't want to be irrelevant, Joe?" she asked with a flash of anger.

"You don't have any choice, love," I said lightly. "Not as you are now. Neither do I. We're just a part of the structure that's been holding up this whole corrupt society. It's got to be broken down before something that might have a chance of being more democratic can be put in its place."

She was silent for a few minutes, the shouts of the crowds filling the gap between us. Then, as we stopped behind some marshals in red armbands who were letting a file of demonstrators across the road, she turned and took me by the arm. "Joe, you're not really serious about it all, are you?"

I felt her fingers pressing into my arm and saw the anxiety in her face. "Oh, yes, I am. I've never been more serious about anything in my life." It was as if my feelings for her were swamped by the excitement that was so tangible all around us. The town was full of euphoria; fear, too, and even panic among those who had sold themselves to foreign styles and values. But for all the men and women who had never even had a chance to think of doing that, there was a new realization that there might be other ways to attain significance, self-respect. Insecurity was blossoming with accidental flowers: customers didn't dare to shout so aggressively at the waiters in restaurants any longer, and only that morning one of the messengers in the office, a broken-down little man who had just come back a second time from the TB sanatorium, had stopped me in the corridor and asked, "Mr. Stewart, is it true there's going to be a Chinese governor?" There was a tense curiosity in his eyes, and he didn't even bother to glance over his shoulder as he talked.

So I was able to ignore Mei's anxiety, to trample over it gaily, callously. I wanted to force her to share my gaiety, and just for moments she would, but in the end it was the world she had built up separately for herself that was going to have to be broken down.

And she, for her part, couldn't believe in my sureness. How could I talk about the struggle, about my commitment to it, when finally I didn't have any roots in the place, any sense of the individual struggle to make it mine?

One night after we had made love, she leaned over and watched me basking. "You're a bastard, Joe; d'you know that?" Her fingers ran lightly along the underside of my chin. "If things turn out badly for you here, you can just get up and go somewhere else, can't you?" And later again, I don't remember where, just the words, less playful, more bitter: "You don't belong here, Joe. You just want to possess it."

In any case her doubts couldn't reach me. I could always get her to admit she didn't really belong here, either. And beyond that, what was the point in all this talk of belonging, roots? Roots were in the past. What I was talking about was the future. It was that simple.

The next Monday it turned to violence.

Down there at the crossroads beneath the balcony that equilibrium had to be destroyed. I was afraid even my voice would disturb it. "How many?" I breathed.

"Close to a thousand in the crowd, I guess. About three hundred cops, with maybe"—Jimmy craned his head round the corner of the balcony wall—"another five hundred or so up the road."

"They don't stand a chance."

What struck me at once was the vulnerability of the demonstrators in the face of all the paraphernalia of the police. They were high school kids mostly, with just a few older men and women among them. The main buildup of the demonstrations hadn't been planned until the afternoon; that was when the great masses of workers would be arriving.

Jimmy followed my thoughts. "The cops must know they've got to do something pretty soon or they'll be in trouble later on."

For the moment, though, there was still this

perfect balance. The police didn't move; just a few officers gesticulated around the loud-hailers; some plain-clothes men walked backwards and forwards, their eyes roving over the crowd, talking into radio-transmitters; the occasional marksman watched the upper-floor windows. And the crowd, too, it seemed, had come to rest. Those at the back still tried to push forward, but the ripples of their pressure were soon absorbed in the middle ranks and didn't even reach those who stood firmly planted in the front just a yard away from the truncheons and riot guns of the police. From all of them there rose up a rhythmic, irresistible chanting,

> Unite
>
> taken up first in one section
>
> *Defeat the imperialist aggressors*
> *And all their running dogs*
>
> spreading through the whole crowd
>
> *Monsters will be destroyed*
> *No rest until victory is won*
>
> like wind in a wheatfield.
>
> *Down with U.S. imperialism*
> *Down with British imperialism*
> *Down with Soviet revisionists*
> *Long live the thought of Mao Tse-tung!*
>
> The voices rose and fell, reaching a climax.
>
> *Long live our great leader Chairman Mao!*
> *A long, long life to him!*

The jerking fists of the crowd were balanced against the metallic hardness of the police. I almost wished it would stay like that, a mirage, forever; I was so afraid of what would happen when it broke. And that, of course, was why it had to break: my fear, the fear of everyone there, demonstrators and police. Somewhere it had to break. You only had to look beneath the surface to see that. At first you saw these two opposing monoliths, but then, just look closer, not at the panorama but at the individuals, one by one. That boy in the front row: he shouts, he believes what he is shouting, but all he sees is a row of black helmets glinting in the sun and other rows behind them for as far as he can see. And look at how his whole body is strained quivering. Mine, too, as I grip the railing. And that English police inspector across from us: he wipes the sweat from his forehead as if he had been in a shower; his whole shirt is stained dark brown as it never would be by the hottest day.

And then, as the moment seemed to go on forever, the break came.

Along the side of the hotel, passing right underneath us, was a pavement separated from the roadway by a steel-mesh railing. No police blocked it. A group at the back of the crowd suddenly saw it as their chance of advancing farther up the hill, bypassing the deadlock in front of them. They came at a trot, orderly, chanting loudly, fifty or sixty of them, maybe more, five abreast, and a cheer rose up from the crowd as they passed the front ranks of the police. But a squad of reinforcements came running round the top end of the railings to cut them off. Another squad vaulted over the railings and wedged up behind them, so now they were caught on their own—police on three sides of them and their backs to the boarded-up windows of the Bank of America just beneath us.

For a moment there was the balance again, everyone waiting, knowing it couldn't last, wanting it not to last; the tension had become so unbearable. Some began jostling—just ordinary pushing and shoving common in the crowded streets of Hong Kong. But here it broke open the anonymity.

The demonstrators began to shout insults, fingers pointing into their enemies' faces. A girl screamed at one of them, a young corporal, "Your mother must be proud of you today, to see what you're doing to your own people. She must have been a whore for the foreigners to get a yellow-skinned running dog like you."

As I looked down on top of him, I could see the blotches of dull red grow across his cheekbones and watched him banging his riot stick nervously into the palm of his hand. Wedged in next to him was a Pakistani sergeant, who had no doubt suffered the racial taunts of the Chinese for years. He reached out and pushed the girl—not a punch, just a push—and she pushed back—just a push. And suddenly the corporal's stick was rising and striking her on the side of the head. And then it was not one riot stick but thirty, forty, the police standing with their feet planted squarely, knees bent, lashing out in front of them like peasants threshing grain. Teeth bared, they moved forward into the pile of bodies, the police in the roadway leaning across the railings to help out. There was nowhere for the demonstrators to go, just back against the boarded-up windows of the bank or down onto the concrete.

And I watched. Watched! What else could I have done? Leaped over the edge of the balcony onto the shoulders of the police like Erroll Flynn? I watched, and my body was paralyzed with the fear and the anger that pulsed through it. An Englishwoman who had come out after us called, "That's the way to deal with them," and I couldn't even speak. What I felt most was a tremendous shame, not of myself, not personal, like the embarrassment you feel for your own weakness or stupidity, but much deeper than that—sickening.

I had never seen blood like that, never known how easily a head splits; the ripeness of it. The blood spurted out at all angles, and the white shirts were soaked with it. And still the chants continued. I saw a man, older than most of the others, still pointing his finger at the police, shouting, "You are traitors to your own people. Why don't you join us?" The riot stick was driven straight into his ear, a crunch, the blood gushing, his hand coming up and the blood gushing around it. But still as he sank to his knees, he was shouting, "Why don't you join us?"

Within minutes there was just a heap of bodies,

some of them groaning, others in a stupor. Those who had come off lightest cradled the ones who had been hurt most seriously, rocking them like babies.

Then the police stood back.

The sound of the main crowd changed. The chanting died down, and in a surge they pressed forward, trying to see, knowing already from the cries what they would see. And the whole force of the police felt themselves being pushed backwards, until the officers in the middle section gave the order for the tear gas to be fired. The canisters came looping across like rockets, bursting into clouds of steam. And the crowd started to break, running back across the square, handkerchiefs over their mouths. Regrouping in alleyways, they could only throw stones now and burn cars and smash windows.

A wisp of gas was blown around us, and I felt myself choking and starting to cry.

"Let's get out of here," said Jimmy.

As we pushed back into the hotel lobby, an American in front of us—a big fat man, balding, a soft, kindly voice—was saying to his wife, "That was really something, eh, Wendy?"

And now the anger, the impotence, broke out of me. Wendy. Wendy! I jumped at him from behind, clawing at his shoulders. He turned to me, horror in his eyes. "Peter fucking Pan!" I shouted at him, tears trickling down my cheeks, as Jimmy Cheung dragged me away.

14

I have never seen the lake in summertime.

When I first came here, it was fall already, maples and birches turning red and golden. Not decay; a last great splurge of vitality that mingled with the heavy survival of spruce and pine. For a few days it really was as beautiful a place as Tom had pretended it would be. I sank into it like a stone.

Along from the cottage, towards the head of the inlet it stands on, the ground turns marshy. I walk there now on the ice among the frozen stumps, but in the fall the water was still full of frogs and carp, a kingfisher sitting on the branch of a dead tree. I remember a bunch of kids having their own private war among the reeds, using the tops of cattails as grenades that burst and filled the air with sticky down.

But I never saw the lake in summertime. Not until last night. In my dream. Till now my dreams have always been of Hong Kong; memories that wouldn't let go, as I came to cling to them. But now there's an immediacy in this place that wasn't here before. There's nothing consoling in that.

It is midsummer, July; the trees are full of hidden birds and the lake is dotted with boats and sails. Small waves ripple its surface while children splash safely in its margins.

But along in the marsh, half-concealed by the reeds, there is a disturbance. The reeds are dense and green, the water full of tangled weeds and roots; and I am barefoot, pulling a flat-bottomed punt among them, mud up to my thighs.

I am afraid because I know what I will find here.

It is marooned like a whale; a distended corpse, slippery as blubber. It has no identity other than what I mold it into. It is lying here at the edge of a small, marshy island, and I am trying to keep it from being discovered by all the other people around the lake. I am afraid they will associate me with it and attack me. I don't know what size it is: sometimes it's enormous, growing as large as the island; at other moments, a tiny speck.

I don't even know if it's dead. I want it to be alive, to hold it and warm it into life with my body, but I'm afraid that it's I who killed it. I pull it out of the reeds, out of the brown stinking swamp water into the sun, but when I look down at my hands, I see that I'm dragging it with a sharp boathook that gashes open its side.

I part the torn edges of this wound, caressing them, pressing closer, kissing, but the body starts to melt away beneath me. I feel it slipping through my fingers into the water, and I splash about trying to gather it together. I can see its image in the waves, and

I am weeping as it spreads out into a thin, distorting film. I bend to pick it up, but it coats my hands. I try to tear it off with my teeth, but it sticks to my skin, my face, becoming me, my tongue.

I wakened. My cheeks were still wet. I lay trying hard to believe in the solidity of the bed beneath me. At last I pushed myself out of it and over to the window, frightened of what I should see outside. But there was only the moon on the ice, the light reversed like a photographic negative, my shadow black against the glass.

15

Sally lay on her back on the studio couch, the detective story she was reading held up above her head. It wasn't the most comfortable position for reading; there was a pain in her neck, and she couldn't get enough light on the pages, even with the lamp twisted round as far as it would go. But she wasn't reading very seriously, anyway. She was thinking much more of Joe sitting opposite her on a cushion on the floor, his back straight against the wall, leafing despondently through an old copy of *Life*.

Every few minutes her eyes would flicker off the page and across towards him, hoping to catch his eyes doing the same thing, but they never did.

"I don't like these American detective stories," she said, putting the book down beside her. "I can never follow what's happening."

He didn't even look up, just grunted.

He had been like this for a couple of weeks now, ever since the inquest, not talking, doing whatever they suggested, but never snapping out of this perpetual moodiness. It puzzled her, and Tom was getting increasingly irritated.

"It's like having a bloody ghost standing behind you all the time," he had said on one of the few nights Joe went out on his own. "Why doesn't he go and haunt somebody else for a change?"

But now that Tom had had to go away, she promised herself she would find a new way of breaking through to Joe again. Just three days ago Tom had come in breezily, shouting, "I've got a job in Tokyo, kiddos," and the expression of obvious relief on his face had made her heart sink a little. Her first reaction was one of anger against Joe, because if it hadn't been for these past two abrasive weeks, Tom would probably have tried to find the money to take her along. Now he just wanted to get away. But afterwards, as she thought about it a little more, it didn't seem so bad after all; Tom would only be gone for about a week, and that would give her a last chance to try to get things back to the way they had been before.

So far she hadn't made any headway at all. She pointed one of her feet up towards the light, the flared leg of her jeans wrinkling back down her calf.

"Do you want to go out for a drink, Joe? I've still got a hundred bucks left from that job I did the other day."

He glanced up with a faint smile on his face and shook his head, then looked back down at some idiotic article about rockets or something. It made her so angry. Somewhere between them the thread must still be there, but how could you ever find it, let alone draw it tighter, with somebody as unresponsive and arrogant as this? It was such a bloody awful bore; its being so unnecessary only made it worse.

She twisted her legs round and sat up, propping her head forward on her hands.

"God, you *are* a bastard, Joe; d'you know that? What makes you so bloody perfect that you can despise everybody else so much?"

He looked up in surprise. Her voice was louder than he had ever heard it. He hadn't even been listening, was hardly conscious of her being there as he sat by himself at the edge of silence. Since the inquest he hadn't really been in contact with anybody else. Winn had come round twice and talked about how he would have to make up his mind and had gone away again, puzzled and irritated. And Joe had phoned Kwan because, he told himself, this was the last person left he could trust. They had gone out for lunch, and Kwan had been unobtrusively kind, wanting to help, but it hadn't made any real difference; in the end, you couldn't take all these people with all their plans for the future —different futures, of course—seriously. All I want, he thought, is a tiny place in the present; no past, no future, just a place where life can pass me by without noticing, without making demands or asking for decisions. An old woman sitting among a pile of cardboard boxes in an alleyway.

He looked up at Sally crying, trying to hold her face together, and saw even that wasn't possible.

"What's the matter, Sally? What have I done?" he asked, going over and sitting beside her.

She leaned against him. "Oh, God, I don't know. It's just that it was all so good at first, and I don't know why it had to go wrong. You seem so different now. Kind of hostile all the time."

He put his arm round her, and she began to sob. "I'm sorry, love, really I am." He suddenly remembered saying the same thing to Mei, her sobs deeper, her whole body shaking, but he hadn't really been sorry at all then. Now he was. Maybe it was easier to be sorry for the things that didn't matter; a way of faking the

216

books so that you could pretend you weren't such a bastard after all. He tried to put the memory out of his mind. "It's just that I wasn't thinking." He could feel the warmth of her body through his shirt. "Look, did you say a drink?"

So they went down to one of the girlie bars just a couple of blocks away, the noise and the sweat and the smell of beer hitting them as they came through the door. It was full of American sailors, most of them drunk and hunched over the bar, or slumped at tables with clinging miniskirted girls coaxing drinks out of them; some were dancing, fat-arsed and elephantine, some sleeping in corners, others huddled together over cardboard boxes filled with garish leather cowboy boots and satin jackets with "Vietnam" embroidered on the backs.

Joe had been in the place just a week ago, trying to get away from himself, but the cloying inhumanity had driven him out after half an hour. As he walked along the edge of the harbor back towards the flat, a little boy came running after him.

"Hey, Joe, you want nice girl? My sister. Virgin. Real tight fuck. You try?" The boy trotting along beside him couldn't have been more than ten.

He knew it was bound to be some poxy, middle-aged whore in a rickety boat so badly lit you couldn't see what you were doing, but suddenly he knew, too, that this was what he wanted. He hadn't had a woman since Evelyne, the night she died—all that time in the hospital, then listening to Sally and Tom making love next door—yet there still wasn't even a flicker of desire in him as he followed the boy down to a small rowing boat at the bottom of some stone steps. No, it was exactly the opposite of desire that he was looking for; it was the coldness that attracted him, the extremity of coldness that would act like a scalpel to cut out this confusion, this conscience, once and for all.

Of course, it hadn't worked out like that at all. The boy had rowed him out to a sampan in the middle of the typhoon shelter, and he had given thirty dollars to an old woman who asked him to wait for a minute inside, where a quilt had been unrolled on the linoleum-covered deck. A bright oil lamp swung overhead. The canvas entrance was pulled back, and a young girl came in, sixteen at the most, shyness mingling with fear in her eyes. Without a word, she took off her trousers and folded them neatly, then unbuttoned the Chinese-style blouse she was wearing so that it hung open to show sharply pointed nipples growing out of an almost flat chest. She lay down on the quilt as far away from him as possible, legs apart.

As he looked down at her, at that completely hairless slit—like a surgical incision—he thought again of Mei, and hatred of himself welled up inside him, tangible as vomit. He got to his feet and fled past the girl, who cowered away from him in alarm, out onto the narrow foredeck, gasping in the dank night air.

But tonight, in the bar with Sally, it was different. There was a band of local high school boys playing clumping rock music, and she started to dance, all arms and legs, like a spider on tiptoe, making the music seem much better than it really was and yet mocking it at the same time. The other people on the floor began to copy her, amused at first, but then drawn out of themselves into a trance that she dictated. Joe could feel it happening to himself as well and followed her, almost hypnotized by the slow-motion dream through which she moved. The only thing that held him back was the pain that shot into his body whenever it twisted, and after a couple of dances he had to give up.

They went and sat by the bar, but soon there were four Americans all asking her to dance.

She looked at Joe nervously. "Do you mind, Joe?"

A relaxed smile reassured her. "Of course not, love."

He sat and watched, feeling himself float away from the suspicion and the self-recrimination that had sucked him down for the past two weeks. He didn't even mind the hands that tried to push their way down inside the top of Sally's jeans whenever there was a slow number; he felt close to her without there being any need to be possessive about it.

Later, half drunk, they walked home holding each other up.

"God, I feel dead," she said collapsing on the couch, wriggling her toes in the air.

"So do I. But it's better than I've felt for ages." And without either of them knowing quite how, they were kissing.

Sally drew back from it first, frightened by the force of his mouth. "I'll go and make some coffee."

When she came back, she sat on the floor at his feet, feeling safer, surer of herself, with just his fingers playing in her hair.

Neither of them wanted to sleep, and she found herself talking about her childhood on the rubber estate in Malaya where her father was a planter: innocence, playing hide-and-seek with the Malay children, swimming with them in a forbidden pool, then being torn away from all that and sent off to school in England where it was always cold and you had to wear woolen underclothes that gave you a rash. The only consolation had been a girl called Joe— "Isn't that funny?"— who had found a book on sex that belonged to her elder brother, and in the absence of boys, in an old chalk-pit near the school, they teased their bodies to life.

"It was those awful underclothes that did it, I'm sure," she giggled. "It was just so marvelous to take them off that you got carried away. We both knew it was wrong, of course, and we kept on swearing that when we were fourteen we would stop, but we never did. Then we got caught, and there was a terrible fuss, and we were both expelled. Joe was sent back to her family in Rhodesia. I don't know what happened to her. I expect she got married." She rubbed her scalp against Joe's fingers. "Like everyone else," she added ruefully.

After school she had gone to work in a film studio for a while, done some modeling, then come out to Hong Kong. "I suppose I was thinking of Malaya when

I came here. It's not the same place at all, but . . . well, I was hoping."

She tilted her head round sadly, and he pressed her pointed chin between his fingers, bending over to kiss her on the forehead. And then they were kissing again, Sally arching back until her head was on the couch while her feet still rested on the floor. He pulled her up beside him, sensing his desire for her lessen now that it was already too late. He felt the awkwardness of her mouth, not full and overflowing like Evelyne's or elastic as Mei's was, but small and hard and breathless.

She groped in his trousers, at the same time saying, "We mustn't, Joe, not here." But she knew she wasn't going to stop, so she told herself instead that this was something that had to be done; she was doing it for Joe.

As she lay beneath him, her pupils flickering anxiously from side to side, he looked down at her small breasts, squashed and shapeless, narrow hips, long, thin thighs. He felt sorry for her, and seeing it in his eyes, she swung her legs up over his shoulders to startle him.

Even then it was still like two pieces of wood being rubbed together, her clinging to him, doing everything she could think of to satisfy him but not managing, until finally, out of sheer fatigue and the pain in his groin, he came in her and rolled over onto his side.

She was glad it was over, glad she had done it for him . . . glad, too, that for her it had been unsatisfactory, because taking nothing for yourself made it seem even more like giving.

"I'm sorry, Joe," she said.

"Don't be silly." He lay there feeling sore, irritated with himself, trying desperately not to let it turn against her. "It's not your fault."

"I'm never any good with men. I want to be, but it's always like this."

"Nonsense!" He put his arm around her, and she edged towards him.

Looking down at her face from this angle with the light behind him, he could see the beginnings of wrinkles at the corners of her mouth, and his irritation was replaced with sadness.

"What were your parents like, Joe?" she asked suddenly, aimlessly, trying to open him out again.

Christ, this is the last thing I want to talk about, he thought. "I can't remember them," he said abruptly.

But it was what she wanted; a way to forget about herself and her own inadequacies. So he found himself having to go over it all again; not an old wound so much as an old emptiness. His parents had been killed in the V-2 raids on London; he was dug out of a pocket of air beneath his bed. He couldn't remember anything of it, not even in his dreams, but maybe that made it worse. After he had gone to live with his grandmother, his mother's mother back in Scotland, he used to lie awake at night trying to force himself down into that blankness, looking for a reason.

"I suppose I learned to live with it," he said. "But it made me feel sort of . . . abnormal, cut off from other people. Like being in a cocoon."

She wriggled closer to him, rubbing her nipples against his arm. Now she knew what it was she wanted to break down. She stretched up and kissed him on the ear. "Joe, do you think we could try again?"

But as he was wearily stretching an aching thigh across her, she stopped him and whispered shyly, "Perhaps if you tried it with your mouth. . . . It's better like that sometimes. Do you mind?"

And that was how Tom found them when he came in. He had got to Tokyo all right and spent the first night drinking on somebody or other's expense account, surrounded by powder-plastered geishas. And then, the next day, the split in the agency he was supposed to be doing the job for had come to the surface, and he, as usual, had been picked by the losing side. But he had got his money, so fuck them!

"Yeah, fuck you, too!" he had said, smiling and bowing to the smiling, bowing, uncomprehending little man who had driven him out to the airport.

When he opened the front door, he was still a bit drunk from all the booze he had had on the plane. But he had remembered to buy a bottle of duty-free brandy, and now he stood brandishing it like a trophy in the air.

"Party time, kiddy-winks," he shouted.

Then he saw them: Sally lying on the bed, arms, legs, mouth wide open, her body twisting, with Joe crouched over her, his head buried between her thighs.

Sally gave a little scream and pulled a cushion across her, banging it into the side of Joe's head on the way. Her eyes were staring, but Joe's, as he looked up, wiping his lips, were dazed, fixed on Tom, seeing Jordan there instead, the clock turning back again, out of control.

Tom looked around wildly, trying to think of what to do, putting the bottle down absent-mindedly on the table.

"Be my guests, you fuckers," he said, swinging back towards the door.

Joe spent the rest of the night in the coffee-shop of one of the big hotels, sitting in front of a glass of bitter Russian tea, watching the drift of faces—night people, queers and lovers and bored waiters—floating round and round their goldfish bowl of neon.

He imagined Tom doing the same thing in another hotel just a few hundred yards away.

"I've got to catch him," he had said as Tom slammed the door. He struggled into his clothes, fingers trembling, and ran out, too. He had no idea what he would do if he did find Tom. It was just an excuse to get away, leaving Sally standing awkwardly in the middle of the room, sniffing and shivering.

He had come in to the coffee-shop knowing he could be by himself.

The images flash through his brain more and more rapidly. He lets them slip by, trying not to look.

He focuses on a drunken German tourist in a blue silk suit, oily blond hair flopping over his forehead, a young—or rather, not-so-young—Eurasian boy whispering intensely into his ear.

He must keep things disjointed; otherwise they might tie up. That's the real danger. Back there in the flat, for instance: Jordan—no, Tom—standing in the door; a gun—no, just a bottle of brandy—in his hand. He wrenches his mind away. To recognize that things repeat themselves would mean admitting he would never learn, never change, never control his life enough to be able to move on from here.

Without his noticing it, the German and his boyfriend have changed into another couple: a large Australian nightclub dancer with thighs like tree trunks growing into the foliage of a frilly little miniskirt, a small man with long black sideburns nuzzling like a rabbit against her neck.

He will never learn; that is the problem. No matter how intensely aware he may be of his mistakes, he will go on making the same ones again. What was it he had said to Sally about being cut off from other people, like being wrapped in a cocoon? Trying to impress her. But the point is that the cocoon is just an illusion: it doesn't protect him from other people; other people from him.

He rubs his finger over the Formica top of the table, but he can't even be sure it's there through the thin coating of grease, the thin layer of skin. He has to hold onto it with both hands to stop it, and the room, from tilting.

A muscle jerks in his arm.

He gets up to go to the toilet, looking into the eyes of the people he passes. The light reflecting.

Piss pouring out of him like water.

He leans forward across the washbasin till his nose touches the mirror, then away. The surface of the glass is cold. He does it again, again.

In the coffee-shop nothing has changed.

Outside, the buildings across the street begin to take on shape, detail in the dawn. Windows, lintels, joints in the stonework. A bus goes past with all its lights on, the passengers huddled into corners, not looking out or in.

Other people's pain. But it's his own he thinks about all the time. He converts other people's suffering into his own so as to feel less guilty for what he does to them: Sally crying hysterically, alone in the flat; Tom . . . God knows where.

Tom had got back to the flat just a few minutes before him.

"Sally's asleep in there," he said, nodding towards Joe's room. He tiptoed over and closed the door. "I'm just making some coffee. Want some?"

"I'm sorry, Tom. Truly I am."

Tom turned towards him, anger in his red eyes, a little man with a streak of dirt on the bald top of his head. "Listen, Joe, you're a prick. Okay? So shut up about it. Stop showing off, for God's sake." He banged a mug of coffee onto the table beside the half-empty bottle of brandy.

They sat in silence, clutching the mugs with both hands, avoiding each other's eyes. But Joe knew he had to say something, had to try to explain.

"Look, Tom. I wish I could explain what it was like. It was just an accident. It didn't mean anything at all."

"I don't want to know what it was like."

"But it's not as if it was even any good."

Tom stood up and walked wearily over to the window, then turned round shaking his head. They had often teased him about being older than them, but until now it had never made him feel different in any way at all. Now, as he looked down at Joe, he felt as though he were talking to a stupid, selfish, ignorant child. He couldn't hate him, and it wasn't because he knew Joe was the stronger that he didn't hit him; he was simply too old and tired to bother to explain. And yet he knew he had to go on trying. "Jesus Christ! You really don't know what a son of a bitch you are, do you, Joe? We take you in because we feel sorry for you, and instead of showing the least bit of gratitude, you treat us like we were dirt. And when I go away on a job, I come back and find you making out with my girl. And you seem to think it's some sort of an excuse to say, 'Oh, never mind, Tommy boy, it's not as if she was any good.'" His voice had been quiet, colorless, but it became more emphatic. "So what does that make you in your own eyes, eh? Some kind of candidate for the Humanity Hall of Fame?"

"Okay, Tom." True as Joe knew they were, Tom's words still forced him to fight back, picking up by reflex whatever weapon he could lay his hands on. He didn't want to quarrel with Tom; he had done him enough harm already, but—"Okay, maybe that's true enough. But don't try to tell me it makes you into some kind of tin god yourself. You're not so bloody innocent, either, let's face it. Taking me in out of the kindness of your heart! You know damn well you only did it because Donald Winn put you up to it."

"What's he got to do with it?" Tom's voice was defensive.

"Oh, come off it, don't give me that. You know what I mean. Donald wanted me somewhere out of Kwan's way, and you were the ideal cover: good old Tom Price with all that crap about Canada. What was it? 'In the fall it's the most beautiful place in the whole world'? Christ! It almost took me in, too."

Joe was watching for a reaction of indignation or guilt; instead there was only puzzlement. Then slowly Tom nodded his head. "Yeah, that figures." He bit his lip. "That morning I went downstairs to the store; we were going out on the boat for a few days. And then when I got to the corner, there was this Mercedes sports car parked there. A young Chinese kid was driving, and Winn was sitting next to him."

"That's right; he can't drive."

"Yeah. So he waved, and I went over. I'd met him a few times around the bars; never really hit it off too well. But that morning he was real friendly. Started talking about Canada. Then he said, 'It sounds like just the sort of place for a pal of mine. Hey, but you must know him, too—Joe Stewart, the poor bugger you picked up the other night and took to the hospital? Well,' he said, 'he's going through a pretty rough time right now. Doesn't have any friends, either.' So I said maybe we'd go up and visit you. And he said, 'Yeah, that'd be nice.' Then I went into the store, and when I came out again, the car was gone." He paused. "I guess he took both of us for a ride, Joe."

They watched each other, both of them suspicious. Tom sensed Joe had turned him away from his rightful anger over Sally onto ground that collapsed beneath his feet. And Joe, for his part, couldn't afford to believe Tom was as innocent as he was making out; that would put him back where he had been before, the only one to blame for all that had happened. No, he didn't believe it; some of it might be true, but not the whole story, surely? There must be more to it. He remembered Mei's words: nobody can afford to tell the truth.

What did it matter, anyway? He got up and went and stood beside Tom at the window, looking down at the junks and sampans in the typhoon shelter beneath them; men repairing fishing nets, children playing sure-footed on the narrow decks, mangy dogs scratching, women cooking and gossiping. A baby was asleep just inches from the side of a boat, and nobody took the least notice. He sensed that some kind of gesture was needed to rise above this mess.

"I'll get my things together and go and find a hotel before Sally wakes up," he said.

"You don't have to go," said Tom, not looking at him. "We're not kids, for God's sake." But there was no conviction in his voice.

"It won't be for long, anyway. I'm going to see Kwan today to get him to fix things up for me to go to

China." He hadn't known what he was going to say until he said it. But in any case, it didn't mean anything. It was just a gesture, and Tom, whom it was meant to impress, didn't give a damn.

16

Outside in the streets there was supposed to be a curfew, but in the basement bar where Winn was waiting for them nothing had changed. Joe had come here once before, what seemed like a long time ago, and it felt as if it would always be just the same: the same loud Filipino rock group in one of the corners, the same bored faces eyeing each other, trying to decide who was worth raising an eyebrow at. It was one of Donald's places, full of the loose fringes of society: reporters, admen, radio announcers, a few tourists after local color, several third-rate Cantonese actors of indeterminate, indiscriminate sex who weren't paid enough for their film work and had to come in here a couple of nights a week to see what they could pick up on the side—down here they were stars. There was nothing here that Joe could even pretend to be interested in any longer.

He lagged behind Mei as she pushed over to the table where Winn was sitting.

Donald jumped up, taking her by the hand, kissing her. "Darling, you're looking just marvelous. What's the secret? Lots of screwing?"

"Shut up, Donald," she giggled, putting her arm round him.

"He's keeping you satisfied, though, is he?" He fixed an eye on Joe over Mei's head.

Joe glared back at him angrily. He shouldn't have come; he had known that all along. Winn had phoned him that morning—in Kwan's office of all places; of all the check, he had wanted to say, but the language was wrong—and as soon as he heard the squeaky, vulnerable voice, Joe had slammed the receiver down. Winn was the last person he wanted to talk to. In the past few weeks too much had happened. Too many of his friends had been dragged out of their beds in the middle of the night, questioned by Winn, then thrown into prison without a trial. Others had been beaten up in the streets by thugs who worked for Winn. The innocence of his absurdity had worn thin.

"Who was that?" Kwan asked.

"Winn." Joe went back to his work.

Kwan stopped what he was doing and came over to the desk.

"Why don't you talk to him?"

Joe switched off the tape recorder. "After all this?" He gestured at the pile of tapes and papers. He had been translating a series of interviews with victims of the police violence. Together with all the letters, many of them anonymous, that had been flooding in, they would make a big impact on the European press. "I mean, how can I, knowing he's behind it all?"

"You might learn something, Joe. Even if it's just a hint of how they're feeling. It could be useful. There's nothing to lose."

Joe looked doubtful.

"After all, you've got nothing to be afraid of," Kwan said gently.

So when the phone rang again, Joe allowed himself to be talked into getting together tonight. For old time's sake! All day he had felt a vague sense of guilt about it, but Mei, when he told her, was overjoyed; it seemed like a break in the confrontation they had been living through together.

"Come on, Joe, sit down." Winn was patting the seat of a chair.

Joe looked around him in disgust. This bar made him feel unclean. He wished he could just walk out.

"What have you been up to, then?" Winn asked.

"You should know."

None of their eyes met.

What the hell was the point of going through this, anyway, Donald wondered. What kind of nostalgia had made him think he wanted to see these two again? Why did he have to bore himself like this, for fuck's sake? Work? A crumb of knowledge? Who cared? He started automatically to tell one of his stories.

"You remember that bank that went bust in sixty-five? The South China Commercial? Well, there's a friend of mine, a lawyer, who's been working on it ever since—two years—just going through all the files and the accounts, trying to sort out the mess. Fucking bore it must be. Anyway, he was telling me one of the things that went wrong was the way they kept on pouring money into companies that had already been losing heavily. Really stupid risks. Good money after bad, you know? Well, the worst of all was this textile factory, Nang See, or something—d'you know the one I mean, love?—and in the end the manager of the bank still couldn't see what was going wrong, but even he knew something had to be done; they were losing so bloody much. So guess what he goes and does? He gets this old fortune-teller from his native village and takes him over to the factory and asks him what's the matter."

He saw Joe sitting back watching him with a smirk on his face, Mei's eyes wandering around the room. "Shit! I've told you this before, haven't I? Anyway, the story's all over the fucking town by now."

Mei leaned across the table and took one of his pudgy hands between her lithe fingers. "No, Donald, you've never told us; honestly. Has he, Joe? Do carry on. It's fabulous." She laughed to show she didn't really mean it, but that didn't matter to him now. He warmed to the touch of her and grasped her hand in his.

"Okay, so we've got this old fortune-teller, right? And he looks at the factory and says, 'Oh, it's very simple; you've got your loading-bay on the wrong side of the fucking factory. The goods are going out in an unlucky direction. If you take them out on the other side, you'll see, in six months' time there'll be a big change in your fortunes.'

"So, would you believe it, the buggers closed the whole factory down and knocked a great big fucking hole through the finishing shop so they could put the loading-bay in there. Cost them hundreds of thousands on top of what they were losing already. And then the bank poured more money in because it was a sure thing now, you see, and they all just sat back and waited for the magic to work.

"Well, you know what happened after that?" Winn caught Mei's eye and winked.

She shook her head, grinning. She was with him now.

"Six months later, exactly, right to the very day, there was the run on the bank, so that all the loans had to be called in, and the whole factory went bust. And so did the fucking bank."

Winn sat back, stirring the ice in his Campari with a ringed finger, then sucked the tip of it slowly.

Joe watched him with distaste.

The Seventh Hexagram

NAME: CHEN YIU-CHEUNG; AGE: FORTY-FIVE;
OCCUPATION: HOUSEWIFE

I've never talked to a reporter before. My husband ought to be here doing this—he's a secretary of the Carpenters' Union, and he's good at this sort of thing—but the police took him away two mornings ago, and I haven't heard a thing about him since.

It was just after six o'clock. We live on the second-top floor of the Kiu Koon Building in North Point. There are nine of us in the flat—the two of us, my mother-in-law, and our six children—and it's a bit cramped in just the two rooms we have. But I don't want to complain because there are lots of people worse off than us, and the rent's very fair, and up there on the second-top floor you get a good breeze from the harbor.

I'm sorry, I'm not doing this very well.

Anyway, I had just wakened up, and I was lying there, thinking about how I would have to get up and light the stove, when there was this terrible racket outside, and the whole building started to shake. It was worse than any typhoon I've ever been in, and I thought it must be an earthquake and the building was falling down. I grabbed the baby, and she started to cry, and my husband jumped out of bed and ran to the window. He shouted to me that there were some enormous helicopters flying up the side of the building —just like giant mosquitos, he said—and that one of them was already landing on the roof. I ran over and looked out, too, just as another one went up past us only a few feet away—so close I could see the white faces of the soldiers inside. Then I looked down into the street, and it was full of soldiers as well, and there were barbed wire barriers across all the corners. And out in the harbor there were police boats with their machine-guns aimed in our direction.

Straight after that we heard the boots on the stairs and kicks against the front door, and six police came barging in, all of them with guns pointing at us —as if we were gangsters.

"Why do you come in here like that as if we were gangsters?" my husband asked them.

But the sergeant shouted, "Shut up! Around here we do as we like."

Then they started to search the flat, pulling out drawers and knocking things down off the shelves. They smashed a bust of Chairman Mao.

There were some Double Happiness cigarettes lying on the table, and one of them said, "Why do you smoke this Communist rubbish? They're made out of chicken shit. They'll give you cancer," and he threw them in the sink.

My daughter had gone to the bathroom, but they just broke the door down with their rifles and pulled her out half naked. My mother-in-law, who's over seventy and a bit deaf, began to shake all over; and my son, who was a tram-worker until he went on strike, shouted at them, "What right have you to come in here abusing people like this?" He tried to push them out of the door, but they hit him over the head three times with their guns, and he fell down on the floor in the corner.

In the kitchen there were some empty bottles my youngest son had brought home with some friends, and they said, "These are weapons, aren't they? You've got them here to make bombs." And there was a big container full of water, and they told us, "You've been wasting water so as to ruin the economy." And they poured a can of kerosene for the stove into the water container. They all laughed at that; they thought it was so clever.

Then they found my husband's tools—chisels, drills, screwdrivers, that sort of thing—and they said that they were weapons as well and that they would see he would get seven years in prison for that. And they took all the union papers that he kept in a desk, and put handcuffs on him and my son, and took them both away, still in their underclothes.

After they had gone, we found that nearly fifty dollars and a gold necklace had been stolen.

Winn felt at ease again. He looked around the bar, recognizing faces, situations.

"What about all these strikes, then, Mei?" he asked suddenly. "What d'you think about them?"

"Me?" She glanced hurriedly at Joe. "Oh, don't ask me, Donald. I don't know. I'm sort of . . . well, caught, but—" she hesitated, pouting her lips, "I don't see what good they do, quite honestly."

"Exactly!" Winn's voice had gone harder now. "So why don't you get this stupid bugger to see that, too. All his mates want to do is break everything down. They're wrecking the economy."

Joe had been waiting for this, knowing all along what Donald was trying to do. But was he always as transparent as this? If he was, he couldn't be much good at his job because all it did was to leave Joe even more sure of himself. There was no way Winn was going to be able to demolish that sureness because it was based on the realities of a situation—the suffering he had seen and been told about, the people he had listened to—not just on theories or ideals. It had been a mistake to come here, but now he was here, he felt good about it, relaxed.

He took his time. "Oh, come off it, Donald. Wrecking the economy! What d'you mean by that? What sort of economy, for Christ's sake? Look at that story he was just telling us." He turned to Mei. "It's an economy based on superstition. They're all just fortune-tellers, every single one of them. It's medieval, and the only reason it makes so much money is because it's got this vast reservoir of poverty to draw on. Poverty, that's what makes it work. Take away that poverty—and that's what we're going to do—and the whole economy collapses. But afterwards you can build things up again, efficiently, scientifically, and there's no need any longer for people to be exploited."

Mei nodded. She knew Joe was right when she

heard him talk like this. For the moment the firmness in his voice quelled all her doubts about how what he said could apply to her, how she could act upon it. She knew that it had to be right. And yet (did there always have to be that "and yet"?) and yet, she couldn't be sure as he seemed to be. And how was he so certain, after all, dammit, how could he be? She remembered that day when she had met him, and what had attracted her to him then was just the opposite of this. It had been the depth of his self-involvement that she had responded to. And now here he was denying that. He seemed to be saying only actions matter, not individuals, just like all the rest of them that he had seemed so different from only a couple of months ago. Was he using this, then, as a means of running away from something? But that would be weakness, wouldn't it? And there was all this strength in him now that her body reacted to so strongly. God, it was just too complicated. Why couldn't she get things straight for once?

She shook her head more fiercely.

"But all these strikes," Winn said in what she thought was a whine. "The workers aren't asking for better wages or conditions or anything. If they were, I'd be the first to support them. Truly I would. But they're purely political. That's why they've got to be broken."

"What's so wrong about that?" Joe came back at him. "Of course they're bloody well political. It's a political issue. There's no point in fighting for a few more cents an hour. You never catch up like that. What they need is a complete restructuring of the whole social system."

"A complete restructuring of the whole social system," Winn repeated sneeringly, struggling to get through to Mei again. "Can't you see it, Mei? It's just so much fucking jargon. He doesn't really mean anything by it. Thank God they don't have a snowball's chance in hell of winning. You don't really think you do, do you, Joe? You're just a bunch of bloody amateurs."

Winn paused, then pushed farther. "What I can't understand, though, is how you could get mixed up with a bunch of fucking racists."

"Racists?" Joe tried to make a joke out of it, kissing Mei on the neck. "Am I a racist, love?"

But Winn wasn't joking. "Shit! Surely your old mate, Kwan, tells you what he prints in his Chinese papers. Didn't you read that poem he had in there the other day?"

Joe hadn't. "Which one?"

"There was only one," Winn said emphatically, sure of himself. "The one attacking 'red-haired, blue-eyed, big-nosed foreign devils.' Let's have a look at you." He put his damp hands on both sides of Joe's face. "Yes, come to think of it, that fits you all right. You've got a big bloody nose, Joe; your eyes are blue; your hair's almost red. It must have been you he was telling his people to ' 'ow up. Workers of the world unite, and all that crap! These buggers don't even make any pretense of that. They're just a bunch of narrow-minded little racists. And they haven't even got the guts to be honest about it. Kwan didn't put that poem in his English paper, just the Chinese one."

Joe felt the argument drifting away from him, and when he spoke, it was more to himself than to anybody else. "No, there's no justification for that. But there is an explanation. Race isn't an issue that Kwan's suddenly injected into the situation . . . arbitrarily. It's been there ever since the British came to Hong Kong. And the racism that's been there all that time has been British racism, our refusal to treat the Chinese as equals. Even today, Mei, how many of the top fifty jobs in the government are held by Chinese, even tame Chinese? You can count them on the fingers of one hand. Well, that silly little poem is just the inevitable response."

"But that's what you lot are saying all the fucking time." Winn held up his hands piously to the smoke-covered ceiling. " 'Please, sir, we didn't start it; you did.' That's what Kwan's always whining."

"It's bloody true, too," said Joe with a flash of certainty. "If anything, it's the only thing that's wrong with him."

Winn nodded sarcastically.

"No, it is; I mean it. Kwan responds too much instead of taking the initiative. But you don't know how lucky that is for you. So far his responses have always been in the direction of peaceful, controlled action. None of yours have."

"Yeah, so what d'you want us to do? Hold the door open for him and say, 'Come on in, Mr. Kwan, and screw us up the arse?' Peaceful, controlled action!" he jeered. "All you're doing is making life impossible for ordinary people. The ones who can't get to work because there are no buses or ferries and who can't eat because the prices of food have doubled. If you go on like this, you won't have any support left. So carry on, Joe baby, be my guest; do my job for me."

"No," Joe said grimly, "the mistake you're making is to think in terms of the bourgeois reaction—"

"There he goes again, for fuck's sake. The same old jargon. The bourgeois fucking reaction. What we're talking about is people, individuals. Everybody in Hong Kong has bourgeois aspirations, even if they haven't made it yet. That's why they're here, you stupid prick. That's why you're here, isn't it, Mei? That's what you want?"

"What I want at the moment," she said, "is for the two of you to stop quarreling so that I can listen to this bloody awful band." She turned away from both of them, as they noticed with astonishment the tears blossoming in the corners of her eyes.

NAME: MA CHIN-LUNG; AGE: SEVENTY-ONE
OCCUPATION: RICE MERCHANT

When you are seventy-one and you have a seven-year sentence stretching out in front of you, sometimes you wonder if you are ever going to see the outside world again. But when I start to feel depressed like that, I promise myself that I will get out of here and that I will live to see the foreigners punished for what they have done to me and my people. Maybe they're thinking that they won't have to put up with me much longer, but they will; they will. For them I'll live forever.

This isn't my first time in prison, and perhaps it isn't my last. The Japanese imprisoned me during the Occupation when I wouldn't support them, and I've had plenty of trouble with the British, too, over the past twenty years. They're all the same. Still I thought that I was going to be able to settle down, to live out my last days peacefully, an old man with a white beard, surrounded by his children and his grandchildren. But when this latest wave of repression began, I knew that I couldn't keep quiet. I put up posters and cartoons all over the front of my store, and I played the great new songs of China on a loudspeaker for my customers.

Then, on the morning of July 25, we got an anonymous phone call to say the police were coming to attack us. I talked to my two young daughters, Yun-ching and Hsi-ming, about what we should do. Should we take down the posters and plead with them to forgive us? No, I said, if you kneel down in front of people like that, they'll just walk over you.

So we piled up a huge wall of rice bags across the entrance and barricaded the back door with sheets of aluminium. Then we gathered all the old bottles we could find into piles and anything else we could use to defend ourselves with—stones, rubbish, anything—and waited for them to arrive. They didn't take long, but I never expected so many of them: lorry-load after lorry-load pulling up in the street outside. There were three hundred of them, so I'm told.

As soon as they began to line up and call on us to surrender, we let them have it with the bottles. My daughters crouched down behind the rice bags, and I stood on top of them with a long cargo hook in my hand. The police stayed well clear of me, I can tell you. What we did was this: as soon as they fired tear gas into the store, we ran into the lavatory, which we sealed off with wet rags; then we wrapped cloths around our faces and came out to hit them with the bottles and stones when they tried to break in. We could have carried on like that all day if they hadn't set the place on fire. As it was, it took them two hours to capture us; not bad for an old man and two teen-age girls! I reckon that if all the people in Hong Kong followed our example, the government would need 300 million police to deal with them!

After that they dragged me off to the police station. "Come along, you old goat," they said, pulling me by the beard.

"At least I'm not a yellow dog that craps in its own kennel," I told them.

They beat me up at the station and threw me into a cell with three other men, all four of us in a space seven feet by five. They wouldn't even let us out to go to the toilet—just a bucket in the corner of the cell. I couldn't speak because my throat was so sore from all the gas I had swallowed, and the food they gave us made me sick—rotten vegetables and rice that I would be ashamed to have in my shop. But I'm not going to ask them for any special treatment just because of my age; I'll take whatever they give me, and it will make me all the stronger.

That was my attitude, too, when they tried to put us on trial.

When we came into the courtroom, all the spectators stood up, but they refused to stand for the judge. That was a good start.

And straight away I told him, "I'm not the one who's on trial here. It's you. You are the guilty one. It was your police who beat me up. It was they who flooded my store with their fire-hoses and ruined my rice. How can you put me on trial and not yourself?"

Then the police announced that they had written

the wrong date on the charge-sheet, June 25 instead of July 25. Three hundred of them and they can't even get the date right! So I said to the judge, "If you can move the days of the year about just as you please, you might as well find us guilty without bothering with the evidence."

But he just went very red and said he was going ahead with the charges, anyway. Charges! I've never heard anything so ridiculous: possession of "dangerous arms" and "inflammatory material" and "unlawful assembly."

I said to him, "Let us see these dangerous arms." And all they had to show was my old cargo hook and a few bottles. So I asked him, "Don't you have any bottles in your home?"

But he said, "Two of these bottles contain a suspicious liquid."

And I told him, "Well, I haven't the faintest idea what kind of liquid it is. It wasn't there when I had them."

So he asked the police witness, "What kind of liquid is it?"

And the policeman said, "It's water, Your Honor."

The whole court just burst into laughter.

And then my daughter Yun-ching asked him what he meant by "inflammatory material." He said it was our posters. And she said, "But these posters merely tell the truth about what you have done to our people." Then she demanded that they read out the posters to show what was inflammatory about them. So the clerk began to read them out very, very softly. But she wouldn't let him get away with that. "Louder," she said, "louder. Nobody can hear them."

So he had to read them all out: "Be resolute, fear no sacrifice, and surmount every difficulty to win victory." "Resolutely counter-attack the provocations of British imperialism." "We shall win. The Fascist authorities will be defeated." More people heard them there in court than had ever seen them in our store. And the interpreter had to translate them all into English for the judge; they sounded like really good posters to me.

Then my other daughter, Hsi-ming, said, "You have charged us with 'unlawful assembly.' Is it unlawful assembly for three members of the same family to live under the same roof? How small does a family have to be for it to be lawful?"

They went on drinking in silence.

Donald Winn glared around him sulkily, but as his eyes found something to fix on, a big grin began to spread across his face. He tapped Mei on the arm. "See that boy over there in the leather jacket?" He pointed quite openly. "That was the reason Gary walked out on me. Don't you think he's gorgeous, Mei? Calls himself a film star like all the rest of them. And he's a star all right, I can tell you. I bumped into him one day at lunchtime, right out here in the middle of Nathan Road, and suddenly I had this fantastic urge to have him right there and then. D'you ever get urges like that, Joe? Well, of course, I couldn't, not quite, anyway, not even me; so I took him back to the flat and then—oh, my God, I get goose-pimples just thinking about it—who should walk in but Gary, right in the middle of it. You should have seen him; it was marvelous, he went absolutely *berserk*. He jumped right on top of me and started screaming and punching and tearing out my hair in handfuls. I thought I was going to die. I was black and blue for days afterwards. And then he got all my clothes out of the drawers and cut them all to shreds and threw them out of the window. I didn't have a stitch left."

As Mei and Joe laughed, he looked at them solemnly. "Laugh, you mean buggers, but it's true; I swear it is. When I went out to buy some more clothes the only thing I had to put on was half a bath towel. Can you imagine me, taking a taxi and going into Lane Craw-

fords wrapped in half a bath towel? All those squealing little salesgirls thinking it was Tarzan come to
deflower them. Christ knows what it's done to my repu-
tation!"

"Poor Donald!" Mei said, her head on Joe's shoulder. "Everybody's against you."

"Too fucking true! Look at that nasty little faggot
he's with now." He stuck out his tongue in their direction.

"Faggot?"

"Yes, the one in drag."

"What? You mean that girl in the weird dress?"
Mei asked incredulously.

"Go on, you didn't think it was a real bird. I don't
expect there's a real woman down here. Apart from
you, of course, sweetie."

She looked around, amazed. "But that probably
means they all think I'm one of them, too."

"That's right. Didn't you see them all whispering
when you came in and sat down over here. They're
all absolutely green with envy."

"But that's horrible," she said, looking at Joe
wide-eyed. "I've a good mind to get up on the table and
take off all my clothes. Just to show them."

"Come on then, darling," Donald egged her on.
"That'll really stir the buggers up."

She sat forwards on the edge of her seat, wriggling, almost tempted. Then she leaned back against
Joe and nestled there. "No, I'll keep it for Joe."

"Jesus wept, you're really getting domesticated,"
Winn mocked her.

She smiled back at him, then ran her tongue along
her lips.

But Winn wasn't interested in Mei any longer. He
turned to Joe, who had been watching them with a nervous, slightly uncomfortable smile. "So, Joe, who's going to burn next?"

Joe's face collapsed.

Mei looked from one to the other. "What are you
talking about, Donald?"

"You knew Yim Bun, didn't you?" he asked grimly.

"No," she said reluctantly, not wanting it to start all over again, "but Joe did." She turned towards him. "Didn't you?"

Joe looked away, down at his hands. "I didn't really know him, just met him a couple of times at parties." Then he looked up at Donald. "He was the most fatuous little cunt I've ever met."

Winn's shallow eyes were suddenly full of a pure anger Mei had never seen there before. "Joe, you're a bastard; d'you know that? The most callous fucking bastard I've ever come across. Just because Joe Stewart finds the man a little—what was it?—fatuous, does that make it okay to burn the bugger? Burn him alive? Just because he's doing the job he's fucking paid for? Which is more than anyone could say for you."

"There are too many Yim Bun's just doing what they're paid for," Joe shouted back at him.

People around them were beginning to listen. Mei noticed Joe's face was all blotchy.

Winn was leaning across the table, his finger pointing at Joe. "I'm just beginning to realize how dangerous you dumb intellectuals are with your half-arsed ideas. But I'm warning you; you and your precious fucking friends had better watch out."

"Don't you threaten me, Donald."

"I'm not threatening you, baby. I don't make threats. I'm just telling you, you don't know what you're getting into, and soon it'll be too late to get you out."

Joe drew back. "You don't even know who did it."

"Who else could it have been, the fucking pixies?" Winn shouted.

Joe got to his feet, and for a moment Mei thought he was going to try to hit Donald. "Listen, I'm sick of you and your hypocrisy. Do you think you can go around threatening and beating and killing people just because you're afraid of their ideas, and nothing's going to happen in return? I saw Leung Kong the night before you killed him." He went on over Winn's protests. "Yes, you, Donald, you, your thugs—they're a part of you, your arms, your legs. Leung was okay when he was arrested—just a bump on the head—and the next morning he was dead, with every one of his ribs broken. And your fucking coroner friend said it was accidental death."

Joe turned and looked around him desperately. "So don't talk to me about that—that mosquito Yim Bun."

He stumbled towards the door. In thirty seconds the bar had returned to what it called normal.

NAME: ANONYMOUS; OCCUPATION:
POLICE DETECTIVE

I am a plainclothes detective, and ever since these atrocities started, my relatives and friends have refused to have anything to do with me. At first I thought I didn't care, but what I have seen with my own eyes in the past few months is something that will haunt me for the rest of my life.

At the beginning of these riots our inspector ordered us to get hooligans to throw stones and burn cars and buses. That way, he said, we would have a good excuse for torturing the leftists, and the government would praise us for our loyalty.

I have seen hundreds of innocent people brought into the police station, and the most lenient treatment any of them can expect is to be beaten until they are unconscious. Our officers showed us how to beat a man so that there would be internal bleeding in the kidneys without any visible bruises or wounds. At times the station looks like a slaughterhouse, with men—and women, too, sometimes—lying on the floor gasping or trying to crawl into a corner because they can't walk. And in the early morning I have seen sacks with the shape of human bodies piled in the corridors. I didn't dare to try to open them because I am a coward and

I was afraid of losing my job and probably my life as well, but the next day these sacks had disappeared without any trace.

I am writing to you now to give you the names of all those who have committed these crimes so that later on I will not be accused of them myself. And when the time comes, I swear that I will turn my gun against the British because I am sick of what they are forcing me to do to my own people.

The street was deserted, covered with litter. The rubbish hadn't been cleared away for days.

Joe had been working with Kwan on some posters that were to be sent to Chinese who lived in Britain and America. As he was leaving, yawning, he asked, "Can I give you a ride home, Wing-leung?"

But Kwan pointed to a camp-bed in the corner: "No thanks, Joe. I sleep here now most nights. It's safer. Did you hear what happened to Tsui Tin-po last week; he got knocked down by a car when he was asleep in his bed in a flat on the seventh floor. So the police said. Strange accidents we have nowadays, Joe." He laughed, exhausted. "Besides, I can work better at nights. There's more time to think." And Joe thought of the report Kwan would still have to write for whoever will be in power in Peking tomorrow, the explanations of the long inconclusiveness of what was happening in Hong Kong. It was a dangerously exposed position he had worked himself into, but it showed hardly at all; just the occasional restlessness, as he turned now from the window. "You know what I'd really like to do? Just go out and sit quietly in a bar and drink some beer." They looked at each other. "Ah, well, good night, Joe. Be careful."

Joe turned into the narrow side street where his car was parked. The streetlamps were so dim you hardly noticed them; some old tenement houses on one side, a building-site with pools of stagnating water on the other. As he walked along to the far end, he found himself trying not to step on the lines between the paving-stones, just as he had done as a child coming up the brae from the village on a dark night, forcing himself not to look over his shoulder.

But as he bent to unlock the car door, he couldn't pretend the noise behind him was just the memory of a childhood fear any longer. He swung round and saw the two shapes coming out of a shop entrance a few yards away, largish men, at least as big as he was himself, with flat, heavy, northern faces. They were both wearing plastic raincoats, plastic hats on the backs of their heads, white shirts, black shoes. One of them had both hands in his trouser pockets, the coat bunched back behind him so that Joe could see—was meant to see—the black police truncheon hanging from his belt. "Unnumbered thugs," the people called them; as opposed to the uniformed police, the ones with numbers.

He didn't have time to be scared as they came and stood silently, intimately, one on either side of him.

"What do you want?" he asked, like an indignant taxpayer.

No reply.

He repeated it in Cantonese, then added as the fear seeped into him, "Mr. Winn's a friend of mine."

One of them said something in a dialect Joe didn't understand; the only word he caught seemed to be Wing Tao-ngan—Winn?—and they both laughed. Joe saw the man's arm begin to bend. He lashed out instinctively, catching him hard in the mouth and feeling the pain in his knuckles and wrist. Before Joe could do any more than watch the man stumble, his arm was caught and wrenched up high behind his head. Bent forwards like that, he saw the man pick himself up slowly, wiping his mouth with the back of his hand, probing his gums with a dirty finger, smiling, smiling as he came up close—stubble on his chin and upper lip, garlic breath—so close that Joe never even saw the knee driving up into his balls. He screamed with the pain as he was kicked twice more, and as he jackknifed forwards, something hard hit him on the back of the neck. His arms were let go, and he fell on the top of his head on the pavement.

Then there were their boots in his side and back, but strangely he was more conscious of his own voice shouting than he was of any pain. In fact, what seemed to hurt most was the wrist he had twisted with the one futile punch he had thrown. He tried to get up once, but they kicked him down again, so that he rolled off the pavement and under the car, grazing the side of his face as he did so. And that was where they left him as they walked off along the street like two men out for a stroll on a Sunday afternoon, not once looking back.

They hadn't even bothered to loosen their truncheons.

After a while Joe crawled out and into the car. He started to drive, pain coming at him from all sides. Twice he had to stop, on the verge of passing out; and when he did get back finally, he sat slumped in the garage for what must have been half an hour before he could find the courage to move.

Mei was asleep, cool, naked, her arms flung out on either side of her. As he saw her, he thought, Now it doesn't matter what happens, and then he collapsed on the bed.

She wakened with a start, conscious immediately, asking questions. "What's the matter, Joe, my love?" Over and over again. She undressed him, but there were hardly any marks on his body that might explain his nightmare: a graze along the side of his face, a swollen wrist, some bruises that hadn't darkened yet. And he didn't want to talk; all he could think of doing was to lie there in the deep darkness, burying himself beside her.

As he was sliding into sleep, she suddenly sat up. "I almost forgot. Donald phoned twice. He sounded incredibly upset—you know, sobbing and angry at the same time? I've never heard him like that before. I couldn't really make out what he was saying. Something to do with a dog. Anyway, I think he said it had been poisoned, and then he said, 'They're a lot of bastards!' And I said, 'Who?' and he put the phone down."

Part 5

17

There is one dream that is final.

It has no meaning. It's a part of nothing. It isn't even a dream.

When I was eight years old or thereabouts, it was the most powerful presence in my life. For what seemed like forever, I lived in its shadow. Everything that gave me pleasure—singing, collecting tadpoles, leaning over railway bridges to get caught in the smoke —all that took place in the intervals between the dream.

In my grandmother's house—demolished now— there was a stair carpet with a blue-and-brown rectangular pattern on every step. It was just an ordinary carpet, a cheap space-filling design, but on the fifth step from the top that pattern filled me with terror. There was nothing strange about it, no snakes or giants; but every night as she took me up to my bed, I would scream in panic when we came to it because I knew that those brown-and-blue furry rectangular lines would trap me in my own death. Some nights it was so bad she would have to put me to sleep in two big armchairs in front of the kitchen range. To curl up there in the warmth, the ashes falling apart, was a great victory.

But most nights she wheedled me up through the pattern—comforting, mocking, a sweetie, a kiss—and for a moment I would believe I had escaped. But then, in my bedroom, there was the wallpaper, salmon pink and covered with a scallop-shaped design. It was all around me: on the walls and the sloping attic ceiling. And after she had turned out the lamp, after I had spun out the ritual of saying good night and her footsteps had retreated down into the light, I would lie there as the design started to move. It expanded like a lung, pressing against my ribs until, with sleep, it spread right through me, over everything.

There was no explaining it. My grandmother could never come close to understanding, and it worried her more than anything else in all those years she cared for me. There were no words for it; perhaps that was what was most frightening. Though I have to smile as I try to describe it, I find the terror still there in this strain in my forearms.

For fifteen years I had forgotten it. Till last night, when I went to sleep. All day a tense frustration had been growing inside me. I knew that everything I had written was becoming a lie. That meeting with Donald Winn, the quarrel over Yim Bun, those interviews—the events had taken place just as I described them, yet they were all false. I had tried to bury the one memory that could make them true, constructing a fiction that would take me around it. Everything I had done all winter—all those tricks to keep me apart from my ac-

tions—everything had been building up to this lie.
Gray drifts of words.

I went uneasily to sleep. And as the light faded,
I began to dream of the scallop design spreading
through me again. It was a part of my body, its im-
print on every cell, vibrating out of my glands. There
was no skin now, no limit to myself. All around this
pulse I had become, whichever way I twisted to try
to ignore it, was the blue-and-brown rectangle of my
death. I could smell its dust in my nostrils again.

I wakened in a fright. But it wasn't a dream—
that was the most terrifying part of all —because as I
lay with the light on now, those patterns of my childhood were radiating out from me like a halo.

18

The film has become jammed. It is burning now. It crinkles, crackles, turns yellow, brown. The picture fades, flares for a moment.

A car far below me, a toy car, turning. Let it stop there.

A shiny blue Volkswagen. Its engine stutters in too high a gear for the tight corner. The driver changes down.

The light bounces off its roof and flashes on the concrete slope above the road.

Joe's fingernails scrape on the concrete railing. Let it be him.

Tai-sun hands me the binoculars. "Here he comes. It's Yim Bun. He's on his own." He runs towards the Opel he stole just this morning.

"We shall give them the biggest fright of their lives," Jordan said.

Put all the blame on Jordan.

I don't even feel the need to deny it now. I'm afraid, and the excitement grows in me. The car is burning again, the man, the smell of flesh, and I don't have to sit and squabble with the memory of Donald Winn any longer.

As Tai-sun ran to the car, Jordan put his hand on Joe's arm. His voice was trembling, "This is it, Joseph. This is what we have to do. I can feel it, here, in my veins."

His whole body was shaking. He couldn't keep it still. His flushed face rocked on his shoulders. There on the edge of that steep, burning road I wanted for a moment to put my arms around him, to hold him and tell him, "Yes, yes, it's all right, Jordan." I looked into his eyes, and I could see the pleading in them; pleading with himself.

"This will be the turning-point," he had said. "Kwan has lost the initiative. All he does is respond to what's done to him. Well, we've got to break away from that. Take control for ourselves. After this, there'll be no going back, Joseph, no going back."

And if Joe, caught up in his own euphoria, hadn't listened, hadn't agreed, they would never have been there waiting for the car.

Tai-sun was beside him with the guns.

As Joe looks down on the top of the car, its sun-roof open, a man's head in the gap, he feels the heat burn into the back of his neck and wipes the sweat out of his eyes.

"Are you sure it's him?" he asks.

He tries to focus the binoculars on the man's skull,

a glimpse of thin hair, glasses; but his fingers twist too far, and the picture blurs. The car goes out of sight behind an outcrop of rock, and he finds his eyes tracing the veins in granite.

"Of course he's sure, Joseph. He's been watching for days," Jordan says irritably; nervous, too.

To their right, the car appears again, jerking at the corner.

"He's a lousy driver," says Tai-sun.

How long does all this last? Two, three seconds. But there's time to be conscious of every variation, every reflex.

"Yes, that's him, all right," I say decisively. "I can see him clearly now."

I remember Yim Bun as he was at the press party less than a month ago, a tiny man with a monstrous ego. I stood on the edges of the group, listening to the effeminate voice that broadcast every day to millions of people about the evil of Communism. He was at it still. "Most of the time it's hard to think of them even as human beings," he was saying. "They're the dregs of our race, a shame to us, people who wouldn't have been tolerated in the old days in China. The Hong Kong government's too soft on them. That's the trouble with the British; they treat their enemies the way they treat their animals: as if they were rational human beings. Well, maybe that works all right with pet dogs, but it's no good with the Communists. They're not rational; they're not even human. What we need, you know, is a petition to the governor to introduce the death penalty for the ringleaders. Round them up, and shoot the lot of them, that's what Chiang Kai-shek would have done."

So he went on, just like this, day after day on the radio, the soft, fragile voice spewing out the message. I watched him then as I watch him again on the dazzling road—the thin wrists and hollow chest, eyes distant behind thick glasses, the head too large for the tiny body to hold—and I wondered what could have happened in him, in his past, to fill him with this obsessive hatred.

"I knew him a little in Shanghai," Kwan had told me. "In all that chaos just after the Japanese left, you met a lot of strange people. I'd been sent there to organize the resistance groups into leftist cells, and Yim used to hang around the fringes pretending to support us. His father was a tailor, a bad tailor. He had always been poor until he picked up a fortune making uniforms for the Japanese. I suppose they didn't care. Anyway, we didn't trust the son, either, of course; we knew he'd sell us out to Chiang Kai-shek for a bowl of rice. We made it pretty humiliating for him in the end."

"Yes, and look at what it did for Chiang Kai-shek," I said loudly. The heads of Yim's cronies swiveled towards me.

His eyes took me in but didn't look at me. He had been talking English, but now he said in Chinese, "My friends, there's only one species worse than a Chinese Communist, and that's an Englishman who joins them just for the chance of going to bed with one of their young whores." They laughed obsequiously at his great wit, but it was so silly and wide of the mark that it didn't reach me, didn't bother me at all at the time. But I remembered it later; coldly, I told myself, not with malice.

And he remembers it now as he watches the car and says, "Yes, that's him, all right. I can see him clearly now." It's there in him as he feels the surge in his blood, the excitement, the superiority. This'll show the little bastard!

But: "It mustn't be something personal," he had protested to Jordan. "We must use him as an example."

As they look down directly in front of them, they see Chang Chi running out into the road from a pile of rocks as the car passes. He is dragging a Road Closed sign behind him. They've already placed another sign farther up the hill. Everything as it was planned. Jordan says impatiently, "Get your mask on now, Joseph," and Joe feels Tai-sun watching him, wondering, Is he going to be all right?

I tug the black cloth hood from my pocket and pull it over my head, blinking in the darkness, smoothing it down to get the eye slits in place. A stab of light; I blink again.

Then I run to the car; one foot on the accelerator, holding it in gear with the other on the clutch, waiting for the Volkswagen to take shape in the mirror.

Why was I there? I don't even know the answer to a simple question like that. Was it, in the end, nothing but the memory of Yim Bun's insult? Revenge?

No, even at the limit of his self-disgust he couldn't say that. But it wasn't impersonal, either. In the Spanish civil war the anarchists in Barcelona took their capitalist victims up onto the cliffs to see the dawn—a dawn that, not being workers, they would never have seen before—and executed them there, facing the sun. That wasn't impersonal, and neither was this. He knew the man who was coming up behind him, and he despised him not just for his ideas but for himself, his body, his voice, his thin wrists, the way he drove a car.

Perhaps that disdain was even more intense than any hatred would have been. Tai-sun hated him; so did Chang Chi; they hated him thoroughly and objectively. And Jordan? I don't think Jordan had even considered Yim as a person; he had no emotional response to him at all; Yim was merely a trifling object caught in the purity of Jordan's pride.

So which of the four was it who was going to kill him?

None of them, of course. They weren't killers. "We shall give them the biggest fright of their lives," Jordan had said. They knew what they were going to do; it was all planned, rationalized; nobody was going to get hurt; that was the beauty of it.

In the mirror the Volkswagen rose from the concrete of the road, flashing sunlight into my eyes.

The Seventh Hexagram

"Who else could it have been?" asked Donald Winn. "The fucking pixies?"

It started with Jordan. Put all the blame on him. No, it started in each of them separately.

But it was Jordan who brought us together, who made the connection.

As I came into the hallway, I looked around automatically for Evelyne, but there was no sign of her.

"Joseph, come along into the study." Jordan took me by the arm. "We won't be disturbed there," he said, though the house seemed to be empty.

A glass of whisky. "Have you any idea why I called you up here?"

I shook my head. I was watching him closely to try and see what had happened to him since we had been together last. It was more than two months, and he had been ill, forced by the doctors to rest for most of that time, but there was hardly any evidence of that in him now. He looked stronger, fitter, so much more in control of himself. There was still a nervous tremor in his right arm, which he tried to hold with his left hand, but his voice had its old depth, and his eyes didn't flit about; they held me steadily, severely.

"What do you think of your friend Kwan now?"

"I haven't changed my mind, Jordan, if that's what you mean." There was assurance in Joe's voice, but beneath it he knew the last two months had changed everything. The days were slipping away from Kwan; in June he had had power just beyond his fingertips—a final push and he could have held it in his grasp—but now it was eluding him in a widening arc. All the work, all the commitment that he could expend weren't enough to find the initiative again. Joe had sensed it, but he hadn't yet been able to admit it to himself.

In any case, Jordan was impervious to anything he heard in Joe's voice. He pressed on. "Good God, you can't still believe you made the right choice, Joseph. You've got to face up to that. The whole movement's collapsing."

"All I can see at the moment," Joe said dully, "is that things are going to take us a lot longer than we thought they would at the beginning."

"That's just typical of you people, you intellectuals, you and Kwan and all the rest of you. You use the future as a refuge. You just didn't know what you wanted from the very beginning, did you? Be honest with me, Joseph; I'm being honest with you. You didn't know what you wanted. Or how to get it. A nice easy victory over a second-rate colonial power, that was all, wasn't it? But it didn't work out like that. Oh, no, right from the start you let them do what they wanted to do. You didn't have any plan for building up the pressure on them. That's what you needed; a number of specific areas you could concentrate on until they crumbled. But no, you took everything as it came and never followed even one thing through to its conclusion. Look at the strikes; you never even made up your mind whether you wanted them to be successful or not. Whether they were to be symbolic, token stoppages, or really to cripple the economy."

He looked at Joe triumphantly, expecting a rebuttal that he would have demolished with ease. But Joe was silent, drained; and suddenly Jordan was conscious of another man, of how deep his thrust must have gone. His voice became more kind. "Believe me, Joseph, people will never follow you if you can't make up your mind. Oh, some will, maybe"—he waved them aside with his hand—"the faithful. They'll follow you down, drown with you. But not your chap in the middle who can't make up his own mind either. He wants somebody to do it for him."

And, yes, I listened. Just a week before, even, the triumph, the glee in his voice would have repelled me. But now again I felt the strength in him, as I had the winter before. I felt the strength, and I sensed the need for it in myself. I knew that the communal euphoria was waning, that when I talked of a long-drawn-out struggle, I was preparing my ground for an ultimate defeat. And so his words seemed to hint at possibilities that until then I would have dismissed as romantic.

"That's why I wanted to see you, Joseph. I know what you've got in you. I know what we can do together." His eyes flared with the madness Joe had seen in them in this same room the first night they met. Yet it didn't repel or puzzle him; it tempted. "This will be the turning point." Jordan took Joe's hands in his; a hard, bony dryness around them. "Kwan has lost the initiative. All he does is respond to what's done to him. Well, we've got to break away from that. Take control for ourselves. After this, there'll be no going back, Joseph, no going back."

I almost missed him, almost let him through.

The car jumped as I let out the unfamiliar clutch —once, twice, a hiccup—my God, it's going to stall. I revved the accelerator furiously, and finally it was in gear, surging forwards, out into the path of the Volkswagen. As his front bumper came level with me, I looked round at Yim just six feet away, his face so close I saw the expression change as he caught sight of the black hood; change in an instant from surprise to fear. The delicate features broke up; I think he shouted. Then he tried to accelerate past me, but it was too late; I was waiting for that and went with him, letting the cars scrape together, mine always angled across in front of his. Inexorably I hooked the steering wheel down towards him, hearing the rasp of metal. He pulled on his wheel, too, trying to turn it away, then threw up his hands in horror as he saw the cliff face rush at him.

The front of the car buckled as he hit the rock at nearly thirty, and I watched over my shoulder as his body smashed forwards, ramming his face through the shattering windscreen.

Joe braked twenty yards farther up on the wrong side of the road. His door was jammed from the impact, and he jumped out on the passenger side. Jordan and Tai-sun were running across the road to the wreckage, guns waving in their hands.

I watch his face as we bump, coyly at first, then join and tear at each other. And he throws his hands into the air, not even trying anymore to escape me; throws his hands in the air as if uncontrol will save him. How I despise him; how he adds to the power in me!

I want to rub it in as I rush back down the road to where Tai-sun is trying to prize his fingers off the steering wheel.

There was a long pause as he went on holding my hands, his face relaxing.

"How are you going to manage that, Jordan?" I asked.

"What? Manage what, Joseph?" His eyes glazed over.

"Well, you know. What you were just saying," I tried to explain, puzzled and slightly afraid for him, "about . . . well, taking control?"

"Yes. Yes, of course." He pulled himself out of the unconsciousness he had been slipping into. "So you want to come in with us, do you? This is your chance to redeem yourself, Joseph; you realize that? To redeem yourself." He enjoyed the savor of the phrase, then looked at Joe sharply. "But there mustn't be a hint of it to anyone; you must give me your word on that."

"Heavens, yes," Joe said lightly, laughing at the mystery, "that's easy enough."

He was about to rebuke me, I think, but stood up instead. "Come along, then, Joseph. There's somebody I want you to meet."

Jordan took me out into the corridor and back along it to that room I had entered by mistake the first night I had come up here. He fumbled in his pocket for a key and bent to unlock the door.

"He won't let go of the steering wheel," Tai-sun grumbled softly.

"Then smash his knuckles with the gun, dammit," Jordan said.

Yim let go straight away and started to shout.

Tai-sun hit him in the face. "Get out of the car and shut up, and you'll be all right."

Look at them as they sit there plotting: Jordan King's declining glamor, Joe Stewart looking for a chance to prove himself, Chen Tai-sun. . . .

"This is Chen Tai-sun," said Jordan. "He's been staying here while the police are looking for him."

The man who got up from the bed must have been in his forties, and the face looked it—lined, eyes bloodshot, unshaven, but the body was lithe and more obviously muscular than in most Cantonese. The hand Joe shook was hard. He felt himself being watched closely as he crossed over to a stool.

Joe had heard his name before; whenever there was talk of terrorism, it was mentioned. Chen Tai-sun had been one of the most active anti-Japanese resistance leaders, a young farmer's son, ranging over the whole area between Canton and Hong Kong with his own tightly knit group of two or three hundred men, throwing the Japanese supply system into disorder. At the end of the war he was a local hero, but he hadn't tried to profit from it politically or financially; he had never settled into the socialist hierarchies. Instead he had left his own people and had gone to live in Macao, working for the casino owners, the smugglers of gold and refugees, the triad gangs, anyone who would pay him. There were still men on the Left who remembered him, who would raise his name whenever there were proposals for bombs or assassinations, but Kwan always resisted. "We can't rely on unreliable elements," he would say, "it's as simple as that."

Chen Tai-sun. My eyes keep on coming back to him. Jordan does most of the talking, and the change that has taken place in him still impresses me; but in Tai-sun there's a force which goes beyond that, perhaps even explains it. It isn't in his face; when I look there, I know what Kwan must have meant: it contains all those years of working for gangsters and cheats. But in his body there's a muscular relaxation, an easy preparedness, that's full of confidence. Perhaps, I find myself thinking, it's his redemption that Jordan's talking about, too.

"There's only one thing that can save us now, Joseph: force, violence. There's no such thing as a peaceful revolution; the violence of the system will always win if we don't oppose it with a greater, more controlled violence. That's the problem now with Kwan. At last he's recognized the need for force, but he doesn't want to get his fingers dirty with it. So he lets it run away from him. All these bombs, they're just scaring off the people we need on our side. That's all they're doing. What we've got to do is find a means of establishing our own control over a situation where violence is unavoidable."

"That's all right, Jordan; I'll go along with that," said Joe. "It's fine in theory. But it's just a theory. It's still just talk."

"No, Joseph, that's where you're wrong." He was full of excitement now, almost laughing with enjoyment. "We have a plan, fully developed, ready to go into effect at once. It's in two stages." He sketched them in the air with his hands. "First, we must silence the leaders of the Chinese community who've been publicly supporting the British. That's our main problem; we have to silence them without harming them. If we kill them, say, or torture them, we'll lose all the people who are lined up behind them." He looked at Tai-sun as if this was an argument they had been over already. "We need them to be present, public, but silent. How are we going to do that? We must frighten them into silence without touching them, without harming them. We must show them what will happen if they are not silent."

"Fine, Jordan, fine. But how do you manage that?"

"We take a man out of his house and blow it up in front of him; we take him out of his car and burn it; we take him out of his lift in his office block and let him watch it fall twenty floors to the ground." He spoke with great sureness now. "We force him to see his own death if he is not silent. All right?"

Joe nodded.

"And once that is done, we have the second stage, which is much easier, no problems there at all. Once we've silenced all the opposition in the Chinese community, we drive out the British authorities. Quite simple. Get a dozen of their top men—snipers, bombs, it doesn't matter how—and the rest'll be on the first plane home; the women'll see to that."

He sat back and looked at me. "That's all it will take, Joseph. It's up to you now. Are you with us?"

Jordan is looking at me, and I know that this isn't just words any longer; I know he is right. This is the only way. But the way to what? I take a deep breath. "Well . . . I'll need time to think about it, Jordan."

He stands above me, bent, threatening, with the naked light bulb behind his tin white curls. "That's not good enough, Joseph. This isn't a time for thought any longer. There's been too much thinking. What we need now is action."

But Tai-sun breaks in on him, quietly, looking into me, talking to Jordan in a Chiuchow accent I don't understand. Then Jordan turns to me again. "He says he doesn't want you in, Joseph; he doesn't trust the British, anybody British. But I want you; I've made that clear, and it's my decision because I'm in control. I'm asking you because I need you with me. Will you come in with us, Joseph?"

And now I have no choice.

I stood and watched.
I stood and watched.
I stood and watched.

Chang Chi ran up the steep road, the sun blinding him. He had to pause to catch his breath, the sweat prickling in his eyes. Damn them. By the time he got up there, it would all be over. The next time he'd make sure he didn't get stuck with some job like this.

. He ran up round the bend where the road flattened out a little, and there in front of him he saw Chen Tai-sun getting the cans of petrol out of the back of the car. He slowed down and sighed with relief. He hadn't missed it.

"So, who do we start with?" Joe asked, all businesslike now that his decision was made.

"Well," Jordan counted them off on his fingers, "there's Lo Hong-lit, the Executive Council member; he'd be an obvious choice. And Auyeung—you know?—the boss of South China Textiles. Or Yim Bun" (my spine shivered at the name), "that little snake on the radio. Or Yu Tsai-ching, the newspaper owner? Any one of them would be good to start with."

"Yim Bun," Joe said softly.

"He's too easy," said Tai-sun. "He's not guarded or anything. We ought to begin with one of them who is because once we've dealt with a couple of them, the others are bound to be more difficult; they'll be in hiding, and there'll be guards everywhere."

"Yes, but Yim would make the biggest impact of all right at the beginning," Joe argued, keeping his eyes on Jordan. "Everybody's listening to him right now, just sucking up his venom—right, Jordan? Millions of people. But just think of what it would be like if he suddenly stopped, from one day to the next, if he went back to attacking the break-down of the family or the dangers of gambling. The effect of it would be fantastic."

"That's true enough," said Jordan. "We'll start with Yim Bun."

"But we'll need more people," Joe went on, still trying to prove himself.

"Of course, Joseph, of course. We haven't been doing nothing, you know. That's all taken care of, isn't it?" He smiled at Tai-sun. "We've got this student from Chung Wah; his name's—what is it? Chang Chi? —anyway, he's very committed, very angry with Kwan, thinks he's a traitor, and he has friends who feel the same way that he can bring in if we need them. And Tai-sun has got a couple of marksmen when we come to that phase of the operation. It's all worked out already, Joseph."

Then Tai-sun, who had shown no response earlier when Jordan had sided with Joe, said quietly, in Cantonese this time, "I still don't think either of you ought to be there."

Jordan turned on him furiously. "I've told you already, Chen, there's no question of that, no question. We've *got* to be there. Both of us."

"But you're too conspicuous."

"Then we'll wear masks. In any case, what will it matter in a month's time? What difference will it make then? Tell me that," he asked scornfully. "There won't be any need for us to hide ourselves then. We've got to be there because it has to be absolutely clear exactly what we're doing. And why. We mustn't be written off as—as vandals, you know. I shall talk to all of them personally. As leader of this group, that's my responsibility. We've got to be clear about that from the very beginning."

Why did Jordan want me with him?

There's a question that might be small enough for me to answer.

Not because he needed Joe, certainly (though that's what he tried to pretend). What use would Joe's inexperience have been in the burning of cars, the dynamiting of houses? It might have appealed to Jordan's own romantic image of himself—was intended to—but there was no reason behind it.

So why, then? As a way of getting back at Kwan? Yes, that must have been it. Jordan's way of proving his victory over Kwan, a way of rubbing it in. As Kwan, ascendant, had taken Joe away from him, he would do the same. Tit for tat, was I nothing more than that?

So here he is, Yim Bun, standing, swaying, in the middle of the road.

Joe held one of his arms loosely; there was no need to do more. He was limp, and Joe held on just to keep him from falling. A small piece of glass was sticking into the corner of his eye, and the blood ran down his cheek. He raised his other hand, not to wipe the blood away, but to feel the edges of the glass.

"Do you think I ought to take it out?" he asked, his voice bewildered and unemphatic.

Nobody answered him.

Tai-sun came down from the car with a can of petrol in either hand, just as Chang Chi ran up to them panting. "What can I do?" he asked. Tai-sun gave him a can of petrol, and they began to sprinkle it over the car seats and the floor.

Jordan stood on his own, a little apart, his head thrown back, a hooded hawk.

As I hold Yim Bun's thin wrist, I feel the pulse beneath my fingers. It's so open to me I could pinch the vein beneath my nails, snap the bone across my knee. But I don't feel dislike or aggression any longer. Just curiosity. What is there underneath this bouncing pulse? A purely anonymous drive? No, surely not. I remember Kwan's words: "We made it pretty humiliating for him in the end." I want to know more about that. What kind of humiliation? His homosexuality? Something to do with that. A young boy betrayed him openly, with laughter? I look into his face, and it has changed, set, composed itself. I've heard of the pain he puts his lovers through.

"Are we ready?" Jordan asked, his head not turning.

"Might as well," said Tai-sun, "but you'd better stand back a bit."

They moved, and Jordan positioned himself directly in front of Yim. He started to speak, the words muffled slightly by the hood. "Yim Bun, you are a traitor: to your country, to your people. The punishment for treachery is death. But we are not vicious as you are; we don't cling to punishment as an end in itself as you do. We want all our compatriots, however misguided, to have a chance to change their ways. We're not so idealistic as to believe that reason will change the mind of a man as steeped in treachery as you are. But fear will. You're a coward, like all of your kind. Jackals. You fear for yourselves. And what we are going to show you now is what will happen to you if you say so much as one more word against your country and your people."

Jordan paused, breathing rapidly, as Tai-sun struck a match. With his head turned away, he threw the match in through the door of the car, and immediately they felt the blast on their faces, saw the flames rise, yellow and purple, and a great billowing cloud of black smoke.

"Come on, let's get out of here," said Tai-sun.

But Jordan went on talking, his voice rising rhetorically, cracking around the edges. "That is what will happen to traitors who don't listen to our warning, Yim Bun. You have been a traitor all your life, but now you will stay silent if you want to remain alive."

And it's my fault. I feel the arm stiffen under my fingers, and I don't do anything about it. The wrist is so pitifully small, harmless. But as I feel that smallness and pity it, he wrenches himself away and throws himself at Jordan, shrieking, "I know you. Who are you to talk about traitors?" Jordan is staring right over him, carried away by his own words, and doesn't see him coming. Yim jumps up on him, one hand reaching for the hood, and pulls it away. "I knew it was you, Jordan King, I knew it was your voice," he shouts, dancing for joy. "But it's you who're the traitor. You're not even Chinese. The police will get you and your French whore; you'll rot in jail, the pair of you."

And Jordan steps back a pace, blinking in the sun.

I don't dream about it, but still, most mornings, it's the first thing that enters my consciousness when I waken. Much of the time it is with me. Yim Bun doesn't haunt me at feasts, but there's his presence around me that time doesn't wipe away.

Joe tried to put it out of his mind. In the weeks immediately after, he did all he could to anaesthetize the memory. But there were private moments of sudden, sweating fear. Sitting at a table eating, lying next to Mei, the normality was paralyzed all at once by a surge of panic he could scarcely contain. There was no cause for it, no predictability. True, it spawned more precise fears in him—of being found out; Kwan, Winn, they must know, must just be playing with him —but those were only symptoms, not the cause. The roots of the panic lay in the instant itself: not fear *of* something, not fear *for* himself, but simply fear: a man struggles to shake the flames like drops of water from his hands.

These moments expand with time; there are days they seem to fill.

Is it guilt that holds them in me? I remember Kwan saying, "The trouble with you Europeans is you've weighed yourselves down with such a burden of metaphysical guilt and sin. There's no way you can free yourselves from it; you don't know what it is to act freely any longer." But no, though I agreed with him and still do, I can't really place anything I would call guilt in my responses. I don't regret Yim's death; I don't feel sorry for him; I'm not afraid of being punished. It's not guilt I feel; it's the horror: the flames grow out of his hands.

I stood and watched.

Jordan stands dazed on the pavement, his eyes blinking, trying to see.

The car is ablaze. The heat burns our faces. A tire bursts like a gunshot.

"We've got to get out of here," says Tai-sun. He

starts to run off up the road but stops when nobody follows him.

Jordan can see now. He can see the little man standing in front of him, blood soaking the white shirt, the look of triumph on the impertinent face.

When Jordan moves, he moves with great speed, pouncing on Yim, one hand clawlike on the scruff of his neck. "How dare you call me a traitor!" he screams, forcing the head down till it touches the ground between his feet. His free hand snatches the can of petrol from Chang Chi and pours it over Yim's back.

We do nothing. We stand and watch as if it isn't really happening.

Yim is whimpering now, pleading incoherently as Jordan drags him towards the car. Still I do nothing. Jordan is full of strength; with one hand he lifts Yim to his feet and pitches him like a sack of rubbish into the center of the flames. And now, when it's too late, when I know it's too late, I run towards them. "No, Jordan," I shout, "no." But the fire's too hot to do anything. As I reach towards Yim, he bursts out past me screaming, and the flames that leap from his clothes scorch my hair and my eyelashes.

"Leave him, Joseph." Jordan holds me by the shoulder, his voice strained, breaking. "Chen was right. This is the only way to deal with these people." As I turn away, I notice the smile on Tai-sun's face.

Yim trips at the curb and flops down on the pavement. I have never heard anyone screaming before—girls in a tantrum, a woman outside the pub in the village—but never anything like this long-drawn-out wailing. I smell him burning; a sweet smell, appetizing. His clothes have gone, black ribbons round his neck; and it's his body, his flesh, that is on fire now. The flames spurt from his arms, and he tries to brush them away, beat them out with his hands; but his hands are on fire, too. The flesh is melting. As I watch, his face runs, coagulates; his nose changes shape; blisters puff up and burst and hiss. I watch; I watch; the skin crackles.

Far off in the distance there's the sound of a police siren. It may be nothing to do with us, but as soon as Jordan hears it, he turns and runs off down the road, away from the car. I go after him, seeing him ahead of me, his long arms and legs jerking high in the air, a lanky schoolboy. I pull off my hood and throw it down. "Come back, Jordan," I shout, and he turns to peer at me, not recognizing who I am. He stumbles backwards, then heads for the rocks at the side of the road and starts to climb up over them. I grab him by the legs and try to pull him back, but he swings round and beats me over the head with his fists.

"Let me go. I order you to let me go. I'm in control here."

But now there's Tai-sun, calm at the back of them. He hands Joe his hood. "Don't leave this behind," he says, then reaches up for Jordan. "I'll look after him."

As they go slowly back, they pass Yim at the side of the road. There are fewer flames from him now; just a black, charring heap with a strange high-pitched growling noise emerging from it. Tai-sun is carrying Jordan in his arms, and Jordan is crying.

19

His life wandered on from there. Simpler. Without direction. There was no real struggle left in it, though he didn't realize that at the time. From then until Christmas the life that he lived was another person's, impenetrable by any self.

For months the energy that had built up in him, making him feel more alive than he had ever been before, had derived from a wider political context, a sense of community, commitment. But then, after the death of Yim Bun, that force deserted him, was spent; and he was left with only the habit of political action, mere gesture. There was no involvement any longer, no euphoria to catch him up and project him into the future.

Jordan was taken home to be mothered, nursed, by a woman thirty years younger. He wouldn't even come to the phone. Chen Tai-sun vanished, and Chang Chi lost himself in the slums. Joe carried on almost, it seemed, as before; but there was nothing, no force inside him, apart perhaps from flashes of panic. He went on working for Kwan, writing, but there was no real meaning in it for him anymore, and often he was paralyzed by an overwhelming sense of dullness, an apathy that nailed him willingly to his bed.

It puzzled Kwan, but the dullness was all around them, and in him, too. For all of them now, their work seemed to be generated out of habit, a track they could see no end to. Kwan himself, the gentlest and most rational of men, found himself refining the techniques of violence, not out of any justifying fire or anger, but simply, belatedly, from the need to keep his movement going. There was nothing else to do. They talked increasingly of the long struggle they were involved in, but the struggle itself was only a gesture. It had failed, they knew it had failed, and they carried it on from fear of inertia. The revolution, which had been born in anger and the rejection of injustice, petered out in boredom and sour frustration.

The martyrs still festered in the prisons: men were beaten, women embroidered handkerchiefs with the thoughts of Chairman Mao. But when they were released, they came home to families that were weakened by hunger, friends who were silently going back to work.

Life went on, diminished. Imperceptibly, summer had disguised itself as autumn, but nothing really changed. The air became drier, cooler, but there was none of the sense of season that he found a year later. No walking down over crunching leaves to fetch water from the lake; no standing on the dock, watching each day as the sun cut out a smaller and smaller segment of sky; no chipmunks or grey squirrels darting like furry shadows across a yellow slope; no lying awake in the night as leaves rattled down on the roof like a shower of rain. No sense of the naturalness in dying, anticipating spring. Just the vague bitterness and dissatisfaction, odd moments of clarity that couldn't be held onto, a gradual putrefaction.

He took refuge from it all, from his part in it all, in Mei. Long ago—four months, six months before it had all started—he had been close enough to her for a few days to think that he loved her. He remembered it remotely. And then he had put her aside for something that must have seemed greater, more meaningful. Meaningful? What did it mean then? Nothing to him now.

Now he came back to her, to resuscitate the past; spent whole days with her again, hours just watching, feeling her body. But it was all so different; this at least had changed, though neither knew how or why. There was so little of the old tenderness between them now, so little of the gentleness he had found, through her, in himself; so little satisfaction, though he fucked her to exhaustion.

When he held her, it was no longer with that constant surprise he had once felt at the variety of her presence. He was no longer afraid of smashing a fragile uniqueness. In a sense, he was closer to her, but a different closeness altogether, his fingers running over her till she screamed for every pore to be penetrated. He wanted to pin her down rather than protect her. Through her, he touched the impersonality of flesh: looking down he saw his body joined to hers; but what were they, these straining bodies, whose were they? What were they made of? He felt the muscles, the blood, the bone, skin; but how did they come together, these parts, into anything knowable? He thrust two fingers up into her, feeling the warmth, the moisture around him, not resting with that, exploring, the insides of the pelvis, veins, tissue stretching. He tried to push farther, his fingers too short, withdrew, his whole fist, a baby's head, holding her legs apart, she groaned, he was all hands, another finger in her arse as she screamed a little, writhed, he held her all in his touch, thrust, pinched. What was it? Mei? The center of her? Hands full of flesh.

When he came in her at last, he had to start again.

And Mei? What did she feel? How could he know, since he sought to annihilate her? But she was tied to him more tightly now. Not closer—that was the wrong word—tighter, more dependent. She hated the pain put upon her, needing it more each day.

As for closeness, the awareness of each other, feeling for the other, they came closest not in sex but in a sense of loss, in moods of sadness.

There's another memory, less exciting to his loneliness perhaps, but warmer, more human.

A Sunday, and the day before it had rained in torrents, leaving low, dense clouds that still clung halfway up the hills. The thick-skinned leaves were heavy with water, and all along the path drops splashed onto them from the overhanging branches. White flowers lay like sodden, crushed-up paper balls beneath trees that two days before had been covered with blossom.

All day, till it was nearly evening, they had wandered restlessly about the flat, irritable and apologetic by turns, not knowing what they wanted and trying not to show it.

"Oh, Joe, if only you'd tell me to do something, for heaven's sake," Mei groaned theatrically. "I ought to be over at the factory, dammit; there's so much to do."

He was lying spread-eagled in a chair. "I know. I should be down at Kwan's. At least I should have phoned. But, fuck it, I can't be bothered." He yawned, and his back ached.

"Well, that's good news, anyway," she said, fiddling with a pile of records.

"It's a bloody sight more important than what you're not doing," he laughed mockingly.

But she didn't want to laugh. She went off into the kitchen, and he could hear her banging about, chopping up vegetables and wishing they were him. But later on she came restlessly back. He tried to shrug her away.

"Oh, come on," she urged him, "let's go for a walk, at least."

So they walked through the limp woods to a small reservoir that nestled in at the foot of the hills. The light was gray; the colors dank. They turned onto a path that led across a low earth dam. On both sides reeds and thick grass grew up above their heads, shutting them in.

Mei clutched at his arm. "Joe, do you remember that story Jordan was telling at Donald's party? You know, the night we met; about the Long March and the Grasslands or whatever it was? Do you think it was like this? God, it must have been awful, claustrophobic."

Jordan: how long was it since he had even thought of Jordan? He hadn't seen him since that afternoon when Tai-sun had carried him whimpering out of the car and left him with the puzzled servants on the doorstep. It had never happened. Like a dream before waking.

"I wonder how Jordan is," Joe found his dull voice saying. "Kwan hasn't heard from him for ages."

"Oh, I met his wife in the town the other day. I forgot to tell you." (Had she? He had told her all about Evelyne.) "She was saying Jordan has to stay in bed now all the time, and he forces her to stay there with him. She only manages to get out when he falls asleep. Poor Evelyne, she seemed pretty desperate." Mei tried to bring Joe closer, her fingers laced in his. "I felt a bit sorry for her, actually. She didn't seem nearly as cold as I used to think she was."

Around them the air was full of the croaking of frogs, everywhere and nowhere; echoes and responses. He didn't want to think of Jordan. He pushed into the grass to see the bullfrog, sure that he knew where it was. But it wasn't there. Off to his right he heard a plop in the black water.

Back on the path there were the snails. The rain

had brought them out into the open, hundreds of them, thousands, crawling on the damp earth with slimy, wandering trails behind them. He picked his way carefully, repelled at the thought of crushing them.

Mei stopped and bent down, peering at the horned head that jutted out of one of the shells. "They're really rather proud-looking, aren't they?" She tilted her own head over on one side. "Imagine it, sixty feet high. How fantastic it would be!"

Joe wasn't listening. His thoughts were with Jordan and Evelyne. Not his feelings; he felt nothing, and in a way that was what he was thinking about—how distant they seemed, how separate from him. Their image in the back of his mind had remained the same as it had been when he was first drawn into their circle—strong, arrogant, glamorous—and to think of Jordan as a petulant child in bed, Evelyne dancing attendance on him, made him want to pity them both; their frustration, their humiliation. But it was an abstract sensation, more the result of the day, the heaviness of the air, than of any emotion. He knew it was not enough, an inadequate response to the strength of feelings that he had once had for them, or they (though he found it hard now even to imagine what it was they might have felt) for him.

"Do you think they ever come out of their shells completely?" Mei asked. She was lying on her side now on the muddy path, her head as close as possible to the snail.

"I've no idea."

"And if they do, can they ever get back inside again?"

Joe leaned down with the stick he was carrying and tapped the snail softly on the top of its shell. Its head drew back in, not jerkily, in panic, nor as slowly as he had expected from seeing them move, but smoothly, like a well-oiled piece of machinery, and with dignity. It was beautiful yet, as a form of self-defense, absurd.

Mei giggled. He bent to do it again, but she

278

pushed his arm away. "No, please?" She stood up beside him. "It's terrible, isn't it? They drag that bloody stupid shell along with them wherever they go, thinking it's going to protect them. And, of course, it's no use at all. By the time they find that out, it's too late."

"Too late for what?" he asked, touched and at the same time laughing at her symbols.

"Well . . . too late for everything," she shrugged, cheerful again. She bent down, her lips forming a kiss. "You stupid bloody snail!"

He put his arm around her shoulders as they walked back, drawing her to him, closer in unfulfilment than in any kind of love.

Till Christmas. It dragged along till Christmas. Christmas Eve he finally saw Evelyne again.

He was a bit drunk when he answered the phone because all afternoon he and Mei had been decorating a scraggy pine tree with tinsel and silk balls; a swig of whisky for each one.

Her voice was serious, direct. "Joe? Do you think you could come up this evening?" He remembered he'd spent Christmas with them the year before. Jordan playing Santa Claus for the servant children. Till now it had gone right out of his head. "It's kind of urgent. Jordan's terribly set on seeing you. He's got a present he says he wants to give you. A secret, he says. I don't know what it is."

"Christ, I really should have phoned, shouldn't I? Look, Evelyne, I'm sorry. How is he now? Mei was telling me she'd met you. Is he any better?" The words came out without his thinking what he meant by them; just an instinctive response to the concern in her voice.

"He's . . . surer of himself, so I suppose in a sense he's better. I don't know, though. . . . But you *can* come, Joe, can't you?"

"Well, the thing is, I'm not sure. We were just—" He looked up and saw Mei shaking her head, her lips saying no. Behind her was that tatty little tree they had laughed so much over, the decorations sticking to it like a fungus. "All right, Evelyne, I'll be up soon."

But when he got there, there was no sign of Evelyne, and Jordan seemed surprised and not especially pleased to see him. He was sitting drawn up close to a low fire, the lights dim, wrapped in a big woolen dressing-gown that looked a couple of sizes too large.

"Ah, Joseph. I was just going to bed. But come in." His voice was deeper even than Joe remembered it, but uncertain, reverberating shakily. "Get yourself a drink. You can get me one, too; weakish." He threw some wood on the fire, and it blazed up.

The wood crackled for a few minutes. Joe couldn't think of anything worth saying, but he kept on glancing sideways at Jordan, trying to stir his memory. Yes, he had changed, grown older, older looking than his age, as before he had seemed younger. When Joe had met him, that thin body had seemed loosely jointed, disorganized, but strikingly vital; now it was just broken fragments held together by the dressing-gown. There was no flesh on him at all, apart from his face, which was fatter. The skin was smoother, if anything, than before; but it was the smoothness that sometimes appears in the faces of the very old, a glow that looks as though it could be washed away, leaving nothing underneath.. The hair at the back of his head, which once had flowed down thick and curly, was now much thinner, too, each single hair seeming to have been separately, artificially implanted. The bones underneath protruded like sharp stones.

"There's nothing like a good fire, Joseph."

Joe flinched from the words, staring at him for a sign of irony or horror.

The face showed nothing. Jordan turned. "Well, are you taking it all in? What do you see?" The eyes were fixed, the skin around them forming a blue-grey hollow half an inch deep. But the pupils themselves were frighteningly intense, as if they were going to burst.

Joe smiled inanely.

"No, I want to know. How do I look to you?"

"Better than I expected, Jordan."

"Dammit, don't prevaricate, boy. I used to like your honesty. You don't have to lie now. I look like a skeleton, don't I?"

Joe nodded. His mouth was dry, and he gulped the last of the whisky.

"This is what my wife looked like before she died." Jordan caught the alarm in Joe's eyes. "Natasya, I mean, my first wife. In Leningrad. She was the most beautiful thing I've ever seen, that girl. On the stage of the Kirov. Like a"—he shook his head, seeking the image—"like an electric flower. I used to go around the textile factories trying to scrape way out of the looms so that she could have a little fat to keep her going. But there were thousands of other people doing the same thing, too, and nobody ever got enough to make much of a difference.

"Have you ever been to Leningrad, Joseph? I went back there in sixty-four, just before they kicked out that old fool, Khrushchev. . . . She's buried in a mass grave outside the city. Quite anonymous." He glanced wildly around him. Then his arms twitched, and some of the whisky Joe had poured for him spilled on the arm of the chair and the front of his dressing-gown. He brushed it angrily away. "Damn, damn, damn!"

For a moment Joe thought he was going to break down and half got to his feet. But then a smile broke across Jordan's face, a surprisingly happy, innocent smile.

"I was right, though, wasn't I, Joseph?"

"Sorry . . . what about, Jordan?"

"About Kwan. Kwan. I may be half dead, but I saw through him right from the start. He made a real fuck-up of everything." He pronounced "fuck-up"—so unusual in his mouth—gleefully, proudly.

"Yes, perhaps you were, Jordan. I'm still not sure. But it's not the end yet."

"Oh, yes, it is; that's where you're wrong again. It's the end. For Kwan, anyway." As he said it, he was triumphant; but then, in the silence afterwards, he slumped straight back into his dejection.

Joe couldn't think what to do with him, what to say. He found himself feeling nervous, even afraid, and he wasn't sure why. On one level it was the kind of fear you have for a tiny child's fragility. But there was more than that, too; he was afraid *of* Jordan as well. There had always been this wildness, this unpredictable force lurking beneath the surface manners, but now it had become more naked, stronger than ever, because the body around it had nearly melted away.

Joe wanted to talk, to break through to him. He felt an intense urge to say something about Yim Bun, and yet he didn't dare. He sensed that Jordan wouldn't remember a single thing. So he searched through his mind for something else. Somewhere there was the echo of what Jordan had said about his being honest; it had pleased Joe grotesquely, like a pat on the head from a childhood hero, even though he was conscious of how unjustified it was. And when he spoke again, he was trying deliberately, crudely, to live up to it.

"Look, Jordan, you can't go on sitting here like this forever."

But all he met was self-pity: "There's nothing else I can do. Truly there isn't. Don't think I haven't tried." Jordan seemed to want to cry.

"But what about all those books you said you never had time to write? All those files in your study? You told me you never had the chance to write them down. All those stories. This could be the chance now, couldn't it?" It was meant to be honesty, but it had come out with the pull-yourself-together tone of a scoutmaster.

Jordan saw that clearly enough, at least. He shook his head slowly. "No, you know it can't."

It was just then that Evelyne came in, into the middle of this hopelessness that was the only bond between them now. She too was different from the way Joe had remembered her. He had idealized her sensuality, her self-possession, but now those images were dispelled—by the actuality, of course, but all the more intensely because of the changes that had taken place

282

in her. He had never before been forced to realize just
how old she was. There was much more of the middle-
aged, middle-class housewife about her now, and cruelly his first instinct was shock that such a short time
before he could have allowed himself to be so dependent on her. The sensuality still clung around her like
perfume, but her body had thickened. Legs and thighs
were still fine and muscular, the face still haughty, but
the muscles of her neck seemed strained to hold it there,
and her breasts sagged beneath the cashmere sweater.
Her skirt was creased and very long in comparison
with Mei's.

As soon as Jordan saw her, he tried to draw himself together; bits of ivory on a string. "Ah, yes." He
managed to call on enough strength—hatred—to make
his voice hard and sharp again. "Here's my nurse."

She breathed deeply. "It *is* your bedtime." Then
she looked at Joe for the first time. "What were you
talking about?"

"About Jordan starting to write again, but—"

"But that's just what I've been telling him, Joe."
He had forgotten how musical her voice could be, with
its wide, lilting range. Just a little too wide now, the top
notes too high, nagging. "If only he would do something. That's what the doctor says he needs most. Something to take an interest in."

She went over and sat on the arm of Jordan's
chair, but he drew away from her into the corner, cow-
ering. "I get tired too quickly. Even writing a letter
tires me out for the rest of the day. You know that well
enough, Evelyne."

"Yes, but we could get you a tape recorder to dic-
tate when you feel like it. Joe would help you, wouldn't
you, Joe?"

Joe nodded. He wished he could get away from all
this.

"No," Jordan said, "no, I've got something much
better than that for Joseph." And now in his voice they
could feel he had got a grip on himself. "Much more
appropriate. Give me that box over there."

283

Evelyne brought it back to Jordan without a word. He handed it to Joe—just a cardboard grocery box. It was full of pieces of paper of different sizes and colors, some dirty, some torn, all of them covered with Chinese writing. Character by character he translated the opening line of the top sheet: "The story of how we crossed the mountains of Szechwan by Lee Fongwing."

He looked up questioningly, and Jordan's eyes seemed to be full of mockery. "I collected them at the end of the Long March. Everybody was writing down these records of what they had been through, and I got as many as possible of them to let me have copies."

"But why give them to me, Jordan, for heaven's sake." Joe held them out in front of him anxiously. "I'm not a historian. I wouldn't know what to do with them."

"I don't want you to do anything with them, Joseph," said Jordan, standing up, an emaciated, suddenly playful bird. "They are to learn from. And now"—he turned abruptly to Evelyne—"you may put me to bed."

Joe sat there after they had gone, the fire dying down, trying to work out what it was that Jordan had been getting at. Articles of faith, these papers were a rebuke, of course, to his own lack of faith; that much he could see at least. But does a man like Jordan give such gifts for purely negative reasons? Surely, he must at the same time have supposed that something really would be learned from them. And yet how? How could that possibly be done? No matter how beautiful these relics might be, how could he, Joe, such a totally different person in so different a context, respond to them in anything more than a purely aesthetic way?

When Evelyne came back, she just flopped down next to him on the large sofa. "Oh, Joe, I feel so exhausted. It's as bad as my sisters with all their kids. They used to make me think they didn't deserve to have any, the way they talked about them. I can remember Claude—she's two years younger than me and had five by the time she was thirty; they're not very well off because she married a Swiss farmer and my father was against the marriage. Anyway, I remember her saying she spent the whole day just longing for the moment when she'd get them all off to bed—to have some time to herself, you know—and then the only thing she could do was go to sleep herself, as well. And I used to tell her she ought to see a doctor!" She laughed wryly and yawned, stretching up off the seat, legs apart. As she did so one of her legs touched Joe's, and he pulled away instinctively. Her mouth turned down sadly. "But what about you, Joe? After all, that's what really matters, isn't it? How are you with Mei? Happy?"

"Yes," he gestured vaguely. "On and off, anyway." He was needled by her assumption of his selfishness and had to prove her wrong. So he tried to show concern. "It must be an awful strain for you having Jordan like this."

And she responded eagerly. "Oh, Joe, if only you knew. It just never stops." Her fingers played with the neck of her sweater. "Sometimes I think I'm going to go mad *with* him. The awful thing is that he's begun to hate me, really hate me, and truly, I don't even know why. I've really tried to do everything I could for him." Joe could see the redness in her eyes and the tears clinging to the corners. "Maybe it was just out of a sense of guilt, I don't know. But the more I do for him, the more he seems to hold it against me."

She got up and went to the tray of drinks, her hand shaking slightly as she poured out some gin. "Did Kwan ever tell you, Joe? Right at the beginning of all this—back in May, was it?—he phoned me about Jordan—to see how he was. Maybe he was just spying. That's what Jordan would say. Anyway, I told him what the doctors had said. Well, I thought nothing more about it, just forgot it completely, until the other night. Jordan was going on and on about how Kwan had tried to destroy him, getting more and more worked up about it. And without thinking—I wanted to calm him down; that was all—I told him how concerned Kwan had seemed on the phone that time. Well, at first he didn't react for about an hour, and then, quite suddenly, he started to scream right out at the top of his voice that I'd been working with Kwan against him. And then that I'd been having an affair with Kwan—"

"With Kwan!"

"I know; it's ridiculous."

Joe watched the tears breaking through the eyelashes and that strong chin beginning to split up. He put his arm along the back of her shoulders, and she leaned over against him.

"And then he talks all the time about Leningrad and his first wife, Natasya, who died in the siege."

Joe could feel the tears on his shoulder, and for a few moments she wasn't able to speak. But she had started, and she couldn't stop.

"The most awful part of it all is . . . making love." She gulped in some air and went on more strongly. "More like hate. He wants to prove that he still can, that he's still young; but he's not, Joe, and, oh, he can't. I've tried to . . . to help him, but, well . . . his body. I keep on remembering what he was like when I met him, and it just makes me so sad. And I don't think he really minds all that much because all he really wants to do is to hurt me."

There, right there, I turned to her again.

I thought of Jordan, of the way the bones at the back of his neck jutted out through the hair, and I could see how the touch of Evelyne's body—breasts, buttocks, thighs that got more full with age—would seem like a constant, obscene rebuke to him. The image of his reassertion, his body forced on and into hers, shocked me. But it fascinated me, too. I felt my own body responding.

I began to stroke her back and, bending down,

kissed the side of her forehead that seemed so exposed, just where the hair was down back. Then we were kissing, and she was standing up, pulling me by the hand towards the corridor.

"What about Jordan?" I whispered.

"He's had his pills," she said gently. "Nothing will disturb him now." She locked the bedroom door, then sat down heavily on the edge of the bed, letting her head slump forward into her hands, a hunched-up, aging woman. But I didn't see that anymore; not cruelly, not from the outside, anyway, as I had always tried to see everything else. If this was hopelessness, it was something I knew I must willingly be a part of.

I reached down to draw her hands away from her face, and her head tilted upwards, the eyes pressed tightly shut.

"Oh, Joe, if only you knew." She sighed and fell back on the bed, gripping my fingers so that I was pulled down beside her.

"What, love?" I murmured, but she didn't answer, just turned towards me, eyes still closed. I touched the lids with my lips and felt them relax, then open.

Relax, then open. I can still feel the touch on my lips, my tongue, even now. The touch of something alive, an insect, a grasshopper, held between cupped palms. Why was it so crucial, that flickering against my mouth?

The life had been sapped out of me in the months before that moment. I'd become an instrument, a tool of action—social action, sexual action—events without meaning, existing only for their own fulfilment. At the beginning Mei had meant something to me, the revolution had meant something, both of them good; but those meanings had been lost, and I was left with only the habits of their observance.

I have to remind myself of that now because here, in my loneliness, I lust after Mei more than I ever desired her then; I long to be with Kwan, planning, projecting, sensing the conflict and the outcome it must lead to. To be part of it again.

But that moment with Evelyne made it impossible to go on living just out of habit. I know that touch, eyes opening beneath my mouth, had meaning, *has* meaning, as all those other memories and hypotheses I may cling to in my nostalgia have not. I don't cling to it. Let it be past. On its own.

I've never been as close to anyone as I was to Evelyne that night, never looked at anyone as closely. I'd begun to think of that face as a mask: beautiful and elegant but suppressing whatever lay beneath. But now the mask was broken, seemed never to have existed, as I looked into, in through, her forehead. Eyes, nose, lips, teeth; those eyes—I'd thought of them as green, but now I can see the flecks of dark brown and blue, hazel, a light moss green as well. Not just as things apart from me; on the contrary, they exist inside me, on my retina, in my brain, as mine exist in hers. In all this face there is movement, change; nothing static about these tiny muscles that tug the lines from nose to mouth outwards into a smile or a twinge of pain. There's no limit to how far I can see, no artificial surface here, no barrier; nothing between me and the molecules we're made of. To think of identity, of separateness, would be absurd.

I must trust myself to these feelings. I'm overcome with the strangeness of it all. A lot of the wonder sprung from that: that it should have been Evelyne, of all people, this Evelyne, whom I'd built up in my imagination into such a figure of stasis, statuesque, controlled. How did it happen? Was it just compassion, just that I felt sorry for her? Yes, that certainly, but it wasn't just pity, from me to her. My own control was broken down, too; my own defenses—the reserve, the distance that I'd kept so firm—were ludicrous. Unnecessary.

The love I'd had with Mei was driven by the need for penetration, the obsession with finding an end, pushing against that barrier of otherness, the bone, tearing at it, causing it pain. But with Evelyne that night everything was expanding. We could open into each other, and there was no end to it because all around us there was an endless expansion. Time for everything, for every pore, hair, blemish. Time to think of all the implications; of how we'd tried this before and failed so dismally, and to know that didn't make any difference at all.

As I came into her, there was a warm, salt sea that engulfed the whole of me, not just my penis, but surrounding every part of my minute body that at the same instant I could feel extending to fill her completely. And just as there had been a slowing down, a relaxation to begin with, so now there was room for laughter, pain, tension, all together, a tangle of limbs, hair, mouths, much more than just two (two?) bodies. Mei I could hold in the crook of my arm, pin down beneath a thumb; but with Evelyne there was so much of us, it seemed we would never come to any end again.

20

INTERLUDE—Spring in the Mountains
Extracts from the story of Ng Man

My name is Ng Man, and I think I am twenty-two years old.

Until our village was liberated by the Red Army at the beginning of the Long March, I lived with my family in Kweichow about fifty miles from Kweiyang, the provincial capital. Ten of us lived in one hut made of mud plastered over grass and bamboo—my grandmother, my father and mother, and their seven children—and we had just under three quarters of an acre of land to farm. We all slept in the same room; my father and mother and the baby on one board supported by broken cooking-pots; my grandmother on another one; and the rest of us on the earth floor around the fire. At least one of us was always ill, and my parents had five other children who died.

We grew rice, but we were too poor to eat it; we had to sell all that we grew to pay the rent and the interest on the money we owed the landlord. The only food we had to eat was corn mixed with cabbage leaves, and most of the time we couldn't even afford to buy salt.

None of us had any education, and I am illiterate. That is why I am telling this story to my comrade, Yu Wah-ming, who is writing it down. But he is teaching me to read, and I hope that soon I shall be able to write things down for myself.

When the Red Army came to our village, they chased the landlords away and executed the worst of them and gave their land to the peasants. We were afraid of them, as we were of all soldiers; but then we saw they paid for everything they took from us, and so when they left the village, it was decided that I should go, too, to repay them for what they had done for us. I am glad of course that that was what I had to do because I have learned so much since then. Really, I am not the same person anymore. And though at times I am still homesick for the South, I know in the end I shall return there again, taking the revolution with me.

It was after that battle in the forest that we came down to the Tatu River. On the way, our commander, Ma Ta-chiu, told us the story of the Taiping Rebellion and said this was where they had finally been defeated by the army of the emperor just seventy-two years before. But the past wasn't going to repeat itself, he said, because we could learn from their mistakes. The reason for their defeat was plain. Their leader, Shih Ta-kai, had waited for three days to celebrate the birth of his son, and that gave the enemy time to trap him with his back to the river. So what we had to do was to avoid the same thing happening to us. We had to get across the river without delay.

The Seventh Hexagram

At first it didn't look too difficult. We were able to take the garrison at the crossing-point of Anshunchang by surprise. They had only bothered to move two of the three ferry-boats over to the north bank of the river. The third boat, the biggest one—it held eighty men at a time—was still on the south side. The Kuomintang general had been so sure it would take us at least another week to get there that he had stayed in the town to have a feast with some of his wife's relatives. He was in bed with his sister-in-law when we captured him!

Anyway, the river was in flood because of the snow melting up in the mountains, and where it comes out of the gorges at Anshunchang it is wider even than the Yangtze and much faster. So we dragged the ferry a long way upstream and mounted machine-guns on the sides and at the front, and General Lin asked for volunteers. Hundreds of us asked to be allowed to go, but there was only room for eighty, and I wasn't among them.

We watched them set off and gradually force their way out from the bank until suddenly the current caught them up and swept them downstream like a leaf. It took them two hours to get across, and all the time the enemy were firing into the boat. I could hardly bear to look; it seemed so certain that they would be sunk, but at last they managed to get ashore on the other side. All we could do was stand there without being able to help at all. Everything was so far away and harmless—tiny feathers of dust or smoke, the noise of a pebble thrown into a pond. But after an hour or so our comrades were able to work their way up onto a steep cliff that overhung the Kuomintang positions, and as soon as the enemy soldiers saw the grenades coming down on top of them, they just stopped firing and ran away. We cheered so loudly I think the noise might even have carried right across the river.

After that time seemed to be our only problem.

On the second day the aeroplanes found us and came back to drop bombs on the ferries, but the bombs just splashed like stones into the river. And it was the river that was our real enemy now. The current was getting stronger, and by the third day it took four hours for a ferry to cross. At that rate I could see it would take months to get the whole army over. I can remember standing on the bank watching the water swirling past and the three tiny ferry-boats struggling against it. It made me feel so helpless, and I began to be afraid the river was going to destroy us as Chiang Kai-shek could never have done.

I was so angry I even picked up a rock and heaved it as far as I could out into the water. But when I looked round, there was Ma Ta-chiu laughing at me. "Why do you waste your energy like that?" he asked. He explained that it was quite clear what we had to do, quite simple; there was no other choice. He had just come back from a meeting where they had decided we would have to march 140 miles upstream to Luting, where there was a chain suspension bridge across the gorge.

We started out at once along the trail that wound thousands of feet up through pine trees and rocks, sometimes so steep that your face was on the same level as the heels of the man just in front. Far below us was the river, rushing white and icy blue, quite different from the muddy yellow field it had been at Anshunchang. Even up where we were, the noise of the waterfalls was almost deafening, and I could see rainbows playing in the spray. At times the sides of the gorge were so close together that we could shout across to our comrades who were trying to keep up with us on the north bank. At other times we would lose sight of them as the path plunged down through thick bushes to the level of the river, and we had to struggle through mud up to our waists where it had overflowed. We marched through the night by the light of pine torches, two long lines of flickering lights strung out along the sides of the cliffs and reflected far down below in the grumbling river. We only stopped for four hours' sleep after marching for fifteen.

The next day the only stops were for periods of ten minutes to have something to eat, and while we ate, Ma Ta-chiu sat on a rock with the rest of us around him and talked about how important this action was. We had to get across the river, he told us; if we didn't make it now, it would be the end of everything we had come so far for already; if we did, nobody could stop us.

As the day went on our comrades on the other bank fell farther behind because they kept on running into small pockets of enemy soldiers. Later, we saw a much larger force, a few hundred at least. Ma Ta-chiu looked at them through the field-glasses he had taken from a Kuomintang officer down near Kunming; he said they must have received an order to get to the bridge before us. At first they wasted a lot of breath shouting insults at us, but when they realized how fast we were going, they kept their mouths shut. For a whole day they tried to keep up, but in the end they began to drop back; and the last time we saw them, they had stopped completely, the whole lot of them lying flat on their backs. They looked like they would never get up again.

At last we came to the bridge. At that point the river is much narrower—only about three hundred yards across—and looking down on it from above, you would think it was boiling, with clouds of spray rising like steam out of a cooking pot. The bridge is made of thirteen heavy iron chains, each one the width of a rice-bowl, about two or three feet apart and embedded in huge piles of cemented rocks. Normally, thick planks of pine wood are tied across the chains to form a road; but when we got there, the enemy had removed these from the side we were on and had drawn back to the cliffs on the other bank. There they had set up a machine-gun post pointing straight across the bridge at us.

The Seventh Hexagram

Volunteers were immediately called for, and this time the whole of my platoon was chosen, with Ma Ta-chiu, of course, as the leader. He told us to strap our guns and swords and grenades on our backs, and then one by one we swung out behind him onto the chains. It seemed to take hours as we moved out so slowly hand over hand, not daring to look down and knowing that all the time we were getting nearer to the hundreds of guns that were firing at us. I don't remember hearing the actual gunshots—the roar of the river was much louder—but all of a sudden I could hear the bullets go hissing past my head or screaming off the iron chains. Ma Ta-chiu was in front and was the first to be hit. I saw him go tumbling over and over, like an acrobat in the opera, and then another man behind him. For a moment I paused, and that was when I was most afraid because Ma Ta-chiu had been like a father to me—only more than a father, since he could see everything so much more clearly than my own father ever could. Without him, I was on my own, and I wanted to turn back. But I remembered what he had said about getting across here—how this was the only way we could survive—and that memory gave me the strength to go on. I was doing it for him, I think, most of all, to prove he had been right.

But as I hung there like a puppet, I suddenly saw it for myself, too; not through somebody else's eyes, but through my own, for the first time. The enemy and the river and the mountains, no matter how strong they were, couldn't possibly defeat us; we could only defeat ourselves.

At last I reached the planks on the far side of the bridge, and that made it a bit easier because they gave me some cover from the guns. But the soldiers at the machine-gun post saw what was happening and ran out and started pouring cans of paraffin over the wood. As soon as they set a match to it, it came streaming down towards me like a wall of fire, and for a moment I was terribly afraid. Once when I was a child I was burned by a pot of oil that tipped over on me—where the scar is on my left shoulder—and all that old fear came alive inside of me again. The only thing to do was to hurl myself right through the flames, so I stood up and started running, pulling a hand-grenade from my belt at the same time. I could feel my right trouser leg burning—and my own leg, too—but I would have been shot if I had stopped to put it out, so I just went on running until I was close enough to be sure of throwing the grenade into the machine-gun nest. The explosion blew me over on my face, and my head was bleeding. And then there were more explosions as my comrades threw their grenades as well, and after that the machine-guns were silent. Once we picked ourselves up, it was quite simple to turn the guns round the other way and drive the rest of the enemy still farther back.

After that we started to replace the planks on the bridge so that the rest of the army could come over, and then our comrades who had crossed the river at Anshunchang appeared, and most of the enemy just turned and ran away into the mountains as fast as they could. But a hundred or so threw down their guns and came towards us with their hands in the air, shouting that they wanted to join us.

Part 6

21

Midwinter, but winter has lost its persistence. It doesn't lock the world in any longer. He senses the restlessness in himself, wanting it to be over.

Last week he saw a pair of raccoons, sluggish and awkward, climbing a maple in search of buds. The sign of an early thaw, says Mrs. McLaren.

The pump in the well has broken, and he's had to waste time melting snow—a laborious process—bringing buckets of the stuff indoors, watching it compact down into a hard grey core of slush. But today, as he walked along the shore, he came on a spring that gushed up out of the rock, then cut like a black blade into the lake. It was hard, a taste of iron in it, numbingly cold. He will get his water there now.

All that is left is the search for an ending. Ends to be cut off.

So: Evelyne.

She was still with him that Christmas morning when he climbed into bed with Mei, her scent still saturating his body. And strangely, as Mei wakened and nuzzled and called him to her, there was more gentleness, more play between the two of them than there had been in the past six months; new love rubbed off on the old.

But he still had to be sure. A day later he phoned Evelyne, trying to keep the nervousness out of his voice, and they arranged to meet halfway down the hillside from her house. So there he was again, walking along past the reservoir he had walked beside with Mei, but with a new eagerness now as he ran at the steep, twisting path that curled through the brush.

He came to an old Japanese guard-post, its concrete scrawled with obscenities in English and Chinese, and stopped there, out of breath, to look back around the ring of hills to the bay and the sea, the currents weaving across its reflecting surface. Everything was startlingly clear in the dry air, each detail emphatic. It was the closest to a winter's day that Hong Kong could manage, and his lungs expanded. The guard-post stank of shit.

He went on past the halfway point with still no sign of her, and just for a second the old frustrations came seeping back in: wasn't she still playing with him, with the power she had over him, just as she had before? Nothing had changed. He paused and looked up at a kite circling about fifty feet away out over the valley, its broad, tattered brown wings flapping slowly a few times in a disorganized way, then soaring, suddenly graceful, as a current of air rose from below.

He glanced back at the path, hoping that somehow she would have materialized there; but no, there was no sign of her. It was all make-believe; probably she wasn't even coming. He felt the disappointment stiffen like an injection in his muscles.

But as he turned a corner, he saw her sitting on a rock in a patch of short grass beside the path. The ground fell away steeply from just in front of her feet, and she was staring out fixedly over the tops of the trees that were rooted in the slope beneath her. He followed her gaze as he came out into the open and saw that she was watching the kite.

His eyes came back to her face in profile, her body hunched forwards, her legs crossed, hands clasped around a knee, and he could see the heaviness across her shoulders, age making its mark in the thickness of her neck. But there was a calmness in her flesh that held him.

As he stepped forward softly into the open, a movement flashed in the corner of his eye, and he caught a glimpse of the kite's dive, down into a minor flurry in the bushes below.

Her eyes, released, turned to him. "I thought I'd wait for you here," she said. "Did you see the kite?"

"Yes, on the way up," he said, out of breath. "I thought you mightn't come."

"Oh, Joe. Still the same old Joe," she laughed and held out a hand to him.

He could see now that he'd been half hoping she wouldn't come, just to prove she was still as he remembered her from six months before; that what had been between them on Christmas Eve was merely temporary, illusory, his drunkenness, her frustration. Instead, it was simple.

She talked a lot about Jordan, not compulsively or guiltily, but as if it was important that Joe should understand. She had been just eighteen when she had first met him: there was a plan for setting up a French steel plant in Shanghai, and Jordan was the contact man with the Chinese government. Her father had asked her to look after him, show him around, expecting the usual dull little state bureaucrat who would make a dutiful tour of the Sacre Coeur, the Mona Lisa, the Tour Eiffel, perhaps the Lido and the Folies Bergères. Instead, Jordan had turned up, so poised and elegant he made her father look like a peasant. He hadn't been to Paris since he was a student, but he knew exactly what he wanted to do: the Jeu de Paume, Racine, Lapérouse. He already knew Malraux and Eluard, and they had taken him and Evelyne to visit Picasso. "They all thought I was his mistress, of course, but I wasn't, not yet, not until we went to Chartres together; that's where he asked me to marry him, and then"—she laughed at the thought—"then he seduced me. He was fifty, but seemed thirty."

Joe felt himself left out again. "What about the steel plant?" he asked dryly.

"Oh, that fell through, of course," she said, her fingers on his cheek. "But don't you see why I'm telling you? That's why I don't feel unfaithful to him now. These past few months have just destroyed what was left of him." There was a long pause; the touch between them. "Of course, he blames it on me."

But there was no need to cry about it now, to wallow in the agony. They looked out over the valley, and Joe pointed to where a kite was climbing towards them again. "There it is again, d'you see? 'Gloomy bird of prey,' " he said with mocking rhetoric.

"What's that?" she asked idly.

"It's a line of Yeats; I'm not sure where from; something about, 'Wisdom is a butterfly and not a gloomy bird of prey.' "

She repeated the words. "What did he mean by that, I wonder?" A silence, and then she went on, seeing the point and getting caught up in it. "Yes, I think I understand. Ireland, and so on; and politics, of course . . . that's what you were thinking of, too, isn't it? If only Jordan and you and Kwan and Donald and everybody else here—me, too—had kept that in our minds in the past six months. . . . Is that what you meant?"

"I suppose so. It's a . . . well, it's a thought, anyway. You don't understand anything by going out and diving down on it with your talons and your beak. You just destroy it. You can't control the chaos all around you; you have to be a part of it, let it find its drift in you, before it can assume any order at all. And that means going off in all directions, turning your back on where you thought you had to go." The idea excited him; he wanted to grip it tighter, pluck the meaning out of it; but then, seeing what he was doing, hawklike already, he drew back, turned away, gloomy for a moment. "Still, it's not as easy as that, either. There are times when the only possible response is to be a bird of prey, a kite, even when you know it will force you to destroy whatever solution you find."

"Perhaps the really dangerous people are the butterflies dressed up as hawks," Evelyne said, teasing him, laughing at the image in her mind.

"I'm not so sure of that; did you know Chen Taisun?"

She tensed. "Too well."

"Jordan told you?"

She stroked his cheek.

And so they went on; fluttering about their past, circling, not really getting anywhere or deciding anything. Afterwards, as Joe walked away from her back down the hill, he was still dazed by the absurdity of it all, so that suddenly he found himself laughing, all alone in the middle of the path, with just the noise of his laughter and the water in the stream below him; laughing like an idiot. Here they were, after all, two people so obviously incompatible, so knowingly incompatible, having already tried less than a year before to find some sort of love between them and made a nasty little failure out of it. Years, upbringing, ideas separated them; they were both tied by force of habit far more closely to two other people than they were to each other. And yet now, he thought, they were emerging, without desire or effort, into an area where the past couldn't even singe their wings.

303

Or so it seemed for four more months, till May began again.

For four more months Joe's life went on collapsing all about him without his even noticing what was happening.

He lost his job, of course. His contract was running out, and naturally the directors weren't going to renew it.

"I'm sorry, Joe. You may not believe that, but I truly am," said Middleton, fiddling with a heavily framed photograph of his frizzy wife. "When I was your age I was a bit—a bit headstrong myself. But you went too far, Joe. Got involved. A good journalist never gets in deep; that's what I always say." Dandruff on his shoulders. (Your mind's flaking away, Middleton!) He'd been telling everybody in the club how he'd see that Joe never got a decent job again, but now he had to pretend to care, leaning forwards, lips moist and quivering. "I'd really like to do something for you, Joe, you know. I feel somehow I'm to blame, too. Not practically, of course," he added hurriedly, "but spiritually, spiritually. It all seems so unnecessary, a combination of circumstances. And now that everything's nearly back to normal—well, it was such a pointless waste, wasn't it?" He had to shake hands. Joe just went away smiling.

And with Kwan and, yes, Mei now, too, he could act suddenly with the same detachment. He could tell them what they wanted to hear; he could lie, please without it seeming like dishonesty at all. It was too distant, too remote for that. Back in the month before Christmas, he had sensed that they were beginning in their different ways to worry about him, about the blackness that they, for their part, sensed in him; but their caring had merely added to his irritability, his aggressiveness towards them. He began to imagine, though he never knew for sure, that Kwan was talking to Mei about him, trying to find out what was going wrong, and though rationally he must have realized that neither of them could trust the other very deeply, it had suited him to go on believing that somehow they were plotting against him. The suspicions spread, penetrated. But now, as the well-being that he drew from Evelyne worked its way into every corner of his life, all that distrust vanished. In their eyes he changed, became more relaxed and confident, listening without a trace of the previous bitterness to whatever plans they proposed. It was as if he had found a deeper sense of security, and in a way of course he had, though before long these roots, which for the moment seemed to give strength to a world of easy compromise, would end up by smashing it completely.

With Kwan, the breakdown of their shared illusions no longer gnawed at their relationship. The obstinate, almost ill-tempered conversations they'd been having—Joe needing to emphasize their failure as Kwan protested, "But this is just the beginning, Joe; impatience is the biggest danger for us now"—all that, abruptly, became unnecessary. Now Joe was able to watch, without reproach, as Kwan himself turned with relief away from Hong Kong. They would have to put all that happened in a wider context, he argued; they'd been making the mistakes of an excessive and bourgeois self-involvement, thinking that their struggle could be an end in itself. How ridiculous, when all the time there was Vietnam, the imminent danger of a Russian attack on China: "Do you think they'd even be capable of that?" As Kwan analysed the new situations, Joe realized how strained he was with insomnia and worry, far more so than in the days of their own struggles just a few months before. He really was more worried about this, the precarious balance of world power, than about the suffering that they had left untreated behind them like an open sore. Joe could see what was happening clearly enough, how this was Kwan's way of not facing up to the reality of their failure, of not admitting that the events they had thrown themselves into had stretched quite beyond their grasp. So he had turned to these abstract threats until they became terrifyingly real. But Joe didn't come out of his corner talking of betrayal as he would have done before. How could he, after all, having made his own escape?

"But what *are* you going to do, Joe?" Kwan asked when Joe told him about the conversation with Middleton.

Joe gestured vaguely, not caring. "I've got no idea."

Kwan's brow creased.

"No, I mean it, Wing-leung. I really don't know. I don't think there's much I can do here. But I'm not sure where else I'd want to go. I guess I'm going to have to reach a decision pretty soon, and yet everything's going to be terribly anticlimactic after this past year."

Kwan ladled out some more soup. "What about China, Joe? Have you thought about that?"

"What use would I be there?" The soup scorched the edges of his tongue.

"Oh, don't write yourself off too easily, Joe. As I see it, you're just the kind of person we're going to be needing most in the next couple of years. We shall have to build up our contacts with other countries again—on our own terms, of course. But to do that, we've got to be able to explain where we stand in the sort of language the non-Communist world can connect with. That's been our big weakness. Semantics. Well, there've been more important considerations, obviously, but all the same we've been too inward-looking, too self-involved. Just as we have been here in Hong Kong on a smaller scale." He smiled. "It will have to be set right now. And that's where you come in, Joe." He reached across the table, not quite touching Joe's hand. "Really, you know, there's a lot you could do."

"It's certainly tempting," Joe mumbled, his mouth full. "Last year there's nothing I'd've rather done. But the trouble is, I can't now, not any longer." He looked around for a reason for not making this choice, any choice, and found one ready-made: "There's Mei now, too, you see."

Mei! Mei, he said, and all the time the touch of Evelyne's body wrapped him like a skin.

Kwan examined Joe for a moment, doubt in his eyes, then stayed on the surface, too. "Yes, Joe, I can see that's a problem. I didn't know exactly how things were between you and Mei; how permanent it was? But you're right, of course; it wouldn't work. Not for her."

And so Joe guided him back to the Russian threat until they had finished the whole bowl of pig's blood soup, each of them as dishonest as the other.

When he told Mei about the conversation that evening, she was overjoyed. This confirmed, brought out into the open, the change she had felt in him; she knew she would win now. The violence that had risen up between them, thrusting itself into their flesh, had been dispelled; it would be just a faint echo in the past. She began to talk about her plans, worried over for weeks but now suddenly released. "Joe, look, we've really got to talk about this. Do you mind?" She came and sat on the arm of the chair beside him. "Sometimes you're so hard to tie down." She started to giggle as he slumped down and held out his hands to her. "No, I really am serious, you idiot. Stop it. I want to talk. Let's look at it logically. You can't stay here; there's nothing for you to do, right? So the only thing that I can see is for us both to go to England—London—for a while. I've got to study textile design sometime, so I could do that there, and you wouldn't find it too hard to get a job if you really wanted to. And even if you didn't, if you wanted to write instead . . . well, we'd still have the money from the factory coming in."

Her voice became apologetic with her fear that it might seem as if she was trying to buy him, hold onto him. But he smiled, nodded: yes, if that was what she really wanted, it was fine by him, they could do it; and as for the money, there was no point in worrying about it now. He drew her over on top of him. "Let's just see how things sort themselves out."

It seems so far away. The people he writes about have become so distant; dwarfs seen from a great height.

All that deception, how can he be so detached from it now? The question puzzles him. But the word is *puzzles;* it doesn't obsess him as such questions once did.

Even at the time, there was a meaninglessness in everything—a sense that it couldn't be real, couldn't matter—that would make any kind of guilt for it contrived. It went on in a daze. The lies may seem cowardly and cruel now when they're dragged up out of the past, but they all—Kwan, Mei, Joe (Evelyne, too, even)—yes, they all needed them then. Obscurely, they knew they needed them. Not just Joe the scapegoat, but a whole society pretending its injuries didn't exist.

It couldn't go on, of course.

It was May, warm in the daytime but the evenings still sweet and cool. He had been with Evelyne, walking along a path below her house, the sky holding just enough haze in it to make the sunset spread from one horizon to the other, to fill everything, their nostrils, their pores, with a penetrating softness. There was a sense of time suspended, and as Evelyne slipped back to Jordan and Joe ran down the hillside, springing from one rock to another, he felt secure, protected. He came to a large jacaranda tree, its blossoms falling, the ground beneath its branches covered with a thick carpet of purple flowers. Their colors seemed to glow even more richly in the last of the light. He walked over them gently.

As he opened the door of the flat, he just had time to call out, "Look at this jacaranda blossom, love; can you get a bowl of water to put it in?" when he heard her sobbing. Not loud, not uncontrollable, just sitting there at the table with her head in her hands and this dead, hiccuping noise seeping out of her. Tears between her fingers.

"Christ, Mei, what's the matter?" He ran to her, hoping it wasn't what it had to be. He tried to put his arm around her, but she pulled away, staring at him with a kind of horror.

"Leave me alone."

"But, Mei, love, it's me; tell me what's the matter."

"You know," she said viciously.

"But I don't. Truly, I don't."

Truly, I don't. It's there, with those words, that the feeling I thought was gone pierces through to me again. A nerve in the surrounding deadness. About all the lies that I had made up for her, played along with before, there's only doubt in my mind: I felt, feel, nothing. So how can I be responsible? But then, as soon as I said in that dreadful, wheedling voice, "Truly, I don't," I was lying just to save myself, to hold something together—my life—which in that instant and because of it, deserved to fall apart. My body pulses with the shame. But still, let the words speak for themselves; they carry their own judgment; need me least of all to judge them.

"Truly, I don't," he said, trying to kneel beside her, but she jumped away and ran like a child to the other side of the room.

"Is that where you've just been?"

"Where? What do you mean?"

"You know. Don't pretend, Joe." She banged her forehead against the wall. "With Evelyne. Fucking that great fat cow."

"For Christ's sake, Mei, who's been telling you this nonsense?"

"What's the matter with me? Aren't I fat enough? Don't I sweat enough for you? Don't I stink enough? God, you stink, too, you bastard. And to think I've put up with it without saying a word."

"Christ, Mei, stop being a bloody stupid little schoolgirl for a moment, will you?" he shouted back at her, getting angry himself now; his only defense.

"Schoolgirl? Maybe I am. But you liked it all right,

didn't you? And what about her? She's old enough to be your mother. Those great tits down to her waist." She picked up a vase from the table beside her and threw it out of the window, nine floors down.

For a moment they were silent, together, waiting for the tinkle of porcelain on concrete.

Then he picked up another vase and held it out to her, lips curling. "Okay, throw this one out, too, then. Throw out all the bloody rubbish for all I care."

She took the vase and put it gently, ever so gently, down beside her. Then she slid down along the wall onto the floor, her skirt up above her thighs, knees under her chin, sobbing deeply now, her whole body wrenched by it.

He turned away from her, back to the other part of the room, picking up a jacaranda flower and dismantling it, looking absent-mindedly out of the window at some children swinging on a seesaw in a playground down below. Others on a slide. It seemed inconceivable that they should still go on playing like that, that old man washing a car, the delivery boy coming up the drive with a basket of groceries on his shoulder, and not know or care what was happening up here. He wanted desperately to be with them, not with Mei, not with himself.

He sat down, taking another flower to keep his hands still, watching Mei hunched up against the wall like a rag doll, her thighs naked and sexless, repugnant.

"Look, Mei, you're just getting hysterical. Can't we talk about it sensibly? Pretend we're adults?" Even then, trying to be kind, not managing to keep the sneer out of his voice.

She just sobbed all the more deeply, rocking backwards and forwards. "You bastard, you bastard, you bastard."

"Oh, come on, Mei, be honest. We're grown up, aren't we? These things happen." His fingers worked away at the petals. "Before we met, there'd been other people for both of us, hadn't there? You used to joke about it even. So what makes this so different? You always said no ties, didn't you?"

It didn't deserve a reply, and he was left sitting there endlessly with the knowledge of his own triviality, sitting watching her, five, ten, twenty minutes. But instead of calming down, as he had thought she must, she seemed to get worse, her whole body heaving, struggling.

He began to panic. "Listen, Mei, love," he said gently, kneeling on the floor beside her. "I'm sorry, love, really I am. I didn't mean to hurt you like this. It's the last thing I wanted."

"Oh, I hate you," she shouted back, her voice deep and rough in her throat, so that she began to cough uncontrollably. "I hate you, I hate you, I hate you," banging tiny fists into her thighs.

"Mei, please, take one of these tranquilizers. Then when you feel better, we can talk about it more. If you still want to."

She snatched the bottle away from him and began to unscrew the top, bending her mouth down to it hungrily. He grabbed hold of her wrist in alarm. "Let go of me, Joe," she hissed, her teeth grinding, her arms surprisingly strong for something so delicate. "It's what you want, isn't it?"

But he could sense the self-dramatization in her voice as she said it, and suddenly he felt exhausted, not caring anymore. He stood up, his body shivering in the void. "All right. Do whatever you want to do."

"No, I'm not going to," she whispered. "Not just to make things easier for you." She clutched the bottle between her breasts and went on weeping, her face swollen and blotched. But he could feel the spring in her unwinding, too, running down into a dead emptiness, more frightening still than the agony it replaced.

22

As Stewart's voice went on trying to explain, Kwan thought he was beginning, after all these years, to understand for the first time what the problem with Europeans really was. Not his problem—theirs. He wasn't consciously a racist, of course; and in practice, when it came down to the point of passing judgments on other people, he paid very little heed to the color of their skins. But that didn't mean he made no distinctions. He had been aware for twenty years or more of the way in which he expected, demanded, more from a Chinese than from a foreigner. It had always seemed quite natural to him; after all, it was a simple matter of fact that the Chinese were more advanced, more civilized, less superstitious than other races, with a longer history of culture and rationalism behind them. He had always been able to persuade himself with perfect ease that there was no arrogance in such an attitude; only the recognition of a greater and more constant need for responsibility. But it did mean that, instinctively, he would judge a European, not on the man's own terms, but by the extent to which he measured up against a Chinese ideal. Which meant, he now realized, that he had never even really bothered to wonder what it was that made somebody like Joe Stewart different. *Different.* A European word. He smiled as it occurred to him that he had always supposed that Europeans were different merely because, to put it crudely, they could never be more than, say, seventy-five per cent Chinese. And left it at that.

But now he asked himself—and it seemed to be almost a moment of insight—what if you couldn't measure them on the same scale at all? Because surely somebody like Joe just wasn't even pointing in the same direction. You used the same words, the same phrases —socialism, necessity, the class struggle—and so it was easy to pretend that you meant the same things by them. But now he could see just how deceptive that was. As he thought of Joe's doubts and confusions, Kwan realized that he had never really been able to take them seriously, not because he didn't feel for him and sympathize, but because they had always seemed to him to be incidental, temporary, a state of mind that sooner or later you worked your way out of. So what mattered, surely, was where you were when you emerged from that state, not the state itself.

But what, he now wondered, if somebody like Joe never did emerge?

It came down in the end—didn't it?—to a question of personality, of self. Somewhere along the line the European had got tied up there, unable to escape from his self-consciousness, his self-pity, his self-awareness. So he became increasingly and inextricably involved in his own problems. The more honest he was, the more painful and devoted was the process of penetrating into his own innermost recesses that spiraled inwards deeper and deeper, more and more blindly, like the inside of a shell. He might talk of the world outside, but he could never really break out into it; not completely, not freely, leaving the shell forgotten far behind him.

Kwan sighed. He had never felt more relieved in the knowledge of his own Chineseness, never more sorry for Joe's contortions. And yet now he was aware of a barrier that had come down between them, whose existence he had never even been conscious of before.

With his finger he traced a spiral over a knot of wood in the top of the table he had been working at. "Round and round," he muttered absent-mindedly.

"Sorry, what did you say?" asked Joe, coming out of his monologue.

"Oh, nothing, nothing." Kwan pulled himself up. "I must have been dreaming."

It was the morning after Tom Price had come back from Japan and found Joe with Sally. Joe had phoned Kwan at his office, and they had said he was at home ill, flu, they thought. It must be serious, too, because nobody could remember his ever having taken a day off before. But Joe couldn't wait for him to get better, not now that his mind was made up, so he took a taxi round to Kwan's apartment. He had never been inside, but as he stood on the pavement, he thought again how out of keeping with Kwan the place was: this great heap of concrete rising out of a street full of the rubbish that fluttered down from a thousand windows. It was so ugly, so depersonalized, with its sterile facing of cheap ceramic tiles that would have looked better on a lavatory wall. On the second floor, as he looked up, he noticed the boarded-up windows of a brothel and remembered Kwan joking about it one night, the worry edging into his voice as he thought of the effect it might have on his children. Joe had met them only once, by chance on the ferry: the son a quiet, intense boy with long hair who played the guitar in a pop group, the girl pretty and respectful but with an underlying strength in her delicate features, the stronger certainly of the two. Kwan hardly ever talked about them, but when he did, his affection was mingled with concern for the mistake he feared he had made by bringing them up in Hong Kong. "It never seemed to be the right time to send them back to school in China. And now, maybe it's too late. I'm not sure they would be able to fit in any longer."

It was Kwan's wife who had wanted to hold onto the children, but he talked about her even less than about them. She was his cousin, and the rumor was that they got on badly. Joe had seen her twice, once in a brief meeting with Kwan in the street, and once again in a restaurant where he and Kwan and a couple of reporters from the paper were having dinner. She had come in with some of her friends, and the two of them had talked politely, amicably, distantly for a couple of minutes before splitting apart, leaving nothing behind them.

That, Joe supposed, was why Kwan never invited people back to his home, and now he hesitated on the landing outside the door. But he had made up his mind, he couldn't wait, and he rang the bell, bringing an eye to the peephole, then a servant's face glaring round the corner of the chained door. The face went away, and Kwan's wife came back and opened it for him. She was wearing a long, heavily embroidered housecoat, her hair drawn tightly back, a striking face with no make-up, middle aged and lined but still beautiful, determined, a match at least for Kwan.

He had just got up, she said, and was working on the balcony. She led Joe through the sitting-room, and at once he was struck by the contrast between this and the outside of the building. Here there was a sense of coolness and proportion, in spite of the basic ordinariness of the room, the uneven plaster, the cheapness of door-handles and window-frames. The furniture was old, austere, made of blackwood, two magnificent scroll paintings of crayfish by Chi Pai-shih on the walls, a cabinet full of Han dynasty jade carvings.

"What a beautiful room."

She didn't smile. "I like to have my own things around me," she said seriously.

Kwan was sitting outside, surrounded by shelves of potted plants: azaleas, geraniums, roses, poinsettias. In spite of the heat he was wearing a dressing-gown over his pyjamas. His face was shiny, a tinge of red in his cheeks, his forehead creased in concentration as he filled up page after page with his neat, incredibly rapid characters.

When he saw Joe, he jumped up, spilling papers on the floor, taking him by the hand, waving apologies away.

"I'm feeling better already," he said.

His wife looked on, then broke off a geranium leaf between her nails, the sudden pungent smell making their nostrils wince.

"Can I get you anything before I carry on with my work?" she asked.

"If you could send Ah Wah out with some more tea——" Kwan suggested, eyebrows raised.

She nodded and tossed the leaf down into the street.

As soon as they were alone, Joe started to explain. "I'm sorry, Wing-leung. I wouldn't have bothered you, but I just had to tell you. You must have thought I'd never make up my mind. Well, now I have. I'm going to China. As soon as you can fix it up for me." It was all so easy. He sat back, feeling a patch of sunshine that fell between the blinds and the plants like a spotlight on his face. "That's why I came."

Kwan leaned forwards and clapped his hands together. "Why, Joe, I'm very pleased." He closed his eyes, feeling suddenly lazy. "What was it that made you decide?"

He had only asked the question out of politeness,

316

but as soon as it was out, he wished he had said something else. He wasn't really interested in the answer at all, but suddenly Joe was launched into a long, confused attempt to explain, that had nothing whatsoever to do with the decision he had come to. He talked about the doubts he had had, the sense of failure after the brief euphoria of last year, his inability to see himself in a wholly Chinese context, his feeling of not being good enough, not strong enough, of having been brought up against a background of such totally different moral and social attitudes that he would never be able to shake them off entirely. And after ten minutes Kwan could see that it was the doubts that remained with him, not the decision.

His finger traced a spiral on the table. "Round and round," Kwan muttered, not even conscious that he said it aloud.

"Sorry, what did you say?"

"Oh. I must have been dreaming." Maybe it was the sun, maybe the fact that he still had a slight fever, but he really did feel as if he was floating. He just couldn't be bothered with all this explaining; he was happy to do anything for Joe, anything at all—to make phone calls, cut through the inevitable delays—but he quite simply couldn't listen to any more of this. Not today.

Joe was enjoying it enormously, though. "How sure can one ever be? That's what worries me, Wing-leung. And yet you have to be sure. Sure that you're doing something for the good reasons, not the bad ones. There are so many stupid, destructive things you get involved in by accident that when you do make up your mind and do something deliberately for once, it's got to be from strength. Not just to escape."

He looked at Kwan's passively smiling face and tried to think of some way to get the point across. "The trouble is it's just so easy to deceive yourself. Sometimes it's as if lies were somehow more natural than the truth." Then an example, an obscure point of shame that had been waiting all this time to be confessed, jumped into his mind. "Do you remember that time—when was it? back at the beginning of March—when you were trying to get me to go to China and I said I couldn't because of Mei?"

Kwan nodded, bored.

"Well, as I said it, it seemed like that really was the reason. I don't think I was consciously trying to be dishonest or anything. It was just the first explanation that came into my mind. Instinctively. But of course it was a lie because by that time I was already in love with Evelyne. So I could only have been using Mei as an excuse, and yet—"

"Yes, I knew that," Kwan murmured.

Momentarily it didn't register—not the words, anyway—and Joe's mind went on trying to formulate this problem that it seemed so necessary suddenly to define. But there was something about the voice, the tone of it, the satisfaction, that pierced through and brought him back into the present. "What do you mean, you *knew* that? How could you?"

"Well." Kwan blinked. "I knew about you and Evelyne. You didn't try to hide it, after all, did you?" Kwan smiled. "That's why I didn't try to press you. There wasn't any point."

Joe leaned back, rubbing his forehead.

Kwan's eyes were drawn down to the unfinished article he was writing about the latest revolutionary Chinese operas. "I wish I was going back to China with you, Joe. It's really exciting, the things that are happening there. You must send us some articles about your impressions, anyway. I'll give you the names of some of my friends in Peking; a couple of them are teachers in the opera school and perhaps you—"

"Look, hold on." Joe's brain whirled: questions he hadn't thought of asking before, possibilities he didn't even want to imagine. He focused on Kwan's eyes, not letting go, and it seemed to him that they had become more attentive, careful.

"I'm sorry." Joe tried to get it into words. "Probably it doesn't really matter any longer, but . . . was it you who told Mei about Evelyne and me?"

And as he said it—was it his imagination?—he saw Kwan relax into a smile again. "Mei? Why, Joe, of course not." A long pause and then—what was it? a moment of calculation?—then a cold little laugh. "She was Donald Winn's friend, you know, not mine."

Joe sighed. So it was Donald, was it? That was all right, then; it really didn't matter. But what about Kwan? There had been that flash of different emotions: watchfulness, then relief, then a kind of shrewd deliberateness.

Kwan stood up, suddenly businesslike. "I'd better make a couple of phone calls, Joe. How soon do you think you'll be ready to leave?"

She was Donald Winn's friend, not mine, he was thinking as he said vaguely, "As soon as you can fix it." She was Donald Winn's friend, not mine. Not mine. He had let Kwan get halfway across the room before he caught up with him, taking him by the arm, holding tight, his voice panicky now. "Jordan was your friend, wasn't he, Wing-leung?"

The eyes retreated. "What's the matter, Joe?" He tried to pull his arm free. "Jordan hated me more than anybody else in Hong Kong. More even than the governor probably." He giggled nervously. "Didn't you know? He even built it up so much in his own mind that he accused me of having an affair with Evelyne. Me!" The voice trailing off, and then just a tremor in his arm.

Their eyes met, but Joe wasn't looking. He could see, hear another scene: Jordan angry, shouting, crazy, banging on Kwan's desk, accusing. And Kwan cool, so superior, saying, "Really, Jordan, you've got it all wrong," then proving it with the miserable truth.

For a moment Kwan was afraid as Joe's fingers dug into his flesh, afraid, though he wasn't a coward, because it was so out of place, so inexplicable, here in this cool, withdrawn room, not like a crowd in the streets, the batons rising and falling, rocks flying, blood, hair sticking on the pavement. Then, just as suddenly as it started, it was all over. He was flying backwards, striking an armchair, falling into it and half out of it onto the floor again. As he looked up, Joe was walking blindly out of the room.

Kwan felt himself all over to make sure he was all right, then called for his wife.

It was another of those days when the sky—the clouds, rather, for there was no sky—seemed tied to the earth. The wetness stuck to windows and clothes and skin. The tarmac glistened. Smoke rose limply from the factory chimneys beside the airport, but it wasn't strong enough to break through the clouds, so it stayed hovering overhead, cutting out the sun, penetrating deep into your lungs. The calendar said that soon it would be autumn, but it seemed more like propaganda to keep up people's faith than something that would ever actually happen.

Donald Winn looked at his watch, then stared back at his reflection in the car window. He could see the sweat standing out on his face, felt the trousers sticking to his legs like rags. This perpetual dampness was bringing him out in spots and boils. "Donald, you look as if you've got the pox," somebody had brayed a couple of nights ago.

"Can't be, darling. Haven't screwed *your* arse for at least three weeks."

But fuck it, he thought, touching his chin and his raw neck, it really did feel like it. What he needed was to get away. Not enough to envy Joe Stewart, though, poor bugger.

Joe had come bursting into his office just yesterday afternoon, upset, almost hysterical.

"Don't think I'm here because I like you, Donald," was the first thing he had said.

It was so vehement, so ridiculously self-assertive,

320

that it had made him laugh. All this insistence on truth-telling, honesty; what a vastly overrated virtue it was! And really, when you come to think about it, it was hardly even a virtue at all; just another form of self-delusion, and a particularly pompous one at that.

His laughter, though, only made Joe even more angry.

"I'm quite sure about it now, so there's no point in pretending any longer. It was you who told Mei about Evelyne, wasn't it?" His face was sweating, too.

Winn pointed at a chair. "Jesus wept, Joe, sit down, and stop making a fucking arsehole of yourself."

He sat down, looking crushed but stubborn. "You can't even deny it, can you?"

Winn took his feet off the desk and heaved himself into an upright position. "Listen, Joe, I don't have to explain anything to you. If you don't like it, you can fuck off out of here." He sighed heavily. "You really are a stupid little prick, you know. You think you're so different. All those ideals. Joe Stewart's going to change the fucking world. And what does it come down to in the end? Screwing in the shrubbery. Okay, fair enough; sex as a substitute for politics. You screw instead of getting screwed; that's fine by me. But why d'you have to exaggerate it all the bloody time. I don't give a shit what you do, Joe, truly I don't; it's the way you have to mess it up with these moral tangles that makes me spew. So Evelyne was a better fuck than Mei; that's good enough for me; end of story. I like a bit of white myself now and again. Pink-grey, rather. Just don't go about trying—"

He never got the sentence finished because Joe was coming at him round the end of the desk. But Winn could move quickly, daintily, when he needed to— hadn't he once won a P & O prize for the paso doble? —and as he jumped up he caught Joe off-balance, grasping his right wrist and twisting it round and up, then catching the other one. For a moment they stood there: Joe trying to struggle free, Winn overpowering him easily, not so much by strength as by sheer bulk, his fat, pustular, grinning face pushing closer and closer until the nose pressed into Joe's cheek.

"That wasn't—" Joe began, breathing Winn's breath, then stopped.

"Wasn't what, darling?" Winn asked and kissed him gently on the mouth before bending him down into the chair.

Joe looked at first as though he was going to cry, then said bitterly, his lips trembling slightly, "Anyway, I've made up my mind. I'm getting out."

"Yes, so I heard. China." Winn looked down at him in disgust. "Aren't you ever going to learn, you—you cunt?"

"Who told you that? Your spy Price?"

Winn shook his head. "Joe, Joe, Joe, can't you see. If somebody rushes around as openly as you do, whether it's screwing Evelyne or plotting with old mother Kwan, nobody needs to tell anybody anything. They all know, anyway."

"You don't know everything, though, do you, Donald?" said Joe, coming to life again with his last tiny particle of independence. "That's why I came to see you. I'm going to Canada."

Winn was so surprised that for once he didn't even bother to try to conceal it. For no reason—no real reason—he was suddenly incredibly happy. This was really going to grind Kwan's face in his own shit. Euphoria swelled in him. He looked at Joe Stewart—this pathetic, stupid, humorless husk rammed down into the chair—and absurdly his pity and disgust began to change into something ridiculously like love. Love? Yes, Joe was his now. Irrevocably. You worked, you infiltrated, you watched and listened and remembered, but in the end you hardly ever saw any real results from what you did because it was all absorbed into the general flux. That was the most you could hope for, the only ideal you could believe in: a state of flux. And that precluded any kind of finality. Whereas this was something you could touch and be sure of holding onto.

And not just for a few days or months, either, but for good because nobody, *but nobody,* baby—he smiled with joy at the thought—ever comes back from the depths of—where was it?—Cobo-fucking-conk!

That had been yesterday afternoon. This morning, standing out on the tarmac, soaked, not by rain or by sun, but by this half-and-half steam, all he felt was a rather vague, hung-over vacancy. Behind him the plane throbbed as little men in white overalls clambered into and through and over it, filling it with petrol and oil and food. And now here were the buses with the other passengers, mainly students, off to find new roots for themselves, and eventually their families, in Edmonton or Saskatoon or sunny Sudbury.

Winn looked at his watch again. If they didn't hurry up, they were going to miss the bloody plane. That was all that was needed to screw everything up; another twenty-four hours and Joe would probably change his mind again and decide he wanted to go to fucking Zanzibar! Shit! He should have looked after him himself. But instead he had hustled Joe off to a hotel, where a watch could be kept on him, and then got on with the other arrangements. A few phone calls fixed up the money and the plane ticket, but then there were the Canadian immigration people to be dealt with: polite, boring, well-meaning men who didn't like to have their arms twisted and who didn't, in this case, have any choice. It took time, though; and when he left them, he felt sapped and heavy and crude, so that instead of going back to see Joe, as he should have, to try to worm something marginally useful out of him—what did he know about Chen Tai-sun, for instance? Or Yim Bun? But fuck that; who cared? Yim was just a sadistic little prick, anyway; bit a kid's left tit off, so he'd heard; getting us all a bad name. Let it lie there, then. Instead of all that, and knowing he was wrong to neglect it, he'd found himself sniffing like a randy dog around the bandstand in a third-rate nightclub. He knew the Filipino drummer in the group was the one thing in the world that could satisfy him when he felt like that; a filthy little beast who would slither all over him for the rest of the night, cooing, "Donald, you have the softest skin I've ever touched."

He watched a family with two young children, and about fifty parcels tied with string, struggling up the steps into the plane's belly. When he turned round, there was the car, with Jamieson, a smooth young army lieutenant, coming towards him, blushing.

"Where the fuck have you been?"

"I'm sorry, sir. Mr. Stewart insisted on going—"

Joe's face was grey underneath the suntan. "It's my fault. I wanted to go to Mei's factory. Just to say good-bye. But she wasn't there."

"You silly bugger, I could have told you if you'd asked. She's in Paris." Having the arse screwed off her by a lot of frogs, most likely, he thought viciously. He pushed Joe roughly up the steps, and saw the door slammed shut. Then, just as they were pulling the steps away, he felt the tissue-paper in his pocket. "Hey, stop." He scrambled up and started to bang like a madman on the outside of the plane until a startled-looking steward pushed open the door again. Winn barged past him and squeezed up the aisle, looking from side to side into the questioning, anxious faces until he reached Joe, who was staring out of a window near the front.

"Here. I forgot to give you this, you bugger." He turned and was gone.

As the plane shuddered and the engines burst into life, Joe unwrapped the paper and came to—what was it? He held it up to the light. Jade, beautifully smooth and white, translucent, cool between the fingers, the moisture from his hand gathering on it like dew. At first the shape seemed to be almost abstract, but then, as he looked closer, he began to make out the figures. Two cats, kittens, their bodies entwined, struggling over —what? He peered at the carving: an enormous dragonfly gripped in both their jaws.

Outside, Donald Winn stood and watched as the plane hurtled down the runway that jutted out into the sea. It looked as though it would never manage to take off in time, and venomously, intensely, he found himself praying it would crash. Just as it seemed too late, the nose tilted back, and it limped like a wounded bird into the clouds, a darker stain of vapor hanging for a few seconds behind it on the thick air.

23

For Donald Winn that was the end. As simple as that. But for Joe there was only the coming back again and again to the beginning, watching over it, keeping it alive.

When he opened the first of these notebooks (a ragged pile of them now) and started to write, there was the one image he had to hold in front of him: the night, the rain, gunshots, a crash. That, he knew for sure, was the one place he would have to begin, the point that focussed it all. But to begin there didn't mean he could ever leave it behind. He knew that was where he would have to end, too, not for the sake of symmetry, but because the pain must be projected forwards into a predictable future.

Now, though, now that he is here once more, he senses it must be for the very last time. What he knows he has to say has somehow become so simple, freed from the contortions he went through to get here.

He can no longer even remember why it should all have been so necessary: the guilt, the hysteria, the heart pounding with the pressure. Thump, thump, thump, the jackboots of the imagination. Why did he have to make it so difficult? The question doesn't even need an answer anymore.

Once Mei had left, he could see no point in trying to control anything.

Ironically it was only then, when it was too late, that he began to realize just how much he had come to depend on her. He had tried to tell himself that what there was between them was habit: the habit of living together, the habit of making a sort of love, the habit of recognition when they wakened to each other in the morning, the habit of laughter, of dissatisfaction. He knew that was all it could be when he saw her one day in the street and his eyes followed her, together with a hundred other eyes, for half a block before he even realized it was Mei. He started to cross the street to catch up with her, to claim her as his; and then, suddenly, he stopped right there in the middle of the traffic, cars going by on either side of him, and he knew that she was a quite separate person, apart. He turned back to the other pavement.

The breaking of such a habit must, then, be easy, unimportant. But when it did happen, he saw at once how wrong he had been, how hard it was, though it was already too late for the recognition to do anything more than add to the confusion.

The first morning there was just the continuing numbness. Mei had phoned her family, an aunt, cousins; and they had come for her even before Joe was up, closing in around her, shutting her off from him. He found them in his study, opening drawers, peering uncomprehending at his papers.

"Fuck off, you bloody vultures!" he shouted at them.

Mei was in the kitchen sitting on a stool, her face pale and bloated, completely alien and unrecognizable as the cousins filled cardboard boxes with her things. He tried to speak to her, to explain, then apologize, but she just stared through him and said something to her aunt in a dialect he had never heard her speak before. The others brushed past him as if he wasn't there, and when they left one of them—an ugly, opaque woman—spat very deliberately at him and missed.

"Christ!" he said to himself aloud as he watched them from the balcony, shouting, scurrying, squeezing into a van, Mei carried along in the middle of it all. "The most civilized race on earth! They're just a bunch of bloody peasants!" Then as he turned away, there was a twinge of self-conscious charity. "Maybe that'll make it easier for Mei, though."

But as the day dragged on, and then the night, he began to realize that this habit—though the word was wrong now, already—this habit of affection wasn't what he had convinced himself it must be. He had built Mei into his life so completely that even the assumption of not caring depended on her presence. He couldn't reason any longer that she didn't matter to him when the very fact of her not being there could force him to concentrate on her so totally.

At night was the worst. As he lay on his own, in his own separate littleness, strangling himself with the sheets and the strands of his thoughts, he began to understand how many different parts of himself had been attached to Mei. Worst of all, though far too late, was the realization of her need for him. Blandly he had assumed that she must be as uninvolved as he imagined himself to be; he couldn't be hurt, so neither could she. The memory of her sobbing washed that away, so that he began to shudder with his own vulnerability. He wandered about the flat from room to room trying to conjure her back, knowing that even if he had the power—which he hadn't—as soon as he had it, he wouldn't have wanted it, anyway.

When he told it all to Evelyne, she was startled, then warm and consoling. But even with her, everything suddenly had to be different. Whereas before he had been happy enough to drift along with all the compromise and secrecy, now the part of her that belonged to Jordan irritated him unbearably. He couldn't stand the thought of them together, wanted her to himself; and soon he was beginning to nag her about it, accusing her of dishonesty, saying she would have to choose.

"I already have, Joe," she said simply.

But even then the words on their own weren't enough because Joe, in the state he was in, wasn't really capable of making a choice himself. So they talked endlessly, round and round, about arrangements, where to go, how to break it to Jordan, without ever drawing close to a decision.

Evelyne was doing all she could to hold the pieces together, pulling Joe into her, in under her wing. "Oh, Joe, you mustn't worry, my love. Listen, it's all quite simple. All you need to do is wait in the evenings till Jordan's had his pills and gone to bed. Then you can come up. We can have every night together now."

One last time he tried to put obstacles in their way. What about the servants? he reminded her. Weren't they bound to find out?

"Yes, of course they will," she explained patiently. "But that doesn't make any difference, either. They won't tell Jordan."

"How can you be so sure?"

"They all hate him."

It couldn't last, of course, but that was exactly what was so attractive about it. One way or another a finality, any finality, was being forced on them. This, even then, was the ending both of them were seeking. Surely that must have been why Evelyne suggested it in the first place. On the surface she seemed so relaxed, calm, nurse to Jordan, mother-mistress to Joe, keeping the different levels of her life carefully, cleverly from running into each other. But underneath she must have been longing to see it all broken up even more strongly than Joe was himself. So they entered into the danger eagerly, kids on a dare. They never even bothered to lock the bedroom door any longer, and every morning Joe would stay on just a little later, one ear waiting for the sound of the bell by Jordan's bed.

Nine days; that was how long it lasted. By the calendar, that is, though still, as he writes, it's all fused together in his mind so that the incidents, the people, can't be separated from each other. He can't remember the order in which anything happened, who said or did or felt what. And it's not just the memory failing, erasing, because even at the time, from one moment to the next, that was how everything was: so intense it had to fade into impersonality.

Then, the tenth day.

It had been raining off and on since morning, in short bursts of five or ten minutes, the water lashing malevolently down and then being turned off again like a tap. Joe stayed transfixed at his bedroom window, watching the curtains of rain being driven in from the sea, feeling more and more empty and cut off, so that eventually he had to pick up the phone and dial her number, not because he had anything to say, but just to make sure that she—somebody—was there. Once he heard her voice at the other end of the line, he put the receiver down.

Towards evening, when the sky seemed to lift a little, he got out the car and started to drive slowly up the twisting road, pausing to look back from time to time at the thin layer of intense light between the black sea and the black sky, exhilarated by the swirling clouds that swooped down like gigantic wings just above his head.

He parked in a corner of the drive where the car

330

would be hidden from the house by a clump of magnolia bushes. As he opened the door, the sky seemed to burst again, and the rain came flooding down more heavily than ever. Instinctively he pulled the door closed, but then he thought, What's the point of keeping dry any longer? Dry for what? So he got out and ran round to the verandah on the far side of the house, where he waited every night for Evelyne to let him in.

He had two hours to wait, standing there in the darkness, soaked through and beginning to shiver in spite of the summer heat, watching the rain seething and spitting off the ground, driving into the cracks in the cement pathway, tearing up flowers and digging rivers through the lawn. Then, almost imperceptibly, it began to ease off until, when Evelyne came out at last, it was just a steady, drifting drizzle.

She leaned her body in relief against his. "Joe, you're soaked."

"It almost washed me away," he said and kissed her.

"It took so long; I'm sorry. I just don't know what's happening to him any longer. This morning he was terrible; all that ridiculous suspicion of me making love to Kwan again. God knows where he gets the idea from. Anyway, he was screaming and crying. And then tonight he was so much better, so relaxed and wanting to talk about going back to France for a holiday. Joe, I nearly told him, but I just couldn't. He seemed too happy. But if he's still the same tomorrow, I will; I promise." She took Joe's hand and began to move towards the door.

"No, let's stay out here." He drew her back to him, kissing her on the neck as her head tilted backwards.

She didn't hesitate, and he felt her fingers firmly on his belt. They undressed each other quickly, the air suddenly cool against their bodies, which had been hot and sticky inside the clothes. He bent towards her, but, "No," she said, "come right out into the garden. Nobody will see us."

So they made love for the last time in the middle

of the lawn, the ground squelchy under their feet, Evelyne standing on tiptoe, then thrusting herself down onto him, her body arched backwards, twisting from side to side. The rain, which seemed to be the only source of light, washed over them, taking their molten flesh and cooling it into form, permanence.

Afterwards, they walked back slowly into the house and turned on the lights in the sitting room, sinking down onto the sofa, with a wet stain spreading out from where they lay, a puddle on the polished floor at their feet. Joe tilted the reading lamp towards them so that he could see her better, then started to kiss her, not with desire, but as a sign of knowing, recognition. Her eyes were closed as he bent to her dark gold curling fur, drops of water still glinting in it. He licked them away.

She opened her eyes and smiled down at him, then closed them again.

He ran his tongue along the curve of her belly. Salt. He felt the appendix scar, the small lines and blemishes of age, the navel, then up to her breasts, no longer firm as she lay on her back with her arms beneath her head, so that without the spreading brown nipples it would have been hard to say where their center lay. He molded them into a point.

He heard the shuffling behind him, felt rather than heard it, whirling round, seeing the slippers first, then the neatly tied silk dressing-gown.

"Jordan!" Evelyne's voice was still soft, unable to shake off the contentment she had sunk into.

Jordan's lips, his head, his whole body were trembling as he tried to mimic her. "Yes, Jordan! What's Jordan doing? Jordan's tucked up in bed, sound asleep. Sleep well, Jordan. Sweet dreams, my love. The devoted little wife!" he sneered. "She's nothing but a cheap tart."

He didn't look down at Joe once. Just stared at Evelyne, his eyes bloodshot, vacant, his hand shaking, too, as it held the gun, the silver gun with an ivory handle, that he had taken from a Kuomintang general thirty-five years before.

Now, as I look back at the scene cast forwards in my mind, it seems that I could so easily have knocked him over without any danger at all. That frail body. He wasn't even looking at me. But the thought just didn't enter my head. I lay there paralyzed at his feet, her feet, the hatred and the fear crossing like arrows just above me. I didn't feel anything. When you dream of something like that, your heart quickens because you sense that what's happening isn't real; so you struggle to prevent it from penetrating into your actual world. But then, when it was really happening, I felt nothing, no fear or panic, only the awareness that this was what we must have been working towards all along. And it was only afterwards, when they were both dead, that the adrenalin pounded belatedly into my bloodstream, threatening to burst veins, heart, brain into tiny pieces.

The first shot shook him from his daze. Evelyne had tried to get to her feet, her legs reaching down beside Joe's left arm.

"Please, Jordan, listen," was what she seemed to start to say, but it was drowned by the noise. Joe was watching Jordan's face as he pulled the trigger: it didn't change at all; no sudden relaxation or pressure, no sign of what was going on inside.

Joe turned to Evelyne, unbelieving. It was such a small hole in her abdomen, but it seemed to have been driven like a nail into a balloon, deflating her, pinning her down like a butterfly, the blood gushing out purple and spitting onto the wet sofa.

But now Joe was awake, scrambling to his feet as two more shots went off, grasping Jordan's arm as it fell to his side.

I don't think he would have tried to kill me if I had left him alone; I don't think he even saw me as a person. His arm as I held it was limp, his body weak

333

and drained, as dry and as light as balsa wood; but then he started to struggle wildly, a strange rasping cry in his throat. It was then that he tried to pull himself away and point the gun at me, but I forced it upwards until it was underneath his chin. We were staring into each other's eyes, and if I had seen anything in his at all, if I had felt anything in mine—vengeance, pity, love—surely I would have wrenched the gun away from him, as I could so easily have done, and thrown it on the floor. But instead there was nothing; in either of us. Meaninglessly, deliberately, I tightened his finger round the trigger and waited for the explosion.

Joe didn't even look as he let go of the body, felt it fall. Already he was running towards the door and the rain and the warm darkness, running, stumbling, getting up, trying to scrape away the blood that had spurted out into his left eye, feeling the grit that was mixed with it and wondering in panic where it could have come from.

24

As they cleared away the table, Mrs. McLaren caught her son's eye and winked. She was a small, plump woman, always on the go: baking, cleaning, keeping the dogs off the chairs, feeding chickens and pigs, mending and making. If you had ever been able to catch her face at rest, frozen, it would have been gruesomely ugly, bloated, twisted off-center like an overripe plum; but it was always in movement, reacting to what was going on around her, creased into laughter or sympathy.

She had been trying to get Joe to come over for a meal for several weeks now. She had kept an eye on him, more closely than he imagined, all winter, watching the moods sweep through him. Recently she had seen the change in him, sensed him struggling to emerge. Yet still there were days when he seemed to be so unobtrusive that he quite simply wasn't there; nothing, no energy emanating from him. It wasn't really good for people, she felt sure, to be shut in the way he was. So she had asked him over. For Sunday dinner. Nothing special; just what they always had.

Standing outside the cottage, Joe glanced around the white lake, patches of slush in the corners where the streams leaked in.

It was finished, his winter book. Ended where it had begun. But already he knew it wouldn't do. The circle was no more complete than the straight line.

Here he was, a different person, different reflections in his eyes and his brain, trying to pretend everything was exactly the same. When he had started, back there in the autumn, it was his own confession he was writing. The more he wrote, the more there always was to tell and feel guilty for. He could look back up above his head and see the things he had said a day or a week before spiraling down on top of him. What made it bearable was that it was all his, him. He had made every word for his own consolation and torment.

But by the end of February, with the drifts of snow diminishing, he knew it couldn't be a part of him any longer. The "I" of the story had come to be more and more unreal, even less actual than the other characters. And that was what they all were now, not people, but characters in a story, gathered into meaning.

It was just history, something he could live without.

A sense of finality, then, of achievement. Surely this must mean he had broken out to a point at which he was free at last from himself.

But one morning he wakened with a sourness spreading down from his brain into his whole body. For two days all he could think of was what he had lost; nothing to put in its place. He began to hate this thing he had made It had cut him off from himself, the one object he could hope to know.

Then that mood had changed, too. All that was left was a modest, almost comforting sadness.

Mrs. McLaren was still there in front of him, still waiting for an answer. "How about it, eh, Joe? If you ask me, you need to get out of yourself a bit."

Around the marsh the ice was turning brown in places. He looked back at her and smiled. "Yes, I think I'd like to."

At first Mrs. McLaren had been worried by the edgy feeling in the air. Joe was fidgeting all the time, hardly saying a word, his eyes prowling around the living-room: the Dresden posy, plaster ducks, the oil company calendar, the twelve-year-old television. It wasn't that he despised what he saw; she had seen that in a visitor's eyes before and knew what to do with it. It was more like fear; a fear of these familiar objects, of being with people. She guessed that was natural enough when you'd been living on your own for so long.

Gord had tried to put him at his ease by talking about Scotland, the auld country, but got no response at all. And Chris, her son—fourteen and restless, the last one left at home—had gone on about his hockey games and asked a few questions about Hong Kong. Joe didn't show a flicker of interest. He didn't mean to be rude, but there was this vagueness in him, just staring at his plate and eating automatically. It seemed like such a shame.

He was relaxing now, though. The beer had helped, of course, and it had certainly helped Gord as well. He was getting into his stride now, not trying to be polite, but just being himself, talking nineteen to the dozen. And Joe, she could tell, was listening, responding. It looked as if they were set for the rest of the afternoon. She went back out to the kitchen. All those whites of egg left over—meringues or an angel cake?

Joe could feel it happening in himself, too. He was

letting go, yet all the time with the reassurance of something solid underneath him. He couldn't define what it was. Perhaps it was just the beer. There didn't seem to be any better, any more rational reason than that. But what he kept coming back to was the voice, Gord McLaren's voice; such a small thing, surely, to make so much difference. There was nothing else about the man that was remarkable; he was large, fat, not as healthy as he looked because he had had a heart attack the year before, a broad face with dark, receding hair and a surprisingly small, delicate chin. Until last year he had been a butcher with the Dominion supermarket in the nearest town, but now he had given that up and just worked the fifty acres he had out here while his wife went out to clean for some of the neighbors. By North American standards he was a failure. But it was his voice that made all the difference. It was the most beautiful voice that Joe had heard since his childhood; deep, but not muscle-bound in its deepness, lilting without being effeminate, rounded and obviously Scots in origin, but with this gentle, lazy, almost lisping slur about it, too. It wasn't what he would ever have thought of as Canadian until then, though in fact Gord's grandfather had been born in this house. Joe could have listened to him all afternoon without bothering what was being said.

You wouldn't have to bother too much, either, not when Gord was carrying on in praise of snowmobiles.

Joe had seen them out across the lake—noisy, growling, pointless machines—and had felt, as the wind blew towards him, the prickle of their fumes in his nostrils.

But Gord would have none of that. "I'm telling you, Joe, they're the best thing ever happened in Canada. You don't have to stay in huddled round the fire watching that darn TV night in, night out. You can really get out into the winter now. Some nights I've seen as many as a dozen of the boys come out here, and we'll just sit around the yard with the barbecue going and cook up some hamburgers. And with these

Skidoo suits you can sit in a snow-drift all night long if you have a mind to and never feel the cold. I used to hate to see the winter come, and now I'm sorry to see it go."

"It'll soon be spring, though, now," said Chris coming in from the kitchen.

"Aw, yes, but that's not really spring," said Gord, knowing one thing, at least, better than his son. Mustn't let these kids get away with everything. "Not like the kind of spring Joe'd be used to. I remember the first spring I saw in England when I was over there; in the war? I could hardly believe my eyes, the way it happened, so gradual like and yet as though you could really see it all going on right there in front of you. Here you've just got the thaw, which is a real messy time of the year, and then it's summer."

He spat into the fire and listened to the sizzling. "No, I'll be sorry to see the winter finish this year. Best winter I ever had. I've got this wine-skin, you know, Joe," he winked, "and I fill it up with vodka and a little drop of orange juice, and that keeps me going all night."

He paused and looked into the flames. "Yes," he said softly, "best times I ever had. Just last month, my cousin Gerry was having a party, and that afternoon I was out on the machine with Doug Ferguson; used to work beside me? Well, I'd had most of a wine-skin of vodka, and we ended up over near Bobcaygeon. There's this fellow I know, name of Charlie Grant, has a chicken farm over there, and I said to Doug, 'Why don't we take a chicken back for Gerry?' Well, this Charlie Grant's a real skinflint, wouldn't give you good day for nothing; and we knew there was no use asking him for the chicken, so we busted open one of the hen-houses and took it for ourselves. Then we walked up to the front door and said, 'Hey, Charlie, we've got ourselves a chicken. How much are you going to charge us for it?' He just stood there looking at his chicken and couldn't open his mouth, didn't know what to say; then he muttered something about the police, and I said the chicken was for Gerry, who's a constable in the OPP, of course, and when we left him there, he was still standing on the doorstep with his mouth opening and closing and not a sound coming out, so we never did pay for the chicken.

"Then we got back to Gerry's, and his wife cooked it up with a creole sauce; but when we sat down to eat it, damn me if that wasn't the toughest, scrawniest old fowl I ever tasted. Doug Ferguson bent his fork in half just trying to get it stuck into it, it was so tough, and we laughed so much about it that Doug couldn't stop laughing in the end. Just went on laughing for a whole half hour, and then his wife, Marg, phoned to see where he was and came over. Well, she can't stand for people drinking, and when she saw him like that, she got this broom handle and drove him home, walking behind him and prodding him like a young steer, though I've never seen a steer that drunk."

Yes, Gord could have gone on all afternoon, but Mrs. McLaren caught the exasperation in her son's eyes as he stood in the kitchen doorway, and came over to them.

"It's a lovely day outside, Joe. You don't want to spend it all cooped up with we old folks in here. Why don't you and Chris here go out for a bit. Then come back for some tea—that's if you've a mind to?"

Gord spat again into the fire, then remembered his wife standing there beside him and glanced up at her apologetically. "Yes, that's a good idea, Joe. Take them skis I picked up last summer, eh, Chris? Over to Herm's place?" He sank back into himself. "There won't be much more snow this year."

It was a good hill, Chris said, considering it only cost a buck. The Dutch farmer who owned the land had thirteen children, and with the ski resorts charging so much had put up his own rope tow, powered by an old Chev. It was a steep hill, Joe could see, especially at the top, curving down in a long sweep, with spruce trees that jutted out from the sides, dark green against the whiteness and the light blue sky. There were a dozen kids up there already, taking turns, building humps of compressed snow to make it more difficult. A few on toboggans as well.

Chris kicked at the snow, and it blew away from them in a flurry. "It's a good day," he said. The snow was loose, the air cold enough to keep it from melting and becoming sticky, but with a layer of ice just beneath the surface.

Joe hadn't skied for five years. He wanted to get the feel of it gradually. "Why don't we walk up the first time? Put on the skis at the top?"

They plodded up the slope, heads down. "I've been coming here ever since I can remember," Chris said. "Mom and Dad used to bring me tobogganing when I was just a kid. They'd hold me in between them."

Then, as Joe paused for breath, Chris waited for him. "This is always the worst part. Getting started."

They had reached the level of the humps the kids had been making and looked up to see a boy hurtling down towards them. He must have been about nine years old, sitting right at the back of a six-foot-long toboggan, not holding on in any way at all, but with his arms stretched out on either side of him like a bird or an angel. As the toboggan hit one of the bumps and took off, separating him from the seat, he let out a great whoop of excitement that turned, as he was smashed back into the ground again, to a loud and joyful shout. "Fuck in the arsehole!"

Chris giggled, then said solemnly. "If old Van Meer hears him, he'll wash his mouth out."

They went on up to the top.

From up there the slope looked much steeper even than from down below, and momentarily Joe was afraid as he saw the snow-bloated trees angled towards him. He tried to forget them in the process of putting on the borrowed skis; they were too long for him and the boots so big his feet shifted about inside.

At last he had them buckled on and stood up near the edge, shuffling uncomfortably, not wanting to look.

"I'll follow you down," Chris said.

Joe nodded.

A kick and he was off, hardly seeing a thing with the icy wind that sprayed into his eyes and nostrils, just this wonderful breath-taking exhilaration in the blind, swooping speed. Then the bump—he had forgotten the bump—a moment of free flight followed by the crunch as he landed, his bones changing places inside his empty body. And suddenly everything was going wrong. The skis were slipping over to one side, the bindings twisting as he slued round, hitting the ground, tumbling over and over in a cloud of snow till his body thudded deadly into the trunk of a tree.

He lay there on the verge of crying and felt the pain shoot outwards from his groin, into his abdomen and right on up his spine, down into his thighs. How are they going to get me out of here? was the first thing he thought. But when he looked up, he saw Chris standing over him, laughter all across his face, offering a hand. "You okay, Joe? It's great, eh?" he said.

For a moment, like a spoilt child, Joe wanted to stay there, moaning, holding himself, cursing, wallowing in the pain. But the hand was still there, so he took it and nearly pulled Chris over on top of him. The boy was strong, though, and braced himself to haul Joe to his feet. Without safety straps, the skis had slid right down to the bottom. "I'll bring them up on the tow," Chris shouted over his shoulder, leaving Joe on his own to plod back up the hill, back up the hill again, discovering to my surprise as I go that the pain isn't unbearable after all.

If you want knowledge, you must take part in the practice of changing reality. If you want to know the taste of a pear, you must change the pear by eating it yourself.

Mao Tse-tung, *On Practice*

ABOUT THE AUTHOR

Born in London, IAN MCLACHLAN attended school on the Isle of Wight, took his degree at Oxford, and in 1960 set out for Hong Kong with his bride, Dominque. He lived and worked there for ten years, and two of his three sons were born in the Crown Colony. For the past seven years he and his family have resided in Ontario, Canada, near the University of Peterborough where he is a professor of comparative literature. Ian McLachlan has traveled widely, most recently to England, France, Turkey, Tibet and Hong Kong.